In 1860, when four million Afro-Americans were enslaved, a quarter-million others, including William Ellison, were "free people of color." But Ellison was remarkable. Born a slave, his experience spans the history of the South from George Washington and Thomas Jefferson to Robert E. Lee and Jefferson Davis. In a day when most Americans, black and white, worked the soil, barely scraping together a living, Ellison was a cotton gin maker—a master craftsman. When nearly all free blacks were destitute, Ellison was wealthy and well established. He owned a large plantation and more slaves than all but the richest white planters.

While Ellison was exceptional in many respects, the story of his life sheds light on the collective experience of Afro-Americans in the antebellum South to whom he remained bound by race. His family history emphasizes the fine line separating freedom from slavery.

Michael P. Johnson is professor of history at the University of California in Irvine and the author of *Toward a Patriarchical Republic: The Secession of Georgia*. James L. Roark is professor of history at Emory University and author of *Masters without Slaves*, winner of the Allan Nevins award.

BLACK MASTERS

BLACK
MASTERS

A FREE FAMILY
OF COLOR IN
THE OLD SOUTH

Michael P. Johnson
and James L. Roark

W·W·NORTON & COMPANY

New York   London

The text of this book is composed in Galliard,
with display type set in Bembo.
Composition and manufacturing by
The Maple-Vail Book Manufacturing Group.
Book design by Margaret Wagner

First Edition

Library of Congress Cataloging in Publication Data

Johnson, Michael P., 1941–
Black masters.

Includes bibliographical references and index.
1. Afro-Americans—South Carolina—Charleston—
History.   2. Afro-Americans—South Carolina—Charleston
—Biography.   3. Ellison, William, b.1790.   4. Ellison
family.   5. Charleston (S.C.)—Race relations.
I. Roark, James L.   II. Title.
F279.C49N43 1984   975.7′91500496073   84–4079

ISBN 0-393-01906-3

W. W. Norton & Company, Inc.,
500 Fifth Avenue, New York, N.Y. 10110
W. W. Norton & Company Ltd.,
37 Great Russell Street, London WC1B 3NU

1 2 3 4 5 6 7 8 9 0

TO OUR FAMILIES,

Anne, Ian, and Sarah

AND

Martha, Michael, and Benjamin

CONTENTS

MAPS AND ILLUSTRATIONS

PREFACE

THIS book aspires to be a history of a remarkable man named William Ellison. In reality, it is both more and less than that. Less, because William Ellison was not a major historical figure whose every act was recorded; much that should be included in a full history of his life remains unknown and unknowable. More, because William Ellison's life was so intimately bound up with his family that his history is inseparable from the history of his family. More also, because William Ellison was inexorably pulled into the maelstrom of antebellum politics by his race. A man of mixed white and black ancestry, Ellison was one of a quarter of a million individuals in the slave states in 1860 whom well-spoken whites referred to as free Negroes or free people of color. Four million other Afro-Americans were slaves in 1860, as Ellison himself had been when he was born in 1790. Ellison's experience in slavery and freedom spans the history of the slave states from George Washington and Thomas Jefferson to Robert E. Lee and Jefferson Davis. Despite Ellison's best efforts to live a quiet, private life of freedom, his fate was linked to other free people of color and, through them, to the politics of the slave South. William Ellison's history, therefore, is his family's life and times.

William Ellison confounds expectations we are tempted to project onto him from our own times. A brown-skinned man who would be called black today, Ellison did not consider himself a black man but a man of color, a mulatto, a man neither black nor white, a brown man. At a time when most Afro-Americans, like other Americans, worked the soil, Ellison was a cotton gin maker, a master craftsman. When nearly all free Afro-Americans were the poorest of the poor, Ellison was one of the wealthiest free persons of color in the South and wealthier than nine out of ten whites. Ninety-four out of one hundred Afro-Americans in the South were slaves in 1860, but Ellison owned a large cotton plantation and more slaves than any other free person of color in the South outside Louisiana, even more than all but the richest white planters.

Although William Ellison was hardly typical, his history sheds light on the collective experience of free Afro-Americans in the antebellum South. By illuminating the prerequisites for rising above the degraded circumstances of most free Negroes, his story reveals the obstacles that prevented other free people of color from prospering as he did. Ellison's economic achievement set him apart from other free Afro-Americans, but he remained bound to them by his race. Elsewhere in the New World, money sometimes whitened. In the American South, the color Ellison shared with four million others proved indelible. Simply to survive as a free person of color in the slave South was no mean feat. William Ellison shared that accomplishment with tens of thousands of free Afro-Americans. His history discloses the thin line separating freedom from slavery, even for those at the pinnacle of worldly success.

Ellison's history would still be hidden if three little white girls had not made a fortuitous discovery in 1935. While playing under their house in the South Carolina upcountry on a hot summer day, the girls found a box containing some old letters that they showed to their father, who saved them. The letters, written by and to members of the Ellison family, had somehow ended up underneath the house where the Ellisons had lived for almost a century. The South Caroliniana Library acquired the letters early in 1979, and we first saw them that spring.[1]

We studied the letters for more than a year before we could imagine writing a history of William Ellison and his family. The letters contain a fascinating tale all their own, and at first we did not recognize it as a pivotal moment in the life of the Ellisons. Furthermore, we simply did not believe sources existed to sustain an account of the private life of an obscure, though extraordinary, free man of color. Gradually, as we searched out documents hinted at in the letters, tracked down leads given us by archivists and colleagues, and looked for and found more than one needle in a haystack, it became clear that we were wrong, that a history of William Ellison was possible.

In 1860, Daniel R. Hundley published *Social Relations in Our Southern States,* which sorted the South's inhabitants into eight categories. Hundley constructed a descending pecking order that ran from gentlemen and cotton snobs through yeomen and poor white trash to the lowly slaves.[2] Nowhere did he find a place for the South's free Negroes. Hundley's omission suggests the anomalous position of free Negroes in the stratified, hierarchical society of the slave South. Negroes were supposed to be slaves. Free people were supposed to be white. People who were free and Negro did not fit neatly into idealizations of Southern society, yet 250,000 of them unquestionably existed in the slave states in 1860. When white Southerners gravitated toward secession as the best defense of slavery, many of them decided it was also time to bring their society into perfect conformity with their ideas by solving, once and for all, the free Negro "problem."

Unlike Hundley, historians of the antebellum South have not neglected free Negroes. Their studies document the harsh repression visited upon free Afro-Americans by the white majority and the abiding assumption of most whites that all Afro-Americans were inferior beings suited only for slavery.[3] Based largely on laws regulating free Negro behavior and on the writings of contemporary whites, these histories focus on how free people of color were thought of by whites and how they were treated by courts and legislatures. Inevitably, these studies tend to portray free Negroes as objects rather than subjects, as people who received rather than participated in their history. The scarcity of records created by free Afro-Americans makes it difficult for historians to avoid this portrait. Their work is a major contribution to a full and honest history of the obfuscations in nineteenth-century white Americans' celebrations of democracy and freedom. But the views of free Afro-Americans are missing.

There are still precious few historical documents that record what free Afro-Americans in the antebellum South did, much less what they thought, believed, feared, or dreamed.[4] Although we had the good fortune to have access to the unique Ellison letters, we ran into countless dead ends in our search for corroborating evidence, systematic comparisons, and many basic facts. We turned up enough evidence to be certain about many matters, but the absence of crucial pieces of evidence has forced us to speculate. The only way to avoid speculation was to ignore important questions, to mimic Hundley. We have chosen to ask questions we cannot fully answer, to consider possibilities, and to imagine what was likely. We have rooted our analysis in what is known about William Ellison and his society, and we have tried to be equally candid about our ignorance and our knowledge. We expect to be held as accountable for our interpretations ventured with meager documentation as for our arguments steadied by a heavier ballast of evidence.

Compared to nearly all other free persons of color, William Ellison left a well-marked trail of documents. Fragments of his experience are scattered among deeds, wills, estate papers, court records, tax books, census lists, parish registers, ledgers, newspaper advertisements, medical records, the diaries and personal letters of white planters and their wives, reminiscences of white and black acquaintances of the Ellisons and their descendants, and among the tombstones in country graveyards. When assembled around the Ellison letters, these pieces allow us to see the antebellum South through the eyes of Ellison, his family, and his free Afro-American friends. Looking through somebody else's eyes is always a tricky business. But unless we have completely mistaken our vision for his, William Ellison saw a South quite different from the one witnessed by white planters and black slaves. What he saw and the sense he made of it defy brief description. We have written a rather long book trying to reconstruct his perspective and to understand it. At the very least, Ellison's story makes clear that he and his free Afro-American friends were active, resourceful human beings who did what they could to make their own history. Like the rest of us, however, they did not have a clean slate to write upon.

It is easy for us to take for granted what Ellison did not and could not: freedom. Freedom was his most prized possession. It allowed him to found, preserve, and endow his

family. But no free person of color could be confident of freedom in the antebellum South. Freedom marked a Negro as
someone whites had to watch. Within the tight constraints
imposed by whites, Ellison used his freedom as he saw fit.
The temptation to define how Ellison and others like him
should have employed their freedom is by no means confined
to antebellum whites. The late twentieth century is not without observers of all colors and political persuasions who are
prepared to pronounce judgment on the Ellisons and their
friends for what they did or failed to do. Contemporary whites
and free people of color considered William Ellison a highly
respectable man; what his slaves thought we do not know.
By today's standards, he may be judged among the worst, not
the best, of men. But his values and his choices originated in
his world, not ours. Although we have our own opinions and
have made no attempt to hide them, we consider our primary
task to explain what Ellison and other free Afro-Americans
did, not what they should have done.

The first step toward understanding Ellison and his world
requires abandoning the language of racial identification
commonly used today. Any person with a discernible trace of
Afro-American ancestry is now usually called "black." Although
Afro-Americans and whites are aware of darker and lighter
shades of black and brown, the racial polarization of our own
society has collapsed these distinctions. The term "Negro"
has fallen into disuse, reserved for formal, noncommittal purposes. The term "colored" is quaint and odious, connoting
the pretensions and evasions that masked racial oppression
within memory of most Americans. The distinctions of color
subsumed today within the term "black" were crucial markers
of both ancestry and status to free Afro-Americans in the
antebellum South. To Ellison and his friends, a "black" person had no white ancestors and was most likely a slave; a
"colored" person was the descendant of white and black
ancestors and was more likely than a black person to be free;
"Negro" was a collective term that encompassed all persons
with any Afro-American ancestry. Some whites understood
what these terms connoted and routinely used them with precision. The vast majority of Southern whites, however, considered the words "Negro," "colored," and "black" synonyms,

for all practical purposes. Those perceptions, which William Ellison could do nothing to alter, were the ones that ultimately counted, a fact we have signified by the word "black" in the title of this book. Elsewhere, however, we have adopted terminology that preserves the racial distinctions significant to Ellison and other free Afro-Americans in the antebellum South. Although we can seldom be certain of ancestry, we have used "black" to mean individuals of unmixed African descent; "colored," "mulatto," and "brown" to mean persons of mixed white and black ancestry; and "Negro" and "Afro-American" to mean all persons with any African ancestors. Once our ears are attuned to these anachronisms, our eyes can open to the world these words describe.

BLACK MASTERS

I

April's Story

ON June 20, 1820, April Ellison appeared on the steps of the Sumter District courthouse in Sumterville, South Carolina. He had left his home and traveled twelve miles east over dusty, rutted roads to present a petition to Judge William Henry DeSaussure. April had a simple request—he wanted a new name. April Ellison, his lawyer explained at the hearing, was a "freed yellow man of about twenty nine years of age." Emancipated four years earlier, he had moved to Stateburg in Sumter District, where he was "endeavoring to preserve a good character and gain a livelihood by honest industry in the trade of Gin making." His name hampered these ambitions because "April" was recognizable to all as a slave name. A change of names, his lawyer argued, "altho' apparently unimportant[,] would yet greatly advance his interest as a tradesman." A new name would also "save him and his children from degradation and contempt which the minds of some do and will attach to the name of April." Because of the "kindness" of his former master, William Ellison, and as a "mark of gratitude and respect for him," he asked to change his name to William.[1]

April Ellison had managed to put behind him the status of slavery but not slavery's stigma. Since April's name accurately evoked his origins, a white judge might consider it perfectly appropriate. It was highly unusual for a free person of color to petition for a new name, but April believed that his slave name would impede his progress as a gin maker and stain his children's future. In the little upcountry courthouse in Sumterville, April was seeking to strip away the last vestige of his former slave status that he could do anything about. Freed from the name April, he would try to let his skill as a crafts-man, his good character, and his ambition speak for them-selves. When Judge DeSaussure granted his request, he now had a free man's name, a name consistent with his status. Yet the new William Ellison's color made the stain of slavery indelible.

When he presented his petition April Ellison lived on the western edge of Sumter District in or near Stateburg, a tiny village perched in the High Hills of the Santee, a narrow ridge of rolling hills along the east bank of the Wateree River. Renowned for beauty, a healthy climate, and fertile soils, the High Hills attracted some of the earliest settlers of the Caro-lina back country. By the first decades of the nineteenth cen-tury the Hills were dense with cotton plantations, planters, and their slaves. In 1820 Afro-Americans made up nearly two-thirds of Sumter District's total population of 25,369, but slaves numbered 16,343 while free Negroes like Ellison numbered only 382.[2] Why did this "freed yellow man" live in the aristo-cratic High Hills, surrounded by wealthy white planters and

their gangs of slaves? Who was April Ellison, and where did he come from?

AS with the vast majority of individuals born into slavery, a nearly impenetrable curtain shrouds April's origins and early life. His tombstone records that he was born in 1790.[3] His birthplace was probably his owner's plantation about forty miles northwest of the High Hills in Fairfield District, a fertile upcountry region lying between the Wateree and Broad rivers.[4] Self-described as a "yellow man," a contemporary term for a light-skinned mulatto, April was of mixed racial origins. Since he was a slave, we can be certain his mother was a slave; since he belonged to a white man named Ellison, she probably did too. White slaveowners named Ellison lived in Fairfield District in 1790, but all that is known of their slaves is their number, making it impossible to determine if a slave woman who could have been April's mother was among them.[5] Of her ancestry or even her name, we know nothing at all.

The identity of April's father is also obscure. Either a mulatto father or mother could account for April's light complexion. But more likely April's father was a white man, either William Ellison, the planter who eventually freed him, or William Ellison's father, Robert Ellison. When April was born in 1790 Robert Ellison owned fifteen slaves on a plantation situated two miles from Winnsboro, the largest town in Fairfield District, a settlement of fifty or sixty houses.[6] April's mother may have been one of the slaves. Robert Ellison was forty-eight years old in 1790, and his youngest child was not yet five.[7] His eldest child, William, was about seventeen. Both men lived on the plantation and had the biological capability to father a slave son. Mulatto children fathered by white planters with their slave women were not uncommon on the Carolina frontier. James Chesnut, an upcountry acquaintance of William Ellison who lived in nearby Camden, was the father of several mulatto children, according to his daughter-in-law Mary Boykin Chesnut.[8] The few slaves masters emancipated tended to be mulattoes, often children of the master.[9]

April Ellison's 1820 petition for a new name declared that William Ellison had owned him "for many years" and had freed him. Just when William Ellison acquired April is not recorded, but it was evidently between 1800 and 1806. In 1800, according to the census, William Ellison owned no slaves; ten years later, he owned nineteen.[10] Upon his father's death in 1806, William received a bequest of a substantial amount of property, but no slaves. William's younger brothers and sisters inherited the slaves their father owned at the time of his death, and, because the will named each slave, we can be certain that April was not among them.[11] William's generous inheritance of land suggests that he was in good standing with his father and thus may have been given some of his father's slaves before 1806, probably April and possibly his mother. In 1800 Robert Ellison owned nine slaves.[12] April could have been one of the nineteen slaves the census enumerator recorded for William Ellison in 1810. Or, more likely, he was the free person of color listed as living on William Ellison's plantation.[13] If so, April still had the legal status of a slave, since he was not formally manumitted until 1816. But by 1810 he may already have begun the transition from slavery to freedom, living *de facto* as a free man.

More direct evidence that April's father was either Robert or William Ellison is the exceptional treatment he received while still a slave. Rather than sending the mulatto boy out to the fields with the other slaves, his master apprenticed him to a trade. The apprenticeship probably began about 1802 when April was twelve, which makes it impossible to surmise whether the decision was made by William or his father. But the most telling evidence for the paternity of one of the white Ellisons is that William Ellison eventually freed April. There is no indication that Ellison ever manumitted any other slave, while there is good evidence that something more than April's craft, color, and talent made him special in his master's eyes. William Ellison owned another artisan, a cabinetmaker named Julius, whom he sold in Charleston in 1813 for $800.[14] The handsome price Julius commanded suggests he was a man of considerable talent and makes clear Ellison did not free all his skilled slaves. Nor, since Julius was a mulatto, did Ellison free all of his mulatto slaves. Instead, for some reason Ellison singled out April for manumission. He may well have had several motives for freeing April, but probably an important one was that April was his half-brother or his son.

When April Ellison was born the South Carolina back

country was barely a generation removed from the frontier. Not until the 1750s did settlers begin to flood the interior, many migrating south from Pennsylvania, Virginia, and North Carolina, and others trekking inland from the Carolina coast. Growth was so rapid that by 1765 the hinterland contained nearly three-quarters of the white population of the colony, but still only a tiny fraction of South Carolina's slaves, who were concentrated on the rice and indigo plantations in the low country. Most men in the back country were hard-scrabble yeoman farmers clearing land, running some livestock, and producing for their families' needs. But a few ambitious, aggressive, and lucky men soon began to emerge from the yeomanry. Eager to make fortunes and found dynasties and not overly fastidious about how, they plunged into any enterprise that promised to turn a shilling. These barons of the back country acquired and sold vast tracts of land, founded towns at the fall line, opened stores, and, above all, began to buy slaves. Slaveholders developed commercial agriculture in the interior and, despite poor means of transportation, began to ship indigo, tobacco, hemp, tar, pitch, turpentine, provisions, cattle, and hogs to the Charleston market.[15] These frontier aristocrats—Wade Hampton I, Thomas Sumter, John Chesnut, John Winn, Joseph Kershaw, and others—rose quickly, and they often retained those qualities that had helped them climb from the pack. They were, contemporaries said, equally tough on horses, slaves, and women. Rustic swashbucklers, they were more at home in the saddle than the drawing room. Their ethos is reflected in the name of the stallion owned by Thomas Sumter and trained by Wade Hampton that beat all comers in the Charleston races in 1791: *Ugly*.[16] Crude in comparison with the coastal nabobs, these back-country men represented the South's new planter class—wealthy, proud, and increasingly powerful.

Robert Ellison hardly ranked in the upper echelons of the frontier aristocracy, but with fifteen slaves in 1790 he was one of the prospering back-country planters. Three out of four inland families owned no slaves in 1790, and two-thirds of the slaveowning minority owned fewer than five.[17] When Robert Ellison first arrived in South Carolina twenty-nine years earlier, he was a member of that slaveless white majority. The Ellison family came to the Carolina upcountry by way of Ireland and Pennsylvania. Originally English, the Ellisons moved across the Irish Sea in the seventeenth century, settling in the northernmost county of Ireland, County Antrim. There in 1742 Robert Ellison had been born. Two years later his father, his mother, his sister, and his four brothers moved to Pennsylvania, where Robert grew up. After the death of his parents in 1761, Robert and the other Ellison children moved to Fairfield District, South Carolina.[18]

According to family tradition, Robert inherited little from his father, a man of "moderate means." But because the young man had a "good English education," he secured the position of surveyor in Fairfield and soon began to buy land.[19] In 1772 he married Elizabeth Potts of Charleston and settled on his farm two miles from what would become in 1785 the town of Winnsboro. During the American Revolution he served as a captain with General William Moultrie. After the war Robert Ellison became an active citizen and respected planter in Fairfield.[20] Several of his sons, including William, followed in his footsteps and became planters in the neighborhood. Another son, John, moved to Charleston, where he became a dry goods merchant on King Street. His daughter Sarah Elizabeth married a young immigrant from northern Ireland named James Adger, whom she met while riding near her father's plantation in 1802.

Adger had spent five or six years in the hardware business in New York City before coming to Charleston in 1802 to supervise a cargo. Once he disposed of the shipment, Adger decided to visit his brother who lived in Fairfield. He traveled upcountry with a white cotton gin maker from Winnsboro named William McCreight.[21] After his marriage to Sarah Ellison, Adger settled in Charleston and became a leading hardware merchant, cotton factor, and wharf owner. In years to come the kinship between the Charleston Adgers and the Fairfield Ellisons would influence one of the young slave boys who belonged to the Ellisons in 1802. But Adger's traveling companion had a far more decisive impact on April Ellison's life.

BY 1790 a tiny planter class made up of small fry like Robert Ellison and great slaveholders like Wade Hampton had emerged in the Carolina back country. But before cotton transformed the region into a plantation society, driving the bears and panthers from the thickets and making fancy plantation balls as common as eye-gouging and ear-biting, someone had to solve a problem. Cotton had been grown in the interior almost from the moment the first white settlers arrived, but commercial production was impossible because cleaning cotton was slow and clumsy. The variety of cotton that grew best in the upcountry—green seed, or short staple—was filled with seeds that clung to the fiber like ticks to the skin. Many a pioneer family spent the long winter evenings seated around the fire tediously plucking the fluff from each seed. The few pounds of clean cotton produced by hour upon hour of handpicking got made up into homespun on family spinning wheels and hand looms.[22]

In 1792 a young New Englander accepted a position as tutor to the children of a Georgia planter. The teaching post did not work out, but Eli Whitney stayed on at Mrs. Catherine Greene's plantation along the Savannah River, where he heard talk about the difficulty of separating those damnable seeds from cotton fibers. Whitney was a practical man, the problem interested him, and he turned his attention to it. He also recognized an opportunity when he saw one. In a world clothed in material made from wool and flax, a machine that would quickly and efficiently remove the seeds from cotton fiber would have immediate economic repercussions on an international scale. The English had already succeeded in mechanizing the manufacture of cotton cloth, but they were unble to get sufficient raw cotton. The South—with its vast acreage, its favorable climate, and its expanding slave labor force—could grow cotton in unimaginable quantities, but cotton stuck to seeds was useless in English textile mills. Early in 1793 Whitney built a simple little device, just wire teeth set in a wooden cylinder that, when rotated, reached through narrow slats to pull cotton fibers away from the seeds, while a brush swept the fibers from the revolving teeth. It was crude, but Whitney knew what he had, and he rushed back north to take out a patent and to begin manufacturing cotton gins.[23]

News of Whitney's invention spread throughout the South like a canebrake fire. In September 1793 the South Carolina planter Pierce Butler wrote a friend, "There is a young Man at Mrs Greene's in Georgia, who has made a Cotton Ginn that with two Boys cleans of the green seed cotton 64 pds of clean cotton in about 9 hours." Butler reported that he "saw the Hand Ginn work. It is much superior to the Ginns we make use of. . . ."[24] Whitney's gin could clean up to 600 pounds of cotton a day when powered by two horses, Butler learned. He calculated that two such gins could clean far more than all thirty-six of the machines he currently used and free the labor of more than thirty slave operatives for use elsewhere on his plantation. Butler itched to replace his gins with Whitney's model. "I am very desirous of getting some other than hand gins for cleaning my Cotton," he wrote in the spring of 1794. "I go more largely on Cotton than any planter in America."[25]

Planters everywhere clamored for the machines, and local craftsmen could sniff out a market as well as Whitney. No mere patent could stop clever backwoods mechanics from building gins of their own. Illegal, locally made gins appeared rapidly in the interior. "The people of the back country almost uniformly prefer making their own gins to using ours," complained Phineas Miller, Whitney's partner, in May 1797.[26] To end the constant litigation caused by the poaching of local entrepreneurs, the South Carolina legislature in 1801 allocated $50,000 to buy from Whitney and Miller "their patent right to the making, using and vending the saw machine within the limits of the State."[27]

Widespread use of the gin broke the bottleneck in commercial production, and cotton quickly pushed out indigo, then tobacco, as the upcountry's major cash crop. Between 1790 and 1800, cotton exports from South Carolina skyrocketed from 9,840 pounds to more than 6,000,000 pounds. Soaring cotton production was made possible by an enormous increase in slaves in the interior. In the twenty years after 1790, the number of slaves beyond the tidewater increased from 29,094 to 85,654.[28] Fairfield and surrounding districts participated in the cotton boom. In 1795 Captain James Kincaid began one of the ripples of change when he set up in his grist mill in Fairfield what is said to be the first operating saw gin in South Carolina.[29] Just a few miles from Kincaid's mill lived a young slave boy named April. Whitney's invention would profoundly alter April Ellison's life. While the commercial production of cotton bound millions of Afro-Americans to perpetual slavery, it would give April an opportunity for education, freedom, and—in time—a fortune.

About 1802 April's master apprenticed him to William McCreight, the young white Winnsboro gin maker who traveled upcountry with James Adger. The McCreight family settled in Fairfield about the same time as the Ellisons, and David McCreight served in Robert Ellison's company during the revolutionary war. While the Ellisons moved into planting, the McCreights gravitated toward the skilled trades. Young William McCreight began his career as a carpenter, building several of the fine houses in early Winnsboro. Sometime after 1795 he began to employ his woodworking skills to build cotton gins, joining the wildcat gin makers throughout the South who seized the new opportunity. McCreight soon gained recognition in Fairfield and surrounding districts as a master craftsman, and his business thrived. McCreight was about twenty-five years old when young April arrived at his shop. The ginwright had no slaves of his own, and he badly needed additional labor to meet the planters' demands for his machines. McCreight had several white apprentices working for him, and his new slave apprentice gave him another useful pair of hands.[30]

April worked in McCreight's gin shop until 1816, growing to manhood between the carpenter's bench and the blacksmith's forge. He was fortunate to have an apprenticeship, and he was doubly fortunate to be apprenticed to McCreight. Training in any trade set him apart from most slaves, who were consigned to grub their lives away with thick-handled hoes. Few slaves had the chance to work with well-wrought tools in an artisan's shop. Even those lucky enough to be trained in a craft usually received only rudimentary apprenticeships, relatively brief periods of instruction designed to prepare them as rough plantation carpenters, blacksmiths, or masons.[31] April, in contrast, spent as many as fourteen years under the tutelage of a master craftman, learning year by year the ways of a complex trade. Gin making required expertise as a carpenter, a blacksmith, and a machinist, plus the rarer ability to integrate the three crafts. April's apprenticeship began his development into a master gin maker.

The craft of gin making was only about ten years old when April arrived at McCreight's shop. As a consequence, his apprenticeship could not have resembled those of ancient craft guilds, where the master was the keeper of an old and highly specialized skill that he passed on to successive generations of apprentices by demonstration and example. With little that could be called tradition, the essence of the craft consisted of an idea, Whitney's. Within the ambit of that original conception almost every feature of the craft was in flux. Gin makers did not manufacture a standardized product, especially in the early years. Each gin was built to the specifications of an individual planter, its size and construction dependent on the planter's needs. Pushed by the planters' insistence on ever bigger and better machines, successful gin makers continually tinkered and fiddled with various combinations of materials, gears, saws, belts, assemblies, brushes, and more, designing and redesigning as they built new gins and repaired old ones.[32] During April's apprenticeship McCreight devised a variant on the Whitney gin, an innovation that gained local renown as the "McCreight plan." The timing of April's apprenticeship could not have been better. He collaborated in the exciting first stages of the evolution of cotton gin technology, as McCreight and his coworkers searched for improvements. Learning the craft at a time when demand greatly outstripped supply also probably meant that April was brought along quickly, pushed into every facet of the trade.

McCreight's shop was a world of tangible objects and physical processes, but it was also a place of creative thought. The complexity of the product combined with the constant experimentation meant that gin making took intellectual power as well as manual prowess. During his training in the gin shop April learned to read, write, and cipher. He acquired basic bookkeeping skills. He figured costs, drew up bills, and kept track of debts and credits. He learned to calculate tolerances, reckon the strength and durability of materials, estimate friction and wear, compute gear ratios, assess stress and torque, measure angles, and lay off distances. As he fashioned wood, metal, leather, and bristle into the hundreds of separate parts that made up a cotton gin, he developed the mechanic's ability to conceptualize the whole, to envision each part meshing with all the others. By the time April left McCreight's shop he had mastered all the skills, intellectual and mechanical, required for independent success in his trade.[33]

The shop served as April's schoolhouse for social as well as mechanical skills. There April met scores of planters who came to negotiate with McCreight for gins. Gins were heavy, cumbersome machines, and once sold and in place on a plantation—usually set up in a specially rigged gin house, sometimes two stories high—they were seldom returned to the shop for maintenance.[34] Instead, somebody trained in the gin shop, like April, traveled out to the plantations to service the machines. On such trips, April reinforced the invaluable network of strategic acquaintances and contacts he had made at the shop. These encounters in the gin shop and on plantations exhibited April's skills before a demanding audience and provided him with valuable experience in how to get along with white planters, not the easiest persons for a young Negro man to please. Self-confidence tempered by tact and deference to white expectations was as important to April as his mechanical ability. Without a flawless education in the ways of white people, April could never hope to prosper as a free colored gin maker in South Carolina.

While William McCreight taught April the craft of gin making, he also gave him lessons in cooperation and trust across racial lines. In the early years when April looked over McCreight's shoulder and later when they reversed positions, April saw that McCreight was a white man he could count on, a white man who did not need constant reassurance of his superiority, who instead recognized, nurtured, and rewarded April for work that equaled or surpassed his own. McCreight allowed April to grow and develop into a master craftsman whom many lesser white men would have regarded as an unwelcome challenger. Over the years, McCreight earned April's trust and respect.[35] He gave April a powerful reason to be optimistic that some whites would not permit his color to cloud their judgment of his character and skill, that they would look beyond what he appeared to be and see what he was.

We do not know with certainty what William Ellison had in mind for his young mulatto slave during his years of training in McCreight's shop, but the evidence suggests that he envisioned freedom for April all along. Given the trade he chose for April, it was impossible for Ellison to employ him full time. A large planter could keep a slave carpenter, blacksmith, or mason busy at home, only occasionally hiring him out to neighbors. But not even the largest planter could provide enough work for a gin maker. Gin makers sold their machines to dozens of slaveholders scattered over an extensive territory, and they traveled as widely to maintain and service the gins. If Ellison intended April to remain a slave, then he was willing for his gin maker to be a slave on a very long leash. More likely, Ellison planned to free April.

Certainly April's extended apprenticeship in gin making prepared him for freedom. He not only obtained specialized training in the craft, but he exercised the discipline and habits necessary to a free man. His education bore similarities to that Robert Ellison designed for his white sons. Like many other self-made upcountry gentry, Ellison hoped to protect his sons from the hazards of a life made too easy by their father's wealth. When he drew up his will in 1806, he gave special attention to his youngest son, Joseph, who had yet to reach his majority. "And as idleness is the parent of vice and always injurious to youth," Robert Ellison declared, "I desire that Joseph shall by his own exertions procure himself food and clothing until he has management of his own property."[36] The classic virtues of the early republic—hard work, thrift, independence, and self-sufficiency—were traits the white Ellisons had to learn, and also ones that—under different circumstances—April acquired during his years in McCreight's shop. If William Ellison did indeed plan to free April, then April probably knew it. While he worked in the shop he probably knew that he was not being trained simply to become a more valuable slave, that all his effort would eventually pay off with freedom. If few slaves had April's talent and training, fewer still had his incentive.

Almost nothing is known about April's life outside the gin shop during these early years, except that in January 1811, when April was twenty, he had a daughter by a sixteen-year-old slave woman named Matilda. Despite the lack of legal provision for the marriage of slaves, Matilda was April's wife. She may have been a slave of William Ellison, but just as likely she was not. By this time April probably lived almost as a free man and could have chosen a wife in town or from one of the plantations he visited as he made his rounds servicing McCreight's gins. His new child, Eliza Ann, was a slave because her mother was.[37] At the time of her birth April was edging toward full freedom. Almost certainly he did not plan for his wife and daughter to remain slaves forever.

ON June 8, 1816, William Ellison appeared with April before a Fairfield District magistrate and five freeholders from the neighborhood. The planter had come to seek permission to emancipate his twenty-six-year-old slave. In 1800 the South Carolina legislature had spelled out in detail the procedure for manumission. To end the practice of freeing slaves of "bad or depraved character" and slaves who "from age or infirmity" were incapacitated, the state required that a master testify under oath to the "good character" of the slave he wished to free and to the slave's "ability to gain a livelihood in an honest way."[38] The outcome of this particular hearing must have been a foregone conclusion. All those sitting in judgment would have known the Ellison family as pillars of the Winnsboro community. They would also have known William McCreight and thus the quality of April's training as a gin maker. And they were probably already acquainted with April himself. They may have observed him at work in McCreight's shop or witnessed his work firsthand on their plantations. Following the brief ceremony April Ellison, master gin maker, had no other master.

According to the testimony of a white South Carolinian who met April many years after his manumission, William Ellison did not give April his freedom. April purchased it. "During the time of his apprenticeship," the white acquaintance stated, "he was allowed, by his master, to do extra work; and from his industry and economy he laid up sufficient money to purchase his freedom from his master."[39] The few slaves who obtained freedom often bought themselves, and April's age of twenty-six suggests that he had spent years working on Sunday and after hours to scrape together his purchase price. Having to buy his own freedom would have been consistent with the stern training for independence that was a tradition in the Ellison family.[40]

In 1816 April Ellison no longer belonged to another man. For the first time in his life he could decide for himself where he would live and work. A wise choice was crucial, and it could not have been an easy decision. Staying in Winnsboro was one possibility, but one that did not promise much advantage. He might have continued as an employee in McCreight's shop, but that would have severely limited his income. It would also mean staying in the dependent position he had occupied as a slave, still under the direct supervision of a white man. Moreover, if April had decided to remain in Winnsboro and set up his own shop, he would have been in the untenable position of competing directly with McCreight. Another option was Charleston. Manumitted slaves often made their way to the city, where they had a range of economic opportunities far broader than that available in the countryside. Charleston also offered the advantages of the largest community of free people of color in the state. But April Ellison was a gin maker, and his gins were designed for the short-staple cotton grown in the interior. To survive as a gin maker, he had to live near his market among upcountry cotton plantations.

Shortly after his emancipation April moved from Winnsboro to Stateburg. McCreight may have suggested that Stateburg would be a promising location, or perhaps planters in the area invited April to settle among them, eager as they were for a good local gin maker. In any case, consistent with the other principal decisions in his life, April's choice of Stateburg was astute. His prospects would not have been better anyplace else in the state. Forty miles from Winnsboro, Stateburg lay near the perimeter of McCreight's territory, though still within it. In Stateburg April was far enough away to escape daily association with those who had seen him grow up a slave and to avoid direct competition with McCreight in Fairfield District yet near enough to exploit contacts made in McCreight's shop and to trade on his reputation.

At least as early as 1813 and probably well before, McCreight built gins for High Hills planters. Richard Singleton, for example, whose "Home Place" was just a few miles south of Stateburg, was a good customer for McCreight. A planter with more than 5,600 acres and 240 slaves, Singleton relied on McCreight to service his heavily used machines. In 1814 Singleton paid McCreight $87.64 for "repairs to two old gins." Two years later, the year April obtained his freedom, Singleton paid McCreight $143.96 ½ for extensive repairs to three gins and ordered another new gin from him.[41] Since these repairs were made on site, someone from the shop in Winnsboro, possibly April, traveled to Singleton's plantation to do this specialized work. As one of the booming plantation districts in the interior, Sumter contained many planters like Singleton who needed the services of a gin maker of proven ability. Most likely, a number of them already knew about April Ellison before 1816, when he came to settle permanently.

Stateburg was located within a few miles of the geographical center of the state, and it stood at a strategic crossroads. One of the state's oldest and most traveled roads from Charleston to the upcountry—the King's Highway of colonial days, later called the Charleston-Camden Road—ran north and south along the narrow ridge of hills. At Stateburg it intersected the Sumterville-Columbia Road that cut across the hills from east to west. For an ambitious gin maker Stateburg provided an ideal location. It allowed easy access to the prosperous plantation districts of the midlands, an opening to the developing cotton regions farther north, and a good connection to Charleston to the south. The Wateree River also offered valuable downstream transportation to Charleston and beyond.

The village had been laid out in 1783 by General Thomas Sumter, revered "Gamecock" of the American Revolution, who hoped to attract the state capital when the legislature moved it from Charleston to some more central location. Not incidentally, General Sumter also hoped to boost the value of the more than 100,000 acres he owned in the area. But the capital went to Columbia, twenty-five miles to the west, and when April Ellison arrived in Stateburg in 1816 he found a sleepy little settlement, with only a tavern, an academy, a store, and a church. Vast estates surrounded the village in the hills to the east and along the swamps of the Wateree River, which

flowed four miles to the west. After the mid-1790s cotton production had increased almost yearly in Sumter District, and
the wealth it generated supported a small aristocracy in splen-
did style.[42] In 1808 David Ramsay, the Charleston physician
and historian, claimed that around Stateburg "refined society
may be enjoyed in great perfection."[43] When South Carolina's preeminent architect and mapmaker, Robert Mills, visited in the early 1820s, he announced that there was "not a
more desirable place of residence, either for health or society,
in any part of the state. . . ." The High Hills were home to
scores of great planters "whose affluence and hospitality give
to the place a character of ease and dignity."[44]

In their rush for accumulation, the back country's first-gen-
eration aristocrats showed little concern for either ease or dignity. Still, they managed to build more than personal empires.
In 1786, for example, General Sumter and several other High
Hills grandees met in Stateburg to organize the Claremont
Society, which quickly founded a local academy and library.
Two years later many of these same gentlemen gathered in
the long room of the Stateburg tavern to establish the Claremont Episcopal Church, and the following year they erected
a building.[45] Nevertheless, the sons and daughters of the
founders were primarily responsible for the elegance and
refinement that so impressed Ramsay, Mills, and others.
Resting comfortably on their fathers' accomplishments, the
second generation could afford to be as concerned with consumption as with accumulation. These sons and daughters
cultivated expensive tastes, kept up with sophisticated fashions, and set extravagant standards of hospitality. Often they
married into the low-country dynasties, and in time they created a plantation culture in the upcountry nearly indistin-
guishable from that of the tidewater.[46]

Sounds of the gracious life in the High Hills echoed through
the aristocrats' spacious homes—at Mathew Singleton's
"Melrose," at John Singleton's "Midway," at Richard Singleton's "Home Place," at "The Ruins" of the Mayrants, at the
Kinlocks' "Acton," and at the Watieses' "Marden."[47] Anna
Waties, daughter of Judge Thomas Waties, who had moved
from Georgetown to Stateburg in 1803, explained that an
attempt to start a local Sunday School failed because "There

are no poor people." Those of the "better class," she said, "were as well qualified to teach their children at home as those who would go to church to do it—so it was given up."[48] Viewed from the piazza of a stately home nestled in the High Hills, life could indeed seem uniformly elegant. Anna Waties did not rub shoulders with many poor people on her rounds of fancy dress balls, or while learning to ride "lanciers," or enjoying the medieval pageantry of a tournament at a local plantation. Nor did she or her friends encounter poor folk while strolling under parasols in the exquisite gardens of the Sumters, Kinlocks, or Richardsons, while worshiping in a pew in Stateburg's Church of the Holy Cross, or while feasting on a late-morning breakfast of eggnog, mint juleps, coffee, buttermilk, chicken, duck, pigeon, sausages, and hot breads, as several servants shooed flies with peacock-tail fans. At home at "Marden" Anna Waties did not even see many slaves. The home places were clustered in the hills where it was cool, breezy, serene, and healthy, and the only slaves in the immediate vicinity were a dozen or two house servants. Plantation fields and gangs of slaves were out of sight several miles away, many of them on the edge of the Wateree's buzzing swamps, managed by overseers.[49]

The opulent society of the planter aristocrats did not attract April Ellison to Stateburg. Instead, he came because their huge plantations required well-made gins as much as slave labor to produce the wealth that supported their elegance. Stateburg's promising market for gins, its excellent location, and its fine road and river transportation would have meant nothing to April Ellison if he, a "freed yellow man," were unwelcome. Presumably, he knew before he arrived that Sumter District tolerated Negroes who were free. Although slaves outnumbered free Afro-Americans more than forty to one, there were more free people of color in Sumter in 1820 than in any other rural district in South Carolina.[50] The free colored population of Sumter was ten times greater than that of Fairfield.[51] It included a group called the Sumter Turks. According to a confused tradition, these dark-skinned people were originally Moors from the Mediterranean who came to South Carolina late in the eighteenth century. Some of them served General Thomas Sumter during the American Revolution, and after the war he invited them to settle in Sumter District.[52] Although most Sumter whites did not consider Turks Negroes, the census listed them as free people of color. A few Turk families and a large fraction of Sumter's other free people of color lived in twenty-four households clustered in the western part of the district. The exact location of this small settlement cannot be determined from the census, but it almost certainly lay within a few miles of Stateburg, though not in the village proper. April Ellison and his family appear in the 1820 census squarely in the middle of this free colored community.[53]

Initially, April chose to live among those who shared his color and his status. Somewhat like a man in a room full of menacing strangers, Ellison positioned himself with his back safely to the wall. While he familiarized himself with the planter barons of Sumter District, his home was nestled among other free people of color. It served to identify him in the white community as a free man and to protect him and his family from being mistaken for slaves. Living in the settlement also insulated him from the thousands of slaves in Sumter whose masters could quickly get the wrong idea from the most innocent association between free Negroes and slaves. Furthermore, April needed free colored friends almost as much as white customers. If he failed to establish good relations with his free Afro-American neighbors, he set himself up as a potential target for damaging rumors spread by a free Negro enemy, rumors that could destroy his chances to establish his business, and worse. As a gin maker, April brought a highly prized skill to the Sumter free Negro community, one that promised to raise the entire community in the estimation of whites. For that reason April may have been welcomed by other free Afro-Americans in Sumter. Certainly no evidence suggests they shunned him. Their existence in the district for decades indicated that April's color and status would not prevent him from practicing his trade.

APRIL began work as a gin maker immediately after settling in Sumter District. In the first few years he primarily repaired gins. Manufacturing new gins on any scale had to wait until he had the capital for a shop of his own and additional skilled laborers. As a gin repairman he probably continued to service

McCreight's old customers, taking care of machines he had helped build in Winnsboro. Now he made the same repairs, but he was his own man and every dollar he earned was his.

In 1819 April presented Richard Singleton with a bill of $42.50 for sharpening saws in his cotton gins. Almost certainly Singleton had purchased these gins a few years earlier from McCreight. At Ellison's rate of 25 cents a saw, he had hand-sharpened 170 saws, representing probably four gins.[54] Forty- and forty-five-saw gins were common, although gins could accommodate sixty or more saws by lengthening the arbor or drive shaft along which the saws were arranged at intervals of roughly three-quarters of an inch. Saws had quickly replaced the wire teeth that Whitney originally devised. A typical saw was a circular piece of iron about eight inches in diameter with an irregular hole in the center for the wooden drive shaft. Teeth serrated the outer edge of the saw, filed to razor-sharp points at about a sixty-degree angle to the perimeter. When the shaft rotated, the saws reached through narrow wooden slats to pull the fiber away from the seeds. The points dulled with use, causing the saw to tear fibers rather than strip them away cleanly. Saws that Ellison later made in his own shop had approximately 160 points evenly spaced around the circumference, each cut at the same angle about a quarter-inch deep.[55] Since each point was filed by hand, it was tedious, painstaking, and painful work. April's hands—dirty, callused, and nicked—would have accurately reflected his trade.

April's repairs involved much more than simply sharpening saws. Two years before repointing Singleton's saws, for example, April completely rebuilt a gin belonging to Judge Thomas Waties. April's itemized bill indicates that he supplied seven new saws and "cut deeper in the teeth" thirty-seven others. He constructed a new drive shaft and removed all the ribs, or slats, "making them wider and polishing them." With use, the ribs became rough, causing the cotton to catch, choking and clogging the gin. April built a new brush assembly, a hollow leather-sheathed cylinder covered by rows of pig-bristle brushes. The cylinder rotated in the opposite direction of the saws to brush the fibers from the saw points. April also made a new brush nut and band nut, probably of

metal, and fabricated new brush and cylinder bearings, either
from soft metal or hard wood. He mended the frame, built a
new hopper board—which fit on top of the gin above the
saws, where the seed-cotton was dropped—and he constructed a new bench on which the slave operators stood as
they fed cotton into the machine. In other words, April completely disassembled, rebuilt, and reassembled Waties's gin.
The work was complicated and intricate, both delicate and

April Ellison's bill for gin repairs, October 6, 1817.
Thomas E. Richardson papers, South Caroliniana Library.

heavy, and it required all the skills of a gin maker. It involved hundreds of parts fitted snugly into a compact, sturdy machine that had to run smoothly from sunup to sundown during the ginning season. For this work, which lasted at least twelve days and possibly more, April submitted a bill for labor and materials of $58.32½.[56]

With each year in Stateburg, April's reputation and list of customers grew. So, too, did his family. Sometime between June 8, 1816, and January 1817, April bought and freed his wife Matilda and his daughter Eliza Ann and brought them to Stateburg.[57] His son Henry was born in or near Stateburg in January 1817, followed two years later by William Jr. and in another two years by Reuben.[58] Unlike their sister Eliza Ann, all the sons were freeborn. Once the boys were old enough, they helped Ellison in his gin business, but until then he occasionally hired the time of skilled slaves who belonged to local planters. When he rebuilt Judge Waties's gin in 1817, for example, he credited the judge $9 "for hire of Carpenter George for 12 days."[59] Hired labor, however, did not suffice.

By 1820 Ellison had somehow managed to buy two adult male slaves between the ages of twenty-six and forty-five who could be put to work at once.[60] April's transition from slave to master, from slave to slaveholder, was nearly immediate. Almost from the beginning he built the economic foundation of his freedom on slave labor. No more than four years after he achieved his freedom, April demonstrated that he did not blink at perpetuating a status he detested for himself and his family. If he began to purchase the slaves soon after he arrived in Stateburg, buying them on credit and paying off the debt as he prospered, then he bought slaves at the same time he bought his wife and daughter out of slavery. By showing that he did not hesitate to own, use, and exploit slave labor, he demonstrated to local whites that, although he was a Negro, although he had only recently been a slave himself, he was no more antislavery than they were—namely, not at all. And Sumter whites were surely alert, for the same year April moved to Stateburg, inhabitants of Camden twenty miles to the north uncovered extensive plans for a slave insurrection.[61] April Ellison lived a wrenching irony. Having struggled to rescue his family from slavery, he was willing to extend that status

A nineteenth-century cotton gin, manufactured in Sumter
District, perhaps by William Ellison.
In the possession of Capt. Richard and Mrs. Mary
Anderson.

A gin saw manufactured by William Ellison.
In the possession of Capt. Richard and Mrs. Mary
Anderson.

to other Afro-Americans. At the age of thirty Ellison was a master gin maker, master of himself, and now a slave master.

In four short years April Ellison, free man of color, had achieved more worldly success than most white people in the South accomplished in a lifetime. He had established himself in the gin trade in the midst of the piedmont cotton boom, and he rode King Cotton just as surely as did the planters. Buoyed by his attainment and ambitious for more, he petitioned the court in 1820 for a new name. Successful, he was now ready to test the outer limits of white toleration as William Ellison. He decided to move from his current status as a mechanic who maintained another man's gins to that of a full-fledged independent artisan, constructing, selling, and servicing Ellison gins. To make that move required a shop. In 1822 he purchased an acre of land from General Thomas Sumter, the largest landholder in the district. Ellison's acre provided him with unquestionably the best location in the area. It sat at the hub of business at the northwest corner of the intersection of the Charleston-Camden and Sumterville-Columbia roads, in the heart of Statesburg. Ellison recognized the value of this strategic location, and so did General Sumter. At a time when the general might have charged $3 to $7 an acre for good land, he sold Ellison the prime crossroads site for $375 cash.[62] Here William Ellison built his gin shop, and he, his children, and his grandson operated it there for decades.

During the same years that Ellison built the foundation for his business, he just as carefully constructed a reputation for respectability. In his petition to change his name he told the court that while he tried to "gain a livelihood by honest industry in the trade of Gin making," he was also "endeavoring to preserve a good character."[63] He recognized that as a free man of color his future prospects depended at least as much upon his standing in the eyes of the established white community as upon his skills as a tradesman. Everything hinged on white perceptions. Achieving respectability was no small task when most whites in South Carolina viewed free Negroes as less diligent, less trustworthy, and less self-disciplined than slaves. These preconceptions made respectability all the more necessary for Ellison.

One path to respectability led just a few hundred yards south of Ellison's gin shop, across the old King's Highway to the Church of the Holy Cross, the Episcopal church founded thirty years earlier. The Stateburg gentry worshiped there and allowed the Ellisons, a handful of other free people of color, and a few slaves to sit in the gallery upstairs. But on August 6, 1824, the vestry and wardens of Holy Cross resolved "that the free colored man—Wm Ellison, be permitted to place a Bench under the Organ Loft, for the use of himself and Family."[64] It hardly seems an auspicious location—under a wheezing organ at the back of the sanctuary, seated on a bench they carried into the church—but it was. The vestry granted the Ellison family the privilege of worshiping on the main floor. Henceforth the Ellisons uttered their prayers and sang their praises on the same level, though behind, the Singletons, the Friersons, the Mayrants, the Watieses, and the other families of the white chivalry.[65]

No evidence exists that the Holy Cross vestry accorded any other free colored person such a place. Since Ellison evidently initiated the request that the vestry approved, it appears that he actively sought confirmation of his status by asking to set himself apart, literally, from the slaves and free people of color in the gallery. Aristocratic whites were his customers, his neighbors, and by the summer of 1824 his parishioners. After the service the Ellisons probably did not linger to mingle with the white members who gathered under the shade trees discussing weather, crops, families, sicknesses, and blooded horses. Nor did the Ellisons receive invitations to join the white families for a grand Sunday supper.[66] Nonetheless, they had their place on the main floor, their symbol of respectability and acceptance.

Ellison probably began attending Holy Cross soon after he arrived in Stateburg. His alternative was the High Hills Baptist Church, about two miles north of the village. It counted among its flock some of Sumter District's most substantial planters as well as a sizable number of free Negroes and Turks.[67] Perhaps Ellison chose the Episcopal church because of proximity or because he had done business with some of its communicants from his earliest days in Stateburg. It may have been Dr. William Wallace Anderson who smoothed his way into Holy Cross.

Holy Cross Episcopal Church, Stateburg.
The South Carolina Historical Society.

Dr. Anderson was master of "Borough House," a magnificent eighteenth-century mansion located on the west side of the Charleston Road, between Ellison's gin shop and the church. Dr. Anderson's father, Richard Anderson, had seen service in South Carolina during the American Revolution and while in Stateburg was befriended by Thomas and Mary MacKenzie Hooper, owners of "Borough House." The elder Anderson returned home to Maryland after the war, but he carried with him memories of the good people of Stateburg. Years later, when his son William Wallace graduated from medical school, Anderson suggested the village as a fine place for a young doctor to hang out his shingle. In 1810 Dr. Anderson did just that and soon afterward married Mary Jane MacKenzie, the Hoopers' niece and adopted daughter. Mary Jane eventually inherited "Borough House," and it remains in the Anderson family to this day.[68] Dr. Anderson's medical

records show that he treated members of the Ellison family
as early as 1824, when, for the fee of one dollar, he pulled one
of William's teeth.[69] Dr. Anderson also operated a plantation, and he may have been one of Ellison's customers in the
early 1820s as he was later. The acquaintance of the white
Anderson and the mulatto Ellison grew into a durable and
trusted relationship.

EIGHT years after he arrived in Stateburg, four years after
he changed his name, and two years after he bought his crossroads acre, Ellison received confirmation that the High Hills
gentry found him acceptable. Behind the decision of the Holy
Cross vestry lay their careful evaluation of his character, his
conduct, and his work. In 1816 Ellison had undergone a similar scrutiny by another body of white men—the magistrate
and freeholders in Fairfield. The first investigation approved
his freedom, the second his move down from the demeaning
gallery. In eight years as a free man he had established that he
was honest, sober, pious, able, respectful, and respectable. His
success required unimpeachable behavior, but that alone would
not have won him acceptance. The key was his trade. As a gin
maker Ellison provided an indispensable service to the planters. He was not the only gin maker in Sumter District, but
he was the only one in Stateburg. He was handy, he was good,
and local planters wanted him to stay. That he built his business with slave labor helped him prove his reliability among
slaveholders. By conceding to him very little—decent treatment, the chance to practice his craft, permission to distin-
guish himself from other Negroes—the Stateburg gentry
gained a great deal.

Because the ground Ellison walked was never more treach-
erous than in his early years as a free man, the action he took
in 1821 had special significance. In March he went to the Court
of Common Pleas in Sumterville to sue a white man for failure to pay a debt. In the case of *William Ellison v. George
McSwain,* Ellison charged that McSwain had bought a horse
from him and still owed him $80.[70] Although South Carolina
law allowed free people of color to make contracts and go to
court, if necessary, to enforce them, Ellison would have
weighed carefully the consequences of appearing in court

against a white man. He could not afford to overstep his bounds. To appear uppity could mean disaster. But how could he afford not to go to court? The respect of whites meant nothing if he could not protect his property. Moreover, how long would white respect last if he did not stand up for what was legally his? To seek redress in court was risky, but to avoid court when it was the last resort was riskier still. His lawsuit against McSwain was bold but not reckless. His decision to bring suit probably reflected his growing confidence in his standing in the eyes of whites. And it probably added to his stature, since the jurors in the case found for Ellison.

Ellison met the test of the jury in 1821 and the vestry in 1824, but he knew that for him the testing would never end. His reputation was only as good as yesterday's behavior. On any day an error in a bill could blemish his name, a botched gin repair could raise questions about his skills, a disrespectful word or a careless gesture could be taken as evidence that he had gotten too big for his britches. Any mistake, no matter how small, could erode white patronage and acceptance and undermine all he had constructed.

II

Freedom Bound

WILLIAM ELLISON'S personal experience was largely confined to the South Carolina upcountry. Nonetheless, the status of Afro-Americans in the Palmetto State and elsewhere throughout the South profoundly altered his life. White laws and white expectations hobbled an Afro-American's every step toward full freedom. In Ellison's world, only a few Negroes entirely escaped bondage when they obtained their liberty.

For almost two centuries before Ellison was born, free Negroes lived in North America. They accompanied the early European explorations as adventurers, sailors, and settlers.[1] Among the indentured servants who served out their terms in the tobacco fields of the Chesapeake Bay region in the seventeenth century were Negroes who, like their white counterparts, became landowning farmers and participants in the local affairs of society.[2] But as the planters of Virginia and Maryland shifted to slave labor in the last quarter of the seventeenth century, freedom for Negroes—like slavery—became a matter of ancestry rather than attainment. Children of the small number of free Negro mothers were allowed by law to retain their freedom. But the vast majority of the thousands of Africans who were brought to the British North American colonies in the eighteenth century were slaves, remained slaves all their lives, and had no choice but to pass that status to their children. Although accurate population figures for the Southern colonies on the eve of the American Revolution are not available, it is certain that free Afro-Americans were few and far between. The tobacco economy of the Chesapeake and the rice and indigo economy of the Carolinas were as firmly committed to slavery as the cotton economy would become in the nineteenth century. The Revolution did nothing to alter that commitment, but it did contribute to an historic increase in the number of slaves who became free.

At the beginning of the revolutionary war in Virginia, the British commander, Lord Dunmore, promised freedom to slaves who would leave their masters and aid the royal cause. Hundreds of slaves rallied to the British standard, and thousands more followed them during the war, including some who belonged to Thomas Jefferson.[3] The patriots did not make a matching counter-offer, though a number of Negroes served as soldiers in Northern units. A good many slaves substituted for their white masters, with the personal promise of freedom after their term of service. A few other slaves obtained their freedom in recognition of their contributions to the hard-fought military campaigns in the Southern back country.[4] By the time of the first federal census in 1790, the year of April Ellison's birth, there were 32,357 free Negroes in the South's Afro-American population of over 680,000.[5] Some of these individuals were the beneficiaries of grants of freedom for their service during the war, but even more benefited from the influence of revolutionary ideas.

The rights to liberty and property were intimately linked in the natural rights ideology of the Revolution.[6] For slaves, the two rights were contradictory. If a slaveowner recognized his slave's right to liberty, he thereby relinquished his own right to slave property. Predictably, nearly all masters found it easier to honor their own property rights than their slaves' human rights. Yet for about thirty years after the Revolution, especially in the states of the Upper South, an unprecedented number of slaveholders tipped the balance in favor of liberty. Between 1790 and 1810 the free Negro population of the Upper South more than tripled, a growth rate more than twice that of the slave population.[7] Although some masters manumitted their slaves outright, most manumissions were made by will after the master's death. George Washington's will freed over 200 slaves upon the death of his wife Martha.[8] This practice was a tidy solution to the conflict between the rights of property, which the master retained during his lifetime, and liberty, which the slave received thereafter. The number of wholesale manumissions of this sort was pitifully small compared to the total number of slaves. Probably not many more than one slaveholder in a thousand manumitted his slaves. Nonetheless, many slaves with neither privileged status nor light skin received their freedom, causing the color of the existing free Negro population to darken. By 1860, almost two-thirds of the free Afro-Americans in the Upper South were black, a consequence of liberalized manumissions a half-century earlier.[9]

Slaves did not passively await their freedom. Thousands simply ran away, and some of them succeeded in slipping into the growing free Negro populations of Baltimore, Richmond, or Charleston. More successful in securing their freedom were the hundreds of slaves who purchased themselves, as April Ellison probably did. As another compromise between property rights and liberty, self-purchase was far preferable to slaves than manumission by will. It may well be that slaves like Ellison who purchased themselves and then bought their family members accounted for the largest portion of the growing free Afro-American population in the Lower South before 1820. However, self-purchase was by its nature restricted to the relatively few slaves who had the skills and ambition necessary to earn extra money, the discipline and self-sacrifice needed to save it, and masters willing to accept it in exchange for freedom. Such slaves were among the slave elite to begin with, and, as the price of all slaves began to climb with the cotton boom after the War of 1812, these slaves became more expensive and their masters less willing to part with them. When Ellison gained his freedom, the era of expanded opportunities for self-purchase was rapidly drawing to a close.

In the Lower South the pace of manumission and self-purchase quickened between 1790 and 1810, but there was little of the wholesale manumission of an entire slave force, blacks and mulattoes, that was common in Virginia and Maryland.[10] Instead, slaves who achieved their freedom in the Lower South were usually special in some way. Typically they were mulattoes, like April Ellison. Often they were the children or the concubines of the masters who manumitted them.[11] Or, if they were not blood relatives of their master, they were likely to be a domestic servant, a nurse, a skilled craftsman, or an overseer—one of the mulatto elite who had frequent personal contact with the master. In addition, the free mulatto population of the Lower South was supplemented in the 1790s by hundreds of mulatto refugees from the bloody revolution in Santo Domingo.[12] Many states refused to allow the refugees to enter, fearing that their slaves were infected with the contagious doctrines of insurrection. Nonetheless, immigrants from Santo Domingo managed to settle in several cities in the Lower South, including Charleston and, especially, New Orleans, where they formed the core of what was by 1860 the largest urban free Negro population in the Lower South.[13] With their contribution, the growth rate of the free colored population in the Lower South actually exceeded that in the Upper South between 1790 and 1810, although the color of the free Negro population did not darken as it had in the Upper South. By 1860, more than three out of four free Afro-Americans in the Lower South were mulattoes.[14]

Soon after 1810 the period of rapid growth of the free Negro population in the South came to an end, brought about by bonanza cotton profits, high slave prices, and the waning influence of revolutionary ideas. The proportion of the Southern Afro-American population that was free reached a peak in 1810 at 8.5 percent; it declined slowly to 8.3 percent by 1830, then slumped more quickly to 6.2 percent by 1860. During the period of slow decline, the free colored population grew at roughly the same rate as the slave population. After 1830 the free Negro growth rate lagged significantly behind the slave growth rate. Few slaves after 1810 could have a glimmer of hope that they might obtain their freedom. Some did, but on the whole the free Afro-American population of the South grew naturally, and even then it did not keep pace with the burgeoning slave population. By 1860, 86 percent of the South's 261,918 free Negroes lived in the Upper South; the Lower South, after the decades of postrevolutionary manumission and subsequent population growth, contained only 36,955 free persons of color, not many more than the 30,158 that lived in the Upper South seventy years earlier.[15]

The small but significant beginning of a trend in favor of freedom for Afro-Americans at the turn of the century was decisively reversed after 1830. For most of William Ellison's life as a free man the trend ran toward slavery, and the pace accelerated with the years. By 1860, all of the quarter-million Negroes in the North were free, but 89 out of every 100 Afro-Americans in the entire nation were slaves. All but 5 percent of the nation's Afro-Americans lived in the South, where 94 out of 100 were slaves. In South Carolina and the rest of the Lower South, the proportion of the Afro-American population that was free had dropped by 1860 to 1.5 percent, less than half what it had been in 1830. In the Lower South free people of color stood on a tiny borderland between slavery and freedom, bounded on one side by over 98 percent of the Afro-Americans who were slaves and on the other side by all of the white population, who outnumbered free people of color ninety-nine to one.[16]

The racial prejudice of whites was constantly reinforced by the debased circumstances of slaves' existence: their utter poverty and dependence on their masters for food, shelter, and—many believed—foresight; the demeaning subservience and unquestioning obedience expected of them by whites; the grinding drudgery of gang labor; and perhaps most damning of all in a nation that celebrated individualism, their irrevocable lifelong sentence to be the property of another person, to be denied virtually everything whites considered their own birthright. As sociologist Orlando Patterson has written, slavery was "social death."[17] During the generation of sectional crisis, Southern politicians boasted that slaves were better off than white workers in Northern factories, but a far more accurate guide to white perceptions of the realities of slave life were the gnawing fears of slave uprisings.[18] Against all odds, slaves managed to create a culture that allowed them more individual expression and collective identity than most whites were even half-aware of. But opportunities for such simple, all-important pleasures as planting a garden, making music with friends, choosing a spouse, or naming a baby could be ended or drastically restricted at any time by the whim of the master.[19] In the context of a society that contained four million slaves, one for every two white Southerners, it is hardly surprising that whites assumed Negroes were inherently inferior and contemptible.

The assumption of black inferiority was so strong that in nearly every Southern state a person whose skin was darker than white was presumed to be a slave, unless the person had documentary proof of free status.[20] The South Carolina law under which April Ellison obtained his freedom was not unusual, although it anticipated by a few years similar laws in the other states. In 1800 the state legislature resolved that "the law heretofore enacted for the government of slaves, free negroes, mulattoes and mestizoes, have been found insufficient for keeping them in due subordination" and set about to remedy the situation. The new legislation included restrictions on manumission. A master who wanted to manumit a slave now had to appear with the slave before a magistrate and five local freeholders, as William Ellison and April did in 1816, and answer under oath all their questions about the slave's character and ability to make an honest living. If the magistrate and freeholders were satisfied, they were authorized to issue a certificate of manumission to the master, who was then required to give a copy of the certificate and of his personal deed of manumission to the slave and to record both documents with the clerk of court. If the master failed to comply with any of these steps, the manumission was void. It was then "lawful for any person whatsoever to seize [an irregularly manumitted slave] and convert [the slave] to his or her own use, and to keep as his or her property. . . ."[21]

These provisions were designed to protect the community from being burdened with the care of old or disabled free Negroes and from being harassed by those who did not maintain "due subordination." Every white person was empowered to enforce the law by confronting a free man or woman of color and demanding to see the required documents, with the promise of an extremely high reward if the documents were unsatisfactory. Doubtful cases were to be resolved in favor of slavery for, as an appeals court judge wrote in 1830, "the presumption of our law is against a Negro's freedom."[22]

William Ellison undoubtedly possessed the necessary documents. But whites probably did not often ask him to produce them since he quickly established himself in Stateburg as a reputable, hard-working free person of good character. In 1832, the informal practice of local whites determining the free status of Afro-Americans was formally accepted as a legal test for the freedom of those who were not subject to the 1800 manumission law, either because they were freed earlier or because they were freeborn, like Ellison's sons Henry, William Jr., and Reuben. In the case of *State v. Harden,* Justice John Belton O'Neall wrote that "Proof that a negro has been suffered to live in a community for years, as a free man, would, *prima facie,* establish the fact of freedom."[23] Although O'Neall's ruling was challenged in subsequent years, it nonetheless illustrates how crucial it was for a free person of color to have a good reputation among his white neighbors. It could mean the difference between freedom and slavery. Legal endorsement of local opinion not only put a premium on free Afro-Americans' relations with local whites but made travel to other regions of the state hazardous unless whites there knew them and accepted their freedom. In effect, the closer one stayed to home, the more secure one's freedom.

Shortly after April Ellison was freed, a new law strengthened the connections between freedom and locale. In 1820 South Carolina prohibited manumission, except by a special act of the legislature. Concerned about the "great and rapid increase of free negroes and mulattoes in this State, by migration and emancipation," the lawmakers also barred all "free negro or mulatto" immigrants from entering.[24] The free Afro-American population in the state had indeed increased by 50 percent between 1810 and 1820, from 4,554 to 6,826.[25] With the 1820 law the legislature attempted to stopper the passageway to freedom within the state and, by preventing free Negroes from leaking in across state boundaries, to create a free Negro population that was known to white South Carolinians, that understood and conformed to the state's racial practices, and that was numerically stable or, preferably, shrinking. Although the free Afro-American population in South Carolina did not shrink, it did grow very slowly after 1820. In the next forty years the number of free persons of color in the state increased only 45 percent, less than in the decade before 1820. Similar laws in almost all the other Southern states contributed to the declining growth rate of the free Afro-American population after 1830.[26]

LIKE Ellison, most free Afro-Americans reached for freedom and security in the society dominated by whites. They took the world as they found it and sought to wring from it whatever they could. Living in a society in which more than nine out of ten Negroes were slaves and in which most whites believed all ten should be, their principal goal was to preserve their freedom. To avoid slipping backward into bondage, they had to give their freedom substance. In the 1820s the free people of color in South Carolina whose success most closely paralleled Ellison's lived in Charleston. Their strategy, like Ellison's, was to accommodate to the boundaries of their existence as set by the white majority and to distance themselves from slaves, even to the point of becoming slaveholders.

But accomodation to whites and separation from blacks was not an acceptable strategy to every free person of color in South Carolina. In the same year that Ellison bought the land for his gin shop, a hundred miles away another remarkably gifted free man of color set out on a radically different path to freedom. In the lovely city of Charleston, with its white steeples, beautiful gardens, and shaded mansions, Denmark Vesey plotted a full-scale insurrection against white power. Rather than allying upward with powerful whites, Vesey chose to reach down to the masses of blacks and lead them in a revolution against slavery. At the age of fifty-five this black Moses would take his people out of the land of bondage or die trying. His own status as a free man and his considerable wealth and standing could not overcome his identification with the oppression and humiliation of slaves. He chose to become a revolutionary assassin rather than to remain a privileged, though disadvantaged, member of a tyrannical regime. The only life he aspired to was one in which all blacks were free.[27]

Until the year 1800, Denmark Vesey was a slave. The first historical record of Vesey dates from 1781, when he was among the human cargo Captain Joseph Vesey transported from St. Thomas to Santo Domingo. This clever fourteen-year-old became a favorite of the crew and was dubbed Telemarque. Captain Vesey sold him, only to have him returned three months later by the purchaser, who declared him unfit. Thereafter Telemarque worked as a seaman on his master's ship in the Caribbean trade. In 1800, back in Captain Vesey's home port of Charleston, Telemarque, now Denmark, had an improbable stroke of good fortune. He won $1,500 in the

East Bay lottery. With his windfall he bought his freedom
and set up a carpenter shop. In time Vesey became a skilled
and respected craftsman, amassing property valued at several
thousand dollars, including a home on Bull Street. A literate
man, he also became a class leader in the African Church of
Charleston. The church was founded in 1818 after more than
three-quarters of the city's 6,000 Afro-American Methodists
withdrew from the white-led Methodist church to form their
own independent congregation under the guidance of Bishop
Morris Brown, who for several years had been in contact with
the leaders of the new African Methodist Episcopal Church
of Philadelphia. Uneasy about the autonomy of these Afro-
American Methodists, Charleston authorities harassed the black
congregation and finally closed the church in 1821.

The decision of Charleston whites to deny black Charlestonians a church of their own helped precipitate Vesey's conspiracy, but other influences also contributed. Vesey read
newspapers regularly and followed national politics. In 1820
the news columns brimmed with debates on the Missouri
question. The political crisis in Washington about the future
of slavery in the West convinced Vesey that whites were badly
divided on the question of the existence of slavery. He spread
the story that Congress had emancipated the slaves but that
white Southerners refused to enforce the law. Vesey knew the
ringing proclamations of the natural rights of freedom and
equality found in the Declaration of Independence and the
Declaration of the Rights of Man. Even more pertinent, he
understood the way these ideals had been translated on the
island of Santo Domingo into a slave rebellion that evolved
into a revolution, ending the institution of slavery and creating the struggling republic of Haiti. As important as any other
influence was Vesey's reading of the Bible, which proved to
him that slavery was contrary to God's will. He was drawn to
the story of Israel delivered rather than to St. Paul's admoni-
tions that servants should obey their masters. Taken together,
Vesey's beliefs convinced him that God's children were called—
by the laws of the nation, of nature, and of God—to battle
for justice and freedom. These ideas put Vesey squarely in the
tradition of the revered founders of the nation. Unlike Thomas
Jefferson, George Washington, and James Madison, how-

ever, Vesey had no doubts that slaves were among God's children.

He gradually gathered around him a cadre of lieutenants: Gullah Jack Pritchard, Monday Gell, Peter Poyas, Rolla Bennett, Mingo Harth, and others. All were slaves, but several were skilled artisans like Vesey. Most belonged to the banned African Church, and some were African-born, as Vesey himself may have been. Gullah Jack, an Angolan, hoped to draw upon the African traditions of the slaves, thousands of whom had been brought to South Carolina when the state reopened the African slave trade from 1804 through 1807. A conjurer, Gullah Jack empowered parched corn, ground nuts, and crab claws to protect those who joined the revolution. The conspirators' plan was evidently quite simple. At midnight on July 14, 1822, they planned to attack the city arsenal, capture its weapons, kill all the whites they encountered, and set fire to the city. When the flames lit up the skyline, rural rebels whom Vesey and his followers had recruited in the months of patient preparation were supposed to rush into the city to complete the victory. What the revolutionaries planned to do with their victory is not clear. Bits of testimony, much of it suspect because it was coerced, indicate that Vesey may have planned to sail away, possibly to Haiti, with as many blacks as he could crowd aboard a ship. It is also conceivable that Vesey believed the rebels could not only take Charleston but hold it and establish a black nation modeled after Haiti. About all that is beyond question is that Vesey and the rebels believed that many whites must die if blacks were to be free.

Exactly what Vesey and his allies would have done with their victory will never be known because, as with dozens of other slave conspiracies in the New World, other Negroes—both slave and free—betrayed it. Slowly at first, then with gathering speed, the conspiracy began to unravel. The first arrests came in May when a slave named Peter Desverney informed his master of an effort to recruit him to the insurrection. One arrest led to another as supects, under the threat of death, implicated others. Shaken by each disclosure, Charleston authorities did all in their power to root out every conspirator. After three months of feverish investigations, 131 Afro-Americans stood accused. In the end 35 received death sentences, 37 others banishment from the state. Peter Desverney and George Wilson, another slave whose disclosures foiled the conspiracy, received their freedom and an annuity from the state legislature. The state also gave cash rewards to two free Negroes, William Pencil and a man named Scott, who alerted whites to the plot.

When the presiding magistrate sentenced Denmark Vesey to death he declared, "It is difficult to imagine what *infatuation* could have prompted you to attempt an enterprise so wild and visionary. You were a free man; were comparatively wealthy; and enjoyed every comfort, compatible with your situation. You had, therefore, much to risk, and little to gain. From your age and experience, you *ought* to have known, that success was impracticable."[28] Vesey's behavior baffled the white judge. The judge's assessment of Vesey's worldly circumstances was accurate enough; he was comparatively well-off and privileged relative to most of his race. But he was also a visionary. As a free man he could have left the slave society of South Carolina at any time. Instead, he chose to stay and try to bring it down. The practicality of a slave insurrection was not Vesey's chief concern. The realists' arguments about matters of power and advantage meant little to this committed revolutionary.

William Ellison was a very different sort of man, despite the resemblances between his biography and Vesey's. Both men personally experienced slavery, Vesey for thirty-three years, Ellison for twenty-six. Both gained their freedom and succeeded in establishing themselves as prosperous tradesmen. Both were intelligent, resourceful men, and neither had a volatile or spontaneous nature. They were deliberate men, and they deliberately chose different paths. While Ellison worshiped with the planter aristocracy, Vesey attended an independent black church. Ellison lived in a beautiful upcountry village of white slaveholders, while Vesey lived among the poor blacks of Charleston. Ellison bought slaves, owned them, and exploited them, while Vesey worked with slaves in the shops and on the wharves of Charleston, associated with them in the churches, taverns, and alleys of the city, and ultimately conspired with them to overthrow the system of slavery. The only slaves Ellison associated with he owned. Ellison may have shared the judge's wonderment that a man like Vesey, with "so much to risk" and "so little to gain," would have attempted what he did. In Ellison we can see the truth of C.L.R. James's observation that in "a slave society the mere possession of personal freedom is a valuable privilege. . . ."[29] Freedom was a privilege Ellison refused to risk. Vesey wanted to remake his world in the name of freedom; Ellison only wanted to make freedom work for him.[30]

As every slave knew, to avoid revolutionary violence did not necessarily mean slavish submission to white power. Ellison struggled to endow his freedom through hard work and careful accommodation. In 1822 he must have had a growing sense of confidence in his strategy. He had only to look around him to see how far he had come in six years. His scrupulous mix of self-assertion and deference paid handsome dividends in increased wealth and respect. Most importantly, his success had secured the freedom of his family. Denmark Vesey could not say the same. Vesey was married to at least one woman who was a slave, and he had several slave children. Just before he was sentenced to death, Monday Gell mentioned that "Vesey said he was satisfied with his own condition, being free, but as all his children were slaves, he wished to see what could be done for them."[31] Ellison also did what he could for his four free children by submitting to what he thought he could not change and by making every effort on their behalf within society's constraints. Gradually, with judicious forethought, he enlarged the boundaries of his family's existence. If Ellison ever had any doubts about the course he was following—and there is no evidence he did—Vesey's fate must have erased them. Accommodation, compromise, and patience, joined with a keen sense of opportunism and a large measure of simple good luck, paid off; revolutionary violence led to the gallows.

Regardless of where it might have gone, Denmark Vesey's path had in fact become a dead end. Nonetheless, Vesey had a powerful impact on the life of every free person of color in South Carolina from 1822 to the Civil War. His leadership of a slave conspiracy linked all free Negroes to the uprising, even though elite free people of color in Charleston cooperated with the city's whites to crush the rebellion. Free people of color became a conspicuous caste, worthy of legislative attention and white watchfulness because they might be tempted to take Vesey's path. The response of white South Carolinians communicated to all free people of color—including the gin maker in Stateburg—the vulnerability of their freedom, the harsh reality of white power, and the depth of the South's commitment to slavery.

THE Vesey conspiracy raised the question of the place of all free Afro-Americans in a slave society. Legislatures throughout the South clamped down on manumissions, expressing a collective judgment that freedom should not be available to any slaves, that the free Negro population would not grow by the incorporation of individuals who had personally made the transition from slavery to freedom, that the line separating slavery and freedom should coincide as closely as possible with that separating whites from Negroes. However, the existing free Afro-American population made it difficult to squeeze Southern society into the rigid categories of whites' racial logic. What should be done with these people? They were free, but they were also Negroes.

As whites came to terms with this question, they defined the extent of freedom for Afro-Americans. The details of the laws governing free Negroes varied from state to state, but the overall pattern was uniform.[32] Whites had a divided mind about free Negroes. On the one hand, whites feared them as disciples of Denmark Vesey and thus wanted to separate them as much as possible from association with slaves and from identification with their plight. On the other hand, whites despised free Negroes (except for the few "respectable" individuals they might know personally) because of the inferiority of their race and thus sought to push them down to the status of slaves, where they would not contravene the assumptions of racial inferiority. Whites never resolved these contradictory impulses. Both were visible in the legislation in every Southern state. While the two imperatives existed in uneasy balance throughout the antebellum years, the inclination to collapse the distance between free Negroes and slaves, to allow racial assumptions to degrade free status, carried more weight.

Vesey's conspiracy provoked the South Carolina legislature

to confront the explosive relationship between slaves and free Negroes. Instead of tightening the restrictions on slaves, the legislature fettered free people of color. Within months of the execution of the last conspirator in Charleston, legislators erected the basic legal structure of white governance of free Negroes. They localized and particularized the freedom of Afro-Americans. Any free person of color who left the state was prohibited from returning, upon penalty of enslavement. Every male free Negro over fifteen who remained in the state was required to obtain a white guardian, "a respectable freeholder of the district" in which the free man of color resided. The guardian had to appear before the clerk of court in his district, attest in writing to the "good character and correct habits" of the free man of color, and record with the clerk his acceptance of the guardianship.[33] The penalty for a free person of color who failed to conform to these provisions was the same as for reentry into the state: enslavement. The clear intent of the legislature was to create a definitive list in every courthouse of each free man of color in the district. If one's name was not on the list, one was not free. The law provided that a white informant who notified authorities that a certain free man of color was not in compliance with the law would be rewarded with half the proceeds of the sale of the man into slavery.

With the 1822 law the very existence of one's freedom, whatever the documentary proof for it under previous laws, was now contingent on having a personal relationship with a reputable white man, a relationship that was close enough for the white man to guarantee to the rest of white society one's "good character and correct habits." It was in the interest of free men of color to have guardians who were as high up the social ladder as possible. No white man would be willing to assume a guardianship for a stranger, and most would be reluctant to become a guardian unless they trusted the man of color enough to risk the possible embarrassment of having their trust betrayed before the white community. Free men of color had to work constantly to curry favor with whites in the hope that they could eventually prove themselves and obtain a suitable guardian. In the eyes of the law, the guardian was not responsible for the acts of his free colored ward. Instead, he agreed to guarantee to the rest of the white community that the free man of color would behave properly. Although the relationship between guardian and free colored ward was different from that between master and slave, the racial distribution of power was much the same. The guardianship law was colored by the same assumptions about white authority and Negro deference that were implicit in slavery.

Most states in the Lower South enacted guardianship laws.[34] Much the same effect was achieved in the other Southern states by laws requiring each free person of color to register with the local court.[35] In South Carolina, free Negro registration dated from a 1792 law that required free persons of color between the ages of sixteen and sixty to pay a two-dollar capitation tax each year.[36] If one neglected to pay the tax, one could be sold for a term of service long enough to cover the arrears.[37] As with the registration laws in the other states, the purpose was not simply to enact a discriminatory tax upon free persons of color. The capitation tax was designed to create an annual accounting of the free colored population in each district. If one's name did not appear on the list, one's freedom was subject to challenge. By the same token, appearance on the tax list was *prima facie* evidence that one was free, without resort to more complicated legal tests. As a practical matter, whites and free persons of color alike tended to refer to the annual registration or tax lists as the pertinent legal evidence for the existence of freedom. In South Carolina, producing the receipt for payment of the annual capitation tax was usually sufficient for a free Negro to convince a skeptical white that he or she was free.

For freedom to be secure from legal challenge, however, a Negro had to be able to prove free birth or manumission before 1820, and each adult male had to have a duly recorded white guardian. Free Afro-American compliance with the guardianship law, unlike that with the capitation tax and annual registration, was irregular. Still, every well-advised free person of color complied with the letter of the law. In Sumter District, where the only list of free Negro guardianships has survived, many free persons of color went beyond the requirements of the law.[38] At least 28 of the 100 Sumter free Afro-Americans who obtained guardians between 1823 and 1842 were females, who were not required by the law to do so. Several of the white guardians accepted guardianships of an entire family of free persons of color, as William Ballard did in 1833 for Mary Johnson and her children William, Jim, John, and Martha, or as Jacob Whiting did in 1840 for James, Harriot, Catherine, and Joseph Smiling.

As the 1822 guardianship law slipped farther into the past, it was not rigorously enforced and many free persons of color were probably entirely unaware of it. In Sumter District, after an initial burst of seventeen guardianships were registered in 1823, only one to four were recorded in subsequent years, fewer than if compliance had been perfect.[39] Most likely, many of those who were freeborn neglected to obtain a guardian under the mistaken assumption that they did not need one, either because their father's guardian was, by extension, theirs or because they simply did not know about the law. So long as they stayed near home, where their freedom was known, they were unlikely to be challenged to prove it; and if they were, they could always show the capitation tax receipt. In general, the security of Afro-Americans' freedom was greatest among whites who knew them on a personal, face-to-face basis. Although the existence of freedom for persons of color was precisely defined in law, in practice the legal complexities were seldom invoked. Instead, informal acceptance of one's freedom by local whites was the crucial determinant.

Since local acceptance overrode the law in daily life, masters continued to manumit some slaves, even after the South Carolina law of 1820 made it illegal. These favored Negroes lived as free persons in the neighborhood where their freedom was accepted, despite its illegality. The practice prevailed throughout the South.[40] Whites were willing to recognize the will of a master as supreme over the law so long as the peace and security of the neighborhood were not disturbed. Although the exact incidence of illegal manumissions cannot be known, Judge O'Neall wrote in 1848 that the South Carolina prohibition on manumission had "caused evasions without number."[41] The freedom of such persons was extremely insecure. A disgruntled heir, an unscrupulous neighbor, or any other white person could challenge a Negro's freedom in court and expect to succeed in returning the person to bondage.

To avoid such a precarious existence for favored ex-slaves,

masters and their legal advisors devised a more reliable way
to evade the law. A master who wanted to manumit a slave
would sell or give the slave to another person in trust, speci-
fying that the slave was to be allowed to live as a free person.
The trust had the legal advantage of pitting the expressed intent
of the master against the 1820 law, a contest masters could
expect to win. The test case was *Carmille v. Administrator of
Carmille,* finally settled in 1842.[42] The trial judge had held
against the freedom given six slaves under a trust on the
grounds that it was an "undisguised attempt to evade the law
of the State, forbidding emancipation." On appeal, the trial
court was overruled, with Justice O'Neall speaking for a
unanimous court in affirming the trust. O'Neall said, *"Kindness to slaves . . . is the true policy. . . . Nothing will more assuredly
defeat our institution of slavery, than harsh legislation rigorously
enforced."* The problem, as O'Neall wrote six years later, was
that, "All laws unnecessarily restraining the rights of owners
are unwise."[43] "The State has nothing to fear from emancipation" under the old law of 1820, he wrote. "Many a master
knows that he has a slave or slaves, for whom he feels it to be
his duty to provide. As the law now stands, that cannot be
done. In a slave country, the good should be especially
rewarded. Who are to judge of this, but the master? Give him
the power of emancipation, under well regulated guards, and
he can dispense the only reward, which either he, or his slave
appreciates."

Despite the opposition of O'Neall and others, the state legislature declared in 1841 that "a trust or confidence, either secret
or expressed, that such slave or slaves shall be held in nominal
servitude only, shall be void."[44] The new law did not apply
to trusts effected before its passage, but after 1841 the trust
loophole to freedom was closed. Some masters continued to
slip around the law and allow a few slaves to live as if they
were free. But after 1841 the freedom of these individuals was
no more secure than those who were manumitted without
the provision of a trustee. Their freedom was totally dependent on local acceptance or indifference, which usually was
available simply because so few slaves were thus "freed."

Free Negroes with impeccable legal credentials were still
subject to many of the same laws as slaves. In South Carolina

they were tried for all criminal offenses before a magistrate's and freeholders' court, a tribunal that only heard cases involving slaves and free Negroes. Their testimony, like that of slaves, was acceptable in this court but never under oath. In the courts that heard cases involving whites, the testimony of free persons of color and slaves was not admissible. Free Afro-Americans could not serve on a jury, nor could they qualify as a freeholder to be included on a magistrate's and freeholders' court. They could be sentenced to the same punishments as slaves, including hanging for capital offenses and, for lesser crimes, whipping, confinement to stocks, imprisonment, and the treadmill. In addition, they could be fined, a punishment slaves could not suffer since they could not own property.[45]

The quality of justice handed down by the magistrate's and freeholders' courts was mixed at best. As an appeals court judge, Justice O'Neall reviewed numerous verdicts against slaves and free Negroes, which led him to conclude that the courts were "the worst system which could be devised . . . [since] the passions and prejudices of the neighborhood, arising from a recent offense, enter into the trial, and often lead to the condemnation of the innocent."[46] The presiding magistrates often did not know or understand the law, resulting in many "errors and abuses of power." O'Neall censured the "whippings inflicted" by the courts as "most enormous—utterly disproportionate to [the] offenses."[47] Despite O'Neall's scathing criticisms, the system was not reformed. Instead, O'Neall was attacked bitterly for publishing his views, which his enemies considered to be both incorrect and impolitic.[48] In a careful study of free Negroes' encounters with the law in Spartanburg District between 1830 and 1860, historian Michael Hindus found that free people of color were prosecuted at six times the rate of slaves. Hindus attributes part of the differential to masters avoiding the courts and dispensing their own version of justice on the plantation, and part to simple harassment of free Negroes. One free Afro-American couple in Spartanburg was prosecuted thirteen times in nineteen years and acquitted each time.[49]

The summary proceedings, harsh sentences, and frequently erroneous verdicts were perfectly acceptable to most whites because they assumed that free Negroes, like slaves, had to be

kept completely subordinate. Furthermore, the courts gave
the force of law to the notion that just as each slave was subject to his master, so each free person of color was subject to
the white community in general. Like the power of masters
over their slaves, legal power over free people of color was
decentralized to each courthouse where the fate of an accused
was decided by six of his white neighbors. There were no
well-defined rights of appeal from these courts, except after
1833 in capital cases.[50] Thus the administration of justice for
free Afro-Americans, like that for slaves, was firmly in the
hands of local whites.

Important as the court system was in linking free Afro-
Americans with slaves and separating them from whites, still
more important was the strict requirement of racial subordination that suffused the entire society. Like slaves, free persons of color were forbidden to strike a white person under
any circumstances. "They cannot repel force by force; that is,
they cannot strike a white man, who may strike any of them,"
Justice O'Neall wrote in 1848.[51] In a case sixteen years earlier,
a white man was convicted of cruelly beating a free Negro
man named Tom Archer without provocation. O'Neall refused
to overturn the conviction on appeal, concluding that "to no
white man does the right belong of correcting, at pleasure, a
free negro." However, for O'Neall—who was a moderate man
in such matters—the problem in this case was not the beating
but the absence of provocation. "Free negroes belong to a
degraded *caste* of society," he wrote; "they are, in no respect,
on a perfect equality with the white man . . . they ought, by
law, to be compelled to demean themselves as inferiors . . .
[and] words of impertinence or insolence addressed by a free
negro to a white man would justify an assault and battery."[52]
Even by this strict standard, O'Neall concluded, Tom Archer
did not deserve to be beaten.

In the daily round of life, every free person of color had to
be constantly on guard against committing some act that a
white person might consider an act of insolence: a sharp word,
a careless boast, failure to remove one's hat, or neglecting to
give a passing white man proper deference on the street. Any
of these and dozens of other acts might be interpreted as
insolence and justify a white man in "correcting" a free person

of color. Of course, not every encounter between a white person and a free Negro was tense and verging on explosion. In a quantitative sense, by far most were calm and unexceptional, primarily because free people of color knew so well the high risks of not conforming to white expectations. In every encounter with a white person, the person of color had to exercise restraint, to discipline spontaneity, to scrutinize each statement and every gesture for anything potentially offensive. The legal definition of insolence was intentionally vague. O'Neall recommended that "As a general rule . . . whatever in the opinion of the jury, would induce them, as reasonable men, to strike a free negro, should, in all cases, be regarded as a legal justification in an indictment. . . ."[53] Slaves were somewhat less subject to this charge since, if a white person corrected them for failure to demean themselves properly, the white person had to answer to the slave's master. If the white person corrected a free Negro, he had no other person to account to, unless, as in the case of Tom Archer, the correction was so outrageous that it aroused whites' sympathy. Each day free Afro-Americans had to convince the whites they saw that they were sufficiently inferior. Each day they had to be prepared to act instinctively toward whites as if they were as subordinate as slaves.

Informal enforcement of racial subordination was supplemented by the formal institution of the patrol. In South Carolina every adult white man was required to participate in (or send a substitute to) the patrol, a group of men charged with riding the local beat several times a month looking for Negroes engaged in suspicious activity. The patrol was primarily designed to police slaves, to prevent them from leaving their home plantation without permission, from stealing crops and livestock, from assembling together secretly for any purpose, and from running away. But any free Negro on the road, especially at night, was likely to be stopped and interrogated by the patrol. If the free person of color could not supply the patrol with proof of freedom, he or she was assumed to be a slave and treated accordingly. In addition, the patrol had the authority to break into any dwelling they suspected of harboring a Negro in violation of the law. In effect, they had no-knock power to harass and intimidate any free colored family.

Privacy for every free Afro-American family depended on being above reproach in the eyes of whites, on never being suspected of aiding a runaway, of trading with slaves, or of meeting secretly with slaves for any purpose. The patrol was also required to look for violations of laws that prohibited free Negroes from carrying a firearm without the written permission of their guardian; from meeting together for any purpose behind closed doors that were locked or barred to prevent quick and easy access to the patrol or any other white person; from keeping a still or selling liquor to slaves; and, after 1834, from keeping a school to teach slave or free colored children to read and write.[54]

All these prohibitions were extensions of restrictions on slave behavior. They reflected the persistent fear of whites that free Afro-Americans might exploit thir freedom to aid slaves to strike against their masters. At the same time, the absolute insistence on racial subordination and the pervasive assumption of racial inferiority pushed free Negroes to the edge of slave status, giving them what a late twentieth-century observer might think were ample reasons to sympathize and identify with the plight of slaves. Thousands did, especially with slaves who were members of their families. But for every free person of color who, like Denmark Vesey, conspired with slaves to undermine slavery, there were thousands of free Afro-Americans throughout the South who saw their fate as separate and distinct from that of slaves as a group, whatever they might think about individual slaves who were their kinfolk. The risks of cooperating in an attempt at insurrection were so great as to be suicidal; whites had most of the people and all of the guns. A less dramatic but much more important risk for free people of color was associating with slaves in their daily lives in any way that raised white suspicions. Suspicions could bring down on free Negroes all the repressive consequences of the mistrust of local white people. Free people of color understood that slaves were the source of their own problem with whites, that their skin color was debased by that of slaves. Thus most free Afro-Americans put what distance they could between themselves and slaves.

FREE Afro-Americans were able to distance themselves from slaves because, despite all the ways the law assimilated them to near-slave status, it also gave invaluable protection to their life, liberty, and property. A white man who murdered a free Negro was guilty in the eyes of the law of the same crime as the murder of a white person. Of greater moment to free Afro-Americans was the possibility of being kidnaped and sold into slavery. Kidnapings were not uncommon, especially in cities where the absence of an individual free person of color was less likely to be noticed quickly. However, most whites deplored kidnapings, and in South Carolina after 1837, the crime was punishable by a fine of not less than $1,000 and imprisonment of not less than one year.[55] Countless guardians filed suits for "ravishment" of their free Negro wards; in other words, they accused another white person of reducing their ward to servitude, a form of kidnaping.[56] Free Negroes could protect themselves from unprovoked assaults by court actions and indictments, including bringing suit against white persons for assault and battery and filing writs of habeas corpus.[57] These protections were sorely limited by the prohibition against free persons of color serving on juries or testifying against whites. Thus an assault upon a free Afro-American that was not witnessed by another white person was unlikely ever to be tried because, even if it had been witnessed by dozens of other free Negroes or slaves, none of them could testify in court. Nonetheless, the legal protections against assaults on life and liberty were invoked numerous times during the antebellum years, and the courts often punished the guilty parties.

While these legal safeguards provided a certain security to those persons of color whose free status was unimpeachable, nothing gave more positive content to freedom than the legal protection of contracts. Free persons of color could make contracts between themselves and with whites. The law stood behind the contracts in every way as if they were between two whites.[58] Above all, protection of contracts meant that the marriage of free Negroes was legal. While slave marriages had no legal status, free persons of color could pass on their precious heritage of freedom. Unlike slaves, free persons of color could protect their families against arbitrary disruption by whites. They could provide for them, shelter them, teach them, and bequeath to them any property they had accumulated, none of which slaves were allowed to do.

Perhaps the single most impressive achievement of free Afro-Americans was keeping their families remarkably intact. In this respect, William Ellison was no exception. In South Carolina in 1860 (outside the city of Charleston), two-thirds of the free Negro households were headed by men.[59] Almost three out of four of these men lived with their wives, and more than eight out of ten of these couples had co-residing children. In the entire state two-thirds of all children were in male-headed households, and 60 percent of all children were in households with both a mother and father present. These statistics are remarkable because they demonstrate how common it was for free Afro-Americans to succeed in maintaining and protecting their families, despite the odds against them.

In addition to the discriminatory laws and social practices, free colored families faced other unique pressures. Masters' policy of selective manumission of only a favored few slaves tended to separate the manumitted from their kinfolk who remained slaves. Like William Ellison, many freed slaves purchased the freedom of a spouse and children. Many other free persons of color had a spouse or children who remained slaves. Few freed slaves could afford to purchase an enslaved family member. Ellison's skill as a gin maker and his ability to generate a considerable income soon after his manumission were rare. The earning potential of freed women was especially low, which helps account for the third of free colored households in South Carolina that were headed by women without a co-residing spouse. Only about half as many male-headed households did not have a spouse.[60] Almost three-quarters of these women had co-residing children, and on the average they had almost as many children as in households with both parents present (3.3 children versus 3.6). Some of these women were undoubtedly widows of free Negro men. But many of them probably had slave husbands. Even if the women had been financially able to purchase their husbands, they were prohibited from freeing them after 1820. Perhaps a few of these women owned their husbands as slaves. If so, the women were still managing to pass along their freedom to their children.

Others among the women without co-residing spouses were concubines of white men. Some of the white men who fathered these women's children were their former masters. Others were white men who chose not to reside with the women who bore their children. In the racial climate of antebellum South Carolina, most white men would not want to acknowledge their mulatto children or their Negro concubine. Although the exact proportion of concubines among the free Afro-American women without co-residing spouses cannot be known, a rough estimate is that they numbered about a third of these women, or about one free colored household in ten.[61] In South Carolina, unlike many other Southern states, a marriage between a free person of color and a white person was perfectly legal.[62]

In 1860 there were just a few co-residing interracial couples in the entire state. About one family in a thousand in South Carolina, some seventy-one in all, was composed of one or more free persons of color and one or more white persons with the same surname.[63] Forty-four of these families were headed by Negro men with white wives; all but two of the men were mulattoes. Seventeen families were headed by a white man with a Negro wife, all but two of whom were mulattoes. Two other families were composed of a white man without a co-residing spouse but with mulatto children. Eight households were headed by a woman; in four instances, a mulatto woman with white children, and in the other four cases, vice versa.

Although these interracial families were found throughout the state, a disproportionate number of white-headed families were in the low country; 27 percent of all free Negro households were in the low country compared to 53 percent of the white-headed interracial families. Typically, the white men were poor farmers, like John Andress, a fifty-one-year-old farmer with $150 in real estate who lived with his mulatto wife Rosanna and one mulatto child in Beaufort District.[64] This regional distribution of the white-headed households is probably the result of the relative scarcity of white women in the densely slave-populated tidewater.

Interracial families headed by free Afro-American men were somewhat underrepresented in the low country and correspondingly overrepresented in the middle districts of the state, in part because of the relatively greater availability of poor white women who were willing to marry a Negro man. More importantly, these women may have been of mixed white and Afro-American ancestry, even though they appeared white. There is no way to be certain whether the census enumerators connoted both ancestry and color by the designation "white." Was Martha Bells, the wife of the propertyless thirty-five-year-old mulatto laborer Henry Bells, of unmixed ancestry, or was she only white in appearance?[65] Evidence that many of the enumerators were guided by color alone is that two of Martha Bells's children, Selena and Ellen, were listed as whites, while William, Zachariah, and Mary—her other three children—were listed as mulattoes. In all of the interracial households headed by Negro men, 65 of the 155 children were listed as whites, strong evidence that appearance, not ancestry, was what counted with many enumerators. Many of these children, their white mothers, and the white men with mulatto wives may have been passing over the racial line, even though they remained part of an identifiably Negro household. At least these households are evidence that as late as the 1850s the color line in South Carolina was not absolutely impenetrable.

Passing was undoubtedly more common than these few families suggest.[66] Unlike most other Southern states, South Carolina never defined precisely who was white. Most other slave states required a "white" person to have no Negro ancestor in the previous two generations, regardless of the person's white appearance.[67] In South Carolina, the determination of whether a person was white was left, as was so much else, to the judgment of the local white community. The question frequently arose in the courts during the antebellum years.[68] It was important because if one were adjudged a free Negro, one could not testify against whites, one was tried in magistrate's and freeholders' courts, and one was subject to the special taxes and harsh restrictions, in addition to the blot on the family name, with all that implied for one's standing in white society. For one white person to accuse another of being a mulatto was an actionable offense. The response was often quick and violent, but if a false accusation reached the courts, it could be punished by awards of up to $500 to the slandered.[69]

But how, exactly, was the crucial determination to be made? If the person in question had, Judge William Harper wrote in 1835, "a visible admixture [of races] evidenced by the color

. . . the hair or [other] features, the person is to be regarded as of the degraded class." On the other hand, if the person "exhibited none of the distinctive marks of the African race," Harper wrote, then he or she was qualified to be considered officially white. In the case Harper was deciding, the individuals whose race was questioned were proven to have had one-sixteenth Negro blood. Yet, Harper wrote, the grandfather of these persons, "although of dark complexion, had been recognized as a white man, received into society, and exercised political privileges as such; their mother was uniformly treated as a white woman; their relations of the same admixture have married into respectable families, and one of them had been a candidate for the legislature." What counted was acceptance by the local white community. Harper thus found the persons in this case to be white. He recommended that "a man of worth . . . should have the rank of a white man, while a vagabond of the same degree of admixture should be confined to the inferior caste."[70] The decision in each case was up to the jury. As Judge O'Neall wrote in 1848, "Whenever the African taint is so far removed, that upon inspection a party may be fairly pronounced to be white, and such has been his or her previous reception into society, and enjoyments of the privileges usually enjoyed by white people, the Jury may rate and regard the person as white."[71] Although William Ellison was regarded by Stateburg whites as a "man of worth," he was not accepted as white because he was clearly a man of color, a "yellow man," as he put it in his petition to change his name. His children were also recognizably persons of color. Even if Ellison's color had been white, however, local white people always had the last word. As a practical matter, white appearance counted for more when the color of one's ancestors was not common knowledge. That meant South Carolina had quite a few individuals known as white colored persons.

SECOND only to the freedom to marry and maintain a family was the freedom to choose an occupation and own property. Again, the legal protection afforded contracts made by free persons of color made it possible for a free Negro to contract for work or payment with any other free person and, if necessary, to resort to the courts for the enforcement of the terms of the agreement, just as William Ellison did.[72] This legal protection did not mean that free Afro-Americans could make contracts as if they were white persons. As members of a degraded caste, they were almost always at a disadvantage in negotiations over wages and prices. Any sharp dealing would test one's respectability and might diminish one's standing in the eyes of some whites. The market for goods and services was never free or unconstrained. It was always conditioned by free Negroes' dependence on local whites.

The economy also put free Afro-Americans at the mercy of local whites. There were simply too few free persons of color for them to trade principally among themselves. They were scattered too widely across the state (with the exception of Charleston) to make extensive trading practical. By necessity they depended on white patronage for what they had to sell, just as they depended on whites to supply them with much of what they needed to buy, from household items to agricultural tools, credit, and, in the case of persons like William Ellison, such specialized services as factoring and banking. Whites, on the other hand, were rarely dependent on free Negroes. In most cases whites had the option to get from other whites in the neighborhood the labor, skills, or products they bought from free persons of color. Ellison's highly prized gins made him an exception. But few other free Afro-Americans enjoyed a position at a critical juncture in the economy. The economic relationship between most free people of color and whites was far from reciprocal. Despite the law's equal protection of contracts, the agreements were always heavily weighted in favor of whites.

Laborers were at the greatest disadvantage in reaching agreements on wages or other compensation. They competed not only with white laborers but also with slaves. As a general rule, free colored laborers were probably employed by whites who could not afford slaves or who had some jobs for which they temporarily needed extra labor. The great majority of South Carolina's free Negroes whose occupations were listed in the 1860 federal census were laborers of one variety or another, some 60 percent in all.[73] One in five free Negro men was a farm laborer; another 23 percent simply listed themselves as laborers or day laborers, although many of them

undoubtedly did agricultural work. A few others had somewhat more specialized laboring jobs: six ditchers, four railroad hands, two timber cutters, two boatmen, two teamsters,
and one ostler, waterman, fisherman, miner, gardener, huck-
ster, and sawmill hand. In addition to these laborers, another
12 percent of free Afro-American men were landless farmers.
Many of them may have been farm laborers; others may have
been tenants. Although tenants probably had more day-to-
day control over their labor than the typical free Negro laborer,
they, like all the others, depended on being hired.

Women were even more concentrated than men at the low-
est occupational levels. Three out of four women were laborers, compared to 55 percent of the men. One-fifth of the women
were simply called laborers; another 16 percent were farm
laborers. The largest group was composed of servant women,
who accounted for one woman in three. In addition to the
thirty-five undifferentiated servants, there were fifty-nine
washers, thirty-two domestics, thirteen cooks, and three
stewardesses. Landless farmers made up another 6 percent.
Servants typically worked around their employers' households, but all the other women laborers probably did agricultural work that was not much different—if it differed at all—
from slave labor. Free colored laborers of both sexes probably
worked side-by-side with slaves much of the time. In many
instances, the census listing of a laboring occupation was a
euphemism for what amounted to a hired field hand.

Artisans enjoyed more control over their work and, because
they possessed a specialized skill, more leverage than laborers
in negotiations for hire. But like laborers, they depended for
their sustenance on being employed by someone else, typically whites. Although they too competed with slave labor, it
was only with the small minority of slaves who were craftsmen. More frequently they competed with white tradesmen.
The 190 free Negro carpenters, for example, competed for
work with 1,515 white carpenters, as well as with the numerous
slave carpenters. To compete effectively and to insure the
patronage of their white customers, free Negroes needed to
be more reliable, more available, and usually cheaper than their
white counterparts. Color had its cost, although it cannot be
calculated precisely.

Like William Ellison, almost a third (31 percent) of free Afro-American men were craftsmen. Unlike Ellison, his three sons, and his first grandson, none of the others was a gin maker. Almost half (47 percent) were carpenters; another 11 percent were blacksmiths. The other tradesmen included twenty-four mechanics, twenty-three shoemakers, twenty-three masons, nineteen tailors, nineteen apprentices, nine wheelwrights, eight painters, four millers, three each of bakers, cabinetmakers, tanners, and millwrights, two each of harness makers and engineers, and a cooper, a carriage maker, a basketmaker, a tinner, a collar maker, a coachmaker, a plasterer, a chairmaker, and a wagonmaker. Among free Negro women, about one in six did artisanal work. Most of them worked with needle and thread, including forty-six seamstresses, eleven mantua makers, and one milliner. Five others worked as weavers, two as bakers, one as a spinner, and another as an apprentice. Although the free colored artisans possessed the autonomy in their work that accompanied their skill, they were no more independent of whites than were laborers. One had to do good work and be compliant to get a job, and to be even more so to keep one. Like laborers, most free colored artisans were easy to replace.

Farmers who owned their land had the greatest independence from whites.[74] They could plant what they chose and dispose of it however they decided. They could provide for most of their families' necessities and some of their desires. While they had to trade with whites and thus suffered from the same white prejudice that afflicted other free Afro-Americans, they did not depend completely on whites for their sustenance. However, only one free person of color in ten was a farmer who owned any real estate. Many of the skilled craftsmen saved enough to acquire some real estate, but often it was no more than a small lot for a home and a garden plot. In the entire state only 29 percent of all free persons of color owned any real estate. The mean value of the real property of these individuals was $824. However, 80 percent of them owned less than $2,000 worth of real estate, and their mean property value was $185, no more than a few acres at best. Only fifty-five free Negroes, 4 percent of all free colored households, owned real estate worth between $2,000 and

$5,000. Those who owned property worth more than $5,000 numbered twenty-seven, 2 percent of the total population. If ownership of real estate is taken as a rough measure of the relative security of the free Afro-American population, then the 71 percent who owned no real estate had the least security, followed by 24 percent who owned an average of $185. In all, 94 percent of the population owned either no land or very little. Only 6 percent owned enough real estate to have at least a small farm and the security and independence it might make possible. In the nation as a whole in 1860, 18 percent of all white men owned real estate worth $2,000 or more, three times as many as among South Carolina's free persons of color.[75] Likewise, the mean value of property owned by white men nationwide in 1860 was more than three times greater than the mean for South Carolina's free Afro-Americans.[76] Clearly, most free persons of color in every occupation, including farming, received little security from the ownership of real estate.

A few free Afro-Americans in South Carolina had occupations that might be termed petty enterprise or nonmanual. Among the women engaged in nonmanual labor were five nurses, five midwives, one governess, and one "Doctress," Mary Rials, a fifty-year-old poor black woman who lived in Marlboro District. Men with nonmanual occupations included four Methodist Protestant ministers in Chesterfield District—John Stephens, a seventy-five-year-old mulatto man and his three sons, J. J., J. W., and Reuben; a prosperous merchant in Barnwell District—Henry Lease, who reported wealth of $7,700; two musicians, a bartender, a trader, an overseer, and H. Simons, a forty-eight-year-old propertyless native-born black man who lived in Georgetown District and was a "Root Doctor." The dependent character of all these occupations suggests that they were concentrated at the bottom of the pyramid in free society. Ninety-eight out of one hundred free Afro-Americans in South Carolina did manual labor of one sort or another. A middle class, defined as those who hired rather than were hired, was virtually nonexistent.

MOST free persons of color in South Carolina were poor. In 1860 the mean total wealth per free Negro household was

$644, one-fifteenth the mean wealth of white families, which was over $10,000.[77] However, most free Negroes were even poorer than the mean value suggests. One-third of all free colored households reported no wealth whatever. Just above the propertyless were another 61 percent of the population who had wealth of less than $2,000; their mean wealth was $414. The overall mean for this bottom 94 percent of all free Negroes was $270. In other words, all but six out of a hundred free Afro-Americans were desperately poor. They owned some clothing, a few household items, some farm tools, rarely a horse, or mule, or cow, and some of them had a little money under the mattress. Their poverty made them all the more dependent on wages. Although they might fish or hunt and raise vegetables, they needed cash to pay the rent, since seven out of ten owned no real estate. In addition, they had to pay the annual capitation tax or risk being sold into servitude for back taxes.

For most, life was a never-ending struggle to make ends meet. William Bing, a fifty-year-old mulatto farmer in Barnwell District, owned no real estate but reported personal property valued at $500. By comparison to most other free Negroes, Bing, his wife Frances, and their seven children were well off. Sarah Callahan, a sixty-seven-year-old black farmer, and her two farm laborer sons in Abbeville District had $60 in personal property. Morgan Collins, a twenty-eight-year-old mulatto laborer in Darlington District, was propertyless. Perlina Morris, a thirty-two-year-old domestic in York District, had $20 worth of personal property. To these individuals and the thousands of others like them, Bing was in an enviable position. He did not have to worry about having enough cash to pay the capitation taxes for himself and his family. Although he was a tenant, he may well have owned his tools and thus have brought to his agreement with his landlord more than just his labor. None of these things was true of people like Callahan, Collins, and Morris. The economic margin that separated them and most other free persons of color from slaves was extremely small, and for many it did not exist. Unlike slaves, they lacked a white master who had an economic interest in their survival and well-being. A white guardian was not a provider. Economic security, autonomy, and independence were hopes and prayers, not realities. Under these conditions, maintaining one's freedom and providing for one's family required hard work, endurance, self-denial, and the ability to improvise constantly—actions that over the course of a lifetime assumed heroic proportions, the heroism of survival.

Color made a difference in the economic welfare of free Afro-Americans. On the average, mulattoes were better off than blacks. The mean wealth of mulattoes was $525, more than twice the mean for blacks, $233. Although blacks made up 35 percent of the potential wealth holders, they owned only 19 percent of all the wealth of free Negroes. Black women were the worst off. They made up 14 percent of the potential wealth holders, but they had only 5 percent of the wealth, a mean of $154. The mean wealth of black men was considerably more, $283, although still pathetically small. The mean wealth of mulatto women was $464, more than three times greater than that of black women. Mulatto men, who made up 47 percent of the potential wealth holders and owned 61 percent of the wealth, had a mean wealth of $549. The difference between mulattoes and blacks was greater than that between the sexes. Women made up 32 percent of all wealth holders and had 25 percent of the wealth, with a mean of $332, while the mean for men was $467.

The major reason for the economic differences between mulattoes and blacks was evidently that whites preferred to deal with mulattoes. The differences cannot be accounted for by mulattoes having a significantly higher proportion of skilled artisans than blacks. The distribution of occupations among black and mulatto men was almost identical: 33 percent of mulatto men were craftsmen, compared to 29 percent of black men; 46 percent of black men were laborers, compared to 43 percent of mulatto men. The largest difference between the occupations of blacks and mulattoes was among women who worked at skilled needlecrafts; 21 percent of mulatto women did such work, compared to 10 percent of black women. The differences between the wealth of mulattoes and blacks also cannot be attributed to more mulattoes being farmers: 23 percent of black men were farmers compared to 25 percent of mulatto men; more black women than mulatto women were farmers, 14 percent to 10 percent. Among the 6 percent of all free Negroes who owned $2,000 or more, however, blacks were significantly underrepresented. While 35 percent of all potential wealth holders were black, blacks made up only 19 percent of the top 6 percent. Furthermore, the wealth owned by these relatively prosperous blacks was less than that owned by mulattoes in the same group. Blacks owned 11 percent of the total wealth owned by those with $2,000 or more; their mean wealth was $3,508, just over half that of mulattoes' $6,544.

Some of the mulatto advantage must have come from favors given by white parents: some cash, some land, some credit, or perhaps most valuable of all, some contacts among white neighbors. This sort of head start undoubtedly aided mulattoes more frequently than blacks. But probably more significant than what mulattoes were given by their white parents or patrons was what they were able to earn for themselves because whites preferred to deal with them rather than with blacks. White prejudice acted as a filter that selectively allowed a few mulattoes to achieve a measure of economic security, while blacks were held back. Among the twenty-nine richest free Negroes, only two were blacks. The richest black man in 1860 was Wade Saunders, a fifty-four-year-old farmer who lived in Newberry District with his eight children. He owned real and personal property worth $12,000.

The top 6 percent of free Afro-American wealth holders— eight out of ten of them mulattoes—owned more than ten times their share of all the wealth owned by free persons of color, 61 percent. Their mean wealth was $5,977, twenty-two times greater than the mean wealth of the bottom 94 percent of the population. At the apex of the economic hierarchy were 2 percent of the population who possessed 41 percent of the wealth; these twenty-nine individuals had a mean wealth of $12,696, which compared favorably with that of whites. Included in this economic elite were ten individuals who owned $10,000 or more. Seven of the ten were farmers, although two of the men also worked as carpenters. The two women, Susan Moore in Edgefield District and Margaret Harris in Georgetown District, were probably widows. Curiously, they owned no real estate. Each of them reported personal property worth $35,000, which made them, after William Ellison, the wealthiest free persons of color in the state outside Charleston. All of the men reported some real estate, but in every instance it was equaled or exceeded by the value of their personal property. The largest real estate holder was Robert Collins, a sixty-year-old mulatto farmer in Georgetown District who owned $10,000 worth.

Members of the economic elite had a disproportionate share of their wealth in personal property. Among the top 2 percent of wealth holders, real estate accounted for only a little over a quarter (28 percent) of their total assets. The next 4 percent of wealth holders had over half (54 percent) of their wealth in real estate. These less prosperous individuals were still concerned with establishing an economic foothold by the purchase of land. The members of the top group were able to divert a large fraction of their wealth to the purchase of slaves. The sixty-five-year-old farmer Lewis Kinsey in Barnwell District, for example, owned nineteen slaves. Another Barnwell farmer, a thirty-eight-year-old mulatto named John Berry, owned ten slaves. The exact number of slaveowners among the free Negro population outside the city of Charleston is not known, but it probably did not exceed one hundred individuals and may have been closer to fifty, most of them among the top 6 percent of wealth holders. In the entire state of North Carolina in 1860 there were only eight free Negro slaveowners.[78] In South Carolina it was certainly true that the ownership of more than two or three slaves was confined to the economic elite. Whatever their desires, very few free Negroes could afford to own slaves.

Thirty years earlier, when slaveownership among free persons of color may have been near its peak, only sixty-nine individuals outside the city of Charleston owned any slaves.[79] Almost two out of three of these individuals owned only one to four slaves, and some of the slaves may have been family members. Ex-slaves like April Ellison who had been freed before the 1820 prohibition on manumission were probably never in a better position to buy family members who were slaves. The price of slaves continued to rise with the demand for cotton, while the economic fortunes of most free Afro-Americans did not rise accordingly. Soon after Ellison purchased his wife Matilda and his daughter Eliza Ann and

immediately freed them, as the law then allowed, he also purchased other slaves and used them in the same ways white
slaveholders did, for their labor. Ellison was not alone. In
1830 one-quarter of the free colored slaveholders owned more
than ten slaves; eight of them owned thirty or more. The two
largest slaveholders, Justus Angel and Mistress L. Horry, both
of Colleton District, each owned eighty-four slaves. For these
free Negro planters, slaveholding was neither a philanthropic
gesture nor a strategy for uniting family members. It was
instead a way to get ahead economically. By 1860 none of
them had done as well as Ellison.

III

Mastering Freedom

PANIC, reprisals, and intense legislative scrutiny of free Negroes followed the discovery of Denmark Vesey's conspiracy. But as nightmares of slave insurrection faded, South Carolina gradually settled down. Whites found it difficult to sustain eternal vigilance when the specter of Vesey failed to materialize in the daily behavior of free people of color. Rigorous enforcement of the laws regulating the lives of the state's free Negro population interfered with ordinary, necessary activity. As white anxieties relaxed, the laws lapsed into dormancy. They remained on the books, however, ready to be invoked any time white fears mounted. After 1822, spasmodic enforcement punctuated long stretches of neglect. Even at the height of the fear in 1822, whites did not deny South Carolina's free Negroes the legal right to property. Had whites formally crushed the economic aspirations of free Afro-Americans, they would have risked driving all free Negroes down Vesey's path into an alliance with slaves. The possibility of economic progress within existing society gave free Negroes a stake in maintaining the distinction between themselves and slaves, even though for most free people of color the stake was more an opportunity than a reality.

William Ellison made the most of the opportunity. Having earned freedom in 1816, he set out to give it an economic foundation. By 1822, at the age of thirty-two, he had already achieved more than most white Southerners attained in their entire lifetimes. His early success served as a springboard to extraordinary advancement in the next two decades. His gin business flourished; his family matured; his reputation among whites grew; and he became a planter. Between 1822 and the mid-1840s he gradually built a small empire, modest by State-burg standards, but by most other measures in the antebellum South, magnificent. Ellison was a living refutation of the dominant white assumption that to be free and Negro inevitably meant to live as a useless, poverty-stricken parasite.

Property rights in the Old South included the right to human property, and exercising that right was the surest means of gaining wealth. As Ellison climbed up from slavery, he acquired slaves in increasing numbers. Owning slaves also provided him a kind of insurance. As a master, he effectively demonstrated to skeptical whites that race did not define his loyalties. Whites could never entirely overcome their suspicion that free Negroes were unsound on the issue of slavery. In Denmark Vesey, they had seen racial loyalty outweigh the law, economic self-interest, and the certainty of ruthless punishment. By owning slaves, Ellison broadcast his orthodoxy on fundamental matters and confirmed that he was motivated by safe, mundane, and thoroughly acceptable acquisitive instincts. Whites could see that William Ellison's primary loyalty was not to the black masses with whom he shared racial ancestry but, like themselves (with whom he also happened to share racial ancestry), to self-advancement within the existing social order.

The magnet of economic self-interest—even of greedy accumulation—probably attracted William Ellison as much as most people. But as a free man of color in a slave society, Ellison had a compelling reason to respond to the attraction. While poverty could snare anyone, white or black, slavery was reserved only for those who were not white. Above all else, Ellison sought to defend his family's freedom, and the primary means available to him was economic advancement. For Ellison, his wife Matilda, and his daughter Eliza Ann, slavery was no vague abstraction. For them and the other members of their family, freedom had no guarantee. Ellison was aware of just how fragile and vulnerable his family's freedom was. He attempted to use his wealth to construct a sanctuary that could provide security and safety. Ultimately, no free Negro was immune to white power, but Ellison did all he could—including becoming the master of others—to buttress his family's position as free people.

Success followed success, but not automatically. Thousands of whites who managed to climb into the master class later fell from it. Perhaps because Ellison was a free man of color and understood that the stakes for him were higher than for most others, his way of approaching business, his way of looking at the world, was profoundly conservative. In any undertaking, he seems to have anticipated all that could go wrong. He moved cautiously, deliberately, measuring each step. Hindsight reveals a pattern in his accumulation, suggesting that from the beginning he adopted a disciplined economic strategy. As an artisan manufacturing the single most important machine in the antebellum South and later as a producer of the South's most important crop, Ellison worked in the mainstream of the region's cotton economy. Seeking success within the dominant economy tied him to white standards, values, and institutions. For more than four decades he blazed an uncharted path in a risky world made all the riskier because, to most whites, he was black.

The trajectory of William Ellison's career inclined upward, not in a series of quick jumps but in a steady, gradual climb. So far as we can tell, his economic ascent was unblemished by even one careless investment or imprudent business decision; few of the wealthy whites he served as ginwright could have claimed as much. Year after year he patiently followed the course he believed offered the most for himself, his children, and their children. On the eve of the Civil War Ellison could stand at his home in the High Hills and look out on a vast panorama of South Carolina geography, and a good fraction of what he could see was his.

"WILLIAM ELLISON, GIN MAKER," reads more than one document.[1] Most white people with whom Ellison did business considered their names sufficient to identify themselves. But Ellison identified himself with his work. It was an accurate label. From his boyhood in William McCreight's shop through his forty-five years in Stateburg, Ellison made his living building cotton gins. Gin making was the foundation of his economic success and the craft he passed on to his three sons and his first grandson. Linking his name to his craft indicated how he wanted to present himself to white society. He did not want his white neighbors to forget the service he provided the community. Gin making gave him and his family much of the security they enjoyed in the slave society of the High Hills. Even after the gin business no longer generated the major part of his family's income, Ellison continued to identify himself as a gin maker.

Ellison's trade tied his economic fate to cotton. In 1816 when he arrived in Stateburg, South Carolina was the leading producer of cotton in the South.[2] In less than a decade, however, contemporaries claimed that the state was finished as a major cotton producer. During the 1820s and 1830s the opening of fresh, fertile cotton lands in the west and heedless agricultural practices at home caused the Palmetto State to tumble from its preeminence in cotton production.[3] Tens of thousands of South Carolinians joined the "cotton rush" to the west. In December 1835, a newspaper in Camden reported that the "tide of emigration still flows westward. During the week . . . no less than *eight hundred persons* passed through this place for the far west[;] of course we include white and colored."[4] One Sumter District resident remembered that the roads were "daily thronged with a continual stream of vehicles of every conceivable class and description, laden with women, children and household stuff, and accompanied by their owners on horseback or foot, with their negroes, dogs, and sometimes cattle, all bound for the new lands in Georgia, Alabama and Mississippi."[5]

South Carolina stubbornly proved the prophets wrong. Despite the warnings and the emigrants, Ellison had not hitched his wagon to a falling star. The state lost its lead in cotton production and may even have suffered a slight decline in its crop in the 1830s and early 1840s, but cotton continued to dominate the economy. Statewide, production more than tripled, from 50,000,000 pounds in 1821 to 168,000,000 by 1859. The middle districts, the principal market for Ellison's gins, showed even greater gains in the last two antebellum decades, advancing from 19,000,000 pounds in 1839 to 79,000,000 in 1859, more than a fourfold increase.[6] Since slaves supplied most of the labor for these bumper crops, the slave population continued to grow, increasing by 144,000 between 1820 and 1860, pushing the state's black majority up to 58 percent.[7] The west's staggering crops did succeed in depressing cotton prices, but that concerned white planters more than William Ellison, ginwright. Production—not profitability—determined the number of gins planters needed. Of course had planters been unable to afford his gins, Ellison would have been in deep trouble. But the price of cotton never sunk so low that it was unprofitable to grow in South Carolina, just less profitable than on the more fertile soils in the west.

Skidding cotton prices may have depressed what Ellison charged for his gins. In 1817 his earliest advertisement offered gins at $3 per saw, and that is the price Mrs. Rebecca Singleton paid Ellison in 1825 for a fifty-saw machine.[8] As early as 1847 and thereafter until the Civil War, Ellison's advertised price was only $2 per saw.[9] The decline in price may have reflected the slump in cotton prices, as well as lower costs of certain materials, small efficiencies in production, and rising competition. Since his gin shop ledgers have not survived, it is impossible to tell. In any case, Ellison at least occasionally sold his gins for more than his advertised price. In 1836, for example, Ellison built a gin for John Singleton's Deer Pond plantation and charged $2.75 per saw, but this elevated price may have reflected the gin's special features, which included "steel saws" and "steel plated ribs."[10] Whether Ellison's gins sold for $3, $2, or some price in between, they continued to return a generous profit.

Expansion to the west put South Carolina's planters at a disadvantage in the cotton market, but it gave William Ellison fresh opportunities. Emigrants from the High Hills were not necessarily lost to Ellison. When his former customers reestablished themselves on new plantations in the west, they sometimes remembered the quality of the Ellison gin. "I have engaged W. Ellison to make me a gin to be sent hiar erly in the spring," Caleb Rembert, a former resident of Sumter District now living in Marengo County, Alabama, wrote to a friend in March 1836. "If you should se him reqest him to hurry with it or our river may becum so low as to prevent the boats from runing, and if that should be the case it will be a disappointment to me as I depend on him intirely."[11] In September, just in time for the ginning season, Rembert announced, "I have got it in my Gin House."[12] For his gin, and crating, hauling, draying, storing it in Charleston, and shipping it by sea, Rembert paid Ellison $184.13.[13] In the same year, H. Vaughan, another former resident of Sumter District who had settled in Benton, Mississippi, informed a Sumterville friend that "Ellison promises to send me another gin." He added proudly, "My crop was 356 bales of about 430 lbs each—220 bales have been sold at an average of about 16½ c.," an announcement likely to warm Ellison's heart and bring tears of envy to the eyes of all but the richest Sumter planters.[14]

How many machines Ellison shipped out of South Carolina is unknown, but only a superior gin could have commanded such loyalty and been worth the extra trouble and expense of shipping and handling. One white resident of Sumter District claimed many years later that Ellison's was "the best cotton gin" made before the Civil War.[15] Another declared that for more than fifty years the Ellisons "manufactured here the standard cotton gin of the south, the Ellison Cotton Gin."[16] Whether or not they were the best, Ellison's gins were good enough to allow him to retain his local market, which in the long run was growing, and to capture a slice of the new market in the west that expanded at a phenomenal rate. Between 1820 and 1860 the South's cotton production multiplied by a factor of ten, and Ellison netted his share of the profits from both the Southeast and the Southwest.[17]

While Ellison sold gins as far away as Mississippi, he probably did most of his business within a thirty- or forty-mile radius of Stateburg. The first Ellison gin for which there is a record traveled only a few miles south from his shop to Mrs. Rebecca Singleton's plantation, an easy wagon trip down the old King's Highway.[18] Mrs. Singleton purchased the new gin in 1825, three years after Ellison bought his shop lot from General Sumter. Exactly when Ellison built his first gin in Stateburg is unknown, but his 1817 advertisement suggests he had the necessary equipment within a year after he became free. Having a shop must have made it easier to use his tools and lay in a store of the necessary iron, lumber, leather, bristles, and other materials. But the new shop did not cause Ellison to neglect his repair business. Between 1822 and 1825, for example, he completed more than $100 worth of repair work for John and Richard Singleton.[19]

Ellison's pursuit of new business included advertising his gins and services in local newspapers. Beginning in February 1817, with his notice in the Camden *Gazette,* he probably advertised continuously until the Civil War. However, because of breaks in the files of extant newspapers, the next surviving advertisement appeared in June 1832 in the Sumter *Southern Whig.* There he announced that he "manufactures, and has consistently on hand, Cotton Saw Gins of the most approved construction," and he emphasized his particular model, with its hand-forged saws and hand-filed teeth. Should a planter not want one of the ready-made gins available in his shop, Ellison promised to "make to order, upon short notice, any description that may be required." Ellison also accommodated cash-strapped planters, declaring that he sold gins "for cash or approved credit, upon very liberal terms."[20] He was eager for business, would do custom work quickly, and was ready to extend credit. None of his advertisements, including notices in the Sumter *Gazette,* Sumter *Banner, Black River Watchman,* and other papers, ever mentioned that he was a man of color.[21] He was just a gin maker by the name of William Ellison, silently exploiting the colorless name "William."

Although not as rare as abolitionists, ginwrights were scarce in antebellum South Carolina. According to the 1860 census, there were only twenty-one gin makers in the entire state.[22] Five of them worked in William Ellison's shop, all members of his family. Still, Ellison never lacked local competition. When he first arrived in Stateburg, Camden had two businesses listed as "gin making, carpentry," and a decade later it still had one.[23] In the late 1840s R. C. McCreight, a Camden ginwright who probably was a relative of Ellison's white mentor, advertised in Sumter newspapers, but by the 1850s his advertisements disappeared.[24] Closer to home, Sumterville twelve miles to the east also housed competitors. In the 1840s Hudson and Brother advertised gins "not surpassed by any made in the State." Their gins, they claimed, "possessed refinements" such as "the Falling Breast and Sliding Ribs, which save a great deal in the way of repairs."[25] Hudson and Brother continued throughout the 1840s, but late in the decade they advertised their skills as cabinetmakers, indicating perhaps that their gin business had slumped.[26] Another challenger, James S. Boatwright, had a shop in Columbia twenty-five miles to the west. Boatwright competed with Ellison in the field, not just in the newspapers. Between 1845 and 1852 he serviced the gins of Richard Singleton, a valuable account that had previously belonged to Ellison. For Singleton's repairs Boatwright received $338.[27]

Spurred perhaps by Boatwright and other rivals, Ellison began to run a different advertisement in the late 1840s. His gins, he announced, were constructed on "the most improved and approved plan, of the most simple construction, of the finest finish, and of the best materials." He noted particularly that his gins had *"Steel Saw[s] and Steel plated Ribs, case hardened."* He also advertised the reasonable price of $2 per saw for his new gins. In addition, he actively bid for repairs, noting that he "repairs old Gins and puts them in complete order, at the shortest notice." And he promised, "All orders for Gins will be promptly and punctually attended to."[28] Ellison ran this notice throughout the 1850s. The only modification was his claim that cotton ginned on one of his gins "of the late improvement" was "worth at least a quarter of a cent more than the cotton ginned on an ordinary gin."[29] That was a substantial boast, for Ellison was saying that a planter who purchased a fifty-saw gin from him for $100 could expect the gin to pay for itself by ginning only 100 bales of cotton, about 40,000 pounds, less than a single year's crop for many Sumter planters.

Although Ellison competed successfully, he never achieved a monopoly of the local market. By 1860 three new gin makers advertised in the Sumterville newspapers. John H. Husband of Florence in Darlington District offered gins at $2.50 per saw, while J. N. Elliot of Winnsboro promised gins at Ellison's price of $2.[30] As early as 1853 a gin maker in distant Columbus, Georgia, also sought business in Ellison's back yard.[31] Sumter planters always had these and other alternatives to Ellison's services. Gins were indispensable, but the free colored gin maker was not. To survive as a ginwright Ellison had to offer the best possible product, which meant constant attention to maintaining and improving the quality of his machines. Tradition has it that Ellison received a patent for some feature of his gin, but existing patent records do not confirm that rumor.[32] Certainly by the 1830s Ellison replaced the standard iron saws and wooden ribs in some of his gins with the steel saws and steel-plated ribs that he later incorporated in all his machines.[33] Only a few years earlier James Boatwright had to turn down orders because his gins did not include steel saws.[34] In addition to gins of the highest quality, Ellison had to offer his customers reliable, speedy service and easy credit. He had to give planters no reason whatever to reject his gins because they were made by a free person of color. Ellison's record makes clear that he succeeded on all counts.

To prosper, he may have had to be more accommodating to planters than his white competitors. Ellison evidently did most of his work on credit. When he died, many of the leading planters in Sumter District had unpaid accounts, and more than a few had personal notes out to him.[35] As a free man of color he probably could not press the planters very hard, and he certainly could not insist they pay promptly. Judging from the accounts of his estate, he kept careful records and simply persisted in his attempts to collect from his customers. He reminded them of their accounts, but he usually waited until they decided to settle up. Sooner or later most of them did, when they had ready cash and were prompted by their sense of fair play, their knowledge of the law, or their desire to maintain access to Ellison's services. In good years, planters paid Ellison for the year's work soon after their cotton crop sold. On January 24, 1824, for example, the executors of the estate of John Singleton paid Ellison $70 cash for work he did the previous September.[36] But some planters paid with promissory notes, not cash. Early in 1848 R. R. Spann gave Ellison his note for $72.61 for work Ellison completed in 1847.[37] Ellison signed Spann's note and turned it over to Dr. W. W. Anderson in partial payment of his medical bill.[38] Dr. Anderson often paid his bills for Ellison's gin services by providing medical care in exchange.[39]

Ellison sometimes found it difficult to collect, whether in cash, notes, or services. It is impossible to determine if he had more trouble collecting than white tradesmen, for planters were notoriously slow to pay creditors, regardless of their color.[40] John W. Buckner, Ellison's grandson who worked as a gin maker, often traveled the neighborhood with a fistful of unpaid bills. At least once he returned without collecting a dime. "John went over the river yesterday," William Ellison wrote his eldest son in March 1857. "He saw Mr. Ledinham. He said that he had not sold but half of his crop of cotton and had not the money but when he got the money and was working on this side of the river that he would send his son with it and take up his account." That same day Buckner had no more success on the eastern side of the Wateree. He "also saw Mr. Van Buren and he was ready to pay but before he did so he wished his overseer to certify it. But John could not find him and, as it became late, he had to leave for home. . . ."[41]

Some planters refused to pay at all. To collect from them Ellison turned to the courts. He did not appear in court often, but he made the twenty-four-mile round trip to Sumterville when necessary. In 1834 the judge of the Court of Common Pleas returned a judgment against William H. Killingsworth for $112.50, a debt he had owed Ellison for a year.[42] Nine years later Ellison secured a judgment against Oran D. Lee for $110, plus interest, for a forty-saw gin Lee had ordered more than two years earlier.[43] Clearly Ellison's work was not over when he built and delivered a gin. Collecting his debts also took time, energy, and, perhaps even more, finesse.

An eyewitness account of Ellison's gin operation was left by Thomas S. Sumter, General Thomas Sumter's great-grandson, who grew up in Stateburg before the Civil War. Sumter remembered that the "frame of the gin, that is the wood work, was made in their work shop by hand, mostly out of white oak, hickory and pine grown on their own lands." The Ellisons "turned and grooved it by hand," he recalled. The "saws that cut the cotton from the seed were made and tempered at their blacksmith shop, and the teeth on them made with a file by hand." Sumter declared that while William Ellison trained his slaves to do the tedious work of filing the saw teeth, the Ellisons did the "delicate work with their own hands."[44] But the slaves must have done some of the delicate work too, for in the 1820s Ellison claimed that a slave gin maker he owned was worth $2,000, far more than the price of a rough carpenter or blacksmith.[45] At times there was apparently more delicate work than even the Ellisons and their skilled slaves could perform, for Ellison employed at least one free Negro gin maker in 1850, an A. Miller who lived with Ellison's son Reuben.[46] Another free man of color, Hale Johnson, a cabinetmaker, may have also worked in Ellison's shop in 1850, since he lived adjacent to the Ellisons.[47] By 1860, however, both these free men of color were gone, suggesting that by then Ellison's family and growing slave force could handle all the work themselves.

Ellison's gin shop also did general blacksmithing and carpentry. No more free from pesky competition in this line of work than he was in gin making, Ellison still enjoyed a brisk local trade. Work done for the Moody family, a large and sometimes rowdy clan of white planters and overseers who lived just north of Stateburg, illustrates something of the diversity of Ellison's operation. Between 1833 and the Civil War, blacksmiths in the Ellison shop made the Moodys' horseshoes, hinges, bolts, nails, hooks, rivets, hoops for tubs, and trace chains. Carpenters built coffins (two for Moody women and several for their slaves), repaired chairs, and finished a fine mahogany table. Blacksmiths and carpenters worked together to make the Moodys a wagon, skimmer and shovel plows, axes, hammers, pitchforks, well buckets, and wagon wheels. Bills for the work ranged from as little as $4.10 one year to $136 in another. The bills were prepared meticulously by either William or Henry Ellison.[48] Unfortunately for Ellison, the Moodys were not nearly so careful in paying them. At least twice Ellison took the Moodys to court, winning judgments of $136 in 1834 and $22.50 in 1860.[49] The settlements evidently left no hard feelings, since the Moodys continued to trade with Ellison.

So important were general blacksmithing and carpentry that in 1850 Ellison estimated they brought in one-half of his shop's income, about $1,500 of an annual revenue of $3,000. The remaining $1,500 came from the gin business, about $1,000 from the manufacture of approximately fifteen gins during the year and the other $500 from repairs.[50] Except for these rough estimates in the 1850 census, there are no records with which to calculate the volume of business done at Ellison's shop or the income he received from it. Most likely his business grew gradually as his reputation attracted more and more customers and as his expanding labor force allowed him to accept more orders.

FROM the 1820s until the Civil War, Ellison's gin shop anchored his economic life. It produced a steady, predictable source of income from which he extracted continuous profits by employing his family members and exploiting his slaves. Without slaves, Ellison could have aspired only to the income of a tradesman, at best a modest existence that promised little security for his family. With slaves, he soared into strata occupied by no other free Afro-American in South Carolina and by only a few whites. Each acquisition of a slave man brought Ellison immediate financial rewards by permitting him to build and repair more gins, to increase his profit margin, and to squeeze the surplus from one more worker. Profits from his gin business allowed him to become a landowner and eventually a planter. William Ellison's fortune derived from his own hard work and that of his family members, but most of all it came from his slaves.

The growth of Ellison's slave force cannot be charted through legal documents as it can for most whites. White planters routinely recorded the purchase or sale of slaves with the court as insurance against later claims, commonly made, that the transaction was somehow imperfect or incomplete. Ellison evidently never registered any of his slave purchases. If he had followed the conventional practice and insisted on registering a purchase, he might have offended the white seller, calling into question the individual's honesty and integrity. The absence of court records of Ellison's slave purchases is an index to Ellison's dependence on the good will of local whites. Ellison did not simply overlook recording his purchases. He understood how to use the courts, he had access to good white lawyers whom he retained when necessary, and—when it was essential, as it was with land—he saw to it that his transaction was thoroughly documented in official records.

Without bills of sale, evidence for the growth of Ellison's slave population must be gleaned from the federal census. The census contains only meager information about Ellison's slaves—their sex, age, and color—and that only at ten-year intervals.[51] Changes that inevitably occurred between visits of the census marshall may be invisible. If a slave died or was sold, and if Ellison replaced him or her with a slave of the same sex and approximately the same age, the census will not reveal it. Because the census often obscures the churning that took place among Ellison's slaves, our estimates of the number of purchases he made are conservative, the smallest number that can account for the total in the census from decade to decade. Despite its limitations, the scanty evidence in the census suggests Ellison's strategy in building his slave force.

In 1820 Ellison owned two adult men, both between the ages of twenty-six and forty-five.[52] Except for those moments when Ellison was arranging business with planters or gathering his supplies, he could have been found working shoulder to shoulder with his bondsmen. Business was good during the 1820s, and not even three men could keep up with it. Since Ellison could not hire white men to work under him, he augmented his labor force with apprentices who, like his slaves, worked for the right price—nothing. A master who wanted a young slave trained as a blacksmith or carpenter sent him to Ellison. In 1822 Ellison paid a Sumterville lawyer $5 for drawing up papers for an unknown number of apprentices.[53] Four years later Ellison paid Dr. W. W. Anderson $2.50 for treating Judge Thomas Waties's "boy," indicating that the slave was temporarily in Ellison's charge, probably as his apprentice.[54] When business was particularly brisk Ellison also hired slaves, as he had before he owned any of his own. In 1825, for example, he gave Dr. Anderson a dollar a day for each of two slaves he employed for fifteen days.[55]

Ellison resorted to apprentices and hired labor because the growth of his business outstripped his limited supply of labor. But apprentices and hired hands meant he depended on transient helpers of varying levels of skill and little training or experience as gin makers. Ideally he would have owned enough slaves to run his shop, slaves he could train methodically and control permanently. Accumulating the capital to buy slaves in the 1820s was difficult, however. He had a wife and four small children to support, and none of them could be of much help in the gin shop. Nevertheless, during his first decade of freedom, Ellison purchased his expensive acre from General Sumter, built and equipped his shop, and somehow managed to buy two more slaves, one man between the ages of ten and twenty-three and another twenty-four years old or over.[56] Presumably Ellison wasted no time putting these men to work in his business, which continued to expand during the 1820s.

Ellison began the 1830s with four slave men, all working in his gin business. Early in the decade he tapped a new source of labor, his sons. Henry turned fourteen in 1831, William Jr. in 1833, and Reuben in 1835. Having three sons was a stroke of luck for the ambitious ginwright, and he saw to it that they learned the trade helping him in the shop, just as he had spent his early years in McCreight's shop. By 1836 Henry, 19, began to assume some special duties, like preparing the shop bills.[57] While valuable, the labor of his sons did not meet Ellison's needs, and he continued to take on apprentices. In 1832, for example, he paid the medical bills of two slaves who belonged to white men.[58] The labor of his sons and apprentices could not compare, however, with that of his slaves. By the end of the decade Ellison owned thirty slaves, twenty-six more than he had in 1830, a spectacular increase of 750 percent.[59] During the 1830s he kept his gin shop in good order, established a solid reputation as a master craftsman, and the work poured in. His profits skyrocketed. Like his planter customers, Ellison invested his income in labor, gambling that it would multiply his future earnings.

During the 1830s Ellison dramatically changed his strategy for acquiring slaves. Previously he had only purchased slave men, who paid immediate dividends in his gin business. When he was just getting started and was short on capital, he wanted quick returns on every investment. But by 1840 he owned nine female slaves. Judging from their ages, Ellison probably bought six women, all but one or perhaps two of them in their fertile years. As a result, Ellison owned slave children for the first time, three girls and five boys under ten years of age. By 1840 he also owned sixteen other male slaves, indicating that he had purchased at least six more men between the ages of twenty-four and thirty-six and four more between the ages of thirty-six and fifty-four. By 1840 he had sixteen male slaves ten or older, old enough to work.[60]

Ellison's decision to buy females was a sharp departure from his previous pattern, but it probably did not represent a change in his primary objective—to acquire labor for his gin business. Although slave women did not work as mechanics, they could and did produce slave children, and the boys at least could become artisans in Ellison's shop. Like white planters, Ellison evidently understood that natural reproduction was a less expensive way to increase one's slave holdings than buying in the marketplace. By acquiring slave women, Ellison adopted the traditional economic strategy of antebellum planters, and, judging by the eight slave children he owned in 1840, it worked. Ellison's decision to sacrifice short-term gain for bigger dividends in the long run reflected his confidence that he had found his place in Stateburg and his intention to sink roots that would nourish his family for generations.

If Ellison's slave women did not work in his gin business, what did they do between births? During the 1830s Ellison began to buy land, most of it fields that provided work for his slave women. In 1835 he initiated the purchase of a home and 54½ acres that belonged to Stephen D. Miller, a Stateburg lawyer and former governor of the state who had decided to move his family to Mississippi. For the sum of $1,120 "paid me by William Ellison, gin maker," Governor Miller sold his home that stood about 150 yards south of Ellison's shop and his land that lay just across the Columbia-Sumterville Road to the west. Ellison bought the Miller property on credit, completing the transaction in November 1838.[61]

He also purchased two larger tracts of land during the 1830s. Both came from the Sumter family, from whom he had bought his original acre. Throughout much of the antebellum period, severe financial distress forced the Sumters to sell off large portions of their vast land holdings. In a transaction he began in January 1833 and completed in July 1838, Ellison paid $581.50 for 65½ acres.[62] The price of about $9 an acre was typical of good farm land in the area. At the end of the decade Ellison bought "Davis Hill," paying the Sumters the huge sum of $5,000 for a parcel of 216 acres.[63] There may have been a dwelling on the property, which could help explain the price of more than $20 an acre.[64] Both tracts—which were just north and east of his shop at the crossroads—abutted his other property.

By 1840 Ellison owned a home, a gin shop, thirty slaves,

and more than 330 prime Sumter District acres. No longer just a tradesman in business for white planters, he was becoming a planter himself. Diversifying into agriculture no doubt created headaches for Ellison, but his farming complemented his manufacturing. Owning land as well as a gin business meant that Ellison had productive work for all his slaves, regardless of sex. In general, the men worked in the shop, the women in the fields. In 1840 eleven members of the Ellison household, mostly female slaves, worked in agriculture.[65] In the same year twelve members of the household, more than half of them slave men, worked in "manufacturing and trades," making Ellison's shop the second largest manufacturing concern in Sumter District.[66] Male slaves produced a substantial income for Ellison in the shop. Female slaves grew provision crops that allowed Ellison to feed from his own fields the more than three dozen persons dependent on him. His slave women also grew cotton, which in time became a major source of income.

A dual career in agriculture and manufacturing gave Ellison flexibility in the use of his slaves. He could assign to his gin shop only those men who showed a talent for mechanical work. The rest he could send to the fields. Certainly a few of the eleven individuals he employed in agriculture in 1840 were slave men. Ellison also was in the enviable position of being able to shift his slave men between agriculture and the gin business according to the seasonal demands of the crops and the pace of business in the shop. Slaves in the shop did not lack for work just because planters temporarily had no need for new gins or repairs. Shop mechanics built gins ahead of demand and had them ready for eager customers.[67] Unlike the gin trade, the blacksmith and carpentry work was fairly steady month to month. Even if there was little work of any kind in the shop and it was lay-by time in the fields, Ellison still had an option. From time to time he hired out his slave men to local planters who needed skilled labor. In 1845, for example, one of the Moody clan hired Carlos, and although the bill did not specify the nature or duration of his work, Ellison received a payment of $5.12½.[68]

In the 1830s Ellison's economic operations achieved a pattern that remained unaltered for the rest of his life. Agriculture and manufacturing meshed effectively, and the combination permitted him maximum exploitation of his labor. With three arenas for productive work—his gin shop, his fields, and neighboring plantations—Ellison's slaves, particularly the men, probably enjoyed even less leisure than most slaves, who enjoyed precious little. The efficiency of the entire operation was greatly increased by Ellison's cautious expansion. He bought no more land than he could use and never before he had sufficient labor to take full advantage of it. Unlike many white planters, Ellison was no land speculator. He benefited in fact from the reverses of one of the area's largest speculators, General Thomas Sumter. Most of Ellison's land came from the general's heirs, who were forced to sell off in their effort to brake their downward economic spiral. Ellison acquired his land over a period of three decades, and once he purchased a tract he never sold an inch. He chose each parcel carefully, buying property only in proximity to the crossroads. Unlike Richard Singleton and other white grandees, Ellison did not have to leave home and ride for days to supervise a sprawling estate. Conservative expansion, along with efficient integration, tight concentration, and direct supervision, increased the probability that Ellison earned the highest return on every dollar he invested.

WILLIAM ELLISON, gin maker, slaveholder, shop owner, and planter, had a private life as husband, father, and family man. His foremost concern was the preservation and extension of his family's freedom. The same unremitting attention, deliberate planning, and steely discipline he displayed in his economic life he also applied to familial matters. Unlike the families of slaves, his family had a legal reality. Unlike the families of the white planters he served, his family's freedom was not guaranteed. Ellison did all he could to assure that whatever respect and acceptance his economic activities could wrest from white society would accrue to his family.

All families are guardians of human survival, but for William and Matilda Ellison the role of guardianship took on special meaning. In addition to the traditional duties of procreation, nurturing, training, and care, these parents had to prepare their children for life in a society in which color and caste predominated.[69] In the antebellum South, race was no fuzzy theory they could push aside and ignore. It impinged on every facet of their lives, including family relationships. For all Southerners, historian Bertram Wyatt-Brown has observed, the "inner life of the family was inseparable from its public appearance."[70] This was particularly true for free Afro-American families who aspired to prosperity and respectability. In the Ellison household, private details of family life were dictated by the need to protect family members from an intrusive, potentially dangerous white society.

Patriarchy structured families throughout the nation in the antebellum years. Southern planters idealized patriarchy as the basis of their authority over their slaves and within their white families.[71] William Ellison had more reason than white planters to act the patriarch. All Southerners were required to take into account community standards of conduct. White communities expected free Negroes in particular to hew to the straight and narrow, and they permitted swift correction of those who strayed. Communities judged entire families by wayward individuals. A single important misstep by an Ellison could undermine the whole family's respectability. As long as family members remained within the orbit of his power, William Ellison compelled them to behave according to his perceptions of the requirements of the white community.

Compared to most Afro-Americans, the Ellisons had privileged lives. But being an Ellison also had its cost. Precisely because so much was at stake, family members forfeited their autonomy and individualism to William Ellison's authority and control. Ellison's economic achievement was so conspicuous that family members could not avoid white scrutiny. Each day, traps and snares awaited a slip by one of the Ellisons. To skirt them successfully—in the shop and fields, at church, on neighboring plantations, in factors' and merchants' stores in Charleston, in the courthouse in Sumterville, and on the roads and trains—the Ellisons had to be sure-footed and nimble. The social terrain in the High Hills shifted from decade to decade. By monitoring his family's behavior as closely as the quality of his gins, William Ellison succeeded in creating a haven in Statesburg. His most important legacy to his family was not the gin business or his slaves, for in time they disappeared. It was not his land, enduring as it was. His most valuable legacy was his good name, the respect he earned in his four and a half decades in Stateburg. His good name outlived him, and long after he was gone it continued to sustain and protect his family in an increasingly harsh and dangerous South.

Eliza Ann, the first of April and Matilda's children, was born in 1811 and lived in bondage until 1816 (or shortly thereafter). Little is known about Eliza Ann's childhood and youth, but it is certain that her early years bore little resemblance to the lives of the young daughters of the planters for whom her father worked. Life in the Ellison household in the 1820s must have been a pinchpenny existence, while the aspiring tradesman scrimped and saved to buy his slaves and land, to build and equip his shop, and to provide a home for his growing family. The luxuries common at "Deer Pond," "The Ruins," "Borough House," and "San Souci" did not exist at the Ellisons'.

Whether Eliza Ann received any formal schooling is unknown. She could read and write, and as an adult she kept us with the Charleston newspapers.[72] There were schools for free people of color in Charleston, but it is doubtful that in the 1820s her father felt he could afford them, even if he accepted the wisdom of investing scarce capital in female education. Most likely, Eliza Ann learned what she knew of reading and writing at home. Whether her mother could have taught her is unclear, for no record by Matilda's hand has survived, and it is not certain she was literate. If William Ellison chose to do so, he could have taken spare moments in the evening or on Sundays to teach his daughter.

White girls in the homes of the local gentry had the advantage of formal education. Increasingly concerned about preparing their daughters for suitable matches, planters either sent them away to school or employed governesses to teach them at home. In 1835 Stephen D. Miller, whose Stateburg home William Ellison bought, sent his daughter Mary Boykin to Madame Ann Marsan Talvande's boarding school in Charleston.[73] But some white families concluded that "schools in Charleston at this time are in low estimation," and made the often painful decision to send their daughters farther from home.[74] A particular favorite of High Hills aristocrats was Mrs. Aurora Greland's fashionable school in Philadelphia. There the girls' training consisted more of learning to be ladies than scholars. When a breath of scandal touched the school in 1830, Mrs. Rebecca Singleton, whose daughters Marion and Angelica were enrolled, quickly announced that "Father and myself request *Mrs Greland* to trust *you* as little as possible from under her *eye.*" To soften the blow she included for each daughter $30 for jewelry and $20 "pocket money."[75] Years later, when Marion married and had children of her own, she chose to educate them in her High Hills home. In 1844 Gabriella Huger congratulated her on her decision to hire a governess, adding, "What a comfort it must be to you to have your children educated under your own eyes, and to have them with you always, instead of sending them off to school."[76] Eliza Ann Ellison probably stayed home too, but she did not receive her instruction from a governess.

Eliza Ann's other youthful activities no more resembled those of her white contemporaries than did her education. She doubtless spent most of her time working alongside her mother, cooking, cleaning, doing laundry, tending the garden, raising poultry, caring for her three brothers (who were six, eight, and ten years younger), and performing the tasks that fell to antebellum women without domestic servants. By contrast, a young white girl stuck in an upcountry village because her father decided not to winter in Charleston, as was his habit, complained of nothing to do. There were "gentlemen" in the village, she admitted, but "no beaux." The two ladies she visited were married, and thus she expected only to become "versed in the management of chickens and children. . . ." She devoted her mornings to reading, sewing, and a little practice on the guitar, her afternoons to walking, riding, or bowling, and "visiting and talking scandal of course occupy most of our evenings." While it was a "very delightful village," she yearned for promenades on Charleston's Battery.[77] Whether Eliza Ann visited in the homes of neighboring free Negroes or found time to gossip and make trips to the coast is doubtful. Unlike her white neighbors, Eliza Ann spent her youth preparing for her future responsibilities as wife and mother.[78]

About all Eliza Ann had in common with local white girls her age was Sunday morning services at Holy Cross Episcopal Church. Each Sabbath, William and Matilda probably made sure that their adolescent daughter was well scrubbed, her dress pressed, and her deportment equally presentable so nothing would give the white parishioners who undoubtedly stole occasional glances over their shoulders any reason to question the wisdom of permitting the colored family to worship on the main floor. The services evidently moved Eliza Ann, for she remained an active, devout Christian throughout her life. Although she did not mingle with the white girls after the service, her behavior was probably as modest, reserved, polite, and ladylike as theirs.

On May 13, 1830, when Eliza Ann was nineteen, she married Willis Buckner in a service in the Holy Cross Church.[79] Her church wedding, conducted by the resident pastor, Augustus L. Converse, suggests that the Ellisons had come far in their quest for respectability, that Eliza Ann had performed her part well and had not been found wanting in the eyes of Stateburg's best people. No evidence exists of the couple's courtship, but Eliza Ann certainly could never have boasted as Marion Singleton did in 1839 that "so far we have had a houseful of agreeable company—and at one time I could muster 9 beaux all staying in the house at the same time."[80] Virtually nothing is known of Eliza Ann's husband. There is no doubt that Willis Buckner was a free man of color. However, the censuses of 1820 and 1830 list no free people of color named Buckner in South Carolina, North Carolina, or Georgia.[81] Whether William Ellison considered Willis a "good choice," as Mrs. Greland of Philadelphia described Brazilia Sumter's new husband, is unknown.[82]

On January 23, 1831, exactly thirty-six weeks after their wedding, Eliza Ann and Willis Buckner had a son, John Wilson Buckner.[83] The new parents probably lived in the Ellison household, but within the year Willis Buckner died.[84] A widowed mother at the age of twenty, Eliza Ann returned to the familiar routines of her youth. Living as she always had, she apparently helped her mother with the housework and the rearing of her brothers and her own infant son. Reuben, her youngest brother, was almost ten when his nephew was born.

John Wilson remained the only small child in his grandfather's house for the first fourteen years of his life. Until the mid-1840s, moreover, Eliza Ann and Matilda were the only free women in the Ellison household. Circumscribed by their race and by a masculine world, they were probably even more confined to the family circle than white women. Visiting, parties, sewing circles, associations, Sunday School—all the occasions that helped white women break out of their domestic isolation—were unavailable because the Ellisons were Negroes.[85] In addition, there were no relatives in the neighborhood during the 1830s, no sisters, aunts, nieces, or cousins to include in a female circle. The relationship between Eliza Ann and her mother was probably strengthened by their living arrangements, common domestic tasks, and isolation. Eliza Ann continued to attend church with her parents, and in 1840 she and her mother stepped forward together to be confirmed in Holy Cross, attesting to the bonds between them.[86]

Unlike their sister, Henry, William Jr., and Reuben Ellison were born free.[87] Their father may have greeted their births as one upcountry gentleman did the arrival of a male child in the home of a Sumterville friend. "I am very glad to hear that the stranger is a son," he declared in 1825. "Boys can take care of themselves; girls are too helpless."[88] Eliza Ann was no invalid, but she could never grow up to work in her father's gin shop. Master of just four slaves in 1830, Ellison no doubt looked forward to the labor of his three young sons, and he demanded it when they were of age. Like their father, the Ellison boys grew up around a gin shop, learning the intricate skills of gin making. Through the business, which entailed trips to various plantations, they became acquainted with the physical geography of Sumter and adjacent districts. They also learned to traverse the area's somewhat trickier social terrain. William Ellison instructed his sons in the behavior, habits, and demeanor whites demanded of free Negro artisans.

The early years of the Ellison boys, like those of their sister, did not look much like the childhood of local white boys. Scions of planter families often enjoyed leisurely, extended adolescences, filled supposedly with reading, traveling, and general cultivation of the higher faculties, all designed to ingrain the manners, bearing, and polish they would need when they eventually assumed their proper stations. To the consternation of their fathers, however, maturing sons often drifted into lazy, dissolute habits, spending their time racing horses, hunting game, fighting gamecocks, playing cards, and drinking wine.[89] While the sons of white planters played, the Ellison boys worked. Rather than enforced idleness, Henry, William Jr., and Reuben learned discipline, industry, and responsibility. Ellison knew his sons' future did not depend on inherited status or gentlemanly airs but on their ability to wield a file, set pig bristles in gin brushes, and hammer out snug-fitting horseshoes. Practical, on-the-job training would teach them skill in the shop and diplomacy in the community. There were no pampered, soft-handed Ellisons, neither men nor women.

High Hills planters regularly provided their sons with extensive formal education. As with their daughters, Louisa Penelope Preston observed in 1835, "Most of our Stateburg & Camden gentry have a proclivity to the North."[90] In the 1830s, James Chesnut Jr. and a number of other local boys attended Princeton University.[91] Even when considering preparatory schools, aristocrats tended to look north. Richard Singleton, for example, after being disappointed in his efforts to persuade a certain Virginia family that reputedly was "fashionable, as well as moral and literary," to send a son to his plantation "to take charge of my two sons and prepare them for College," bundled young John and Matthew off to a school in New Jersey.[92] Both Singleton boys eventually entered the University of Virginia, a Southern institution that attracted several Sumterians, including Richard I. Manning, who lived a few miles south of Stateburg.[93] Many young aristocrats treated universities as new places to sow their wild oats. Most Southern colleges and universities annually dismissed a fair number of students for one or another form of "indecency" that came naturally to the headstrong young planters-in-the-making.[94]

According to local tradition, William Ellison shared the gentry's proclivity to the North and sent his sons to school in Canada.[95] Available evidence neither confirms nor contradicts the story. Ellison's finances were less cramped in the 1830s than in the 1820s when Eliza Ann was young. He could

afford expensive educations, and he was probably more willing to invest in schooling for his sons than for his daughter.
All three boys were literate, and it is almost certain they
attended school. Henry, the eldest, had an excellent com-
mand of written English as an adult.[96] William Jr., the middle
son, was less accomplished, suggesting that Ellison may have
favored his eldest son with a better formal education.[97] The
boys may have gone to school in Canada, but far more likely
they went a hundred miles south to Charleston, where private
schools for free people of color were taught by leading free
mulattoes like Thomas S. Bonneau and Daniel Payne. Even
after South Carolina outlawed schools for free Negroes in
1834, several continued to operate, quietly teaching the children of the free colored elite.[98] If the boys did go away to
school, it was not for an extended period, making Canada less
likely than Charleston. All three were in Stateburg in 1830 and
1840 when the census marshall called, and the medical records
of Dr. W. W. Anderson indicate that between 1832 and 1840
none of the boys went more than two years without a visit
from the doctor.[99]

Regardless of their formal training, the three Ellison boys
had their most useful teacher at home. Free Afro-American
parents, like slave parents, instructed their children in the arts
of survival. William Ellison knew that superior mechanical
skills meant little without social dexterity. Ellison's instruction may have resembled the lessons taught by the wealthy
white planter James Henry Hammond, in his way another
outsider in the upper reaches of South Carolina society. In
1840 Hammond declared that his younger brother could make
something of himself if only he displayed *"energy, enterprize,
and determination."*[100] Five years later, he told another younger
brother that grit and hard work were not enough. Hammond
said he had encountered a raft of problems in rising to "a
position to which I had not been bred" and surrounded by
"people who *looked down on me.*" To succeed, he developed
certain social habits that he outlined for the edification of his
brother. "Unless you fawn & flatter, every one you meet in
every grade, you are damned," he said. "This can be done
without degradation. Every man's vanity & self-love can be
touched without any loss of character & dignity." In South-

ern society, "Sensible men study to do it handsomely." The key, Hammond concluded, was to be "conciliating" and to display "politeness & aminity."[101]

This litany of advice came from a white man who, through marriage and hard-driving management, had become one of South Carolina's richest planters and, just before delivering this homily, had concluded a term as governor of the state.[102] Viewed from William Ellison's social stratum, James Henry Hammond was a silver-spooned, blue-blooded aristocrat. Ellison knew at least as well as Hammond that "sensible men" study humankind, especially the aristocratic species native to the High Hills. As much as Hammond, Ellison ordered his life according to a self-conscious design, and he was not backward in demanding that his sons adhere to it. Fathers in the antebellum South regularly bombarded their sons with advice, but whether Ellison lectured pompously like Hammond or taught silently by example is not known. However he taught, he demanded that his sons acquire the habits of deference, tact, and circumspection they needed to elicit the respect and patronage of white planters. By every measure, Ellison proved a more effective teacher than Hammond. The master of "Redcliffe" constantly found fault with his sons' lackluster performances. Ellison's sons learned their lessons.

Just as the sons were creatures of their father's drive and ambition, the father's success was in some measure the creation of his sons. During the 1830s all three sons began to pull their weight in Ellison's business. Henry turned eighteen in 1835, William in 1837, and Reuben in 1839. Ellison integrated each of them into the family economy as gin makers. The 1830s were years of enormous expansion in Ellison's business, and his three sons made important contributions keeping up with the work in the shop, supervising slaves, making repairs in the field, procuring raw materials, tallying accounts, and chasing down customers who had not paid their bills.

Each day Henry, William Jr., and Reuben worked under their father's direction, and each night they slept under his roof. Before 1835 the Ellison home was probably a cabin attached to the gin shop on the solitary acre at the crossroads Ellison bought in 1822. Sometime between 1835, when Ellison contracted to buy 54½ acres from Stephen D. Miller, and 1838,

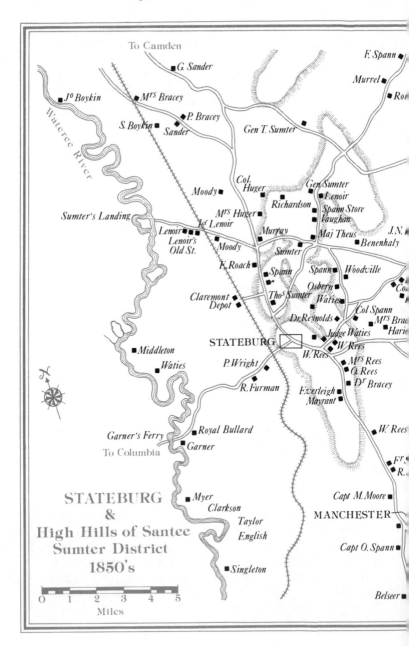

To Camden

G. Sander

F. Spann

Murrel

Ro[

J⁰ Boykin

Mʳˢ Bracey

S. Boykin

P. Bracey

Sander

Gen T. Sumter

Wateree River

Moody

Col. Huger

Gen Sumter

Lenoir

Richardson

Spann Store

Vaughan

J.N.

Sumter's Landing

Mʳˢ Huger

Iˢᵗ Lenoir

Lenoir

Lenoir's Old St.

Moody

Murray

Maj Theus

Benenhaly

Sumter

F. Roach

Spann

Spann

Woodville

Tho⁵ Sumter

Osbern

Waties

Co[

Claremont Depot

Dr. Reynolds

Col Spann

Mʳˢ Brac[

Harie[

Judge Waties

W. Rees

STATEBURG

W. Rees

Middleton

Waties

P. Wright

Mʳˢ Rees

O. Rees

Dʳ Bracey

R. Furman

Everleigh

Mayrant

W. Rees

Garner's Ferry

Royal Bullard

To Columbia

Garner

Fʳ

R.

STATEBURG & High Hills of Santee Sumter District 1850's

Myer

Clarkson

Capt M. Moore

MANCHESTER

Taylor

English

Capt O. Spann

Singleton

0 1 2 3 4 5

Miles

Belseer

when he recorded the deed, the Ellisons moved into a fine house.[103] The Miller land included Miller's home, which stood just south of Ellison's shop and a few hundred yards north of the Anderson's magnificent Borough House. What made the acquisition remarkable was not just that it was the home of a white man but that it was the home of one of South Carolina's most illustrious citizens. Miller had served in the South Carolina legislature and the United States House of Representatives and Senate and, while a resident of Stateburg, had been inaugurated governor of the state. In 1823 Miller and his wife Mary Boykin had a daughter, Mary Boykin Miller, born a few miles north of Stateburg at the home of her mother's parents.[104] Mary Boykin Miller ultimately married James Chesnut Jr. and became the South's most famous diarist of the Civil War.[105] She evidently spent several years of her girlhood in her father's Stateburg home, while the Ellison boys were growing up nearby. Mary's playmate was Dr. W. W. Anderson's son Richard, who won fame during the Civil War as "Fighting Dick" Anderson. Mary Chesnut later remembered that her mother's personal servant married an Anderson slave, a match eased because the "Anderson house was next door."[106]

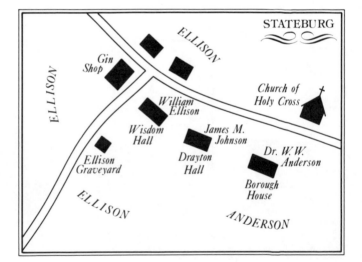

Stephen D. Miller's decision to sell his Stateburg land and home to Ellison must have been based on his estimation of Ellison's ability to pay and on his knowledge of the artisan's good standing in the community.[107] Ellison's decision to buy rested on similar economic and social considerations. The price of $1,120 was steep, but by the mid-1830s Ellison could afford it. Still, without confidence that the white people of State-burg would approve, neither Miller nor Ellison would have entered the agreement. Ellison would never have risked the purchase if Stateburg whites considered it arrogant or pre-sumptuous. Both Miller's decision to sell and Ellison's to buy confirmed the ginwright's economic and social achievement in two decades in the High Hills.

Set back from the southwest corner of the intersection of the Columbia-Sumter and Camden-Charleston highways, the house was clearly visible to all who passed. Travelers may have paused and taken notice of the celebrity of its former owner or the color of its new residents but not its architectural ele-gance. The large two-story frame structure was not ostenta-tious. Soaring white pillars would have strained Ellison's pocketbook and white Stateburg's tolerance. One local his-torian claimed the house was built before 1760, but another, noting its "Hand wrought hinges, hand made nails, wain-scoting of side single boards, small window panes and a nar-row central hall," ventured an origin later in the eighteenth century.[108] A broad-roofed porch extended across the entire front of the house, and three evenly-spaced windows opened above it onto the second floor. Four exposed brick chimneys, two at each end of the house, jutted above the roof line and provided a fireplace for each of the eight rooms. When the Ellisons arrived, there were probably four bedrooms upstairs and a parlor, dining room, living room, and perhaps another bedroom downstairs.[109] Detached behind the house were a kitchen and several outbuildings. Spacious and comfortable, it was appropriate for a wealthy tradesman and his respect-able family.

Within months of recording the deed to the Miller prop-erty, William Ellison returned to the Sumterville courthouse to record a second document, one even more important to him than the deed on his property. On July 12, 1838, with Dr.

W. W. Anderson certifying that his statements were true, Ellison registered the birthdates of all his children and his grandson.[110] The purpose of this seemingly unnecessary act was to establish beyond any doubt that they were all free persons. By recording Eliza Ann's birthdate and her free status, Ellison documented that she was free before the 1820 ban on emancipation. Her freedom meant that John Buckner, Ellison's grandson, was born to a free woman and was thus himself free. By recording evidence that his sons were born after their mother's manumission, Ellison established their free status. The timing of the registrations suggests they were prompted by Ellison's major land purchases. Taking title to large tracts of real estate may have impressed Ellison with the need to establish conclusively that his children and grandson were legally free and thus capable of owning and inheriting property. Whatever his motivation, Ellison went out of his way to create a public, legal record that proved his family's freedom.

"Wisdom Hall," the Ellison family home.
From *The State,* October 4, 1931.

THE village of Stateburg and the old cotton country in the surrounding hills tended to cling to the planter families who had been successful in the early years of the cotton boom. Even in the 1830s and 1840s when the High Hills and the rest of the upcountry experienced an exodus to richer lands, individuals left, rarely entire families. The same aristocratic family names that Robert Mills sprinkled over the High Hills in his famous 1827 map of South Carolina persisted decade after decade. The codes, customs, and values that regulated community life were primarily those of the gentry who from generation to generation dominated the political economy of the area. Unified by race, class, religion, economic interests, and over time by blood, planters were the arbiters of community standards and judges of community behavior.

The Ellison family was as rooted as the white gentry. Race set the Ellisons apart from the white community, but they were never insulated from community judgment. Just as individuals were compelled to act within the framework of family obligations, families operated within the web of community control.[111] When a white person failed to conform to the will of the community, the miscreant usually tarnished the family reputation and brought its social standing down a peg or two. More was at stake for the Ellisons than admission to the sitting rooms of the leading white families. Community disapproval could destroy all the Ellisons had built. Without patronage the Ellisons could not work in Stateburg. Withdrawal of their welcome also meant loss of protection from those willing to light the firebrand and knot the lynch rope. Ostracism was tantamount to banishment, and neither was a mere hypothetical threat. In 1860 the Ellisons received a letter from a free man of color named Jack Thomas, who had left Stateburg seventeen years earlier for Central America. "It seems as there has been a curse upon us ever since we left home," he declared. "I wish I was back home," he wrote. "*Would to God* I was there now."[112] The reason Thomas was forced to leave the village is not clear, but some serious infraction drove him from the community. One member of the Ellison family recalled that just before he departed Thomas "awakened with the prospect of an abundant final siesta."[113]

Even a hawk-eyed observer like William Ellison could not

always be sure of community norms. They were not formulated into rules. White men had to guess and improvise, and sometimes they misjudged.[114] Ellison's social assignment was murkier. Some of the standards that applied to whites—moral uprightness, piety, and honesty—also applied to him. But some traits accounted virtues in whites—manliness and the various assertive manifestations of freedom—were dangerous in a Negro. Moreover, Negroes were held to additional standards, such as humility and deference. White men had difficulty staying on the path to honor and status, but at least others had gone before them and trampled down the grass. Every day William Ellison explored new territory. He was a Negro who worked in a white man's trade, a former slave who owned more slaves than most white Southerners, an artisan whose wealth dwarfed that of most whites, a man born in the slave quarters who now lived in the home of a former governor.

The Ellisons' color, status, and eye-catching achievement made them unavoidably conspicuous. Because of the location of their new home, they lived in a fishbowl. The crossroads site was wonderful for business, but it meant that daily life in the shop and fields and on the porch could be observed by peering travelers. Directly across the old King's Highway from the Ellison home stood a tavern. "It was here the tobacco wagoners, cattle dealers, and travelers from the upcountry on their way to Charleston would meet and rest," one Stateburg resident remembered, "and all the surrounding country would gather to fight chickens, run race horses, play cards, trade and drink corn whiskey from North Carolina and Virginia, and also fine wines. . . . "[115] Public and private life overlapped for everyone in the antebellum South, but the Ellisons were on display constantly, even at home. Self-scrutiny and self-regulation had to become habitual.

In small, stable rural communities like Stateburg, everyone literally knew everyone else. Prying, judgmental neighbors with long memories and short tempers presented free families of color with real dangers. But the human familiarity that permitted community standards to be defined and enforced also protected those who conformed. Historian David M. Potter termed Southern society a "folk culture" characterized by "personalism," a dense network of human relations, person to person, face to face.[116] Direct, personal knowledge of one's neighbors probably intensified both hatreds and allegiances, but it also accustomed people to take the measure of a man or woman, white or Negro, and trust it more than any abstraction about men or women, whites or Negroes. For free Afro-Americans, this amounted to an opportunity to be judged as human beings, and they seized it. Free Afro-Americans knew white communities could be brutal to those who failed to live up to expectations, while they supported, defended, and rewarded those they found worthy.

Each day William Ellison cultivated personal relations with powerful white men. As long as the Ellisons stayed in State-burg among people who knew them personally, who valued them and their work, they had all the security the antebellum South offered to free people of color. As he established his reputation in the High Hills, Ellison had advantages few other free people of color could exploit. When he arrived in 1816, he bore the family name of a respected white planter in Fair-field District, and local white people, knowing about such things, probably silently assumed shared blood. When April Ellison took his former owner's first name four years later, he strengthened that suspicion. The fact that Ellison was a mulatto proved a continuing asset. Most whites were biased in favor of light-skinned Negroes.[117] If they had to deal at all with Negroes who were not slaves, they preferred them light. In the long run, however, the bedrock of Ellison's acceptance was his trade. Any white man who needed a shoe for his horse, a new bucket for his well, or a hinge for a sagging door appre-ciated the convenience of having Ellison around. The quality of his work and the steady reliability of his service were cru-cial to the unspoken white decision that he deserved to stay. Every gin saw he forged fastened another link to High Hills planters. Each planter's promissory note embedded him in the complex system of credit that entangled white men.[118] Few colored men could claim as many business relationships with white planters as William Ellison.

Ellison made certain that the white men who came to the gin shop encountered free people of color who measured up. The Ellisons had to master the subtle rituals of racial etiquette in the midst of serious business negotiations. Each Ellison had to be deferential but not obsequious, sensitive to planters' wishes but not sycophantic, attentive to planters' demands but not slavishly obedient, ingratiating but not groveling. Aggressive independence and haughty self-assertion would jeopardize planters' patronage, while bootlicking and kowtowing would destroy planters' confidence and respect. As black businessmen rather than slaves, correct behavior for the Ellisons lay somewhere in between. Just where, however, must have been difficult to determine. The shop's prosperity confirms the Ellisons' ability to find the tightrope and walk it.

Because wealth was generally esteemed and often assumed to be the mark of merit, Ellison's economic success helped win the respect of the white community. However, in the antebellum South prosperity was reserved almost exclusively for fortunate whites. Each advance by Ellison nudged him farther from most other free Afro-Americans and closer to the white elite, heightening the disjunction between the social connotations of his color and the visible reality of his success. Lesser whites in particular may have viewed his ascent with resentment and jealousy. A former slave on Richard Singleton's plantation remembered that the overseer there considered slave artisans a personal affront. "Ye think because ye have a trade ye are as good as ye master," he would scream before whipping them, "but I will show ye that ye are nothing but a nigger."[119] In Mississippi, a dispute over property led a white man to murder William Johnson, the free Negro barber and diarist of Natchez.[120] Prosperity had its risks, but it was better than poverty. Poor free Negroes found it more difficult to attach themselves to powerful whites. Ellison's wealth made it easier for wealthy whites to respect him, despite his color.

The 1822 law requiring each free man of color to have a white guardian formalized the personal relationships between the races. Legislators wanted every free Negro man in South Carolina beholden to some upstanding white man. On January 7, 1828, five years after the law became effective, William Ellison appeared before the clerk of court in Sumterville with Dr. W. W. Anderson. Anderson swore that he had "known William Ellison a free man of colour for several years and

believe him to be of good character and correct habits."
Declaring himself a "free holder" in Sumter, as required by
the law, Anderson formally accepted the guardianship of the
mulatto ginwright.[121] Anderson probably knew Ellison as well,
or better, than any white man in the High Hills. Since 1822
Ellison's gin shop had stood within a few hundred yards of
Anderson's "Borough House." By doing business with each
other, the two men developed mutual respect that the guardianship formalized.[122]

Why William Ellison waited five years to secure a white
guardian is unclear. It is unlikely that he was ignorant of the
1822 law. He never lacked sound legal advice on essential matters. His delay probably came from his instinctive caution about
entering a binding agreement with a white man that could—
if it were with the wrong white man—compromise his newly
won freedom. Only six years after he had slipped free from
his white master, the law told him to find a white guardian.
His caution about making the decision was probably buttressed by a growing confidence that things were working out
in Stateburg, a feeling that he could afford to take his time to
look over white men just as they were looking him over. By
choosing Dr. Anderson, Ellison selected the white man who
came to his house frequently on medical calls, who knew his
family, who did business with him, and who worshiped in his
company each Sunday at Holy Cross.

Whether Ellison ever called upon Dr. Anderson to do anything in his capacity as guardian is unknown. A former slave
of John Frierson, whose plantation "Pudden Swamp" was in
the eastern part of Sumter District, remembered that his master, a "kind-hearted man," was "chosen by some of these free
colored people as their guardian," and he "never failed to
respond to the call of distress." All free Negroes, he recalled,
"had to have some white man to be their guardian. That is,
some white man to look after their interest to see that they
got their rights, and to protect them, if necessary."[123] Although
the legislature passed the guardianship law to force each free
Negro man to find his own personal policeman, free men of
color did what they could to twist the law in their favor. They
hoped their guardians would instead safeguard them and their
interests.

Other Stateburg whites also accorded Ellison the recognition and respect he sought. In an article on the "Governor Miller home" in 1931, the Columbia *State* reported that "There are many people now living who remembered these [Ellison] gins when in use in every part of this and other states," and that the gin maker William Ellison "is said to have been a mechanical genius. . . . "[124] Two decades later, Thomas S. Sumter, a descendant of the founding father of the district, recalled that William Ellison "was well respected by all, and he and his sons patronized for their gins." He even claimed to remember that every person buried in the Ellison family graveyard had been laid to rest by white "friends" who acted as attendants and pallbearers.[125]

Contemporary evidence from the nineteenth century confirms these twentieth-century reminiscences. When Dr. Anderson drew up his early accounts for the Ellison family, he sometimes headed them "William Ellison—colored man." Over the years, he dropped all references to race, and he treated William Ellison and "Mrs Ellison," an unorthodox appellation for a free Negro woman in the antebellum South.[126] In 1838, a Mr. C. Cross presented William Ellison with an expensive three-volume *Life of Napoleon Bonaparte,* published in 1827 in Philadelphia.[127] Although it has proved impossible to identify Mr. Cross, he obviously believed Ellison deserved such a gift and would appreciate good history.

One of the most revealing illustrations of how Ellison operated in the white community comes from the diary of Natalie Delage Sumter. No white family other than the Andersons had a more enduring relationship with Ellison than the Sumters. In 1802 Thomas Sumter, Jr., the general's son, married Natalie Delage while he was in France on a diplomatic mission. After a tour of duty in Brazil, the Sumters returned to Stateburg to live at "Home House," the plantation the general gave his son. "Home House" was located two miles from Ellison's shop, and the ginwright did good business with its owner.[128] When Thomas Sumter, Jr., died in 1840, Natalie Delage Sumter took over the management of the plantation. To help order her chaotic life, she began to keep a diary. On July 14, 1840, she made the following entry: "Ellison est venu[;] j'ai arrange mes affairs avec lui. he is a

very honest man for he came to tell me about 144d [$1.44?]—
that no one knew but him[;] he is to get me 3 locks. I gave
him 75 cts."[129] Like a brown Abraham Lincoln, Ellison made
a four-mile trip to return a small sum he discovered he had
inadvertently overcharged Mrs. Sumter. This particular customer—hassled by unruly slaves and gouged by opportunistic
tradesmen—could not have been more appreciative. The story
of Ellison's utter honesty almost certainly made the rounds,
for "Home House" was a hub of High Hills society, and Mrs.
Sumter was a regular visitor in the parlors of leading citizens.[130] Her story probably sparked other ladies and gentlemen to recount their experiences with the remarkable colored
man who lived in the Miller house in Stateburg.

ONE important feature of Ellison's life never entered those
cozy conversations among the Stateburg aristocracy. Like so
many other free persons of color, Ellison remained tied to
slavery by a family member. He had a fifth child, a daughter
named Maria Ann, who remained a slave all his life.

On November 17, 1830, Ellison purchased Maria from her
owner, Dr. David J. Means of Winnsboro, "in consideration
of the love and affection which I have for my natural daughter Maria a woman of colour . . . with a view to procure &
affect her emancipation."[131] Since manumission had been
outlawed ten years earlier, Ellison resorted to the legal tech-
nique of vesting her ownership in trust to another person.
The day after he purchased Maria from Means, he sold her
for one cent to Col. William McCreight in Winnsboro, the
white man he had served as an apprentice fifteen years earlier.
The trust bound McCreight to hold Maria under carefully
prescribed conditions: she was to be "allowed to live with
William Ellison or whomever he directs"; Ellison retained "the
right at any time to emancipate" her in South Carolina or any
other state; if Ellison died, then McCreight was to "secure
her emancipation as soon as possible here or in another state";
all expenses for these arrangements were to be paid by Ellison's estate, and his executors were prohibited from contesting this provision and from themselves holding Maria "in
bondage"; and finally, McCreight and his family had "no right
to the services of Maria during or after the life of William

Ellison," and this was to extend to any children she might have. The trust, in short, allowed Maria to live as a free woman of color, although legally she remained McCreight's slave.

Why Ellison did not purchase Maria soon after he was freed in 1816, when he bought Matilda and Eliza Ann, is not clear. According to Maria's age in the 1850 and 1860 censuses, she was born in 1815, only a year before Ellison became a free man. Whether she belonged to the Means family at the time of her birth is unknown. John Means and Thomas Means were white planters who lived in Fairfield District in 1810 in the vicinity of Winnsboro. Both of them were large slaveholders, with ninety-five and eighty-six slaves, respectively.[132] Maria may have belonged to one of them, through whom she passed to David Means, who owned thirty-three slaves at the time he sold Maria to her father.[133] It is possible that whoever owned Maria refused to sell her to Ellison shortly after he obtained his freedom. However, that seems unlikely. There is no obvious reason, other than unpredictable personal preferences, why Maria's owner would refuse to sell a very young child who would be a financial drain until she was nine or ten years old.

Ellison's own mother lived until 1837, when she died in Fairfield.[134] No evidence exists that he purchased her freedom. All that is known is that at his mother's death he returned to Winnsboro to bury her. Ellison paid James and Robert McCreight, white carpenters and gin makers, the substantial sum of $12 for a "Covered Coffin."[135] It was no simple pine box. The coffin was apparently adorned on the inside with a fine cloth covering. In 1843 the McCreight brothers charged white William Ellison (a son of April's owner) $5 for a plain coffin; in 1841 the coffin they built for the white planter's daughter cost $13.[136] Ellison had not forgotten his mother. He had traveled a considerable distance to give her a decent burial and had provided a coffin comparable to one suitable for Fairfield's white gentry.

In the years just before her death, Ellison's mother may have been one of nine free women of color approximately her age in Fairfield District.[137] More likely, she was one of several slave women about that age owned by white William Ellison.[138] At the time of April's birth in 1790 she was probably a favored slave of white William Ellison or his father Robert, one of whom apparently fathered April. During the 1820s and 1830s, while her son was making a name for himself in State-burg, her favored status probably persisted, either in the form of mild servitude or *de facto* freedom. An old woman who had lived in the district since the late eighteenth century, she may have had no desire to leave her long-time home or to obtain formal freedom. Evidently, neither was true of Maria.

Ellison probably delayed buying Maria for fourteen years after he bought his other family members because his wife Matilda was not her mother. If Matilda had been the mother of Maria, the mother and child almost certainly would have been owned by the same person. If that person allowed Ellison to buy Matilda, he or she would probably also have sold Maria at the same time, since the child would have been no older than two. It seems reasonable to suppose that Matilda and Maria had different owners, and that suggests Matilda was not Maria's mother. If Maria was born to another slave woman, she was only a step-daughter to Matilda, and a half-sister to Eliza Ann, Henry, William Jr., and Reuben. Circumstantial evidence suggests that is exactly how she was treated after Ellison sold her to McCreight in 1830.

It is unlikely that Maria ever lived with William Ellison and the rest of his family in Stateburg. She certainly did not live there at the time of the federal census in 1830. The 1840 census, however, noted that two free women of color between twenty-four and thirty-six years old were in Ellison's household.[139] One of them was certainly Eliza Ann, 29. Conceivably, the other was Maria, 25. However, it was probably somebody else. If Maria was living with the Ellisons between 1830 and 1840, it is odd that she did not appear in the medical records of Dr. Anderson, who regularly visited and treated all the other family members during these years.[140] By 1850, when the census first recorded the name of each person in the household, Maria definitely did not live with the Ellisons. Instead, she resided in Winnsboro, married to a thirty-five-year-old free mulatto carriage maker named Henry Jacobs.[141] Jacobs was born in Lancaster District, which borders the northeast corner of Fairfield, Maria's birthplace. Jacobs evidently owned his home. He reported real estate worth $500. He lived near several white carriage makers and a white cotton gin maker. His skilled trade and his proximity to a gin maker suggests that he may have known Maria's new owner, McCreight. Most significant of all, however, was that Maria was living as a free woman of color more than forty miles from all the other Ellisons in Stateburg. Every other child of William Ellison lived in the family compound after marriage, and even after having children of their own. If Maria was a family member like all the others, why didn't she?

By 1860 Henry Jacobs had prospered. He owned real estate worth $1,200 and personal property worth $2,500.[142] He was within the economic elite of free Afro-Americans in the state. He still lived in Winnsboro working as a carriage maker. Maria still lived with him, along with a sixty-seven-year-old free mulatto woman named Ann Jacobs (probably Henry's mother), and two teen-age girls, Mary Ann and Sarah, who were probably Henry and Maria's daughters. The girls' ages, seventeen and fifteen, respectively, suggest that Henry and Maria married about 1842. In any case, Maria and Henry did not move to Stateburg during the 1850s.

Evidence from William Ellison's will suggests that more than geographical space separated Maria from all the other Ellisons. In the will he drew up in 1851, Ellison bequeathed parcels of land to Henry, William Jr., Reuben, and Eliza Ann. He provided that "the rest and residue of my Estate, both real and personal . . . be equally divided between my four children." To "Maria Ann Jacobs of Fairfield District," not identified in any way as a relative, he left five hundred dollars. Furthermore, Ellison named all of his children except Maria as executors of his estate.[143] After his death, the meticulous records of his estate contain an entry for May 25, 1863, noting that $466.55 was paid "to Maria Jacobs for Balance of Bequest made by William Ellison." On the same day, 75 cents were paid "to Express Agent for transmitting the above" to Maria.[144] The bequest was paid, it appears, at arm's length.

Although the evidence is not conclusive, it is sufficient to suppose that Maria was Ellison's daughter by a slave woman other than Matilda. If that was true, Ellison had sexual intercourse with the woman as late as 1814, three years after Eliza Ann was born to Matilda and two years before he became free. It is certainly true that by 1820, after he had purchased his wife and daughter, fathered two free-born sons, and bought two adult male slaves, he left enslaved in Fairfield his young child Maria. It was not because he lacked the money or the desire to free his family that he failed to buy her.

Why he finally bought her is not known. Dr. Means, her owner, moved to Alabama in 1830.[145] Perhaps Ellison heard of the impending move and sought to prevent Maria from being taken so far away. Or his decision to buy Maria could have been influenced by any number of other considerations: an accumulating sense of responsibility for her; a gnawing guilt for having fathered her and then abandoned her in slavery; a growing ability to afford to buy her; a feeling that he was losing his other daughter, who married Willis Buckner in 1830. Or perhaps it was as simple as Maria asking him to buy her and allow her to live as a free woman. There is no way to know.

Ellison's motivation in selling Maria in trust to McCreight is only slightly less obscure. The 1820 law banning manumission allowed the legislature to grant exceptions, but the chances of obtaining legislative approval were almost nil. In 1838, for example, James Patterson, a free man of color who lived in Columbia, petitioned to be allowed to free his wife Sarah and his two children, George and Mary, whom he had purchased and currently owned as his slaves. Patterson asked the legislators to grant his request "so that honest industry, the unwearied pains and untiring efforts of a Father & Husband may not be lossed to him entirely."[146] Sixteen prominent white citizens of Columbia supported Patterson's petition, pointing out that "He is an honest careful industrious man." Pierce M. Butler added a personal endorsement of Patterson as "an industrious well behaved boy, respectful & always knowing his place."[147] Despite this chorus of praise, the Committee on the Colored Population denied Patterson's request.[148] William Ellison could not hope to succeed with a petition to set Maria free.

By selling Maria to McCreight rather than retaining her himself, Ellison gave her *de facto* freedom the strongest possible protection in the law. Without selling her to somebody, he could not specify the terms of her trust. Had he simply allowed her to live as a free person, he risked having her claimed as a slave by any white person who challenged her freedom, a risk that was far greater if her nominal owner was a free person of color instead of a respected white man. Having worked with McCreight for so many years, Ellison was confident that he could be relied on to carry out the terms specified in the trust.[149] Ellison also had confidence in his white guardian, Dr. Anderson. But admitting to Dr. Anderson that he had an illegitimate slave child would call into question the good character and correct habits Anderson had attested to in court. Ellison had to create a legal record to insure Maria's *de facto* freedom. By selling her to McCreight, he made certain that record appeared in the courts of Fairfield District forty miles away from Stateburg. It may well be that Maria's existence was unknown in Stateburg before Ellison's death, even to members of his family. Maria is not mentioned in the stories about Ellison that have been handed down over the generations by Stateburg residents. When he carefully recorded the names and birthdates of all his other children in the Sumter District courthouse in 1838, he did not mention Maria. By naming her in his will, Ellison announced her existence, but there is no evidence he ever acknowledged her relationship to him in any way other than the sale to McCreight.

If Maria was Ellison's daughter by some unknown slave woman, then she represented the only notable misstep in Ellison's disciplined march toward freedom and respectability. That the misstep was taken only two years before he was free may have haunted him with memories of how easy it was to stray from the path out of slavery. It was a mark of his character that he acknowledged her as his daughter, purchased her in 1830, and did what he could to secure her freedom. But Maria and her mother must also have left their mark on Ellison, constantly reminding him that absolute rectitude was the price of freedom and that, despite all his efforts, he could never completely put slavery behind him.

I V

"Wisdom Hall"

B Y his fiftieth birthday, in 1840, William Ellison had reached a plateau. In the first thirty years of his life, he climbed from slave to master, and in the next twenty years, from master to planter. The owner of thirty slaves, a half-section of High Hills land, a flourishing cotton gin business, and a handsome home, he had amassed an impressive fortune. No evidence directly reveals Ellison's assessment of his achievement, but it is difficult to imagine that he felt disappointed. In a half-century his efforts had taken him from a starting point below all whites to the economic level of the white ruling class. The pace of his acquisitions during the next two decades leaves no doubt about his unquenched ambition. But as he grew older and his sons came of age, he had to channel more of his ambition through them. Since 1816, his ultimate ambition had been to secure and endow the freedom of his family. His legacy of land and slaves could underwrite the freedom of the second generation of Ellisons, but only the efforts of his children could pass his most cherished possession to subsequent generations.

Between 1844 and 1847, when they were in their mid- to late twenties, Henry, William Jr., and Reuben each chose a bride from a prominent family of color in Charleston. William Jr. probably married first. His new wife, Mary Thomson Mishaw, was nine years younger than he.[1] She was the daughter of John Mishaw, a prosperous free mulatto shoemaker who belonged to the Brown Fellowship Society, Charleston's most exclusive free mulatto benevolent society.[2] Henry and Reuben married sisters. Henry's wife, Mary Elizabeth Bonneau, and Reuben's, Harriett Ann Bonneau, were daughters of Thomas S. Bonneau, the respected free mulatto schoolmaster and community leader, who was also a member of the Brown Fellowship Society.[3] Mary Elizabeth was seven years younger than Henry, and Harriett was probably younger than Reuben, though her age is unknown.[4] Through their marriages, the three brothers joined the Ellison family with the brown aristocracy of Charleston.

In the tradition their white neighbors had established a generation earlier, the Ellison brothers married upcountry wealth to tidewater society. As sons of one of the state's wealthiest free men of color, the Ellisons did not need to restrict their choice of spouses to the few eligible free women of color in Sumter District. The field of choice in Charleston was not only larger, but more fashionable. Although the brothers stood to inherit their father's estate, red clay probably showed in the stitches of their boots. They lacked the polish, refinement, and cosmopolitan associations an elite spouse from Charleston could bring them. By marrying into established free mulatto families in the city, the Ellison brothers broke out of the social isolation of Stateburg and gained kinfolk among the prosperous mulatto artisans and slaveholders who composed Charleston's free colored aristocracy. That the brothers successfully courted daughters of the upper crust of Charleston's Afro-American society suggests how well their father's wealth traveled.

William Ellison presumably gave his blessing to these advantageous marriages, since in all other important matters the sons had to reckon with their father's wishes. They may also have had to meet certain demands of their brides' families. Thomas Bonneau and his wife Jeannette and John Mishaw and his wife Elizabeth were active parishioners in St. Philip's Episcopal Church, a congregation elegant enough, for example, to witness the baptism in 1822 of Wade and Ann Hampton's son Christopher Fitzsimons.[5] When the Bonneaus baptized their own son Thomas Collins in 1814, one of the sponsors was William Pencil, the free Negro man who became an official hero of South Carolina for betraying the Vesey conspiracy.[6] The respect accorded the Bonneaus' piety is evident in their sponsorship of numerous baptisms of free mulatto children in St. Phillip's. It may well be that the Ellison brothers' prospective in-laws insisted that the suitors establish their religious credentials before they consented to their daughters' marriages. In 1843, shortly before the Ellison brothers married, all three were baptised at Holy Cross in Stateburg.[7] Two years later, after William Jr. had married Mary Thomson Mishaw, all three of the brothers, their father, and Mary were confirmed at Holy Cross, suggesting that maybe even old William Ellison had to knuckle under to the Bonneaus' religiosity.[8] For a quarter of a century he had faithfully attended services at Holy Cross without stepping forward for confirmation. He and Matilda were baptized together in 1836, and now, nine years later, he made the confirmation of his sons another family occasion.

How the Ellison brothers met the Bonneau sisters and Mary Mishaw is unknown. The brothers may have attended Thomas Bonneau's school in Charleston and been introduced into free colored society by their teacher. But since Bonneau died in 1831, Reuben was almost certainly too young to have been one of his students. He and his two brothers may instead have gone to Daniel Payne's school early in the 1830s and made contacts through Payne, who taught several of Bonneau's daughters.[9] Or the Ellisons may have become acquainted with Charleston's free mulatto families when they came to the city on family business, picking up supplies, looking after the shipment of cotton gins bound for the Southwest, and making certain their father's cotton was properly consigned to his factors. They may also have come to know the city's free colored elite through their new brother-in-law, James Marsh Johnson.

On February 26, 1845, after nearly fourteen years as a widow, Eliza Ann (Ellison) Buckner married James M. Johnson, the son of another member of Charleston's free mulatto elite, James Drayton Johnson, a respected tailor.[10] Young Johnson, who was about nine years younger than Eliza Ann, had moved to Stateburg in 1842.[11] An experienced, well-trained tailor, he may have learned of the market for hand-sewn fashions among the planters in Sumter from a long-standing friendship with the Ellison brothers that dated from school days in Charleston. It is also possible that William Ellison suggested the move, since the senior Ellison may have been a friend of Johnson's father as early as the 1820s.[12] If Johnson had no previous contact or knowledge of the Ellisons, he surely met them quickly after he arrived in Stateburg, since he was baptized in Holy Cross along with the three Ellison brothers in 1843 and received confirmation shortly thereafter, two years before Henry, William Jr., and Reuben.[13] While her brothers evidently married in their wives' home church in Charleston, Eliza Ann's wedding took place in Holy Cross, with Reverend Converse officiating again.

Rather than losing a daughter and three sons, William and Matilda Ellison gained a son-in-law and three daughters-in-law. All four Ellison children brought their spouses home to live in their father's household. They were more than Ellison's eight-room house could comfortably accommodate. Sometime in the 1840s he and James D. Johnson purchased a frame house about seventy-five yards south of the main residence, possibly as a wedding present for Eliza Ann and James M. Johnson, although the two patriarchs retained ownership of it.[14] The house was not a cozy honeymoon cottage, however. In 1850 it housed, in addition to Eliza Ann and James, Johnson's stepson John Buckner, Reuben Ellison and his wife Harriett Ann, and Peter Turner, a seventeen-year-old free colored tailor who probably worked as Johnson's apprentice.[15] Residing in Ellison's own house were he and his wife Matilda, Henry and his wife Mary Elizabeth and their three-year-old daughter Matilda, and William Jr. and Mary Thomson and their three children, William John, Henrietta Inglis, and Elizabeth Anna.[16] Within the family, the Johnsons' residence was referred to as "Drayton Hall," evidently in honor of Eliza Ann's father-in-law. William Ellison's home was called "Wisdom Hall."[17]

Just as their residences attested to the strength of family bonds, so did the names the Ellisons chose for their children. Between 1845 and 1852 William Jr. and Mary Thomson had five children. Their son William John was named for his grandfathers, William Ellison and John Mishaw. Elizabeth Anna bore her aunt's name. Another daughter, Henrietta Inglis, was evidently named for Henry and the Inglis family, a free colored family in Sumter District who also attended Holy

Cross.[18] Their son Henry McKensie carried the names of his uncle Henry and another member of the Inglis family.[19] Their youngest son, Robert Mishaw, was given Mary's maiden name combined with the name of one of her uncles.[20] Henry and Mary Elizabeth named their only child after Henry's mother, Matilda. Reuben and Harriett Ann's only child evidently died shortly after birth, before it was named, and Eliza Ann and James M. Johnson had no children of their own.[21] In the entire family only one name—John Wilson Buckner—does not conform to the familiar pattern, possibly because his father, Willis Buckner, named him. The name of every other member of the third generation of free Ellisons commemorated the network of love, respect, and authority that knit the family.

WILLIAM ELLISON presided over his sprawling family compound that in 1850 contained sixteen family members spanning three generations. While Ellison's three sons and his grandson John Buckner worked in his business, they were by no means equal partners. William Ellison never relaxed his grip on the economic empire his family helped build. The sons' marriages did not fracture the unity of the family, nor did they alter their father's patriarchal authority. By 1860, when William Ellison was seventy and his sons mature men in or near their forties, the sons shouldered much of the responsibility for the daily operation of the business, but Ellison steadfastly refused to share ownership or control. In 1860, when Ellison's fortune was at its peak, only Henry owned any land, a measly thirty acres.[22] The sons had become slaveowners, but William Jr. owned only one slave, Henry three, and Reuben five.[23] They did not own the houses they lived in or the shop where they worked. One day they expected to inherit their father's wealth, but until then they lived and worked almost entirely under their father's direction.

The Ellison brothers first became slaveowners during the 1840s, but their slaves were house servants, not income-producing artisans. In 1850 William Jr. owned a sixteen-year-old black woman, and Reuben, a nineteen-year-old black woman. Henry owned a fourteen-year-old girl and a boy, eleven, both black.[24] Their father probably gave them the slaves, who most likely did chores around the house and yard, looked after the young Ellison children, and served the children's mothers. The Charleston brides were no strangers to house servants and may well have expected them as necessary parts of family life, especially in the country. By 1860 William Jr. still owned one slave woman, probably the same woman he had in 1850. Henry's three slaves included a man, twenty-one, a woman, twenty, and an eight-month-old child. Reuben's slaves had increased to five, the twenty-eight-year-old black woman Hannah whom he had owned previously, and her four small children five years old and younger.[25]

William Ellison's land and slaveholdings multiplied during the 1850s, suggesting that most of the income generated by the family business funneled into his hands. Although Ellison dominated the family economy, he permitted his sons and grandson a small measure of economic independence. From his thirty acres of land, Henry collected the profits from thirteen bales of cotton in 1860.[26] William Jr. also made some "cotton money," evidently from farming a corner of his father's estate. He also had his own bank account in Charleston. In 1857 he asked Henry, who was in Charleston on business, to withdraw "three hundred dollars that you will see in the W. J. Elison Saving Bank Book with the dividends and surplus dividends that it have drawn," and leave it at the Ellison's factors' office, "subject to Father's order."[27] His father repeated to Henry that he was to give the factors "the money I have borrowed from William."[28] The three Ellison sons and John Buckner probably took a number of small carpentry and blacksmith jobs on their own account, pocketing the money they earned. Without question Reuben did dozens of small jobs in the 1850s, the largest paying him $45.29 and most of them something between $5 and $20.[29] Another scrap of evidence of a measure of financial independence comes from Dr. Anderson's medical records. Until a few years after the brothers married, Anderson charged their bills to their father. By 1849 each son had a separate account with the doctor, which each presumably paid himself.[30]

However, these tokens of economic independence illustrate the Ellison brothers' subordination to their father. He took the lion's share of the income and reinvested in more land and slaves. He paid them wages, allowed them to grow a little cotton of their own, and permitted them to use the shop tools (and possibly slaves) for some sideline accounts of their own. But they had little opportunity to accumulate their own wealth. On the eve of the Civil War, for example, Reuben—who was forty years old—owned his family of slaves, furniture valued at less than $50, an old shotgun, some books, brushes, and three head of cattle.[31] If Reuben and his brothers had relied solely on their own private incomes, their lives would have been nearly as barebones as those of other free people of color.

The one male member of the family who did not work for William Ellison was his son-in-law, the tailor James M. Johnson. Johnson probably did his sewing in his home, "Drayton Hall." Planters interested in Ellison's gins were men who appreciated handmade clothing and could afford it. On a visit to the gin shop, they could saunter over to Johnson's house to be measured for a new outfit. The Moodys, who lived just north of the crossroads, were among Johnson's regular customers. In 1853 one member of the family bought a plain drill frock coat and pants for $4.50. Two years earlier, he paid $7.00 for a black alpaca frock coat and gray cashmere pants and vest.[32] Thanks to Johnson, some Stateburg house servants dressed as smartly as any in Charleston. In January 1851, Richard Singleton had Johnson make a broadcloth jacket, pants, and vest for his butler, William.[33] To planters like Singleton, having a tailor from one of Charleston's best shops just up the road in Stateburg was a delightful convenience. In 1859, when Johnson temporarily returned to Charleston, several Stateburg planters continued to patronize him.[34] Another planter "regretted he did not know I was in Town so as he might have got his work done," and, Johnson reported, the man tried to persuade him to accompany him back to his place in Summerton, a small town in Clarendon District, about twenty miles south of Sumter.[35]

Like his brothers-in-law, Johnson did not escape dependence on the family patriarch. In addition to tapping Ellison's list of customers and working out of the family compound, Johnson farmed a few acres of Ellison's land and grew a bit of cotton. Late in 1859, Johnson wrote Henry from Charleston that he had sold his cotton and thus "will be able to settle up with your Father for Bagging, Rope, &c."[36] A month later he decided to sell his cotton seed too, since he expected to reside in the city for the year and could not plant a crop.[37] Johnson also teamed up with William Ellison in the "Ellison & Johnson" shoe business. Most likely, Ellison provided the shop, tools, an occasional slave, and supplies of leather—which he used extensively in his gins—while Johnson supplied the skills and probably much of the labor. Johnson made shoes for the same prominent white families he clothed. In 1854 he made a pair of "fine shoes" for $2.50 for one of the Moodys and four years later a pair of "negro shoes" for $1.12½ for one of the Moodys' slaves. Johnson also repaired shoes, charging 75 cents for half-soles for "fine shoes," for example.[38] Although he worked as a tailor, cobbler, and farmer, Johnson remained another of William Ellison's dependents.

THE crowded, bustling Ellison compound should have been ripe for intrafamily tension. Jealousy, envy, and competition for family rank were common in aristocratic white house-holds, especially between brothers and brothers-in-law.[39] When Johnson married Eliza Ann and moved into the Ellison com-pound, he might have become a prime target of hostility from the Ellison brothers. All the evidence points in the opposite direction, however. Johnson seems to have been on friendly terms with all the brothers, and he was especially close to Henry. Letters exchanged between the two when Johnson returned to Charleston in 1859 reveal a warm, affectionate friendship. The long, chatty letters contained gossip and jests as well as candid discussions of marriage, religious faith, and politics. They disclose two men who enjoyed each other's company. When James ended a letter with "Give my Love to All at Wisdom Hall & accept for yourself the same," the sen-timent was more than perfunctory.[40]

Johnson's presence in the Ellison family failed to engender the provocations that tore at other families. To begin with, Eliza Ann did not bring home a stranger. In fact, Johnson may have met Eliza Ann through his friendship with her brothers, documented in their collective baptism at Holy Cross in 1843. Perhaps more important in the long run, Johnson posed no economic threat to the brothers. Had he joined the gin business, the brothers might have had to settle for a smaller share of the proceeds. And, since James and Eliza Ann had no children, the brothers did not confront new heirs challenging their own children for places in the family enterprise and portions of their father's estate. When Ellison made his will in 1851, he made it clear that Johnson would not obtain a share of his estate. Ellison decreed that his property would follow blood, not marriage. Eliza Ann would inherit her father's half-interest in "Drayton Hall," a certain slave, and one quarter of the property that remained after her brothers received certain specific bequests. At her death, her inheritance would pass to her children, and if no child of hers survived, it would return to her brothers, not to her husband.[41] Johnson threatened no heir; instead he was a family asset. His crafts generated a cash income, and his acumen in the community buttressed the family's standing with dominant whites. Johnson made the family compound a busier and more productive place.

Almost no evidence indicates conflict between the Ellison brothers and their father, which at first glance is curious. In aristocratic white families, the concentration of wealth and power in the hands of the patriarch often devastated father-son relationships. The father's refusal to surrender power created resentment and frustration among those waiting for their turn at the reins.[42] Since few white patriarchs were as miserly with property and authority as William Ellison, it would be understandable if the Ellison household had been ripped by generational strife. If the Ellison sons chafed at their father's dominion, they did so secretly. The evidence indicates a family bound by mutual respect, love, and understanding. Why did the sons submit without taking offense?

William Ellison's monopoly of productive wealth helped mold obedient, subservient sons. In his 1851 will, Ellison bequeathed to his sons, jointly, "Wisdom Hall," the gin shop, and shop lot. After Eliza Ann had received her specified portion, each son received an equal share of the remaining property.[43] At least by 1851 the sons knew that rebelliousness could lead to disinheritance and the loss of a fortune. Potent as such a threat may appear, similar threats did not always deter the sons of white planters from standing up to their fathers. It is unlikely that Ellison's control over his property was sufficient to dictate the lifelong deference of his sons.

Unlike planters' sons who sometimes had nothing to do, the Ellison sons were never idle. From the time they were boys, they turned their hands to every task in their father's business. As participants rather than observers, they experienced work rather than enforced idleness. They escaped hostility bred by unwanted leisure and thwarted ambition. They received the satisfactions of craftsmanship, and their father allowed them enough work on their own account—in the fields and the shop—to soothe some of the sting of his economic mastery.

The sons of white planters sometimes complained that they could do better if they took over, but the Ellison sons could not fault their father's performance. Working beside him each day, they could see him handle with equal skill the assembly of a cotton gin, the instruction of a slave, and the shade-tree conversations with white planters about nothing in particular that were crucial to business in the shop and acceptance in the community. An almost flawless leader, Ellison was evidently a humane father. Tough and demanding without apology, Ellison was not like James Henry Hammond, whose haughty arrogance withered his sons' affections and damaged their lives.[44] Ellison appears to have held his sons to standards no higher than those he met each day. As in his relations with the white community, he may have let his deeds do much of his talking. At least, his sons respected him, and instead of becoming passive, self-pitying, ineffectual individuals, they grew into energetic, mature, productive men. It is doubtful that they detected even a tinge of irony in the name "Wisdom Hall."

Rather than break his sons to his will, William Ellison raised them in his own image. For that reason, they may have thought from time to time about leaving Stateburg and moving far enough away to set up a shop and become their own men. But if they learned nothing else from their father, they learned to calculate the odds against any plan. Anybody other than a reckless adventurer could see that outside Stateburg economic opportunity was constricted and personal safety questionable. To avoid competing with their father, they would have to move outside the High Hills, where they would be unknown free colored artisans competing head to head with white gin makers and blacksmiths. Their chances of duplicating their father's achievement were slight. When April Ellison came to Stateburg, the cotton boom was in full force, and planters were on the lookout for a good gin maker, even if he was a Negro. A generation later, the cotton boom had moved half a continent to the west, and resentment of free Negro artisans had grown.

The economic balance sheet gave the Ellison sons little reason to take such a risk. Although they did not own much property, they lived comfortably. They did not have to leave the family compound to escape poverty. And while the sons of many planters looked forward to a reduced patrimony as static agricultural estates were subdivided among several heirs, the Ellison brothers anticipated an inheritance that continued to grow vigorously and showed no signs of faltering. Continued subjection to the mastery of their father was entirely consistent with their present and future economic welfare.

If the sons sought greater personal autonomy, abandoning "Wisdom Hall" offered bleak prospects of obtaining it. Free people of color could not hope to establish autonomy in the antebellum South. The freedom of Afro-Americans required white sponsors and protectors. Flight from William Ellison would have cut off the sons from the leading white planters of the High Hills who knew them and valued their work. Successful free men of color shortened rather than stretched the distance between themselves and powerful white friends. Only by assuming a dependent position in a patron-client relationship with whites could free people of color secure their freedom and seek to expand the limits of their circumscribed lives. Stateburg was the locus of the Ellison brothers' security. Staying there meant remaining their father's sons. Whatever the stresses of life at "Wisdom Hall," they were never great enough to drive any of the sons away from home.

William Ellison was obsessed with preserving the freedom of his entire family, and his sons seemed to identify their welfare as individuals with that of the family as a whole. They seemed to share their father's belief that the best way to confront the family's vulnerability was solidarity. Unity meant a communal economic life and acceptance of William Ellison's leadership. The corrosive reality of white society lay just beyond William Ellison's front yard, and his sons knew it. The Ellison brothers understood the place of free Negroes in Southern society. That understanding shaped their response to their father's rule. They chose to follow him and hoped eventually to succeed him.

LIFE in the Ellison household was almost too good to be true. Even the three young Charleston women evidently made a satisfactory adjustment to Stateburg. When John L. Manning married Sallie Clarke of Virginia in 1848 and brought her back to his family's palatial "Millford," just a few miles south of Stateburg, Sallie described the experience as an "ordeal," the "severest to which a young girl can be subjected." She received "the very greatest kindness & affection as a member of the family," and she said "every effort has been made to make me feel as one of them." Family members called her "daughter," "Sister," "Cousin," and "Aunt," but she still felt isolated in "a land of strangers."[45] For the young Ellison wives—accustomed to strolls along the Charleston waterfront, shopping in stores on King Street, and visiting in the parlors of dozens of free colored homes—the family compound in Stateburg made a small world. The upcountry was a trial for young white women from Charleston who fled there during the Civil War. One who settled near Camden grumbled about the lack of amenities and society. Few "seek us socially to walk or ride in the afternoons or come over to see us after tea," she fussed. "If we go out to walk, we find a disagreeable sandy uneven road and scarcely ever meet an acquaintance to enliven the way. . . . " She found the neighborhood all "dullness & monotony."[46] The Ellisons' Charleston brides had even fewer resources in the surrounding community, but their growing families and the activities in the Ellison compound evidently kept them occupied, for they stayed.

Moving to Stateburg did not require the young women to sever their connections to family and friends in Charleston. The lives of the upcountry Ellisons intertwined with the Charleston Bonneaus, Mishaws, Johnsons, and their assorted friends and kinfolk. The hundred-mile trip to Charleston was a hard, dusty journey before the railroad pushed into the interior. By the 1840s, the South Carolina Railroad snaked along the eastern edge of the Wateree Swamp just below "Wisdom Hall." Trains to and from Charleston stopped at the Claremont Depot, less than a three-mile buggy ride from the Stateburg crossroads. Ellison slaves carried family members to the station and fetched them when they returned.[47] Just enough evidence survives to suggest that a trip to Charleston was a special occasion but one that the Ellisons indulged in freely, both for pleasure and business. In December 1859 Henry and Mary Elizabeth's daughter Matilda went down to spend time with her grandmother, Mrs. Jeanette Bonneau.[48] In previous years Mrs. Bonneau had come to Stateburg for a long visit, and a sister of Henry's and Reuben's wives announced her intention to "pay Stateburg a visit" and bring along her daughter Jany.[49] Family traffic clearly went both ways.

Economic ties also stretched between Stateburg and Charleston. In 1848 John F. Weston, a free mulatto machinist who married another of Thomas S. Bonneau's daughters, consulted with Henry and Reuben about the impending sale of their father-in-law's estate. Six town lots, the buildings on them, and four slaves were scheduled for the auction block. Weston proposed that the heirs adopt some plan "to get the value or nearly" for the Bonneau property, which was being sold because of a lawsuit against the estate by Bonneau's son, Thomas Collins Bonneau.[50] Weston suggested that the family "procure a Bidder to run the property to what we consider to be a fair price." He wanted Henry and Reuben to agree to the plan before he proceeded, since the scheme could backfire if the property were "knocked down to us."[51]

The Ellisons also were in a position to lend a hand to needy relatives on occasion. In 1855 Jacob Weston, a free mulatto tailor who had married yet another Bonneau daughter, wrote Henry thanking him for the money he had sent for Mrs. Jeanette Bonneau. It had arrived, he said, "just in time."[52] In time for what is unknown. After her husband's death and the disposal of his estate, Mrs. Bonneau lived in a modest house on Coming Street, paying taxes in 1860 on one slave and real estate worth $1,000.[53] The aid she received from one of her Ellison sons-in-law, via another son-in-law who could give it to her personally and smooth her acceptance of it, is a tangible illustration of the emotions that laced Ellison kin.

The Ellisons traveled to Charleston often to deal with cotton factors, supply merchants, and bankers. For example, in 1857 Henry went to the city with instructions from his father to deposit money with E. L. Adams and E. H. Frost, white commission merchants and factors on Adger's north wharf who had handled Ellison cotton for years. William Ellison also asked Henry to stop by Joseph Ellison Adger's hardware store on East Bay and buy a half-dozen weeding hoes, two hand saws, and eight bags of guano.[54] Adger's middle name came from his mother, Sarah Elizabeth Ellison, the sister of white William Ellison, the Fairfield District planter who owned April until 1816.[55] The marriage bonds within the white family may have had something to do with William Ellison of Stateburg taking his trade to Adger's hardware store. While he was in the city, Henry had several other errands to do for his brother William. He had orders to withdraw money from William Jr.'s bank account and give it to Adams and Frost, to arrange to have a pair of trousers made for John Buckner, to buy a handkerchief and some boots for slaves, and to pick up a pound of starch and four pounds of bird shot.[56]

Family members were not the only ones who sent him traipsing from one shop to another in the city. When Henry was in town in 1858 he received a letter from a family friend among the Sumter Turks, passing on a request from Louisa Murrell, General Thomas Sumter's elderly granddaughter who lived near the Ellisons in Stateburg.[57] She "asks you to bring a paper of green glazed cabbage & one or two of Leek seed & she prefers them from Landreths seed store," Henry was told by his friend. He added, "She will give me the money to hand you."[58] Whether Landreth's seed store had previously been on Henry's list of stops, he doubtless added it, even if it was a bother. The willing performance of small favors, especially those attentive to preferences, cemented personal relations with important white people and constituted a social obligation as well as a familial duty.

Trips to Charleston were not all business, however. We know virtually nothing about what the Ellisons did for fun, but they certainly took pleasure in visiting kinfolk and friends every time they came to the city. They evidently attended church with the Johnsons, and probably enjoyed renewing friendships with the city's many free colored tradesmen, who brought the Ellisons up to date on the latest news from their distinctive perspective. And the Ellisons never neglected to stop and see Mrs. Bonneau. After the early 1850s, however, those visit must have been tempered by sadness.

BREEZES and a moderate climate gave the High Hills a reputation for health, but beginning in 1850 the Ellison family compound was touched repeatedly by death. On January 14, 1850, Matilda Ellison died. Fifty-six years old, the matriarch of the Ellison clan became seriously ill in October 1849. She received scores of visits from Dr. Anderson before she finally succumbed.[59] Her husband made the arrangements for a funeral at Holy Cross and laid her to rest beneath towering oaks that grew a hundred yards north of "Wisdom Hall" at the bottom of a gentle slope. Matilda's grave was the first in what became the family graveyard.

Two years later, on September 15, 1852, Henry's twenty-eight-year-old wife died, after a debilitating illness. On her granite tombstone Henry had the stone cutter inscribe:

> Thy Race though Short is done Mary
> And thou art gone to rest
> In Heaven that Bright and blissful land
>   Upon they Savior's breast
> No More shall torturing pain, Mary
> Disturb or rack thy frame
> No more shall tears of sorrow fall
>   Upon thy cheek Again
> Rest Mary Rest for Christ Himself
> Was Once the Dark Grave's Quest
> This Heavenly One the Prison changed
> Into a place of Rest.[60]

Less than eight months later, Mary Elizabeth was followed by Mary Thomson, William Jr.'s twenty-four-year-old wife. The inscription cut on her tombstone reads, in part:

> In the Prime of life and the
> Vigor of Youth, she was Visited with

A painful and lingering disease
And as a Christian, she bore
With patience through faith
In her Redeemer, Until her
Spirit was called away unto
Him that gave it.[61]

The ordeal continued. Seven weeks after the death of his wife, William Jr. lost his infant son Henry McKensie.[62] In December 1853 Reuben's wife Harriett Ann died, evidently from complications of childbirth.[63] The next May, William Jr.'s three-year-old son Robert Mishaw passed away.[64] In less than four years the family suffered six deaths, five of them in only twenty months. Some may have been victims of a terrible epidemic that ravaged the South Carolina upcountry between 1852 and 1854. The pestilence was so deadly that in September 1853 the governor of the state set a day of fasting, humiliation, and prayer to seek deliverance from the scourge.[65]

All six of the Ellisons received church burials. The services were held in Holy Cross's beautiful new building, constructed in Gothic design from the unusual material of Stateburg earth tamped into thick, buff-colored walls. Light filtered into the cool, dark sanctuary through imported stained glass windows.[66] Harriett Ann's body was evidently returned to Charleston for interment. But after each of the other services, the Ellisons and their friends accompanied the deceased family member back across the road and down the hill to the family burying ground, where the coffin was lowered into the grave.

After 1853, Eliza Ann was the only free woman left in the family compound. To her duties as mother of John Buckner and wife of James M. Johnson were added all the obligations of her deceased mother and three sisters-in-law. She became the mistress of the household, supervising the household slaves, taking care of her bereaved brothers and father, and stepping in as surrogate mother for her young nieces and nephews. All the children may have moved into her house. At least they stayed with her when they were sick. In Henry's account with Dr. Anderson, an entry for September 27, 1852, notes, "Visit for daughter at Johnsons."[67] William Jr.'s account includes an entry for May 9, 1854, reading, "Two visits for your child at Johnsons."[68] In 1857 a new free woman of color from Charleston joined the family circle. John Buckner married Jane Johnson, who was evidently the sister of his stepfather, James M. Johnson.[69] The Buckners lived in "Drayton Hall" with the Johnsons, but in 1860 both Jane Buckner and her infant son died, leaving the couple's two-year-old daughter Harriet Ann for the care of Eliza Ann.[70] Again, Eliza Ann was the solitary mistress of both "Drayton Hall" and "Wisdom Hall."

Eight deaths in one decade threatened the Ellison family with disintegration. But it did not disintegrate. Despite all the heartache of the 1850s, the family compound remained a refuge and a source of strength. An iron-willed patriarch could not stop death, but he could defy it. Under William Ellison's direction, three generations continued to live and work together. Although William Ellison was in his seventh decade, he refused to relinquish mastery.

IN 1860 leading citizens of Stateburg considered William Ellison a gin maker. Ellison advertised that identity in local newspapers, and in both 1850 and 1860 censuses he reported that as his occupation. The report was accurate as far as it went, but it bespoke a studied modesty. Over the years, Ellison had expanded his economic activity far beyond the gin shop. Judged by the size of his slave force, his acreage, and his annual cotton crop, Ellison had become a large cotton planter as early as the 1840s. There is no reason to doubt Ellison's pride in his status as a planter. But he did not parade it. Had he stopped working as a sweat-stained mechanic, had he sold off the gin shop and become a full-time planter, he would have suggested to the white community that he had forgotten his place, that he was pushing for equality. Whites may have decided that he needed to be taught he was not white. As a gin maker he provided a service to the white planters and stayed visibly tied to his origins and his place. Ellison's white neighbors knew he had a cotton plantation and many slaves, but his gin shop depended on their business, served their needs, and convinced them that old William Ellison was their kind of colored man.

At first glance, the 1840s were far less bountiful for Ellison than the 1830s. After striding forward in seven-league boots in the thirties, he slowed the pace of his acquisitions of slaves and land. In 1850 as in 1840, the gin shop employed twelve adult men, presumably Ellison himself, his three sons, his grandson John Buckner, one or two free men of color, and five or six slaves, plus an uncounted swarm of slave boys.[71] Clearly, the gin business was not infinitely expandable. Ellison's territory in the High Hills could absorb just so many gins. The radius of his blacksmith and carpentry business was shorter still, attracting many small jobs from planters within easy travel distance and occasionally a major project from a planter who did not trust it to his slave artisans.

Records that would permit an estimation of the profitability of Ellison's shop have not survived. The only evidence comes from Ellison's report in the 1850 census, and it is misleading. Ellison told the census enumerator that his income from the gin shop was $3,000 a year and that his expenses included $240 a month for labor and $580 a year for raw materials.[72] According to these figures, Ellison's annual expenses exceeded his income by $460. Ellison's estimates of his costs are probably fairly accurate, but the implication that he lost money is false without question. Ellison said he paid $280 for 2,000 pounds of iron and steel, which he probably purchased in Charleston. He estimated his lumber costs at $200. He cut a good deal of lumber from his own land, but he also bought additional lumber locally. In 1860, for example, he paid Dr. W. W. Anderson $117.08 for lumber from his sawmill on Rafting Creek.[73] Ellison estimated his expenses for "other articles," which would have included such things as leather belting and pig bristles, at $100. Ellison bought pig bristles, a lowly but crucial component of gin brushes, from local planters, who realized a little pocket money, or perhaps credit with Ellison, for this otherwise useless commodity.

Ellison's largest expense by far was for labor, which amounted to $2,880 for the year. He did not pay his slaves a wage, and their subsistence costs were almost negligible because by 1850 he produced most of their food on his plantation. The wages Ellison paid were divided among the five or six free men of color who worked in his shop in 1850, all but one or two of whom were Ellisons. Assuming a wage of $40 a month, a reasonable rate for a gin maker, Ellison's $240 monthly out-lay for labor went into his pocket and that of his three sons, possibly his grandson, and maybe one or two other free Negro tradesmen. Depending upon whether a full month's wages went to him and his grandson, he paid somewhere between $120 and $200 of his monthly wages to family members. Since all the Ellisons lived together in the family compound, the elder Ellison had access to his sons' labor around the clock to aid him on his other income-producing activities, principally his plantation. By marking off to the gin business all the wages he paid his sons, he exaggerated his gin shop labor expenses to the extent that his sons helped him make money in other ways. For example, although Ellison had a large number of slaves, there is no evidence he ever employed an overseer. Presumably he and his sons shared that responsibility, saving him a sizable expense. No doubt such considerations did not enter the estimate he gave the census marshal. Yet it was pre-cisely such considerations that made his family enterprise prof-itable. Furthermore, by paying his sons wages he presumably was allowing them to buy for themselves what he would have otherwise paid for and had in fact paid for until they estab-lished their own families in the middle 1840s.

By the 1850s and probably well before, Ellison's plantation eclipsed the gin shop as a source of income. The shop kept busy and continued to turn a profit. But perhaps most valu-able of all, it moored Ellison to his beginnings as a tradesman. Paradoxically, Ellison's gin shop bound him to his slave origins and set him apart from white planters while its profits drew him into the planter class. Ellison's prudent behavior throughout his life suggests that he understood that his money could buy him a great deal, including trouble.

In 1847 Ellison boosted his land to a little over 350 acres. He paid the Sumter family $270 for a tract of 22 and one-half acres that lay just north of the gin shop.[74] During the 1840s his slave force grew to thirty-six, six more than in 1840. His slaves were still predominantly males (twenty-six of thirty-six), and sixteen of them were over ten years of age. Ellison's decision to buy females in the 1830s continued to pay off in slave children. In 1850 he owned eleven slaves under the age of ten. Although much of the change that occurred within his slave population may be hidden by the census reports, we can say with certainty that during the decade he acquired five new females in their twenties and lost four older women and one girl who was under ten when the decade began. Ellison's male slaves increased by five, but most were boys, and he lost at least two older men and one in his middle years.[75] The only extant record of Ellison adding to his slave force comes from February 1845, when he bought January for $545 at an auction of the personal property of Thomas Sumter, Jr. Thirty-three slaves changed hands that day, and, like the other buyers, Ellison put down a little cash—$41.85—and gave his bond for the rest.[76]

Despite only modest gains in land and slaves, Ellison experienced no economic difficulty in the 1840s. The marriage of his sons followed shortly by new grandchildren increased his expenses. However, the most important reason for the modest growth of his empire was his decision to divert income from the acquisition of property and slaves to the accumulation of capital. Ellison fattened his savings during the forties, preparing for his spectacular expansion during the 1850s.

By 1860 Ellison had increased his slave population by a stunning 75 percent, from thirty-six in 1850 to sixty-three in 1860. His twenty slaves under ten years of age indicate that he continued to profit from natural increase, but he was also active in the market. At a minimum, he purchased during the decade three females between the ages of ten and twenty-nine and seven males in their twenties.[77]

Except for his acquisition of January at Sumter's auction in 1845, we do not know where Ellison acquired the slaves he purchased. As he did when he bought January, he may have ridden a few miles to some High Hills plantation where there was a sale, prompted by migration to the west, economic hard times, or the division of an estate following the death of the owner. When Colonel Richard Singleton died in the 1850s, for example, his creditors descended, forcing the sale of slaves from his huge slave community.[78] When Thomas S. Bonneau's estate was auctioned off in Charleston in 1848, Ellison evidently purchased one of Bonneau's slaves, a young boy named Isaac.[79] But Ellison did not need to travel all the way to Charleston to buy slaves. Slave sales occurred regularly in the neighboring towns of Columbia, Camden, and Sumterville. On December 22, 1853, Isaac Lenoir of Statebug publicly announced that he would be at the Sumterville courthouse the following Monday to sell fifty slaves, nine mules, and a mare.[80] Local planters also sold individual slaves whom they found redundant, or wanted married to a spouse on a neighboring place, or with whom they were displeased. Perhaps most often they sold slaves simply because they needed cash. Ellison could have arranged a private sale, as William Benbow did in March 1857, when he bought Jack for $1,112 from a Stateburg slaveholder.[81] Although we cannot establish the manner or place of Ellison's purchases, he had plenty of opportunities to strike a deal without venturing far from home.

As he had during the 1830s, Ellison matched his slave purchases with land. In 1852 the Sumter family sold him "Keith Hill" and "Hickory Hill," together more than 540 acres. In a single transaction, the largest of his life, Ellison more than doubled his real estate. The land stretched out to the north and west of Ellison's other property at the Stateburg crossroads. His mortgage stipulated a price of $9,560, to be paid in five annual payments. Ellison, however, paid off the entire amount after only one year.[82]

In 1860, for the fifth and final time, a federal census marshal visited William Ellison. Ellison told the marshal that his personal estate, comprised mainly of his slaves, had a value of $53,000, and that his real estate, which he said consisted of 800 acres, was worth $8,250.[83] In fact, Ellison understated his worth. Even if his personal wealth had been made up exclusively of his slaves, which it was not, his estimate of the average value of his slaves was $840. That was about right for a typical plantation where almost all adult slaves were field hands. But Ellison's operation was not typical. Many of his twenty adult slave men were highly skilled craftsmen, and their value in the market could easily have been two or three times higher than average. Ellison also underrepresented the size and worth of his real estate. Instead of the 800 acres he declared, he owned nearly 900 acres. And his estimation of its value—$8,250—was less than half the amount he paid for it.[84] High Hills real estate no longer appreciated rapidly, but neither did it depreciate.

Even judged by the questionable census figures, Ellison's economic achievement was impressive. Compared to his free Negro neighbors in Sumter District, Ellison possessed princely wealth. Almost half (45 percent) of the free persons of color in Sumter were propertyless. The mean wealth of all free Afro-Americans in Sumter, excluding the Ellisons, was $205. The sum of the real estate owned by all the free persons of color in Sumter did not equal Ellison's. His personal property exceeded the total personal estate of all 328 other free Negroes in the district by a factor of seven. Ellison's real estate was worth 80 times more than the mean of free persons of color in Sumter; his personal estate was more than 500 times greater.[85] Ellison's wealth topped the total wealth of all the free persons of color in twenty-five of the state's thirty districts.[86]

Ellison had also outdistanced 90 percent of his white neighbors in Sumter. In 1860 the mean wealth of the free families in Sumter was $21,100, higher than in any other district in the state.[87] Twenty-six white planters owned 1,000 or more acres, and twenty-one held 100 or more slaves.[88] Dr. Anderson, for example, owned real estate worth $30,000 and personal property valued at $100,000, including 149 slaves.[89] George Cooper, another white planter in Sumter, possessed real estate worth $70,000, $350,000 in personal property, and 374 slaves.[90] Although Ellison's wealth did not rival the white aristocracy's, he was among the top 10 percent of all Sumter slaveholders and landowners. In the entire state, only 5 percent of the population owned as much real estate as Ellison. Only 3 percent of the state's slaveholders owned as many slaves. Compared to the mean wealth of white men in the entire South, Ellison's was fifteen times greater.[91] Ninety-nine percent of the South's slaveholders owned fewer slaves than he did.[92]

However, Ellison was neither the richest free person of color in the South nor the largest slaveholder. Louisiana contained six free Negro planters who were wealthier and owned more slaves.[93] The richest was Auguste Dubuclet, a sugar planter whose estate was valued at $264,000. The largest slaveholders were the widow C. Richard and her son P. C. Richard, also sugar planters, who together owned 152 slaves. Outside Louisiana, only one free Negro in 1860 is known to have reported greater wealth than Ellison. London Berry, a thirty-eight-year-old mulatto steward in St. Louis, owned real estate worth $67,000, a sum larger than the wealth Ellison reported in the census but not above the actual value of his property.[94] No free person of color outside Louisiana is known to have owned more slaves than Ellison in 1860. Since the Louisiana planters tended to be second- and third-generation free people, it is likely that Ellison was the richest Afro-American in the South who began life as a slave.

OVER the decades, Ellison spent an enormous sum to acquire his real and personal property. Calculating the cost of his real estate is straightforward. Between 1822 and 1852, the dates of his first and last purchases, he paid $16,900 for land.[95] Figuring his outlay for slaves is more speculative. From his first acquisition sometime before 1820 to his final purchase in the 1850s, Ellison bought an absolute minimum of thirty-five slaves, and he may have bought twice that number.[96] If their average purchase price was $500, a conservative estimate considering that he usually bought young adult men and women, then he spent at least $17,500 and as much as $35,000 or possibly more for slaves.

Estimating the cost of Ellison's investments is easier than figuring his income. Existing evidence permits only the roughest estimate, and then only toward the end of his career. By far the most important source of revenue over the years was Ellison's shop, which he claimed in 1850 produced an annual income of about $3,000 before the costs of labor and raw materials were subtracted.[97] Agriculture provided Ellison's second major source of income. He produced cotton, his only important cash crop, beginning in the 1830s, but his largest crops came in the 1850s, after he had more than doubled his acreage and nearly doubled his slave force. In 1860 Ellison stated that his fields yielded eighty 400-pound bales of cotton, which at ten cents a pound had a value of about $3,200.[98] After Adams and Frost, his factors in Charleston, had deducted the charges for transportation, storage, insurance, and their fees, Ellison would have ended up with somewhat less.[99] His 500 acres of improved land also produced

2,000 bushels of corn, 1,000 bushels of sweet potatoes, 200 bushels of peas and beans, and forage for forty hogs, twenty-one sheep, and ten cattle, all of which made his plantation self-sufficient in provisions.[100] Hiring out slaves and a few other minor enterprises also brought Ellison some income, but only in trivial amounts.

How did Ellison save enough of the income from his shop and fields to pay for the property he bought? The records of his purchases do not even hint that he received special favors, under-the-table gifts, or reduced prices. If anything, he paid a premium. No white benefactor lined Ellison's pockets. That Ellison paid his own way is certain, but how is not. He invested something between $35,000 and $50,000 during his lifetime, and his peak annual income, that of 1860, was roughly $6,200 before expenses. His expenses were substantial, they underwent important changes during his career, and they are impossible to estimate with any confidence. Just maintaining his large extended family was a major expense. In addition he had to pay for the maintenance of his slaves, stock his plantation and shop with tools and supplies, cover court and legal fees, and foot the bill for expensive medical care, property taxes, factors' charges, transportation, special taxes on free Negroes, pew rental at Holy Cross, and a hundred and one other items. Nevertheless, after making all these payments Ellison had enough left over to stash away money for more land and slaves. His income was not large enough to have made saving that much money easy, especially in the first two or three decades. Besides working hard and working his slaves hard, Ellison followed two other practices that seem to have been particularly important in allowing him to amass his capital.

The first simply was that, after paying the expenses of production, Ellison did not spend very much. He scrimped, saved, and squirreled away every dime he could. His standards of consumption were in fact limited by his race. Unlike white planters, he did not try to cut a fine figure, build and furnish a mansion, or underwrite tours of the continent. "Wisdom Hall" was not ostentatious. Ellison's household furniture was serviceable but hardly grand; it was worth $230 altogether, little more than a white planter might pay for a piano. Although

the Ellisons had house servants, they did not maintain a reti-
nue of the dozen or more common in white households in
Stateburg. Ellison owned both a carriage and a gig that carried him and his family to church and the train depot, but
their combined value of $20 does not suggest ornate convey-
ances. The Ellison brothers took an interest in horse racing—
the obsession of several High Hills grandees—but the family
owned only horses that never set foot on a racetrack. Ellison's
best horse, a sorrel mare, was worth $150, the same value as
Burtrand, one of his mules. The only display Ellison permitted himself was a gold watch and chain, valued at $100.[101]

A racial ceiling also hung over the aspirations of his children. His sons did not need expensive medical or legal educations, since their race closed those professions to them. His
daughter did not need a closetful of fancy gowns and an
attractive dowry to find a husband. Ellison had no need to
copy the expensive hospitality of the white planters, bar-
bequeing a side of beef and tapping a barrel of whiskey for
his lesser neighbors while he enjoyed a glass of Madiera with
his peers. Expenses that white planters considered necessities
were luxuries for Ellison, even dangerous luxuries. Ellison saved
more than all other free people of color because he had a
larger income, and he spent far less of it than whites who had
larger incomes and appetites. When Ellison spent money he
seems to have kept his eye constantly on buying production,
on capital expenditures that ultimately would increase, not
reduce, the bottom line.

Ellison probably had another source of income, however,
one revealed only in the composition of his slave population.
Every census indicates that Ellison's slave population had an
unusual structure. In each decade his male slaves heavily outnumbered his females. In 1820 and 1830 he owned only adult
men. In 1840 the ratio of adult men to adult women (including the age category of ten to twenty-four as "adult") was 16
to 6, almost 3 to 1. In 1850 the adult sex ratio (using twenty
years and over as "adult") was 14 to 7, or 2 to 1. In 1860 Ellison
owned twenty-three adult males and sixteen adult females, a
ratio of nearly 3 to 2. The sexual imbalance among Ellison's
adult slaves also appeared in more extreme form among his
slave children. In 1840 he owned eight children, five of them

boys. In 1850 nine of his ten slave children were boys. In 1860 boys comprised fifteen of his twenty slave youngsters. In Ellison's quarters, female slaves were few and young females were rare. In 1850, after owning several slave women in their child-bearing years for more than a decade, Ellison had only one female slave under the age of 18.[102]

Assuming that nature presented approximately equal numbers of little girls and little boys to slave mothers belonging to Ellison, there is a shortage of about twenty young girls in Ellison's census rosters. The best explanation of that shortage is that Ellison sold slave girls. The evidence is not conclusive, since, as with his slave purchases, records of his slave sales do not exist. Certainly Ellison did not object to selling slaves. In his will he directed his executors to sell a young woman named Sarah and to divide the proceeds among his heirs.[103] Grim as it is, selling is the most plausible way to explain the missing slave girls. No evidence exists of a mysterious sex- and age-specific disease sweeping decade after decade through Ellison's quarters.

Nor is there any evidence that Ellison created the imbalance by purchasing additional boys. If the boys who appear in the census were bought, Ellison's slave women were nearly barren. The census figures already suggest very low birth rates. If Ellison's slave women had produced equal numbers of girls and boys (that is, an additional twenty children), their fertility rates would still be lower than we might expect on a plantation with a high ratio of men.[104] Assuming that the mothers of the twenty slave youngsters who appear in the 1860 census were the eight women between the ages of eighteen and twenty-nine in the 1850 census plus the three additional women of childbearing years Ellison acquired during the 1850s, they would have had to produce fewer than three children each during the decade to account for the fifteen boys and five girls in the census and the ten absent little girls. Moreover, the census of 1860 lists children with their mothers, at least with women whose ages allow us to believe that they were the mothers of the children who follow them on the slave schedules. For example, a thirty-two-year-old female is followed by males aged thirteen, ten, eight, six, and four months. A forty-year-old slave woman is followed by males aged twenty-one, thirteen, seven, and four.[105] These age patterns would be unlikely if Ellison bought slave boys of random ages in the market. The listings even leave spaces for the births of missing girls.

The whereabouts of the girls could be easily explained if Ellison had given them to his children. But Eliza Ann never possessed any slaves of her own, and while Ellison's three sons were slaveholders by 1860, each owned only one female whose age could possibly have allowed her to come from the group of missing children.[106] The final alternative explanation is that Ellison was a closet abolitionist who secretly freed his young females. This possibility is farfetched. There is no evidence whatever that Ellison ever freed one of his slaves, either while he lived or by his will after his death. He dedicated his life to accumulating property, not dispersing it. To Ellison, slaves were property, without question. Besides, being a Negro emancipator would hardly have added luster to his reputation in Stateburg. To free slaves, which was illegal in any case after 1820, would have destroyed a lifetime's effort to prove himself a reliable, solid citizen.

Why would Ellison sell off black girls? The best answer is that he sold them to help raise the large sums he needed to buy more adult slaves and more land. By turning human capital into cash, he was able to sustain an aggressive program of expansion. To him, slaves were a source of labor, and the laborers he needed most were adult men who could work in his gin shop. Men, as a rule, were also stronger workers in the fields. Even though slave women often had less strength and endurance, they did valuable work for Ellison in his fields, but it was not as valuable as having babies.[107] Their boys could grow up to be workers in Ellison's shop or full hands in his fields, but in Ellison's eyes their girls could never provide the labor he most wanted.

Rather than accumulate slaves he could not exploit to the fullest, he probably sold twenty or more girls, retaining only a few who could eventually have more children, cultivate his fields, and in a few cases work in his home as domestics. To Ellison, slave children were either future labor or ready cash, depending on their sex. If Ellison sold twenty slave girls for an average price of $400, he obtained an additional $8,000 cash, a sum large enough to have made a major contribution to the land and slave purchases that made him a planter. Evidently, Ellison's economic empire was in large part constructed by slave labor and paid for by the sale of slave girls.

SURELY, it might seem, selling little girls would have stigmatized William Ellison in the eyes of influential whites in Stateburg. Certain standards for the treatment of slaves had taken root in the South in the decades before the Civil War.[108] The code of paternalism—at minimum the exchange of decent care in return for obedience and hard work—was honored in the breach more often than not, but there were planters in Sumter District who felt constrained to try to abide by its tenets. The code did not normally countenance selling children away from their immediate families. A former slave of John Frierson, master of "Pudden Swamp" a few miles east of Sumterville, remembered that his former owner was never "known to separate mother and children." Frierson simply "did not believe in this kind of business."[109] J. K. Douglas of Camden did not believe in that kind of business either. In February 1848 he wrote John B. Miller of Sumterville to explain the plight of "that valuable Christian man of colour, Charles," who was about to be sold and separated from his wife and children because of the death of his master. Separation would make Charles "miserable," Douglas explained, and he asked if Miller could not possibly buy the slave and preserve the family.[110] Sumter District planters did their share of buying and selling, but most resisted breaking up families, at least as a conscious policy. Someone who was entirely dependent on the good opinion of the white community could not afford to be blind to prevailing practices.

White planters may have reserved their paternalistic expectations for each other and exempted a free man of color like Ellison from their strictures. More likely, however, the planters' paternalism was a very forgiving standard. What protected Ellison from public censure was his economic situation, not his race. Owners who sold slaves had to have a reasonable excuse, and Ellison had one. Unlike white planters who prized the laboring capacity of slave girls only slightly less than that of boys, Ellison had no use for girls in his shop and only a limited use in his fields. For him girls were a financial burden. Paternalism was never so rigid a code as to cause any slave-holder economic distress. Even staunch defenders of the duties of planters believed that slave sales, however regrettable, were sometimes unavoidable. Perhaps the fact that no town gossip latched on to Ellison's sales is indirect evidence that Stateburg residents understood and accepted Ellison's very different labor requirements. Some, like John Frierson of "Pudden Swamp," may have disapproved, but there is no evidence that anyone ever branded Ellison a heartless monster for separating girls from their mothers and selling them. They considered Ellison a respectable man, a reputation he had worked hard to earn and one he would not have risked for the world, certainly not for a few more acres of it. Far from condemning practices like Ellison's as barbaric, white planters condoned them.

Local tradition is silent about Ellison's slave sales but out-spoken about his reputation as a harsh master.[111] His slaves were said to be the district's worst fed and worst clothed. The story jibes with certain of Ellison's character traits and with his circumstances. Year after year Ellison drove himself relentlessly. In January 1841, for example, Natalie Delage Sumter, widow of Thomas Sumter, Jr., recorded in her diary that the previous night she had gone to bed at eleven o'clock, only to be awakened by her house servants, who told her that William Ellison "had come to settle his accts."[112] A fifty-one-year-old tradesman who was still out collecting at midnight in the dead of winter probably had few qualms about stretch-ing his slaves' workday from before sunup to after sundown. Hungry for more land and slaves, Ellison and his family lived frugally, and he probably was even more tightfisted in provid-ing food, clothing, and housing for his slaves. If he did treat his slaves harshly, it may have been because he dealt with an unusually hostile slave community, bitter men and women who had seen their daughters sold away. Harsh treatment could also have stemmed from Ellison's need to prove to whites that, despite his history and color, he was not soft on slaves. A reputation for harshness was less dangerous than a reputa-tion for indulgence.

Although the rumor that Ellison was a cruel master is plau-sible, there is no evidence to confirm it. Aside from his apparent practice of selling girls, Ellison probably acted about like any other High Hills slaveholder, no better, no worse. Sensitive to public opinion, he probably did not stray too far from prevailing practices. Stern discipline and stingy maintenance hardly distinguished his mastery from whites'. Most slaves endured such treatment regardless of the race of their masters.[113] The origin of Ellison's reputation as a tough skinflint of a master may rest partly in the white community's familiarity with Ellison's slaves, who worked in tattered garments in the fields or shop near the crossroads, visible to all who passed. His slaves were not isolated on plantations miles away down along the Wateree swamp or scattered through the hills.[114] The way Ellison treated his slaves was on public display every day, and white observers took notice. What they saw is impossible to tell; what they noticed says as much about them as about Ellison. It is also possible that the story of Ellison's harshness was no more than a self-serving tale begun by whites eager to defend their own stewardship of slaves by contrasting it with the cruelty of a black master, the meanest slaveholder in the district.

In reality, little is known about Ellison's slaves or his relationship with them. The census, however, reveals that all of Ellison's slaves were black. None was ever listed as a mulatto.[115] Normally a slave population the size of Ellison's would have included a sprinkling of light-skinned Negroes. Mulattoes made up 5 percent of South Carolina's slaves in 1860.[116] If Ellison's slaves had reflected that proportion, three of them would have been mulattoes. His all-black quarters may have been the result of a conscious decision. A mulatto owning other mulattoes as slaves may have been too much of a contradiction for Ellison. Or his dependence on the good opinion of whites may have convinced him that he could not risk having tongues wag about the paternity of mulattoes on his plantation the way they did about the mulattoes who belonged to white masters. By color coding his plantation, Ellison created a safe distance between his family and his slaves. On his plantation, like almost all others, both status and color differentiated the master from his slaves.

Ellison's slaves sometimes ran away, as did slaves on neighboring plantations. The historian of Sumter District reported that from time to time Ellison advertised for the return of his runaways.[117] On at least one occasion he hired the services of a slave catcher. According to Robert W. Andrews, a white man who purchased a small hotel in Statesburg in the 1820s, "a valuable slave, who was a fine mechanic, a cotton-gin maker, belonging to Mr. William Ellison, made a break for the Free States." Andrews remembered that "Mr. Ellison offered me five dollars a day [and] to find me a horse and pay my expenses, if I would bring back the slave, whom he estimated at two thousand dollars value." Andrews first inquired in Manchester, a small town about ten miles south of Statesburg, where he heard that the runaway had joined a group of jockeys headed for Virginia. Following the trail, Andrews caught up with the slave in Belleville, Virginia. "I was paid on returning home," Andrews said, "$77.50, and $74.00 for expenses."[118] In the same decade, another High Hills slaveholder—Richard Singleton—was willing to track a runaway even farther. In April 1822 James Usher informed Singleton that "your boy William" had been captured in New York City and that the slave was in jail in Wilmington, North Carolina, awaiting shipment home. Usher added that "your boy Davis" had also been spotted in New York, where he was married to a free woman, and that he expected Davis would soon be collared.[119]

While most of Ellison's slaves never ran away, some were out on the road on business. A few skilled men probably traveled to local plantations to make repairs, just as Ellison himself had while he was a slave in Fairfield District. Many of Ellison's men would have had to be abroad if they were married. The sexual imbalance among his slaves made it impossible for them to find a wife at home. If they married off the plantation, Ellison would have to give his permission and provide them special passes for occasional visits to their spouses. The practice of marrying off the plantation was common in the High Hills. Remembering Statesburg in the 1830s, Samuel McGill said, "In those old times one might travel a whole day without meeting anyone, because there was not many people except on plantations, and they had little or no business out of it; colored husbands excepted, having wives on neighbors' places."[120]

Grueling as their lives were, the slave men who worked in

Ellison's gin business may actually have had certain advantages. Their work as mechanics was exhausting, but they probably preferred it to monotonous, back-breaking days in the fields. As one Camden planter observed in 1831, "Negroes are fond of acquiring trades as it gives them an opportunity of making something for themselves."[121] Masters sometimes allowed their skilled artisans to work a little on their own after hours and to keep their earnings. One bit of evidence suggests that Ellison permitted at least one of his slaves such a privilege. The ledger of the tavern that stood directly across the old King's Highway from Ellison's home lists a small account—just a few dollars in 1837—for "Ellison's Stephen." For a little molasses, tobacco, and whiskey, Stephen repaired and sharpened several plows.[122] Although Ellison allowed Stephen to work for a few luxuries, he clearly was not offering him the same opportunity the white William Ellison had provided his slave April. For any slave who reached for more, William Ellison of Stateburg turned to a slave catcher.

While Ellison withheld the ultimate reward, he did not scrimp on his slaves' medical care. They received the best medical attention available, administered by Dr. Anderson, who began treating the Ellisons and their slaves as early as 1824. From then until the Civil War, Dr. Anderson's meticulous records indicate that he made hundreds of visits, sometimes at night, to Ellison's slaves, almost fifty of whom he mentioned by name.[123] Among other things, the doctor extracted Sam's tooth, purged Augustus, cupped John, dressed Tom's hand, lanced Washington's whitlow, amputated Abram's leg, bled Ben, delivered Elsey, "cured" Tunic's gonorrhea, lanced a "negro man's abcess," delivered Charlotte "with instruments in [a] case of difficult labor," set the fractured arm of a child, set the fractured thigh bone of a man, removed a splinter from a boy's arm, and treated Stephen's "case of syphilis." He also prescribed a wonderful variety of medicines, including laudanum, hartshorn, sulphur soda, blistering plasters, cathartic powders, Peruvian bark, camphoratic mixtures, gum camphor, spirit of nitrate, cream tartar, myrrh, calomel, spirit of lavender, quinine bitters, and "blue pills." While it is questionable whether such close attention was always a blessing, Ellison clearly did not neglect his slaves' health.

Nor did he give up quickly when a slave failed to respond to treatment. In 1837, for instance, Dr. Anderson made twenty-nine visits to Jacob. Whether Ellison acted out of financial self-interest or personal concern or both, he spent as much on his slaves' medical care as most planters. Even the lordly Hamptons, whose plantations just east of Columbia held several times as many slaves, spent little more. In 1833 Dr. Josiah Nott charged Wade Hampton II $329 for treating his slaves at "Woodlands," "Millwood," and elsewhere.[124] In 1844 William Ellison paid Dr. Anderson $212, most of it for attending his slaves.[125]

Ellison furnished medical care for all his slaves, but he was more selective in providing for their spiritual lives. Reverend Augustus L. Converse and other rectors of Holy Cross Episcopal Church ministered to only a few of Ellison's slaves. Ellison saw to the baptism of six of his slaves in his own church. In 1844 John was baptized; in 1850, Sarah and Nancy Ann; in 1853, Jacob; and in 1861, Sarah Ann and Virginia.[126] These baptized slaves were somehow favored by their master, perhaps because they were house servants (as Sarah almost certainly was) or because they were hard-working craftsmen who had earned Ellison's respect. Other Ellison slaves may have attended services at Holy Cross, either on Sundays, when they would have sat in the gallery, or on those rare evenings when the Reverend Converse preached a special service for slaves.[127] Since Ellison's church stood within a mile of his slave quarters and the services never conflicted with the work day, attention to the religious lives of his slaves would not have cost Ellison a cent. The difference between the dozens of slaves treated by Dr. Anderson and the half-dozen baptized by the rectors of Holy Cross is a rough index of the distance that stood between Ellison and his slaves, a distance both parties probably helped maintain, each for their own reasons. Given the choice, many of Ellison's slaves may not have seen spending Sunday at his church as something that would do as much for their souls as playing with their children, visiting with friends, or doing almost anything to keep a few hours for themselves.

The Ellisons indulged certain slaves in small ways, much as white planters occasionally granted little favors. Correspondence between members of the Ellison family reveals that from time to time on their visits to Charleston they picked up items for their slaves. In 1857, for example, William Jr. asked his brother Henry to "Get a hankerchief *[sic]* for Charlotte." He also passed on a request from Gabriel, who asked Henry to bring back some "lether booties" for his wife.[128] When the Ellisons wanted to send something to a family member in Charleston, they sometimes chose a slave to deliver it, and their choice of messengers indicates a certain sensitivity. "This will inform you that Isaac has arrived safe bringing the shoes, for which you have my thanks," James D. Johnson, William Ellison's old friend, wrote from Charleston in December 1858.[129] Johnson said that Isaac had "reported himself daily to me and has conducted himself properly according to request." After mentioning that he expected to send Isaac by train the next day, Johnson added, "His parents begs to present their thanks to you for permitting him to see them. The old man has been working for me and requested me to write you to let him come. I intended to have done so, but your sending him has made it unnecessary." Young Isaac evidently made the trip to the city more than once and may have grown a bit bold, for in February 1860, Johnson's son, James M. Johnson, wrote, "I was glad to hear that Isaac returned and hope he has seen his folly."[130] By the end of the year Isaac was back in the Ellison family's good graces, for Johnson declared, "I expect to bring something for Isaac from Fanny, which may be an inducement for him to bring the cart to the depot."[131]

These small favors must have been reserved for a special few, and even for them, rare. A privileged relationship with the Ellison family had its little rewards, but it also brought special demands and dangers. While on a trip to Charleston, Eliza Ann instructed Sarah, who belonged to Eliza Ann's father but who served her, to "clean out the Fowl house properly & bury the contents in the poultry lot adjoining."[132] Eliza Ann's husband, James M. Johnson, demanded, "Do see that Sarah behaves herself & salts the creatures regularly."[133] Somehow Sarah failed to behave herself to William Ellison's satisfaction, and she was the only slave he singled out to be sold at his death.[134] Ellison's field hands did not receive handkerchiefs and boots from Charleston or special instructions from 100 miles away, but, so far as we know, they were not sold away either.

What little evidence we have suggests that Ellison's mastery was neither particularly mild not particularly harsh. With the major exception of the apparent sale of slave girls, his slaves suffered the usual rigors of bondage. Despite his own history, Ellison did not view his shop and plantation as halfway houses to freedom. He never permitted a single slave of his to duplicate his own experience. No shred of evidence indicates that he felt the tug of racial affinity, no document hints that he considered his slaves members of an extended plantation family. Ellison's ancestry offered immunity to no slave, and his definition of family stopped far short of the quarters. Everything suggests that Ellison held his slaves to exploit them, to profit from them, just as white slaveholders did.

But William Ellison was not white. What kind of man buys himself, his wife, and his eldest child from bondage and then does not hesitate to buy, hold, sell, and exploit others as slaves? It will not do to argue simply that his heart was as callused as his hands. Nor is it sufficient to imagine that he merely shrugged his shoulders and muttered something to the effect that some were just unfortunate in their condition and some were not. We know little about Ellison's view of himself as a slaveholder, but what little we know suggests that he must have had a rationale, some explanation that was personally satisfying and that allowed him to persist in the course he followed all his life as a free man. Nothing suggests that under his calm exterior he wrestled with a moral dilemma. There is no evidence that he spent restless nights anguishing over being a black master. Nothing indicates he fought back floods of guilt or even doubt. Instead, he appears as confident in his behavior as white planters, who in general had a clear conscience about owning other human beings.[135]

At first it seems impossible that Ellison might have associated slavery with racial inferiority. A former slave with some African ancestry, he could hardly proclaim that Negroes were natural slaves and whites natural masters. While this straight-out white racist argument held little comfort for Ellison, it is possible he entertained a variant of this common Southern refrain. Ellison was not white, but he was partly white. Whites in the antebellum South had confused ideas about mulattoes.[136] Some believed mulattoes' mixed blood sapped their vitality and destined them for extinction. Others thought mulattoes were in certain respects superior to Negroes of purely African ancestry, to approximately the same extent as they had white blood. Some light-skinned Negroes shared the latter view. In Charleston, color-conscious free mulattoes formed exclusive mulatto organizations that shunned blacks, slave or free. [137] If Ellison partook of this mulatto snobbery, he could have used his mixed blood as a basis for a racial defense of his mastery and his slaves' servitude. He and all of his family members were brown; all of his slaves were black.

To a racial defense of slaveholding Ellison could have joined a version of the planters' most common rationalization—paternalism. In the South the two dovetailed nicely, for the notion of reciprocal obligations between unequal partners was especially powerful when the lesser partner was perceived as inherently inferior, a childlike being in need of special protection and guidance.[138] Ellison no doubt considered his behavior toward his slaves honorable, possibly even generous. He could claim that he provided them with basic care, necessary discipline, and useful work. By fulfilling his sense of responsibility as their guardian, he legitimized his authority as master. White Southerners buttressed their racial and paternalistic arguments with evidence from the Bible, history, science, political theory, and elsewhere, all of which made the mature proslavery argument less a consistent theory than a collage, a Southern patchwork of self-serving illusions.[139] Ellison owned a Bible, attended church, and read history. If his conclusions about slavery differed substantially from his white neighbors', none of his actions ever betrayed his secret thoughts. More likely, he had no reservations about his mastery.

Ellison's defense of slaveholding may have been as much a jumble of myths as whites'. At bottom, however, his answer to the question of how he, a free man of color, could own slaves probably had a hard-edged precision no white man needed. No white person ever had to fear that his freedom could be alienated. No free Afro-American could ever be confident that his would not be. For Ellison, mastering slaves was central to his drive to master freedom. Patriarch of three generations of free Ellisons, he saw his primary responsibility as the preservation of his most precious asset. His family's freedom, like that of all free people of color, rested on a trap door, and white hands gripped the lever. Free Negroes could do little to influence their destinies other than to impress whites with their economic achievement, to persuade them that they were respectable and useful members of society, and to assure them that they were trustworthy and loyal Southerners. In the antebellum South, nothing was more lucrative, more respectable, and more patriotic than owning slaves. Along with his land and shop, Ellison's slaves formed a barrier against degradation and an endowment that he hoped would guarantee that his family continued to live as free people. Ellison did not make the rules of Southern society. Owning slaves attached him and his family to the dominant class of the South, who, if they would, could protect and defend his family's freedom.

WHITE planters in the High Hills held Ellison in high regard. One measure of their esteem is their acceptance of Ellison as a full-fledged member of Holy Cross Church. By 1844, twenty years after he had been allowed to come down from the gallery and sit with his family on a bench under the organ at the back of the church, the vestry of Holy Cross rented a pew to Ellison just as it did to white Singletons, Friersons, Watieses, Spanns, and Andersons. For his pew at the back of the sanctuary Ellison paid $35 a year, the same fee Dr. Anderson paid for his pew at the front of the church near the right hand of the rector. Only eight choice pews rented for more than Ellison's, seven of them directly in front of him in the center of the building. All but four of the other twenty-one pews rented for less than Ellison's. Although his $35 fee indicated his wealth and acceptance by the congregation, the location of the pew at the back of the church and its number—30 out of 30— indicated his bottom rank.[140]

The communicants of Holy Cross welcomed the Ellisons into their midst. Rector Augustus L. Converse no doubt appreciated their contributions, for his white parishioners were not always forthcoming. Converse complained to a friend, "It is a very common notion that a subscription for the salary of

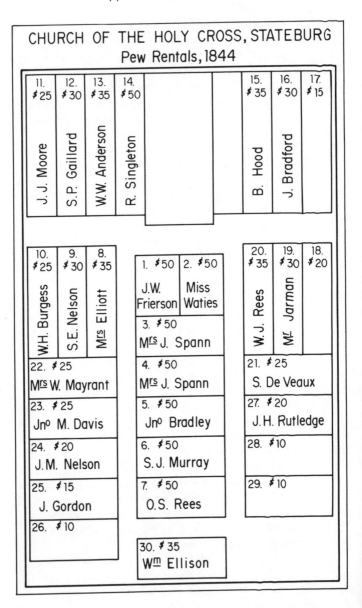

CHURCH OF THE HOLY CROSS, STATEBURG
Pew Rentals, 1844

11. $25	12. $30	13. $35	14. $50			15. $35	16. $30	17. $15
J. J. Moore	S.P. Gaillard	W.W. Anderson	R. Singleton			B. Hood	J. Bradford	

10. $25	9. $30	8. $35				20. $35	19. $30	18. $20
W.H. Burgess	S.E. Nelson	Mrs Elliott	1. $50 J.W. Frierson	2. $50 Miss Waties		W.J. Rees	Mr Jarman	
			3. $50 Mrs J. Spann					

22. $25 Mrs W. Mayrant	4. $50 Mrs J. Spann	21. $25 S. De Veaux
23. $25 Jno M. Davis	5. $50 Jno Bradley	27. $20 J.H. Rutledge
24. $20 J.M. Nelson	6. $50 S.J. Murray	28. $10
25. $15 J. Gordon	7. $50 O.S. Rees	29. $10
26. $10		

30. $35
Wm Ellison

a clergyman is one of those debts (if debt it is allowed to be) the payment of which may be indefinitely postponed."[141] The delinquincy of his white parishioners notwithstanding, Rector Converse and the congregation welcomed the Ellisons only so long as they stayed in their place. Only one other free family of color, the Inglises, received the privilege of a Holy Cross pew, but they were not as favored as the Ellisons. The vestry directed that the Inglises' pew "should be placed in the gallery."[142] Every Sunday the Ellisons' distinctive position in the social hierarchy of Stateburg was made visible to all as families filed into their pews. Back in pew number 30, the Ellisons were the first of the last, who congregated in the gallery, and the last of the first, who occupied the main floor.

Marking the social boundary between white and black and free and slave, the Ellisons' pew suggests the loneliness of their position. In Stateburg and elsewhere in Sumter District the Ellisons had no free colored peers. With the exception of the Inglis family, with whom the Ellisons were on friendly terms, no evidence exists of close relations between the Ellisons and other Sumter free Negroes. Had the Ellisons reached out to other free people of color who worked as farm hands and domestic servants, they would have jeopardized their reputation for respectability, since most local whites considered the typical free Negro an idler or a thief.

The one local group with whom the Ellisons could safely enjoy social relations was the Turks, whose racial status was ambiguous. The Turks professed to be Caucasians, and for generations the white Sumter family steadfastly defended the claim. Most other whites in Sumter District perceived the swarthy Turks as people of color.[143] Elsewhere in the state, other groups—variously called Brass Ankles, Red Bones, Red Legs, and Buckheads—shared the Turks' indeterminate race. Most of these individuals descended from remnants of Indian tribes who intermarried with poor whites and freed or escaped slaves.[144] Whites discriminated against them as if they were Negroes, but they tried to give themselves a separate status, aloof from blacks.

The Sumter Turks socialized with neither whites nor blacks. Clannish, they married almost exclusively within the seven lineages that comprised the group. Most of them poor, uneducated farmers and their families, the Turks could not begin to match the wealth and accomplishments of the Ellisons. However, despite the economic status the Turks shared with almost all free people of color, they themselves were not definitely Negroes. Since consorting with Negroes would imperil their shaky claims to whiteness, they stayed to themselves, most of them living in a settlement a few miles northeast of Stateburg. The Ellisons' respectability and light color made them attractive friends for Turks, and the Turks' racial indeterminancy made them uncontroversial associates for the Ellisons. Both the Ellisons and the Turks occupied unusual social terrain, and it appears that they gravitated toward one another.

A glimpse of the nature of the friendship between the families is provided by an 1858 letter that S. Benenhaly, a member of the Turks, wrote to Henry Ellison, who was in Charleston. The letter mentioned numerous personal matters—a recent communication from Henry's brother Reuben, Benenhaly's poor health, and his request for a "cheap shawl" from the city. Benenhaly also referred to local white people known to him and Henry. Isaac Lenoir, an elderly planter who lived near the Benenhaly's, "is sinking daily"; another planter had recently died of "disease of the heart." Among other tidbits, Benenhaly told Henry that a white man asked "very particularly when you would return." Revealing the calculated reserve that both he and Henry understood and practiced habitually, Benenhaly said, "I could not tell [the man] & [I] did not like to show any curiosity by enquiring why he wished to know."[145]

Benenhaly's letter contained no news of free Negroes in Stateburg, but it did mention members of the free colored community in Charleston. Benenhaly asked that Henry "remember me kindly [to] Mrs. Bonneau & her family & to Mr Johnson & his."[146] Probably through their friendship with the Ellisons, the Benenhalys had come to know the Ellisons' elite kinfolk in the city. The relationship between the Bonneaus and the Benenhalys dated at least from the early 1850s. In 1852 Frances Pinckney (Bonneau) Holloway asked her sister Mary Elizabeth Ellison in Stateburg to "Tell Old Mrs Benenhaly . . . I will write soon and whenever I pay Statesburgh a visit I will bring Jany to see her."[147] Frances's willingness to take her daughter and travel over to Mrs. Benenhaly's suggests the friendship that connected the families.

The association of the Turks and Ellisons eventually solid-ified into kinship. Regardless of their aversion to marrying outside the clan, particularly into colored families, two Turks married grandchildren of William Ellison.[148] When Ellison's grandson John Buckner lost his first wife in 1860, he quickly remarried Sarah Oxendine, a Turk.[149] Many years later, Henry Ellison's daughter Matilda, whom S. Benenhaly had asked Henry to kiss for him and to remind her "not to be too much pleased with Charleston & averse to returning to old friends in Sumter," married a Benenhaly.[150]

The Ellisons' relationship with the Turks did not tarnish their standing in the eyes of local whites. On two occasions the testimony to Ellison's respectability that white planters typically confined to their private conversations made their way into print. In 1849 Benson J. Lossing came to Stateburg to gather information on the career of General Thomas Sum-ter, whom he intended to include in his volume *Eminent Americans*, a collection of biographical sketches. As he inquired about General Sumter, he encountered tales about Ellison, and he shoehorned a glowing reference to the gin maker in his thumbnail biography of the general. Lossing observed that much of Sumter's property was now in the hands of "a mulatto named Ellison." The free Negro artisan "had purchased the freedom of himself and family in early life," Lossing wrote, and now he was "the owner of a large estate in land, and about sixty slaves." Lossing's error about the precise number of Ellison's slaves (he owned thirty-six in 1850) suggests that the white planters who informed him did not count Ellison's slaves but were impressed that he owned many. In Stateburg, Lossing reported, Ellison was "a man greatly esteemed."[151]

Lossing's book appeared after William Ellison died. Another public statement by a contemporary appeared in print while Ellison lived, and it reached a national audience. William H. Bowen was a long-time resident of Sumter District who fled to the West in the 1840s. With his wife and four children, Bowen settled in Union Church, Mississippi, a small village about fifty miles east of Natchez, where he worked as a druggist.[152] Like many other Americans, Bowen read the *Sat-urday Evening Post,* a weekly periodical devoted to serialized romances, tips on farming and homemaking, brief news items, and such esoterica as discussions of the poetry of asparagus. In March 1856 an item in the *Post* about a Negro in the North who had reared a large family and prospered caught Bowen's eye. Bowen remembered William Ellison and composed a letter to the editor of the *Post*.

Here was a "case that deserves notice," Bowen began. "A negro man, by name William Ellison, was bound out by his master to a gin wright, in Winnsborough, South Carolina," he explained. "During the time of his apprenticeship he was allowed, by his master, to do extra work; and from his industry and economy he laid up sufficient money to purchase his freedom from his master." Once free, Ellison moved to Stateburg "and commenced gin making and repairing, and in a short time he was able to purchase his wife and children." In 1845, when Bowen left South Carolina, "William Ellison owned 40 or 50 negroes, (among them 15 or 20 workmen,) a large cotton plantation, and owns nearly half the town of Stateburg; and I expect by this time (if he is living) he is worth eighty to one hundred thousand dollars." In Stateburg, Bowen concluded, "William Ellison is respected by all classes of citizens, and is honorable in all his dealings." He added an intriguing postscript, suggesting that if the *Post* published his letter, a copy be sent to Ellison, "and if you wish it, he will send you a statement of his rise and progress in a slave State, in the most aristocratic district in South Carolina."[153]

Although sectional rivalry may have prompted Bowen to write his letter, claiming Ellison's success as evidence of Southern superiority, Bowen clearly remembered Ellison's story fifteen years after he left Stateburg. There is no evidence that the editor of the *Post* ever followed up Bowen's suggestion about writing to Ellison, but Ellison probably saw Bowen's letter anyway, since on May 7, 1856, the Sumter *Watchman* reprinted it. The Sumter paper showed no embarrassment about a local Negro receiving national attention. It did, however, refer to Ellison as "a somewhat remarkable personage" and contrast his ambition with the laziness of most blacks.[154]

The significance of Bowen's letter lies in its assessment of Ellison's major achievements from the perspective of a white man who had been his neighbor. Bowen emphasized that "industry and economy" were responsible for Ellison's phenomenal success. Ellison personified the self-made man, the archetypical American. But unlike many other self-made men, he was esteemed as "honorable in all his dealings," earning him the respect of "all classes of citizens." Bowen, whose own wealth was just a fifth that of Ellison's, did not resent Ellison's accomplishment or find him arrogant or pushy.[155] Bowen did not attach any special meaning to a "negro" like Ellison owning "negro" slaves. However, Bowen may not have been typical of his class of white men. In 1823, while he still resided in Sumter District, Bowen accepted the guardianship of a free man of color named Richard Mack, an uncommon trust that set him apart from most white men, especially those who were not wealthy planters.[156]

At the same time a white man testified to Ellison's acceptance in the "most aristocratic district in South Carolina," Ellison himself publicly affirmed his loyalty to the community and its peculiar institution. Whites knew that Ellison's allegiance to slavery was as solid as the anvil in his shop, but during the Kansas crisis he reaffirmed his commitment to it. In May 1856, just as the *Post* item was appearing in the Sumter newspaper, a group of planters met at the Sumterville courthouse and formed the Kansas Association of Sumter. The association planned to raise money to support guerrillas fighting to make Kansas safe for slavery. A committee of the association solicited funds in the district, and twenty-four individuals pledged $100 each, among them William Ellison. With the money, the association dispatched twelve young men to do battle with the Free Soilers. Whether Ellison's contribution represented his heartfelt conviction or was a cheap way to buy more insurance is not clear. If asked directly to contribute, he could not refuse, particularly since the *Post* item had just made him a pawn in the sectional confrontation. Whatever Ellison's motivation, his pledge expressed his devotion to the protection and expansion of slavery. A century later the historian of Sumter District pointed proudly to this evidence that on fundamentals a black man had stood shoulder to shoulder with his white neighbors.[157]

For all his professions of loyalty to the South and all the polite nods to "Mr. Ellison" by local whites, what was said of

Jeem Whitaker, a free man of color in Camden, was also true of William Ellison—he was "as good as white, but not quite."[158] Ellison's climb up from slavery demonstrated that hard work and exquisite racial diplomacy could mine a razor-thin seam of opportunity. It did not show that the South was a color-blind, classless society open to merit. Ellison succeeded not as a representative of a race but as an individual, the great exception. His ancestry made him a perpetual outsider, distanced by his color. Neither wealth, refinement, nor loyalty to slavery could close the gap. Nothing could.

Ellison built his refuge in Stateburg at a very high price. He enslaved other Afro-Americans, ignored most free people of color, dominated members of his own family, and spent his life trying to please whites. The cost, however, did not include the sacrifice of his personality or the elimination of his will. He behaved deliberately, according to his judgment of the demands of his society. As a young man he decided that the route to security lay through accommodation and sweat. His tools were calipers and files, deference and circumspection. He stood as far from the river of heroic, militant black protest as any man in his era.[159] He did not challenge Southern society, but he did seek to defend himself from the degradation it reserved for people of color. He contradicted the basic notions white Southerners had about Negroes. In that modest, quiet way he led a life of protest. Whites, however, saw him only as the exception that proved the rule. His example did not budge their attitudes toward race or slavery. Ellison's success benefited only those who lived in his compound. That is what he set out to achieve. To do it, he participated in an oppressive regime and helped perpetuate it. His experience shows what antebellum Southern whites demanded of an Afro-American who wanted freedom and security for himself and his family.

ALL the dangers did not lie outside the Ellison family compound, as the deaths during the 1850s showed. The last few years of the 1850s apparently revealed to Ellison disturbing new evidence of the fragility of his dynasty. According to the historian of Sumter County, Ellison's son Reuben fathered slave children born to Hannah, his young slave woman.[160]

Hannah's eldest child, Dianna, was born in 1853, the year Reuben's wife Harriett Ann died. At two-year intervals thereafter Hannah gave birth to Susan, Marcus, John, and Virginia.[161] According to the 1860 census, all the children were black, like their mother.[162] When Marcus, John, and Virginia were baptized in Holy Cross in 1858, 1860, and 1861, Hannah was listed as the mother, but no father was indicated, which was not unusual for slave children.[163] Reuben was listed as the master of these children, but whether he was also the father cannot be proven. A Stateburg informant said many years later that Reuben's children continued to live in the neighborhood after the Civil War and married into the local black community.[164]

Reuben's backsliding, according to Stateburg tradition, displeased his father. If Reuben was in fact the father of four or five of his slave children, "displeased" may not be strong enough to describe William Ellison's emotions. He had devoted his life to pulling himself and his family up from slavery, and now—if the story is true—Reuben was dragging them all back down. Third-generation Stateburg Ellisons were slaves. Aside from what it implied about the family, it looked even worse in the community. All the barriers Ellison had erected between his family and slavery were weakened, though not destroyed. Ellison's reputation in Stateburg in the 1850s could withstand gossip about Reuben's slave children that strongly resembled him; after all, such rumors were not unknown in white families. But were the children Reuben's?

They probably were. The timing of their births makes it plausible that Reuben was the father, and the baptisms suggest the children were somehow special to Reuben, for he was connected to no other slave baptisms. And one other piece of evidence is consistent with the likelihood of Reuben's paternity. Reuben died in the spring of 1861, just a few weeks before the firing on Fort Sumter.[165] His father had not disowned him or driven him out of "Wisdom Hall."[166] Perhaps the old man's censure was tempered by his memory of Maria and his own surrender to temptation. Like all the other Ellisons, Reuben received a funeral service in Holy Cross. But he is the only Ellison without a headstone or marker of any kind in the family burying ground.[167] William Ellison had never scrimped on gravestones before. The arrangement of the other stones makes it unlikely that Ellison set a stone for Reuben that was later removed by vandals. There is no spot for Reuben in the carefully plotted rows. It is true that in the spring of 1861 the Ellisons, like all other free people of color, had other things on their minds that might have made a tombstone seem an irrelevance. But it is also possible that the absence of a stone reflects William Ellison's final judgment on Reuben's paternity of slave children. Ellison took no steps whatever to acknowledge kinship or even regard for Hannah's children. Perhaps when he buried Reuben he hoped quietly to put to rest the distressing truth about slave Ellisons.

That truth was doubly distressing in 1861, for the Afro-American ancestry of the Ellisons and the South's commitment to slavery had come to mean that Reuben's slave children may have represented not the final remnants of the Ellisons' bondage but harbingers of the future. In South Carolina and elsewhere throughout the South, free Negroes were under attack from rural planters who wanted to eliminate or enslave them and from white mechanics who coveted their jobs. Propelled by the impending sectional crisis, the assault was nowhere more ominous than in the city of Charleston.

V

Freedom Besieged

S HORTLY before Thanksgiving 1859, James M. Johnson left Stateburg, where he had lived for seventeen years, and returned to Charleston, the city of his youth. He came back to help his father, James D. Johnson, who was preparing to retire from his lifelong work as a tailor. The old man had lived in the city for most, if not all, of his life. He was a native of South Carolina and a mulatto, but whether he was born a slave like William Ellison is not known.[1] He may have moved to Charleston sometime before 1820, possibly from Stateburg. In 1810, when Johnson was about seventeen, two free Afro-American households in Sumter District were headed by men named James Johnson. One family contained eleven free persons of color, the other, seven.[2] James D. Johnson may have been among them. By 1820 Johnson evidently resided in Charleston, where his eldest son, James M., was born.[3] But Johnson and his family first appear in the surviving records of the city ten years later, in 1830.[4]

Charleston was an ideal place for James D. Johnson to capitalize on his skills as a tailor. In one season more potential customers passed Johnson's shop on upper King Street, in the heart of the retail district of the city, than a tailor would be likely to see in a decade in a rural village.[5] As the hub of trade and fashion in South Carolina, Charleston was as vital to a tailor like Johnson as the cotton fields of the upcountry were to a gin maker. In 1830 Johnson probably lived above the shop with his wife Delia, their children, and several boarders. One or two free Negro boarders probably worked for Johnson as journeyman tailors or apprentices, as did the

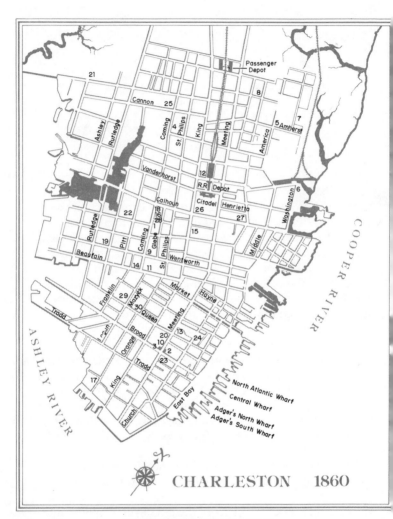

CHARLESTON 1860

KEY TO MAP OF CHARLESTON

1. Jeanette Boneau
2. City Hall
3. Court House
4. John DeLarge
5. Joseph Dereef
6. Richard E. Dereef
7. James Eason
8. Eason's Foundry
9. Grace Episcopal Church
10. Hibernian Hall
11. Richard Holloway
12. Robert Houston
13. Institute Hall
14. James D. Johnson
15. Johnson's Tailor Shop
16. Benjamin K. Kinloch
17. Charles Macbeth
18. William McKinlay
19. Christopher G. Memminger
20. Mills House
21. Henry T. Peake
22. John Schnierle
23. St. Michael's Episcopal Churc
24. St. Philip's Episcopal Church
25. Thomas L. Webb
26. Anthony Weston
27. Furman Weston
28. Jacob Weston
29. Samuel Weston
30. Westons' Tailor Shop

six slaves who were also listed in his household.[6] Four of the slaves were young boys less than ten years old, and the other two were young men between ten and twenty-three. Although the slaves lived with Johnson, he probably did not own them. Most likely, their masters hired out or apprenticed them to Johnson. While he trained slave apprentices, he also taught his craft to his sons James and Charles, whom the family called Charley. When young James moved to Stateburg in 1842, he had ten or twelve years of experience as a tailor in the competitive Charleston market. For more than fifteen years afterward his brother Charley continued to work in their father's shop on King Street. With Charley's help, along with the journeymen and apprentices, James D. Johnson managed to keep his head above water.

By 1834 he had set aside enough money to buy a small lot on Coming Street for $250. He purchased the lot in the name of his sons as a speculative venture for their benefit. Two years later it paid off handsomely when Johnson sold the lot for $1,800.[7] In 1836, perhaps with some of the windfall from the Coming Street lot, Johnson bought property on King Street for $6,000, the seller agreeing to hold a mortgage until Johnson paid off the note.[8] The lot probably contained Johnson's tailor shop and his residence. The high price reflected the prime location of the property, and the mortgage demonstrated Johnson's reputation as a solid, hard-working artisan. Three years later Johnson made another speculative investment, this time in a lot in the northeast suburbs of the city, for which he paid $3,000, once again with a mortgage to the seller until the debt was settled.[9] His tailoring business did well enough for him to pay off this mortgage, but whether he ever amortized the mortgage on his King Street property is unknown.

Johnson also bought four slaves during the 1830s. In 1834 he purchased the nineteen-year-old Judy and her nine-month-old daughter Caroline.[10] Two years later he bought a mulatto woman named Florence.[11] The next year he acquired Billy, who was about nineteen.[12] Johnson probably employed Billy in his shop, but his two slave women most likely worked as domestic servants, relieving Delia of some household chores.

Johnson did well enough during the 1830s to afford a half-interest in "Drayton Hall" in Stateburg, where his son James lived with his wife Eliza Ann.[13] He helped provide his son with a comfortable country residence, and James M. Johnson returned the favor by giving the house his father's name. However, Johnson's investment in Charleston real estate turned sour during the 1840s. Less than ten years after he had purchased his lots, he sold them both at a heavy loss. In 1846 he sold his suburban lot for $1,500, half what he paid for it.[14] A year later he sold his King Street property for $3,400, again, little more than half the purchase price.[15] He also sold his two slave women, Florence and Judy, perhaps to obtain some badly needed cash.[16] Rather than move his shop, he stayed on in his valuable King Street location, evidently paying rent.

In 1850 he decided to move his family, including Charley and his wife Sarah, into two houses on the west side of Coming Street that he bought for $1,400.[17] Numbers 7 and 9 Coming, where the Johnsons continue to live during the 1850s, were in a pleasant residential section of the city populated by many of the leading free Afro-American families. Nearby stood Grace Episcopal Church, an outgrowth of the overcrowded congregation of St. Philip's. At Grace, the Johnsons and a score of other free mulatto families worshiped among the 200 white parishioners. Johnson's shop on King Street was a six-block walk from his Coming Street home. The large public market, the railroad depot, and even the courthouse were also within convenient walking distance. By 1860 Johnson paid city taxes on his houses, assessed at $4,000, and on three slaves.[18] By a lifetime of labor he had managed to hold his own and do a little better.

Johnson's modest economic success was probably overshadowed by his pride in his family. He and Delia reared and educated their two sons and two daughters.[19] Charley married first, evidently in 1843. He and his new wife Sarah continued to live with his parents on Coming Street.[20] Perhaps the best evidence of the respect Johnson's children had for him was the name Charley and Sarah chose for their young son who was baptized in Grace Episcopal Church on April 4, 1851: James Drayton Johnson.[21] Shortly after the child's baptism, he and his mother died. In November 1852 Charley remarried. His bride, Gabriella Miller, was a light-skinned young woman from a free colored family resident in Charleston for many years.[22] Charley and Gabriella celebrated their wedding in Grace Church, and they continued to play an active part in the life of the congregation, serving as sponsors of baptisms of free colored infants and confirmations of free colored adults.

From Stateburg, James M. kept in close touch with his brother and father in Charleston. John Buckner probably came to know his stepfather's sister Jane Johnson during the visits back and forth between the country and the city. John and Jane married in Stateburg in 1857, and in March of the next year Jane gave birth to Harriet Ann, James D. Johnson's first granddaughter and William Ellison's first great-grandchild, the first member of Ellison's fourth generation of freedom.[23]

The family ties between the Johnsons and the Ellisons were constantly reinforced by exchanges of letters, gifts, favors, and visits. Henry's only child, Matilda, lived in Charleston during the late 1850s, usually staying with her maternal grandmother, Mrs. Jeannette Bonneau, who lived three blocks up Coming Street from the Johnsons.[24] Matilda dined with the Johnsons from time to time, and they looked in on her and her grandmother. When Henry or any of the other Ellisons came to Charleston, they always visited the Johnsons, and more often than not they stayed with them. A few weeks before John Buckner married, William Ellison Jr. placed an order with Charley for a new pair of trousers as a wedding gift, probably not the first time and certainly not the last that Charley made clothing for one of the Ellison clan.[25] Slaves shuttled back and forth between the two households with messages and with items plentiful in one place and scarce in the other.[26]

In December 1858, James D. Johnson sent the Ellisons greetings "from all of our Canada folks." Charley and his family had recently moved to Toronto, where he worked as a tailor. He was "busy," his father wrote. Perhaps referring to the reason Charley went north, Johnson added that Charley "has never enjoyed better health although he is sewing." Charley found the cold weather in Toronto "bracing," but he missed his family and friends in South Carolina. "In every letter they begged to be remembered to all thier *[sic]* friends, especially those of Stateburg," Johnson wrote Henry.[27]

Charley was also missed by his father. Charley's absence seems to have precipitated his father's decision to retire. Charley left South Carolina sometime between March 1857 and December 1858.[28] Without his help in the tailor shop, the old man evidently concluded that he could no longer run the business by himself. Johnson needed somebody to help meet customers, take measurements, cut patterns, stitch seams, buy supplies, pay merchants, collect accounts, and supervise the work of the journeymen, apprentices, and slaves. He was sixty-five and not in the best of health. In his letter to Henry in December 1858, he noted that he was "quite unwell at present although not laid up since the 21st but hope soon to be better."[29] Within the next several months Johnson hatched his plans for retirement. He could not afford simply to quit working. His shop had been his livelihood for thirty years, and he still needed any income he could get from it. He could hire other tailors to work for him, and he could depend upon the clientele he had built up over the years to continue to patronize his shop. Eventually he might sell the business to an enterprising younger man. But in the meantime, he would withdraw from the business gradually. He may have asked his son James to leave Stateburg and return to Charleston to take Charley's place and ease his own transition to retirement. Or James may have volunteered to come down. In any case, late in the fall of 1859 James M. Johnson moved to Charleston and stayed for more than a year.

After seventeen years in rural Stateburg, Johnson was an upcountry transplant in the bustling city. He wrote frequent letters back to his close friend Henry, passing along news of relatives and friends in the large free mulatto community and commenting on his fresh exposure to urban life. Just before Christmas 1859, about a month after he had arrived in the city, James wrote Henry that he and Eliza Ann had recently attended a fashionable wedding that "came off in style." The free colored bride and groom, each with ten attendants, were married by Reverend Christopher P. Gadsden, the white rector of St. Luke's Protestant Episcopal Church. Several bridesmaids had come all the way from Savannah. The wedding supper was a grand affair catered by Nat Fuller, a free mulatto man who often catered the parties of the city's white aristocrats. Although James and Eliza Ann left early, before the wedding cake was cut, they stayed long enough to share in two bottles of champagne and for Eliza Ann to have the oysters Fuller served especially for her. After the reception the bride and groom left on a honeymoon "Tour in the country." "You must come down," James invited Henry, "& follow the fashion."[30]

Lavish weddings were hardly the fashion among the free Afro-Americans in Sumter District. The less glamorous routines of rural life surfaced in Johnson's letter when he asked Henry to make certain the slave girl Sarah "behaves herself & salts the creatures regularly." Salting the livestock in Stateburg and serving champagne and oysters in Charleston— Johnson's contrast between country and city life, though doubtless unintentional, could hardly have been sharper. With his letter Johnson sent along "some little nick nacks" for Christmas gifts for the children in the Ellison family compound, William Jr.'s son and two daughters and John Buckner's little girl. Cheerily, Johnson closed his letter by wishing Henry and "all at Wisdom Hall a Merry Christmas" from himself, his father, mother, wife, and Charley's wife Gabriella, who was visiting from Canada.[31]

Johnson's chatty family letter contains only one hint that he wrote it when the outlook for free Negroes was increasingly ominous. Johnson asked Henry to "tender my congratulations to your Father on the adjournment of the Legislature." Congratulations were in order because a bill to enslave all free persons of color in South Carolina had failed to pass. He urged William Ellison to read the account in the Charleston *Courier* of the speech made against the bill by Christopher G. Memminger, a wealthy lawyer, planter, and politician in the Charleston delegation to the legislature. Johnson and the Ellisons had evidently discussed this and several other bills under consideration in Columbia that were designed to repress and further restrict free Afro-Americans. The Ellisons' viewpoint cannot be inferred from Johnson's letter, but his own confidence and optimism are unmistakable. "I prophesied from the onset that nothing would be done affecting our position," he declared.[32] Despite proposals to eliminate all free Negroes by enslaving them or expelling them from the state, despite the increasing political turbulence throughout the nation, Johnson did not express the slightest foreboding. This

Christmas, as in Christmases past, he looked forward to the future with confidence that things would not change. His father would retire. His life and the lives of the Ellisons and the Johnsons would go on as they always had.

MANY white South Carolinians were determined to make the changes Johnson was certain would never come. In 1859 citizens throughout the state petitioned the legislature to enact some law that would eliminate free persons of color either by forcing them to leave or by enslaving them. The petition from upcountry York District spoke of the "great evil and mis-chief" of free Negroes "every day mixing and mingling with the slave population," and urged the legislators to "adopt such measures as may in your wisdom remove this evil and reduce the colored population of this state to one uniform condi-tion."[33] Petitioners from Ellison's home district echoed the York proposal, citing the "continuous dificulties *[sic]* arising from the association of slaves and free negroes."[34] Abbeville petitioners agreed that free persons of color "have decidedly a demoralizing effect upon our slave population," and they spelled out the racial logic for action. Free Negroes were "the most degraded people that live in a civilized community," they proclaimed. "We know that naturally they are indolent, lazy, improvident, destitute of forethought, and totally incapable of supporting themselves and should have someone to arouse their dormant energies and direct their labor." The petition-ers appealed to the legislators to place South Carolina's free Negroes "in a happy state of bondage, the place where God designed the African race to be." If the legislature was "not disposed to grant this boon," they asked the lawmakers to "appropriate a fund, and have them removed to Liberia, and thus relieve the State of their contaminating influence."[35] Free Afro-Americans contaminated slaves because, as petitioners from St. Helena Parish had argued almost thirty years earlier, "the example of indolence and vice exhibited by the coloured free persons is perpetually before the slave. They encourage insubordination by precept as well as by example."[36]

The argument for the elimination of free Negroes had been percolating through the minds of white Southerners for years. As the number of free Afro-Americans grew rapidly in the years after the American Revolution, many leading whites concluded that free Negroes had no future in the United States. "Why not retain and incorporate the blacks into the state . . . ?" Thomas Jefferson asked rhetorically in his *Notes on the State of Virginia,* published in 1787.[37] The apocalyptic reason he gave seemed plausible to many white Americans at the time and continued to haunt white Southerners who contemplated the likely evolution of a biracial free society. "Deep rooted prejudices entertained by the whites; ten thousand recollections, by the blacks, of the injuries they sustained; new provocations; the real distinctions which nature has made; and many other circumstances, will divide us into parties, and produce convulsions, which will probably never end but in the extermination of the one or the other race," Jefferson said.[38]

The only practical way to avoid this cataclysm was to remove free Negroes from the United States and colonize them in their African "homeland," many white leaders believed. The American Colonization Society was founded for this purpose in 1817, and it was instrumental in establishing Liberia and in sending thousands of free Afro-Americans to settle there. Colonization was completely impractical, however. The money and ships necessary to transport the free Negro population to foreign shores were far greater than the resources available, even to the federal government. Furthermore, enthusiasm for colonization sagged during the late 1820s and early 1830s as the cotton boom emphasized the value of Negro laborers, as free Afro-Americans in the North bitterly attacked the idea that Africa was their homeland and insisted that they were as American as whites, as the colonization movement itself began to take on a subdued anti-slavery coloration, and as the South became increasingly hostile to any suggestion that slavery was undesirable.[39] Instead of supporting colonization, the South began in the 1820s to prohibit manumission and to restrict the liberties of free Afro-Americans.

The assumption that free Afro-Americans were neither integral nor desirable members of American society survived among most whites in both the North and South. The problem was to accommodate that assumption with the reality of a half-million free Negro Americans. Some abolitionists and religious humanitarians hoped to replace white assumptions about racial inferiority with affirmations of the brotherhood of mankind.[40] But these reformers were always a tiny minority in the North. The predominant view among Northern whites mirrored that among white Southerners. The rallying cry of free soil, free labor, and free men was composed of almost equal parts of anti-slavery and anti-Negro sentiment.[41] Most white Northerners did not want Negroes in their society any more than they wanted slaves. Several Northern states restricted Negroes from entering, and most hoped that free persons of color already there would sooner or later leave.[42] A few, like Abraham Lincoln, clung to the chimera of colonization. In August 1862, in the midst of the Civil War, after Lincoln had decided to issue the Emancipation Proclamation, he called five black leaders to the White House and urged them to support the return to Africa. "Even when you cease to be slaves, you are yet far removed from being placed on an equality with the white race," Lincoln said; "on this broad continent not a single man of your race is made the equal of a single man of ours. . . . I cannot alter it if I would. It is a fact."[43]

Although white Southerners shared the racial prejudice of their Northern counterparts, slavery made the proper social policy toward free Negroes a momentous issue in the South. After the 1820s, Southerners dropped the argument that slavery was a necessary evil bequeathed to them by their forefathers and replaced it with the defense that slavery was a positive good.[44] Slavery was ordained by God, sanctioned by the Bible and all of human history, and it benefited the entire society, even the slaves. Since Negroes were inferior, the argument went, they were incapable of withstanding the rigors of freedom, as proved by the degraded circumstances of nearly all free Negroes. Afro-Americans were far better off as slaves, where masters could take care of their needs and direct their labor. Although the proslavery argument was grounded on the unshakable conviction that all Negroes were inferior to whites, the case was not compelling enough before the late 1850s to cause whites to consider seriously the enslavement of free Afro-Americans. In "What Shall Be Done With the Free Negroes," published in 1851, the proslavery theorist George Fitzhugh rehearsed the case that, "Humanity, self-interest,

[and] consistency, all require that we should enslave the free negro."[45]

Part of the reason why racial assumptions were not pushed to their logical conclusion before the late 1850s was that many white Southerners continued to think of enslavement as a form of punishment, an extreme one at that. According to state laws, freedom was something an Afro-American could forfeit by committing certain acts that states defined as criminal. But could a state confiscate the freedom of Negroes simply as a matter of social policy, in the absence of an overt, prohibited act by each individual free Afro-American? If many white Southerners were willing to answer yes, they nevertheless did not begin to try to carry out their plans until decades after the proslavery argument matured.

Whites also delayed serious discussion of the enslavement of free Negroes because it was not at all clear that enslavement was within the law. While the statutes in every Southern state defined a second-class status for free Afro-Americans, they also recognized and to a certain degree protected their freedom. Would a new law usurping the freedom of persons of color be constitutional? Would it be prohibited by the Fifth Amendment's guarantee that "No person shall be . . . deprived of life, liberty, or property, without due process of law. . . ."? The ambiguity of free Negroes' legal status in each Southern state was compounded by such questions as whether a free person of color was even a "person" within the meaning of the Constitution. If free Afro-Americans were not first-class citizens, were they citizens at all? Were they under the jurisdiction of the federal constitution or not?

These questions were settled by the Dred Scott decision of the United States Supreme Court in 1857.[46] Chief Justice Roger B. Taney, in a long, rambling opinion riddled with misinformation and internal contradictions, concluded in part that Negroes were not citizens within the meaning of the Constitution, and that, slave or free, the Constitution simply did not apply to them, except as they were considered property. Although the major question Taney was deciding dealt with the status of slaves, free Afro-Americans entered his opinion as part of his argument that they were not then, nor had they ever been, considered part of the American "people." He used this argument to buttress his conclusion that since Negroes like Dred Scott never were citizens under the Constitution, regardless of where they resided, they had no right to bring suit in the federal courts, a crucial issue in Scott's plea for freedom.

While Taney's opinion created a storm of protest in the North, it was calmly accepted in the South. Southerners seemed to understand what Don E. Fehrenbacher, the foremost historian of the Dred Scott decision, has called Taney's "true purpose," namely, "to launch a sweeping counterattack on the antislavery movement and to reinforce the bastions of slavery at every rampart and parapet."[47] The highest tribunal in the land endorsed the most extreme Southern position in the sectional controversy. The prospects for Afro-Americans had "never appeared so hopeless," Abraham Lincoln believed. "All the powers of earth seem rapidly combining against" Negroes, Lincoln told an audience in Springfield, Illinois, in September 1857. He evoked a terrifying image of Afro-American imprisonment:

Mammon is after him; ambition follows, and philosophy follows, and the Theology of the day is fast joining the cry. They have him in his prison house; they have searched his person, and left no prying instrument with him. One after another they have closed the heavy iron doors upon him, and now they have him, as it were, bolted in with a lock of a hundred keys, which can never be unlocked without the concurrence of every key; the keys in the hands of a hundred different men, and they scattered to a hundred different and distant places; and they stand musing as to what invention, in all the dominions of mind and matter, can be produced to make the impossibility of his escape more complete than it is.[48]

One invention to which the Southern states quickly turned was enslavement. Arkansas was the first state to consider legislation to enslave free Negroes.[49] Made in 1856, the proposal was narrowly defeated, partly because of doubts about its constitutionality. After the Dred Scott decision those doubts vanished. The legislature debated the law in the 1858 session and passed it early in 1859. It provided that any free Negro in the state by January 1, 1860, would be enslaved. Arkansas had the smallest free Afro-American population in the South, and most free Negroes left soon after the law passed. Far more important to the South's other free persons of color was the Arkansas precedent. Within months, nearly every legislature in the South deliberated the wisdom of outlawing freedom for Negroes.

John Brown's raid on Harpers Ferry, Virginia, quickened the pace of their deliberations. In October 1859 Brown led a small band of followers, including five free Negroes, on a pre-dawn seizure of the federal arsenal at Harpers Ferry. The self-appointed leader of what he envisioned as an army of liberation for slaves, Brown managed only to get most of his followers killed and the rest captured, tried, and hanged.[50] Bungled though it was, Brown's raid frightened white Southerners. Here again were free Afro-Americans ready to carry on the work of Denmark Vesey. Once again men prepared to arm slaves and lead them in rebellion. The rather easy interaction between slaves and free Negroes that white Southerners had previously considered a nuisance now seemed to be intolerably dangerous.[51] Free Negroes might be abolitionist emissaries spreading unrest among slaves and conspiring with them to rise up against their white masters. Some Southerners believed these fears exaggerated, but none could discount them entirely. Racial anxieties impelled Southerners to consider whether to make their policies toward Negroes, as they put it, "consistent" with proslavery ideology.

For whites, the most satisfying way to attain consistency was to have free Afro-Americans volunteer to become slaves. In South Carolina, several free Negroes sought legislative permission to forfeit their free status. In December 1859 an illiterate free man of color named William Bass petitioned the legislature to allow him to become the slave of Philip W. Pledger, who owned his stepfather and other kin. Bass's petition conformed perfectly to the reasoning of many whites about the proper place for free Afro-Americans. Bass said his "condition as a free person of color, a negro, is more degrading and involves more suffering in this State, than that of a slave, who is under the care, protection and ownership of a kind and good master." Bass emphasized less the advantages of slavery than the hardships of freedom. He said that "as a free negro he is preyed upon by every sharper with whom he comes in contact, and that he is very poor, though an able-bodied man, and is charged with and punished for every offence, guilty or not, committed in his neighborhood, and lives a thousand times harder, and in more destitution, than the slaves of many of the planters in [Marlborough] District."[52] Bass's petition was featured prominently in newspapers throughout South Carolina and celebrated as a promising harbinger of enslavement by consent. The legislature's Committee on the Colored Population considered Bass's petition and several others and recommended the passage of a law to grant the wishes of the petitioners.[53] Legislators knew perfectly well, however, that although most free Negroes shared Bass's poverty, they had no desire whatever to surrender their freedom. White notions of racial consistency could not be realized by the consent of free Afro-Americans.

In the South Carolina legislature in 1859, Edward Moore, a representative from York District, introduced a bill to compel consistency. Moore's proposal provided that any free person of color in South Carolina on the first of March 1860 would be sold into slavery. "The whole of these trifling vagabonds should be sold or compelled to leave the State," Moore argued. He opposed voluntary enslavement or any other attempt to "discriminate" between free Negroes and slaves. Slaves were not allowed to choose their masters. Why should free Negroes be given the privilege? Many legislators considered Moore's bill "ultra and extravagant," according to the Columbia correspondent of the *Courier*. But Moore asserted that his opponents "might just as well say that it is wrong to take the liberty of a slave as that of a free negro; the one is as much entitled to it as the other. . . ."[54]

The "unusually warm" three-hour debate in the legislature disclosed that many of the lawmakers were sympathetic to Moore's plan, though not to the ruthless logic with which he intended to carry it out. A somewhat less extreme proposal was introduced by John Henry Screven, who represented St. Luke's Parish in the low country. Screven's bill provided that free persons of color who were convicted of crimes that currently were punished by fines or imprisonment would henceforth be enslaved. Screven said that he was "not disposed to encourage any sweeping remedy" or "to produce any new revulsion in the country." His bill would respond to the complaints of citizens throughout the state about the "trouble, inconvenience and often injury" caused by free Negroes. It would "prevent these people from becoming a tax upon the country from idleness and vagrancy." At the same time, Screven pointed out, he opposed "any measure calculated to injure those people who do behave themselves, or to impair what is the obligation upon South Carolina to extend protection to those who are good citizens."[55]

In effect, Screven's bill gave the magistrate's and freeholders' courts local option on whether to enslave free persons of color. In many districts the number of free Negroes enslaved under Screven's bill probably would have been almost the same as under Moore's plan. The advantage of Screven's bill was that it did not eliminate freedom without cause. If a free Negro man stole a chicken or traded with a slave, he thereby forfeited his freedom. Screven argued that he did not "believe that the country and people are prepared" for Moore's proposal to "sell the whole class." The alternative, he said, was that "where this class are disposed to be idle and vicious, reduce them to that position where they can have a master who can make them work. This would disturb no commonwealth and this population, instead of being an evil, would be protected."[56]

Christopher G. Memminger argued against both the Moore and Screven bills and defended free persons of color on grounds of justice and sound policy. Memminger expressed "utmost confidence" that slavery was based on "principles of right and justice," principles compromised by the two bills. He ridiculed Moore's assertion "that it is consistent with Justice to take those reared and standing among us free, and from who we are encouraged to look for everything becoming and proper, and reduce them" to slavery. Screven's proposal was flawed because, Memminger argued, it made slavery a punishment for crimes when "we maintain [it] to be the proper condition of the slave." The state had protected free Negroes for years, Memminger pointed out. Although free persons of color were not citizens, they were still "entitled to the protection of our laws." Furthermore, Memminger asserted, the real threats to slavery did not come from free people of color. Referring to the Vesey conspiracy, he asked, "Was it not through the instrumentality of a free colored man that a formidable insurrection was discovered and quelled"?[57] Indeed, only two years earlier the legislature had voted to increase to $200 the annual pension paid to Peter Desverney, the former slave emancipated by the state for betraying the Vesey conspiracy.[58] "Have we not again and again voted testimonials to people of that class," Memminger reminded the lawmakers. In fact, Memminger declared, working-class whites were a greater threat to slavery than were free Negroes. In Charleston, Memminger said, "there were [free colored] men of most estimable character, and as a general rule, take an equal number of them and an equal number of those [white men] who come nearest to them, and there will be found more amongst the latter who are demoralizing our slaves." Memminger concluded that it was "not the policy of the State to set those people who are our friends against us." He moved for the indefinite postponement of Screven's bill.[59] Although the Charleston delegation in the Assembly supported Memminger's motion, a 66–50 majority voted to send the Screven bill on to the Senate and to table Moore's bill and the more than twenty others dealing with free Negroes.[60]

James M. Johnson's letter to Henry Ellison just after the legislature adjourned suggests that free Afro-Americans throughout the state followed the debate on their status with more than casual interest. When the Screven bill was bottled up in the Senate Committee on the Judiciary and, like all the other free Negro bills, failed to pass, the Johnsons and the Ellisons breathed a sigh of relief. However, none of the bills was rejected by the legislature. They remained in the hopper, ready to be called up at the next session. From the perspective of Johnson and others among the free colored elite, the legislature appeared to be involved in little more than another of its periodic spasms of repression. Members of the free colored elite were cautious and concerned, but their outlook was tempered by the conviction that, as in the past, their status would not change.

DURING the preceding generation the South Carolina legislature had made only minor changes in laws governing free

Negroes. After the passage of the 1822 law responding to the Vesey scare, the most notable modifications were the 1834 law prohibiting free Negroes from teaching free Afro-Americans or slaves to read or write, and the 1841 ban on the use of trusts to evade the law against manumission. At moments of sectional tension, legislators proposed more sweeping changes. In 1835 the distribution of inflammatory abolitionist literature through the mail prompted bills to prohibit free persons of color from owning slaves, to outlaw marriages between whites and free Negroes, and to require every free colored mechanic to work under the supervision of a white tradesman.[61] Lawmakers debated the bills, but they passed none of them. The *Mercury* called the proposals "tyrannical and impolitic" and reported that an "overwhelming majority of the citizens of Charleston" opposed them.[62] The *Courier* agreed, noting that "such extreme severity is not demanded by the crisis."[63]

The *Courier* explained in some detail why the proposed laws were "false policy." "The true policy of the State is to foster slave labor," the *Courier* postulated, and all else followed from that. The free Negro's "right to hold slaves gives him a stake in the institution of slavery, and makes it his interest as well as his duty to uphold it. It identifies his interests and his feelings, in this particular, with those of the white population. . . ." In addition, owning slaves was often the only way a free person of color could bring parent or child, husband or wife "into the bosom of the family." The proposal to prevent free colored artisans from working for themselves would either drive free Afro-Americans out of the state, the *Courier* argued, or it would make them "exchange their habits of honesty and industry, for those of idleness and profligacy." Those who stayed would become "moral pests in our community." Forcing free persons of color to work under white supervision just like slaves would create rather than solve a problem, the *Courier* said. Prohibiting free Negroes from working independently would have the "inevitable result of breaking down the barrier, which now separates the free colored man from the slave, and assigns him an intermediate *caste* between the slave and his master," the *Courier* pointed out. "It is this intermediate position in society, that has given the free colored man of the South a degree of self-respect, which has placed him, in industry and morals, so far above his degraded fellow of the North. . . ." Furthermore, the *Courier* declared, the free colored population of Charleston had long been upright and trustworthy: "the conduct of the free-colored people of this city, if not of the State, has been for the most part so correct, evincing so much civility, subordination, industry and propriety, that unless their conduct should change for the worse, or some stern necessity demand it, we are unwilling to see them deprived of those immunities, which they have enjoyed for centuries, without the slightest detriment to the commonwealth."[64]

Attempts to alter the laws governing free persons of color ran up against what might be called the Charleston defense. Powerful Charlestonians argued that any blanket restriction on free Negroes fell with unnecessary and unfair harshness on free persons of color in Charleston, whose conduct was exemplary. This argument prevailed in almost every attempt by country planters to solve the free Negro problem as they saw it. As the *Courier* was careful to point out in 1835, free Negroes in Charleston were different from those elsewhere in the state. Outside the city, the argument that free Afro-Americans were an intermediate caste between slaves and whites made little sense simply because the number of free Negroes was so small. Outside Charleston, free persons of color comprised 1 percent of the population; they were hardly visible as a boundary between slaves and whites, much less an intermediate class. In the country only one Afro-American in fifty was free. In the city, the proportion of free persons among the Afro-American population was ten times greater, about one out of five. Charleston was the unofficial capital of the free colored population of the state. Although the city contained in 1860 only 3 percent of the state's slave population and 8 percent of the state's whites, it harbored 33 percent of all free persons of color. Free Afro-Americans made up only 8 percent of the total inhabitants of the city, but they were numerous enough to constitute a separate class, and they were visible enough to appear to be intermediate between the mass of slaves and the white majority.

When country planters visited Charleston, they could see that the free colored people in the city were different from their rural counterparts. In the 1859 debate in the legislature, Screven acknowledged that in some sections of the state free Negroes were "neither vicious, idle, nor guilty of crime."[65] So long as free persons of color were favored by Charleston's delegates to the legislature and by the city's newspapers, they had powerful allies. Although Charlestonians did not control the legislature, the leadership and prestige of Charleston politicians and their influence with friends and kin throughout the state gave the city more influence than its population warranted. Charlestonians' views were especially influential when new restrictions on free Negroes were considered, a fact that frustrated many country planters. The proper response to the complaints of rural planters, the Charleston defenders implied, was to use the time-tested magistrate's and freeholders' courts to govern unruly free Negroes. Any other response caused more problems in Charleston than it solved elsewhere in the state.

The success with which Memminger and the other members of the Charleston delegation deployed the Charleston defense in 1859 contributed to the confidence of the free colored elite that their status was secure. It must also have been satisfying to be praised in the legislature for an "estimable character" and for "everything becoming and proper." To have these sentiments printed in the *Courier* was even sweeter. These testimonials, however, did not cause Charleston's free persons of color to sit back.

Johnson and other leading members of Charleston's free colored community took positive steps to encourage their defenders and to win their continued support. Early in January 1860 Johnson sent Henry a copy of Memminger's remarks in the legislature and reported that "I have pledged your Father as a Contributor to a present to be sent him."[66] What was purchased with the contributions of William Ellison and other free persons of color is not known. Surely it was something fine enough to reflect their appreciation for Memminger's help, as well as their own gentility and good taste. Under what circumstances the gift was presented to Memminger is also unknown. It is certain, however, that a leading representative of Charleston's free colored community supplemented the gift by personally thanking Memminger for his support. When

Memminger was in the city for a few days before he left to undertake his duties as commissioner to Virginia to make the case for secession, Johnson accompanied Robert Houston, a highly respected free mulatto tailor, when he expressed to Memminger the appreciation of the free colored community. "I was present when Mr Houston Returned him thanks in behalf of our people," Johnson wrote Henry.[67]

Perhaps Houston, Johnson, and others called on Memminger at his home on Wentworth Street, just a few blocks away from Johnson's residence on Coming. Perhaps they went to his law office or encountered him at church. Houston and Johnson were certainly not total strangers to Memminger. All three men were active members of Grace Episcopal Church. The church stood on Wentworth, just east of Memminger's home and a few blocks from Johnson's. In 1853 the Memmingers' daughter Fanny was baptized in the church, as was Robert and Sarah Houston's son Richard.[68] Houston, Johnson, and the other twenty or so free colored families among the Grace Church parishioners were familiar faces to Memminger. Perhaps they had a nodding acquaintance, perhaps more.

Exactly what Houston said to Memminger cannot be known, but he was certainly well qualified to speak for, as Johnson put it, "our people." Houston had lived in Charleston for many years working in his tailor shop on King Street a few blocks north of James D. Johnson's shop.[69] Although Houston owned only a modest $2,000 worth of real estate in 1860, his high standing in the free colored community was reflected by his membership in the exclusive Brown Fellowship Society, an organization restricted to fifty of the leading free mulatto men in the city.[70] Possibly Houston was selected by a group of free men of color to thank Memminger, perhaps as they pledged contributions for Memminger's gift. Houston's reputation for respectability and piety would have made his thanks credible to Memminger. Johnson wrote Henry that Memminger received Houston's thanks "very cordially and throws the blame [for the agitation against free Negroes] on the up country members [of the legislature]."[71] Pleased by Houston's remarks, Memminger probably enjoyed the role of protector of the relatively powerless free colored community.

Such cordial, face-to-face exchanges and the bonds of mutual respect they symbolized were common among members of Charleston's free colored elite and leading white families. White men like Memminger were customers of free mulatto men like Houston and Johnson. Doing business with one another and worshiping together, they came to know each other personally. These personal relationships helped bridge the chasm between the races. Powerful white friends gave the free colored elite confidence that their position was secure. Respectable, trusted free persons of color reinforced white leaders' convictions that free Negroes deserved their freedom. However, most whites in Charleston did not have satisfying personal relationships with free Negroes. Johnson, Houston, and Memminger all knew that upcountry legislators were not the only ones behind the campaign to eliminate freedom for Afro-Americans. The most numerous opponents of free Negroes were among the white planters in the upcountry, but the most threatening opponents were among the white workingmen in Charleston.

IN October 1858, just over a year before Memminger's conversation with Houston and Johnson, white workingmen in Charleston organized a campaign to petition the state legislature for relief from competition with slaves. A "large and enthusiastic" group of white mechanics gathered at Masonic Hall on King Street at Wentworth on the evening of October 8 for the purpose, as they announced in an advertisement for the meeting, "of considering matters involving their own interests."[72] The men denounced the "baneful evil" of slaves who hired their own time and complained that the laws prohibiting the practice were "dead letters upon the Statute Book." They resolved to petition the legislature for "more rigid enforcement" of existing laws and for increased penalties for violators.[73] When they presented their petition to the legislature in November, it contained 163 signatures and was supported by resolutions from the Charleston Mechanics' Society, the South Carolina Mechanics' Association, and the Charleston Grand Jury.[74]

Slaves who hired out were a perennial problem for white workingmen in Charleston. Unlike rural planters, many urban employers needed a number of hands for short periods of time to unload a ship, to haul goods between the railroad depot and the wharves, or to work on a construction project. Hiring laborers for the duration of a specific job was economical and practical for these employers. But a man who stacked cotton bales in the hold of a ship one day might be walking the streets of the city the next day, looking for work. For most white workers, unemployment was a familiar experience. Any white laborer could look around the city and see scores of slaves who had been hired to do jobs that might otherwise have gone to whites. Every time a white laborer faced the prospect of losing his job he simultaneously faced slave competition.

Urban masters often found it both convenient and lucrative to hire out their slaves.[75] Especially during the busy fall and winter months when the year's rice and cotton crops funneled through the city on their way to northern and European markets, masters took advantage of the increased demand for laborers and hired out any of their slaves they could do without. By confiscating most or all of the slaves' wages, the masters pocketed cash without selling the slaves or supervising their labor.

Employers were not at all reluctant to hire slaves. They were a handy source of reserve labor, and they could not walk off the job or leave the city, as white workingmen sometimes did. Best of all from the employers' point of view, slaves were usually cheaper to hire. Since their masters were obliged to feed and house them regardless of whether they were hired out, hired slaves did not necessarily need to earn wages that covered the cost of subsistence. Their wages were essentially a cash bonus to their masters, rather than a source of their own livelihood.

Profitable and convenient for masters and employers, slave hiring created severe competition for white workers. Since the eighteenth-century white workingmen had periodically sought to limit slave hiring. Ideally, they wanted to monopolize the labor market. That ideal was impossible to realize since it ran head-on into masters' prerogative to use their slaves in any way they chose, including hiring them out. The most that white workers were able to achieve was a combination of municipal and state laws regulating slave hiring.

In Charleston every slave who was hired out was required to have a badge, purchased annually by his or her owner. The badge law of 1800 limited the number of badges a master could purchase (and hence the number of slaves he or she could hire out) to six.[76] Although that limit was lifted in the city's comprehensive revision of the badge law in 1843, the price of the badges still served as a minor restriction on the number of slaves who were hired out.[77] At seven dollars, a badge for a "handicraft tradesman" was the most expensive; a badge for a carter, a porter, or a day laborer was four dollars.[78] Since the price of a badge was little more than the wages a hired slave would be expected to earn in a week or two, the badge law only discouraged masters from hiring out slaves for a few weeks during the year. The 1843 law may well have increased the number of slaves in the city who were looking for work because, once a master had purchased a badge, he or she stood to gain from having the slave hired out for as much of the year as possible. This indirect incentive for masters to hire out their slaves only applied to Charleston residents. Nonresidents had to pay three times as much for slave badges. From the standpoint of white workingmen in the city, the badge law merely limited their competition to slaves of Charleston residents.

More than it limited slave hiring, the badge law checked the activities of slaves. Hiring loosened the bonds between slave and master. A hired slave had greater freedom of movement in the city than a slave who worked directly under a master's supervision. The badge law, however, made each white person in the city an extension of the hired slave's master. The badge identified the wearer as a slave rather than one of the city's free colored population. Simply by noting the slave's badge number, any white person could report suspicious behavior to the slave's master, since the master's name was recorded, along with the slave's name and occupation, at the time the owner purchased the badge. A master who undermined this system of control by failing to buy a badge for a slave who worked out was subject to a fine of twenty dollars for each offense. An employer who hired a slave without a badge faced a much stiffer fine, twice the cost of the badge for each day he employed the slave.[79] By penalizing the hirer more than the master, the badge law attempted to eliminate illegal employment opportunities rather than hold masters solely responsible for the slaves' actions.

White workingmen were in an ideal position to observe employers who violated the badge law. However, if they ever hoped to be hired by that person, they were unlikely to report the hirer to the authorities. White workers' need for jobs compromised their willingness to insist that the law be enforced to the letter. On balance, the badge law probably did more to cause white workers to chafe at slave competition than it did to limit it.

Of far greater potential significance to white workingmen were laws prohibiting the slaves from hiring their own time. A master who wanted to hire out a slave was supposed to negotiate directly with the hirer about the terms of the slave's employment. If a slave carpenter, for example, reached an agreement about work and wages with an employer without the intervention of his master, then the slave was hiring his own time. He was, in a sense, participating in the labor market as if he were free. A municipal ordinance of 1796 prohibited slave mechanics from hiring their own time and an 1822 law extended the ban to all male slaves.[80] A master who violated the 1822 law was subject to the extreme penalty of forfeiting any slave who was allowed to hire his own time. This stringent sanction promised to benefit white workingmen in Charleston by making it impractical for masters to hire out their slaves for short periods of time. To comply with the law, a master had to act as an employment agent for his slaves. As soon as one job ended, the master needed to find the slave another one, a burdensome, time-consuming chore that made the whole hiring-out process considerably less attractive to masters. On the face of it, the law should have worked to reduce the number of slaves who were hired out and to open up a corresponding number of jobs to white workingmen.

Because the law was rarely enforced, it had no such effect. The law was not intended to benefit white workers but to prevent slaves from having the freedom of movement and association that, as the Vesey conspiracy vividly proved, could threaten the peace and security of the community. As the memory of the Vesey conspiracy faded, the initial motivation for the prohibition on slaves hiring their own time lapsed, and the law fell into disuse. In 1849 the legislature amended the 1822 law to prohibit all slaves—male and female—from hiring their own time, and to reduce the penalty for an offending slaveowner to a fine of fifty dollars.[81] Yet even this law was neglected. Speeding its neglect was the cumbersome procedure it required masters to follow in hiring out their slaves. While the liberties allowed to slaves who hired their own time were potentially dangerous to white society, they were in practice quite convenient for the slaves' owners. The principal effect of the ban on slaves hiring their own time was to create a thriving black market in slave labor, supported by slaveowners and employers who winked at the impractical law. When white workingmen complained in their October 1858 meeting that the laws regulating slave hiring were dead letters, they knew what they were talking about.

White mechanics' attempts to protect themselves from slave competition were hindered by their small numbers in the state and the specialized nature of their concerns. Most white men lived in the country, and their problems were far removed from the hiring practices in the streets of Charleston. Rural slaveholders were also inordinately sensitive to any move to limit their prerogatives as masters. Furthermore, every white workingman could avoid slave competition by leaving for the North. The turnover among white workingmen in the city was compounded by the seasonal job market in the city, as hundreds of white laborers migrated South for the winter, then left during the spring and summer lull. Many of these men were recent immigrants from Ireland or Germany, which distanced them from the native-born majority of the state.[82] Working under these handicaps, Charleston's white mechanics did not succeed before 1858 in altering the laws or the practices of slave hiring.

By then, important changes had prepared the way for a new attempt. During the 1850s the city acquired a white majority for the first time in its history. The high price of cotton and continued expansion into the fertile lands of the Southwest created a strong demand for slave labor, pushing the prices of slaves to new highs. Urban masters in Charleston and other Southern cities sold many of their slaves, a large number of whom had probably been hired out.[83] Between 1850 and 1860 the slave population of Charleston fell by more than 5,600 while the city's white population increased by more than 3,300. Thirty years earlier slaves made up 51 percent of the city's population, whites, 42 percent.[84] Now the balance had reversed. In 1860 slaves comprised 34 percent of the city's inhabitants, whites, 58 percent. There were nearly 10,000 more whites than slaves in the city. Never before had whites so greatly outnumbered slaves on the Charleston peninsula. Racially, Charleston had become an enclave of the upcountry in the low country, where slaves outnumbered whites five to one. Actually, the city had become even whiter than the upcountry, where in 1860 whites were still a minority.

As white workingmen took over some of the jobs previously done by slaves, the new racial balance in the city was visible to all. When Yankee author John W. DeForrest visited Charleston in 1855, he wrote his brother that "the crowd of porters & coachmen that met us on the dock presented not above half a dozen black faces. Instead I saw the familiar Irish & German visages whom I could have met on a dock at Boston or New York." A Charleston friend explained to DeForrest that "This was different years ago . . . and it is only lately that the whites have begun to crowd the blacks out of the more responsible lower employments."[85] Whether white workingmen crowded out blacks or filled a vaccuum created by the departure of slaves who were sold away mattered less than the new importance of white mechanics in the life of the city. Aspiring politicians courted them, proslavery ideologues calculated their loyalty to slavery, and Southern nationalists hoped they would buttress the South's independence by manning shops that would produce the goods currently imported from the North.

White mechanics in Charleston seemed to hold the key to the city's economic expansion. Newspaper commentators argued that if the city was to regain the prosperity it had enjoyed thirty years earlier, domestic industry had to be encouraged. Southern-built steam engines should power Southern-built rice mills and cotton gins. Southern-built railroad cars should roll on Southern-built rails connecting backcountry plantations to the Charleston harbor. To complete the connection, the city contracted with the local foundry of James M. Eason to dredge the channel leading from the harbor to the open sea, removing the mud and sand that clogged Charleston's artery of trade with the world.[86] By the late 1850s the city's economic fate was literally in the hands of the city's white mechanics.

Leaders of the white workingmen recognized that they were in a strong position to try once again to limit competition with slaves. A few weeks after the sixty-seventh anniversary meeting of the Charleston Mechanics' Society in February 1858, the city council entertained a proposal to forbid slaves to hire their own time.[87] The text of the proposal has not survived, but more than likely it was an attempt to restrict the black market in slave hiring and to increase the penalties for both slaveowners and hirers. Exactly what precipitated the proposal is uncertain, but the current economic downturn in the North may well have been a contributing factor.[88] As unemployed laborers from Northern cities flocked south looking for work in the winter of 1857–58, they intensified the competition for existing jobs in Charleston and other Southern cities. As competition increased among whites, workingmen again envied the jobs held by hired slaves. They argued that the way to increase the number of jobs for white men was not to restrict the immigration of white laborers but to prevent employers from hiring black market slave laborers. When the city council debated and voted on the mechanics' proposal in May, they rejected it by postponing it indefinitely. The correspondent of the *Mercury* found the "long and able discussion" of the proposal "one of the most interesting debates of the present Council" but concluded that since the bill did not pass, "We do not now conceive that the public interest would be benefitted by . . . publication [of the debate]."[89]

Stymied by the council in the spring, the white mechanics were struck in the fall by a yellow fever epidemic that raged through the city for three months. Yellow fever deaths of whites climbed from 6 in the second week of August to 122 in the second week of September and then slowly declined back to 6 by the second week of November.[90] In that period, 645 whites died from the disease. Hundreds more were stricken and eventually recovered. At the height of the epidemic, the

Howard Association, a charitable organization devoted to providing medical aid and relief to needy sufferers and their families, noted that "As we are all aware, it is the laboring class of our community, whose life is one long battle with want, that the scourge whose ravages we now deplore affects most severely."[91] Five out of six of those who died were newcomers to Charleston. Immigrants from Ireland and Germany were especially hard-hit.[92] Nearly 300 representatives of the Howard Association visited the homes of the sick throughout the city. They solicited contributions from the community and raised almost $20,000 to aid the victims. The city council set aside Thursday, September 23, as a day of humiliation and prayer for relief from the plague.[93] But the deaths continued for another six weeks.

In starkest terms, the epidemic dramatized the common plight of white workingmen. Poor white laborers did what they could to help themselves, their families, and their friends. Nursing a sick friend during the weeks of the epidemic, taking in a widowed mother and her children, sharing a meager board, and other acts of self-help reinforced the solidarity of white workingmen and reaffirmed the necessity of cooperation and sacrifice. The work of the Howard Association reminded the larger white community of the poverty and suffering in their midst, generated sympathy and contributions for relief, and fostered a mutual awareness of the interdependence of white mechanics and all other white Charlestonians. And, as hundreds of poor white laborers lay sick and dying, their jobs were filled by blacks, who were almost immune to yellow fever. During the entire three months of the epidemic, only thirty-one blacks died from the disease, fewer than the number of whites who died each week between mid-August and mid-October.[94] For every Negro who succumbed to yellow fever, twenty-one whites died. The epidemic made it more urgent than ever for white workingmen to consider "matters involving their own interests," as they did in their meeting in Masonic Hall early in October while the epidemic waned.[95]

Four out of five of the men who signed the petition framed in that meeting were common laborers or tradesmen.[96] Twenty other signers had nonmanual occupations. Some, like John Gotgen, who ran a grocery and barroom at the corner of East

Bay and Tradd, catered to white mechanics. A few employed them, like L. F. LeBleux, a civil engineer and architect at the new Custom House, which was under construction. At least nine signers worked there, including three carpenters, a stone cutter, a clerk, a foreman, and several laborers. Although the petitioners were not entirely confined to the working class, support for white mechanics was almost entirely confined to working-class neighborhoods.

The petitioners included virtually none of the wealthy planters, merchants, and lawyers in the city and very few of the prosperous white tradesmen. Only seven signers owned $5,000 or more, and more than three-quarters were property-less.[97] Just a handful of the signers owned slaves. More than 1,200 slaveholders lived in the city, but only four of them signed the white mechanics' petition.[98] That, it became clear, was the crux of the mechanics' problem.

The mechanics proposed two bills to the legislature. The more moderate bill asked that the penalty on the owner of a slave who hired his own time be extended to the employer and that the fine for each violation be doubled to $100. The more drastic measure prohibited slaves from working at any "mechanical pursuit" and from being hired out, either on their own or by their master. After considering the bills, the Committee on the Colored Population issued a report that was printed in pamphlet form and reprinted in the Charleston newspapers.[99] The report embodied the sober reflections of the state's elected leaders on the problems of Charleston's white mechanics.

According to the committee, neither of the bills fully grasped the nature of the problem of slave hiring. The white mechanics complained "that slaves are permitted to go at large, exercise all the privileges of free persons, make contracts, do work, and in every way live and conduct themselves as if they were not slaves." The committee agreed that this was an "evil" but asserted that the character of the evil was "more general than the specific one" of slave competition. "The evil lies in the breaking down of the relation between master and slave," the committee announced. The breakdown resulted in "the removal of the slave from the master's discipline and control, and the assumption of freedom and independence, on the part of the slave, the idleness, disorder and crime which are consequential, and the necessity thereby created for additional police regulations to keep them in subjection and order, and the trouble and expense which they involve." Despite these evils, the committee concluded that it was impossible to provide the remedy proposed by the white workingmen. "We are, as a slaveholding people, habituated to slave labor," they said. Yet in the "towns and villages" of the state there was "ordinary labor . . . to be performed which can be done either by whites or negroes." To agree to the mechanics' more radical proposal or even to enforce "to the full" the existing laws against slave hiring "would create a revolution." It would "drive away all slave labor from any employment in the towns and villages of the State."[100]

The committee's reasoning directly contradicted their diagnosis of the evil as the collapse of the relation between master and slave. In effect, they said that labor would be driven away if masters were required to maintain close supervision of their slaves. "It would be impossible to have this sort of slave labor, if there must be a contract with the owner for every specific job—as for instance, the transportation of a load in a wagon or dray, the carrying of a passenger's trunk to or from a railroad, &c." In short, although slave hiring made it more difficult to control the slave population, masters could not be expected to conform to the impractical demands of the law against slaves hiring their own time. "The subject . . . is full of difficulty, and until you can change the direction of the public prejudice, prepossession and habit, you can never enforce a law which conflicts with them."[101]

The committee recommended that, as the white mechanics asked, the penalty for violations of the existing laws be extended to employers, but they did not recommend an increased fine. Worse, from the point of view of the mechanics, the committee recommended gutting the existing laws by exempting from the prohibition on slaves hiring their own time those slaves who worked as domestic servants, common laborers, porters, draymen, wagoners, carters, or stevedores—in sum, most of the slaves with whom Charleston's white workingmen competed.[102] In essence, the committee proposed to make the law conform to everyday practice. Rather than providing white mechanics with relief from slave competition, they offered slaveowners relief from inconvenient laws. The recommendations made clear what the committee meant when it said that the white mechanics had only a limited understanding of the problem. Despite the committee's recommendations, none of the proposals came to a vote in the 1858 session of the legislature, and all were carried over to the next session. The bills were considered again in 1859, along with the bills to enslave free Negroes, and again they were shelved for reconsideration in 1860.

Thwarted by the legislature, the white workingmen went back to the Charleston City Council to try to overrule the Committee on the Colored Population's endorsement of slave-hiring practices. In mid-January 1860, just two weeks after Robert Houston and James M. Johnson thanked Memminger for his defense of free people of color, Alderman John Kenifick, a druggist, introduced an ordinance that banned slaves from hiring their own time, with $50 fines for both master and employer.[103] The council referred the proposal to a special committee composed of Kenifick, E. W. Edgerton, a wealthy Broad Street draper and tailor, and William Ravenal, a rich East Bay merchant. After deliberating for six weeks, the special committee reported at the end of February that passage of the proposed ordinance would be "both inexpedient and improper."[104]

Their reasoning echoed that of the Committee on the Colored Population. The proposal was inexpedient because, "In all large cities, the successful prosecution of trade and commerce requires a great number of laborers, by the day or by the hour, and during the business season. They are generally employed and constantly changing their employers; at times, almost everyone engaged in business are *[sic]* obliged to employ *this* kind of labor, but very few require it permanently." If the proposed ordinance were adopted, the committee pointed out, "stevedores, barbers, chimney-sweeps, wood sawyers, and laborers, who are slaves, would be stopped, and the business thrown into other hands." That, of course, was precisely the point of the white mechanics' proposal. But, the committee argued, the proposal would inconvenience families as well as businesses. "Mantua makers, nurses, seamstresses, and washerwomen must necessarily change their employment, and [white] families would be compelled to seek another source to supply their places. . . ." Furthermore, if the proposal were enacted, "the evident result would be the depreciation of slave labor, which your Committee are of the opinion is by no means desirable." In fact, the proposal was improper because "The slave is the property of the owner, and like all other property which he holds, subject to his own management and control."[105] The members of the committee, all of them slaveholders, utterly rejected the white mechanics' request. The council accepted the report and gave semiofficial local approval to the existing black market in slave hiring.

For their efforts at the state and local levels, white workingmen in Charleston had obtained less than nothing. Not only were their proposed remedies denied, but so were their grievances. Although the mechanics had the law on their side, the legislature and the city council agreed that the law had to be violated to carry on the business of the city and to protect the rights of masters. By trying to reduce slave competition, white workingmen came into open conflict with slaveowners, a battle that, seen in retrospect, they were sure to lose. Having failed to penetrate slaveowners' defense of slave-hiring practices, white mechanics shifted their attack. They turned to competitors who were much less numerous but much more vulnerable.

White workingmen did not entirely overlook free Negroes in their 1858 campaign in the state legislature. The mechanics' petition did not mention free people of color, but the presentment of the Charleston Grand Jury linked slave hiring and "the practice so extensively prevailing among free persons of color—carrying on business on their own account, making contracts for the erection of houses and other undertakings" as "evils which demand the prompt intervention of the law."[106] The resolution of the South Carolina Mechanics' Association also complained about competition with free Negroes. It asked the legislature to impose a tax on free persons of color or to enact "some other remedy . . . that shall at least place us in such a position that we may be able to compete with them, if they are to be on an equality with us."[107] Neither request was incorporated into the proposed laws, which dealt only with slave hiring. That reflected the secondary importance of free Negro competition to Charleston's white mechanics. It was troublesome and annoying but not ruinous.

Free people of color were less important competitors than slaves because there were fewer of them in the city. Slaves outnumbered free Negroes more than four to one in 1860, and the ratio had been even higher in earlier years. Free men and women of color were also clustered a notch higher on the occupational scale than slaves who were hired out. Most hired slaves worked as common laborers or domestics, and only a small but important fraction worked as skilled tradesmen.[108] Among free people of color in Charleston, the pattern was the reverse.

Like the Ellisons in Stateburg, most free men of color in Charleston made their living as artisans. In 1860 more than two-thirds of Charleston's free men of color were skilled tradesmen.[109] Carpenters were the most numerous (139), tailors were a distant second (55), and ranking in descending order were painters (24), barbers (22), butchers (22), bricklayers (19), shoemakers (19), and blacksmiths (16). Fewer than one out of five free men of color worked as common laborers.[110] Only one man in twenty had a nonmanual occupation as a shopkeeper. A similar pattern prevailed in New Orleans, but it contrasted sharply with the occupations of free Afro-Americans in Northern cities, where about three-quarters of them worked as common laborers.[111]

Free women of color in Charleston also exhibited this distinctive occupational profile.[112] Six out of ten were dressmakers, mantua makers, seamstresses, or other skilled needleworkers. The rest either worked as laundresses (24 percent) or as other domestic servants (13 percent), together composing almost twice the proportion of free Afro-American men in the city who were at the bottom of the occupational ladder. Still, the women, like the men, were far more frequently employed at skilled crafts than were free women of color elsewhere in the state.

Between 1850 and 1860 the number of free colored artisans in the city had increased modestly by 14 percent, from 370 to 420.[113] The number of carpenters increased by 38, more than any other trade. The number of painters increased by 12, bakers by 11. The number of other tradesmen, such as bricklayers, butchers, and blacksmiths, increased less, while the number of millwrights, barbers, and wheelwrights stayed about the same or declined slightly. The number of shoemakers, however, declined by half, and the number of tailors fell by more than a third. This net, though uneven, growth in the number of free Afro-American tradesmen in the city indicates that white artisans made few inroads during the 1850s in crafts occupied by free colored tradesmen. White mechanics' complaints about free Negro competition, like those about slave competition, arose not from men who were being encroached upon but from men who wanted to encroach.

Free people of color not only blocked the occupational aspirations of white workingmen but were also the focus of more complex class and racial resentments. Since free Afro-Americans in Charleston were not required to wear badges or any other sign of their status, white workingmen often mistook them for slaves. When a white mechanic reported what he thought was a slave working without the badge required by law, the person would often turn out to be free. This source of confusion was complicated by the numerous Afro-Americans in the city who had been illegally freed after the 1820 ban on manumission. Although these individuals were technically slaves and subject to the city's badge law, they could evade the law by establishing their free status, typically by showing their receipt for the capitation tax on free Negroes.[114] Or, if the person had not paid the capitation tax but could in some other way satisfy city officials that he or she was free, the individual could pay the tax with a penalty and, again, foil the white person's attempt to enforce the badge law. From the perspective of white workingmen, the distinction between slavery and freedom was a slippery technicality protected by the willful blindness of many slaveowners to the legal prohibitions on manumission and slaves hiring their own time.

City law enforcement officials—the police and the mayor, who presided over the court that heard cases involving slaves and free persons of color—responded to the white mechanics' grievances with crackdowns on Afro-Americans suspected of violating the capitation tax or slave badge laws. When white workingmen petitioned for relief from slave competition in

October 1858, city police arrested fifty-three free persons of color for failure to pay the capitation tax, after having made only five such arrests in the previous four months.[115] After the October crackdown, police made only sporadic arrests for capitation tax violations, averaging less than three per month until December 1859, when the repressive free Negro laws were debated in Columbia. Then, while James M. Johnson was celebrating a peaceful Christmas in the city, police swept up thirty-two free persons of color for not paying the capitation tax.

Both crackdowns were evidently timed to reassure white workingmen that city officials were sensitive to their demands. During those same months, police also arrested slaves who were working out without badges. But for every two such slaves arrested in the months between October 1858 and December 1859, three free persons of color were picked up, even though slaves vastly outnumbered free Negroes. The crackdowns hit free Afro-Americans harder partly because whites were sometimes confused about their status but mostly because they were more vulnerable. A free man of color who failed to pay the capitation tax had to pay his own taxes and fines. The fine for a slave arrested for violation of the badge law was assessed against the slave's master, who had many ways to make the process of collecting difficult and unpleasant for city officials.

THE vulnerability of free Afro-Americans and the deep resentments many whites felt toward them were rooted in the same simple fact: they were Negroes who were free. Unlike slaves, they did not have a powerful class of whites with a compelling personal interest in protecting them. In addition, they refused to act like slaves. Even in the explosive racial climate following the raid on Harpers Ferry, they insisted on exercising their freedom. Their behavior rankled many whites and sparked intensified scrutiny of free people of color throughout the South.

In Charleston, some whites still saw free Negroes as the heirs of Denmark Vesey. One planter pointed out that Harpers Ferry was "no insurrection but an invasion of abolitionists and free negroes" and warned that only by constant vigilance could whites prevent free persons of color from tampering with slaves.[116] In mid-December a group of white Charlestonians formed a Committee of Safety to search out and arrest "all Abolition sympathizers and emissaries."[117] A member of the committee pointed out the numerous activities in the city that were potentially subversive, such as the "negro schools kept by white persons," the Northern papers received every week by free people of color, the circulation among the city's Afro-American population of an illustrated life of John Brown, and Yankee pedlers "publicly expressing their peculiar opinions."[118] Although some white Charlestonians ridiculed the Committee of Safety for overreacting, Harpers Ferry proved to many whites that "A free negro in a slave country is a natural incendiary."[119]

Despite the shortage of inflammatory behavior by free people of color in Charleston, anxious whites saw plenty of evidence that they were not staying in their place. Many whites felt that city officials and the white community in general had become too lenient about Negroes' abuses of law and propriety. The importance of their views was magnified by the election campaign for mayor and city councilmen that was under way as the news of Harpers Ferry reached the city. Several writers catalogued Afro-Americans' transgressions in a series of letters in the newspapers. The letters sizzled with racial hostility. Was it wise to permit Negroes to have "privileges"?

One slaveholder declared that every day he observed open violations of the laws. He saw "crowds of black children who throng our streets every morning on their way to school . . . the crowds who congregate at nightly 'sittings up' . . . negro visitors to northern cities and watering places, who go and come regularly every season under the *very eye* of the *law*, and who return, possibly, with the personal acquaintance of the black Douglas *[sic]* and the white Greeley . . . [and] violations of State laws and civil ordinances in regard to the liquor traffic with slaves." All these illegal activities could be repressed by enforcing existing laws. There remained, however, the perfectly legal, but still offensive, social behavior of Negroes in the city. What about "the 'nuptials of *blacks*' [which] are celebrated in a spacious temple of the most High—where a bridal party of a score and ten in numbers are transported to this

modern centre of fashion and false philanthropy in gay equipages—and where hundreds of others, robed in extravagant
costumes, witness, possibly with eyeglass in hand, this the
dawn of a new fashioned sentiment, and where harangues are
delivered on 'rights'?"[120]

Another slaveholder catalogued the offenses of free Negroes.
He argued that the 1820 ban on manumission "is daily violated in spirit and in fact, both through the aid of negro class
societies and associations, and also by the aid of our own
citizens." He asked why "the slave of yesterday is the master
of today . . . traveling with impunity North and South, and
entering successfully into competition with the worthy white
citizen for the best patronage of the city—made the subjects
of editorial puff and notice, and driving through our thoroughfares in stylish equipages, rivalling those of the less favored
white man."[121] The alarming erosion of racial boundaries could
be seen everywhere, another Charlestonian said. He asked,
"Why our public hacks, in the hands of negroes, aye, and
some white men, are daily filled with black and mulatto males
and females, slaves and free, indulging in the privilege of taking the air, in violation of known public sentiment? Why are
they permitted to attend balls, churches, and funerals in carriages, to assume to themselves prerogatives and distinctions
which have been, and ought to be, among the landmarks separating the classes?" The problem with Charleston's Afro-
Americans was that they were uppity. "Shall the slave and free
negroes be permitted to lay aside all respect, and put all proper
restraint at defiance. Shall they, in silks and laces, promenade
our principal thoroughfares, with the arrogance of equals—
by their insolent bearing making the modest lady yield them
on the walk, and the poor white woman to feel that to be
virtuous and honest gives her place, in appearances, below
the slaves, in the gratification of her desire for dress and distinction?" In 1859 these questions were more potent than ever.
Racial identity shared by the demure lady and the poor white
woman was the basis of the South's political solidarity. If the
poor white woman felt humiliated by Negroes, would she
and her husband conclude that the problem was the slaves?
Or the masters? The writer asked if the provocative behavior
of Negroes continued to be tolerated by city officials, "Is it

thus that the institution is to be strengthened in public esteem, and made to conduce to the general welfare and benefit of the whole community?"[122]

These sentiments propelled the crackdown on free Negroes in Charleston in December 1859, following Mayor Charles Macbeth's reelection in November. They also contributed to the urgency of the state legislature's December debates about enslaving free persons of color. Moreover, they signaled a shift in the political balance favorable to white workingmen. So long as white mechanics sought protection from slave competition, they aligned themselves in opposition to slaveholders, the most powerful class in Southern society. When the white workingmen began to turn their attention to free people of color, they found large and influential segments of the white community lining up with them. In the winter of 1859–60, as white workingmen were learning once again the futility of contesting with slaveholders, they were also beginning to sense the promise in the repeated appeals for white solidarity. White mechanics were becoming more important to other white Charlestonians than ever before. The sectional crisis made it imperative for white Southerners to stand together against their enemies. The need for white unity strengthened the claims of the white mechanics, so long as they directed their attack against free Negroes rather than slaves. For this reason, the enslavement proposals debated in the legislature in December 1859 were not simply the latest in a series of crackdowns, as James M. Johnson concluded. Instead, they were the beginning of a new era of searching analysis of the place of free Afro-Americans in a slave society under siege.

At the beginning of 1860 white Charlestonians were on edge, alert to dangers they sensed were all around them, yet greeting them with all too familiar faces. How much freedom should they allow free Afro-Americans? Not enough, the city council decided in December 1859, to attend Donnetti and Wood's troupe of performing dogs, monkeys, and goats at the Charleston Theater or to see Archibald McKenzie's exhibit of trained canaries.[123] But it was acceptable, they decided in January 1860, to allow free Negroes to enjoy Rumsey's and Newcomb's Band of Campbell Minstrels.[124] If the logic behind these distinctions was ineffable, it was nevertheless clear that the spotlight was on Charleston's free Afro-Americans. Whites watched their actions, noticed their gestures, monitored their expressions, and pondered their loyalties. When the Grand Jury met early in January 1860, it declared a nuisance the common practice of free persons of color and slaves riding in public carriages, often driven by white men. The Grand Jury noted that this reversal of racial roles was "loudly complained of by all classes of our [white] citizens; it is proper that the line of demarcation between the castes should be clear and distinct, more particularly at this time. . . . It is fully time that slaves and free persons of color should know and understand their position. . . ."[125]

Whites throughout the state shared the grand jury's concern. Late in November 1859 a well-attended public meeting in Sumter (the new name of Sumterville) unanimously supported a resolution urging the legislature to prevent slaves from hiring their own time. The Sumterians declared their determination "to ferret out and rid us of every element in our social system which is inimical to the safety and perpetuity of our institutions." The citizens of Sumter had a specific element in mind, one "countenanced by law" yet one that "lurks under a covering . . . concealed from observation," namely, the "free colored population of our country." The assembled white men, who included J. S. Richardson and J. D. Frierson, looked upon free Negroes as a "dangerous and inimical element—an element at once the parent of idleness, of dissatisfaction, of vice and crime among our slaves." They asked the legislature "to devise a plan, whereby in the course of time, we may free ourselves of its dangers, and our institutions of its pestilential influence."[126]

Three weeks later the agitation struck even closer to "Wisdom Hall." On December 10, 1859, white men gathered in a public meeting in Stateburg to form an association to prevent tampering with their slaves. Similar meetings were held elsewhere in Sumter District. The Stateburgians formed a committee to which suspicious persons could be reported. The committee was supposed to examine such troublemakers, particularly when the evidence against them was not strong enough to stand up in a regularly constituted court. The committee was composed of Ellison's white neighbors and customers: Dr. W. W. Anderson, B. Moody, W. Sanders, I. N. Lenoir, and J. N. Frierson.[127] Although Ellison had no reason to believe these men suspected him, he could not ignore the racial tension crackling through the village.

IN Charleston, whites who defended free Afro-Americans emphasized the social value of their intermediate status. As Memminger pointed out in the legislative debate on enslavement, free Negroes stood between slaves and whites and, as the foiled Vesey conspiracy had shown, could be counted upon to identify with the interests of whites rather than blacks. Free Afro-Americans were intermediate in another crucial way, some white Charlestonians began to acknowledge privately in the midst of the white mechanics' campaign against slave competition.

In December 1858, as the proposals to restrict or eliminate slave hiring were before the legislature, Alfred Huger, the postmaster of Charleston and member of one of the city's most aristocratic families, wrote a friend that the legislature was taking up "every foolish remedy for Evils connected with the free colour'd population!"[128] The supposed evils did not exist, Huger said. He defended free Negroes as a valuable buffer between whites and slaves. "I believe there is not a better intermediate class in the world than the free colour'd people in this city[;] they are singularly respectable[;] they are our natural allies, tho they can never be our Equals[;] they make an insurmountable barrier between the right of the master and the sedition of the slave." Even more important to Huger, free people of color stood between working-class whites and the white gentry. "They are a check upon the insolence and profligacy that is poured out upon us by every ship that comes here, either from Ireland or the North and they create a becoming respect for the higher classes, or I should say better classes," he wrote. Free Afro-Americans worked hard and, unlike white mechanics, had the merit of being disfranchised. "Although they are degraded themselves," Huger noted, "they work faithfully and more economically than those [white men] who would supplant them. They are in many instances worthy and pious people who acquire property by their own industry and who having *no votes* are not bought and sold as is the case with their persecutors and enemies." Free Negroes, he declared, "are the last remnant or speck in our society not injured themselves and not inflicting injury upon the Public by the 'general suffrage law.' "[129]

Huger believed that manhood suffrage produced "the deep and burning injustice of giving men without property, the privilege of deciding how far property *can* bear to be taxed."[130] A few years earlier he had supported a conservative candidate for governor because, he wrote a friend, "Those who have *no* Property are already sufficiently willing to be the Enemies of those who *have*. In a country like ours, it is of the last importance to protect the landholder and the slaveholder!"[131] To Huger, the white mechanics' attack on slave hiring was a perfect example of the general problem. "The Eternal meddling between a Master and his slave, by saying how the slave shall be hired or used, it is only a domestic 'Higher Law' in disguise," he wrote. In fact, Huger often allowed his own slaves to hire themselves out. In the spring of 1858, for example, he sent two of his mulatto carpenters, Ned and George, to look for work.[132] But Huger's fear of the politics of white workingmen extended beyond his personal self-interest. At bottom he believed white mechanics threatened the stability of slave society. They had "no sympathy for the Negroe . . . [and] treat him not as an humble friend but as the deadliest Enemy." Compared to white mechanics, Huger believed, the anti-slavery politician William H. "Seward and his gang are innocent."[133]

Free Negroes were a valuable intermediate class precisely because they posed no such threats. They had the supreme virtue of being a working class that was politically docile. "They are attached to the soil and they confer a greater benefit upon the community than any other men who receive so little," Huger observed. "They are the most easily managed and controul'd—and when you consider them as a people who are disfranchised forever—not daring even to ask for political privileges, yet paying their taxes with punctuality and humility, it does seem to me at variance with all justice and mercy and subversive of our true policy thus to tyrranize [*sic*] over them or crush them."[134]

To Huger and other aristocratic whites in Charleston, free

people of color were an ideal working class. Unlike slaves, they were respectable, hard-working, skilled, pious, and loyal. Yet like slaves, they were Negroes, and thus could never aspire to full participation in society as the equals of whites. That made them the "natural allies" of the "better classes" of whites, for they had a common enemy in the white working class, whose aspirations were exactly those closed to free Negroes. White mechanics' votes gave them the political opportunity to pursue their goals and to resist being "easily managed and controul'd" by their social betters. The white mechanics' campaign to limit slave competition by interfering with slave-hiring practices brought home to Charleston's white aristocrats the dangers of class conflict and the virtues of free people of color.

In 1858 and 1859 Charleston's white leaders successfully defended both existing slave-hiring practices and the existing intermediate position of free Negroes. In 1860, as the sectional crisis deepened, they began to reexamine their political alliances. In the end, they were forced to choose whether their greater enemy was among the white mechanics in Charleston or the "Black Republicans" in the North. The fate of the city's free people of color hung on their choice.

Just before Christmas in 1859, James M. Johnson was confident that their choice would be what it had always been during his lifetime, that "nothing would be done affecting our position."[135] His father agreed. He planned to travel to Toronto during the coming year to visit his son Charley, to see the sights, and to celebrate his retirement. For a free man of color to leave the state and return risked the legal punishment of enslavement. James D. Johnson's plans are a measure of the confidence with which he and other members of the free mulatto elite faced the new year. Their white friends would continue to defend them and they would ride out the attacks on their freedom just as they had in the past.

VI

The Middle Ground

THREE times during the twelve months beginning in April 1860 the nation's attention focused on Charleston. Each time events in the city severed yet another tie between the South and the rest of the country. When the Democratic party convened in Charleston late in April 1860, Southern delegates bolted and split the only national political party into two separate parties, each appealing to a sectional constituency. About seven months later, after the November elections gave Abraham Lincoln the victory, secessionists in South Carolina organized a campaign to lead the South out of the Union, a campaign that culminated in Charleston late in December with the passage of the state's ordinance of secession. During the next five months, as six other slave states followed South Carolina, sectional tensions stretched to the breaking point. In mid-April 1861 the uneasy peace finally ended when the shore batteries opened fire on Fort Sumter in Charleston harbor and plunged the nation into full-scale civil war. In no other twelve-month period before or since have events in Charleston been so important in the life of the nation.

The Democrats came to Charleston in April 1860 hoping to repeat their 1856 success. At their convention that year in Cincinnati they nominated James Buchanan to head the ticket, to the dismay of some Southern Democrats who had hoped for a candidate more closely identified with the South. To placate Southerners and promote party harmony, the party's committee on the national convention decided to meet in 1860 in the heart of the South, in Charleston. In the fall elections in 1856, Buchanan proved to be the ideal Democratic candidate, a Northern man with Southern principles. He won with the support of five Northern states and every Southern state except Maryland. Another Democratic victory seemed within reach in 1860 if the party could nominate a candidate on a platform that appealed to Southern Democrats without alienating too many Northern Democrats. In Charleston, however, the Democrats' Southern strategy fell apart. When Southern delegates failed to obtain a platform plank that guaranteed federal protection of slavery in the territories, most of them walked out of the convention. Their supporters in Charleston applauded the move and filled the seceders' empty seats in the convention hall with bouquets of fresh flowers. Unable to heal the rift or nominate a candidate, the convention adjourned in early May. The remaining delegates left Charleston hoping that time would allow the party to reunite and to choose a nominee in harmony when the delegates reconvened in Baltimore in June.[1]

From his vantage point in Charleston, James M. Johnson watched the Democratic convention, but he kept his distance. He did not want to satisfy his curiosity at the risk of arousing the suspicion of the police and possibly being thrown in jail, staining his good reputation. Two weeks before the convention began, the city added seventy-five men to the police force of 150 to keep an eye on the expected crowds and on the gamblers, thieves, and pickpockets they were sure to attract. As convention visitors disembarked from steamers and made their way along the wharves into the city, they passed under the gaze of uniformed mounted policemen armed with swords, pistols, and instructions to bar entry to undesirables.[2] Although Johnson was no threat to the good order of the city, he was a colored man, and he took care to stay away from the center of convention activities at Institute Hall on Meeting Street and the nearby Mills House and Hibernian Hall, where many of the delegates stayed. The day the convention began, the police passed Johnson's tailor shop twice "making arrests of suspicious & rowdy characters," he wrote Henry Ellison. Prudently, Johnson kept off the streets as much as possible. He wrote Henry, "If you have lost the Rights you ought to find solace in making a Retreat from the Heat," a statement that could almost stand as a general description of the defensive political posture of the free Afro-American community.[3]

Keeping a low profile did not prevent Johnson from enjoying the excitement the convention brought to Charleston. He followed the formal proceedings of the convention in the daily reports in the local newspapers, which he then forwarded to the Ellisons in Stateburg. He kept up with the far more interesting unofficial activities of the conventioneers through reports from acquaintances, both Negro and white, who dropped by his tailor shop. He heard about the numerous public concerts of Boston's Gilmore Brass Band, which came to Charleston with the New England delegation. An old free man of color told him about a local militia unit that marched to the railroad depot to celebrate the opening of the Charleston and Savannah Railroad and to salute Fernando Wood, the mayor of New York City, who was campaigning for the Democratic nomination. Curious about the increased business Charleston's hotel and saloon keepers anticipated from the convention, Johnson monitored reports that at the beginning the convention crowd was thin and the city's merchants had to reduce prices they had only recently jacked up. After the convention was under way, business was as brisk as expected, and Johnson heard that the convention district on Meeting Street was jammed with people around the clock. At a speech to the crowd in front of the Mills House hotel one evening, General John Schnierle—a neighbor of Johnson's and a former mayor of Charleston—objected to the remarks of a Virginian and, Johnson was told, threatened to beat the man with a stick. Johnson savored the rumor, partially corroborated by a report in the *Mercury,* but he did not take the political speechifying too seriously. A man who witnessed the incident told Johnson that one man "got up & delivered himself thus, 'What fools we are. Here we are in Convention & what is it all but Humbug, Humbug,' & sat down." Johnson half-seriously noted that "Allowance must be made for them that after imbibing hot punches, inhaling fresh air will confuse one's ideas."[4]

The one public festivity Johnson personally witnessed during the convention was the annual parade of the city's volunteer fire companies. Virtually the entire city turned out to watch the uniformed white firemen march beside their brightly decorated engines.[5] In such a large and local crowd Johnson and other Afro-American Charlestonians could safely enjoy the occasion, despite the vigilant police.

Not every free man of color in Charleston was as circumspect as Johnson. On the second day of the convention William P. Dacoster, a prominent free mulatto machinist, was so drunk on King Street that he was arrested and "pulled thro the streets to the Guard House," Johnson reported to Henry, who knew Dacoster.[6] The authorities fined Dacoster and allowed him to go free the next day, thanks to the intervention of his neighbor, James Johnston (not Johnson), a free mulatto tailor who, like Henry and Reuben Ellison, had married one of Thomas S. Bonneau's daughters. But Dacoster was soon drunk again and stayed drunk. He "disgraced his family," Johnson noted, adding, "His wife is to be pitied."[7] Johnson's reproach suggested that he also felt Dacoster's indiscreet behavior reflected unfavorably on the entire free colored community, especially when they were under such close scrutiny.

When the Democratic convention adjourned without making a nomination, Johnson accurately reported to Henry that the seceding delegates were taken by surprise, since they were still willing to return to the fold once the concessions they sought were granted. Even more surprised by the adjournment were the hotel keepers of Charleston, who were stuck with an unusually large liquor inventory. But Johnson registered neither dismay nor foreboding about the disruption of the Democratic party. He seemed to regard it as nothing more than an unexpected outcome of traditional political maneuvers.

The bustling free colored community, not politics, preoccupied Johnson in the days and weeks following the adjournment of the convention. Like most other Americans, Johnson did not foresee the coming national cataclysm. Nor could he predict the ominous local and personal repercussions of the next nine months of deepening sectional crisis. When the Democrats met in Charleston in the spring of 1860, Johnson and others among the free Afro-American community were taking care of their usual business, aware of the attack on their freedom by upcountry planters and the city's white mechanics but optimistic that they could survive. By the winter of 1860 their confidence had withered. By then, Johnson, the Ellisons, and the rest of the free colored community stood on the brink of extinction and despaired of their survival.

IN April 1860, a few weeks after the Charleston City Council rejected the white mechanics' latest proposal to limit slave competition, the police began to enforce the slave badge law more rigorously than at any time since the mechanics began their campaign almost two years earlier. In April the police arrested twenty-seven slaves for working without badges, whereas in the previous three months—while the city council considered the mechanics' request to curb slave hiring—the police had not made a single arrest for violation of the badge law. Who took the initiative in enforcing the badge law is not known. Perhaps the white workingmen decided to report every suspected violation they saw. Or, more likely, the newly reelected mayor, Charles Macbeth, with the support of the city council, ordered the police to make a visible display of enforcing the law as a way to show the mechanics that city authorities were not entirely unresponsive to their needs. Although strict enforcement of the badge law did little to reduce the number of slaves competing with white workers, it at least demonstrated that the city was unwilling to allow masters to ignore the slave laws with impunity, and it reassured all whites that the city's racial priorities were in order. The tempo of the crackdown on slaves working without badges accelerated in May, when police made forty-five arrests, and it stayed at record levels during June and July, when a total of seventy-two arrests were made. In just four months almost twice as many slaves were arrested for badge law violations as during the preceding twenty months.[8]

At first, few free Afro-Americans were caught up in the new wave of arrests. Only three free persons of color were arrested in April for failure to pay the capitation tax required of free Negroes. But beginning in May and continuing through June and July, the police swept up seventy free persons of color for not paying the capitation tax, more than in the previous crackdowns in October 1858 (when the white mechanics began their campaign against slave hiring) and in December

1859 (when the state legislature debated proposals to enslave or expel free Negroes). Still more ominous, the pace of arrests did not abate within a few weeks, as it had previously. Instead, it continued through the late spring and summer with little sign of slackening.[9] The cumulative effect of events of the last six months—Harpers Ferry, the local mayoral election, the proposals before the 1859 legislature, the white mechanics' failure to obtain relief from the legislature or the city council—raised racial tensions in Charleston to a pitch unequaled in many years. All Afro-Americans, both slave and free, were put on notice that they were being watched closely.

Nevertheless, James M. Johnson failed to mention the worsening racial climate in Charleston in his letters to Henry Ellison. He saw nothing alarming about the numerous arrests of slaves and free persons of color. The police were not picking up his elite friends and acquaintances. The likelihood that he would be threatened in any way seemed remote. He was throughly enjoying his stay in the big city.

In mid-May he invited Henry to come down to Charleston for a series of special morning services at Grace Episcopal Church. He tried to entice him with the promise that, if he came, he would "hear fine preaching, see fine Ladies," and have a chance to listen to music by the Christian and Convivial Society and to take part in two maroons, festive picnics in the country that were a springtime ritual of Charlestonians of all classes and colors.[10] Johnson himself "spent a very pleasant afternoon" with a friend at the May Festival of the German Rifle Club and Turners' Association. The festival took place at the club's "Sporting ground," an eighteen-acre site on the outskirts of the city complete with a large clubhouse that contained a dance hall, a billiard room, a bowling alley, and a bar. The festival attracted hundreds of Charlestonians. "The crowd was immense," Johnson reported to Henry, "& the Fun was of a novel & diverting kind." Johnson saw a young black man climb a fifty-foot greased pole and get the valuable watch waiting at the top, which many others had tried to reach. He watched sharpshooters compete, and he was impressed by the feats of gymnasts, especially when they locked arms and made "their evolutions like a wheel Rocket."[11]

For Johnson, race relations in the city were not dangerously tense. He felt at ease in the predominantly white crowd at the German's May festival, even though many of the whites did not know him. So long as he and the other Afro-Americans in the crowd observed the conventional rules of racial etiquette, nobody objected to their coming to the festival and having a good time. Doubtless they had to remain on the periphery of activities and be careful not to do anything that some white person might interpret as too familiar—like showing up on the dance floor. But cautious, discreet behavior was nothing new to Johnson and most other free persons of color.

Uppermost in Johnson's mind was his daily round of work, family, and social activities. He put in long hours at the tailor shop sewing for the city's white merchants and professional men and for the white planters who were in town for their spring provisions. Work at the shop allowed plenty of opportunities for socializing, and Johnson relished them. He enjoyed the friendly banter with his white customers. When the white factor and planter James Caldwell came to the shop in mid-May to pick up his suits and pay his bill, Johnson "joked him about gallanting the Ladies" and later reported proudly to Henry that Caldwell "was quite pleased at it."[12] Conversations with white customers had to be kept safely deferential. But much of the time the only people in the shop were Afro-Americans—Johnson, two or three free colored journeymen who worked with him, one or two of his father's slaves, and an occasional free colored visitor. Then conversations could be less guarded, more frank; they could range across travel, religion, and politics viewed from the perspective of free men of color. They could be about rather than with whites. At such times Johnson's shop was part of the grapevine by which members of the free colored community kept themselves informed. Johnson prized the morsels of news and gossip that free colored men and women passed along when they dropped by the shop. He relayed the most interesting material to Henry, and, after the Democrats left town, he did not write a single word about the crackdown on slaves and free Negroes.

As portrayed in Johnson's letters, the world of Charleston's free people of color was placid and benign. Instead of writing about who was being arrested, Johnson kept Henry up to date on the eligible young free colored women in the city: who was being courted; who was engaged; who was not yet spoken for. This information interested Henry because, after eight years as a widower, he was on the lookout for a new wife. Johnson's attention to such matters testified to his belief that things in Charleston were normal. The most noteworthy crisis among Johnson's free colored acquaintances was a shot-gun wedding. The reluctant bridegroom, Rixy Gordon, a twenty-one-year-old free mulatto butcher, was hauled to the altar by the mother of his deceased wife. Gordon's former mother-in-law, in cooperation with the friends of the preg-nant bride-to-be, Christiana Leman, an eighteen-year-old free mulatto mantua maker, confronted him with a formidable wedding party: a white Methodist minister, one of the city's most respectable free men of color (a Weston), and two other less reputable free men of color (Johnson called them "Bull Dogs") who gave Gordon a choice, "Marry or Die."[13]

Springtime in Charleston was anything but dull. Johnson attended a lavish reception at the Weston home, where he talked with his father's good friend Richard E. Dereef, the proprietor of a wood business and one of the wealthiest free men of color in the city, and Frederick Sasportas, a well-known free mulatto millwright, both of whom asked to be remem-bered to Henry. Another notable social event in May was a supper given by William McKinlay, a wealthy free mulatto tailor, for some visiting free men of color from Georgia.[14] Since it was illegal for the Georgians to enter South Carolina, McKinlay's supper in their honor was another sign that Charleston's free mulatto leaders anticipated no trouble from the police. In fact, free people of color in the city took advan-tage of the lovely spring weather to organize their own maroons, at least one of which Johnson attended. Their behavior at the picnics bespoke the lightheartedness (and lightheadedness) of a spring day full of promise. Johnson watched some of his free Negro neighbors leave for their maroon with wagonloads of "Luxuries," including so much liquor that in the city, he joked to Henry, "Corn Juice was at a Premium." Several hours later the revelers returned, tipsy and gorged, since the luxuries had been "too soon transferred to copper fastened vessels made of Flesh." One man "looked like a cask," Johnson wrote, "& methinks a tapping would have caused a rise to set the coach afloat."[15]

THE blithe spirit of Johnson and his friends in the midst of the police crackdown on slaves and free Negroes is a measure of the distance that separated them from most other Afro-Americans in the city. Johnson and his circle of associates comprised an Afro-American aristocracy set apart from the rest of Charleston's Negroes by their freedom, their color, and their wealth. Free status elevated them above eight out of ten Afro-Americans in the city who were slaves. A visible mark of their freedom was their brown skin. It distinguished them not only from slaves—more than 80 percent of whom were black—but also from the one in three free Negroes in the city who was dark-skinned.[16] What put them at the top of the free colored community was their wealth. Most free people of color in the city, like those elsewhere in the state, were desperately poor. More than three out of four were propertyless. In contrast, the free mulatto aristocrats owned both real estate and slaves.[17]

James Drayton Johnson was not a wealthy man by any standard, but he ranked securely in the middle of the free mulatto aristocracy. His two houses at 7 and 9 Coming Street were valued at $4,000 in 1860, which put him within the top 5 percent of free colored real estate owners. By virtue of his three slaves he also ranked among the city's top free colored slaveholders. Only forty-one free persons of color owned real estate worth as much or more than Johnson's. Only fifty-three owned as many or more slaves. At the pinnacle of the wealth pyramid were several of Johnson's friends. The wealthiest free person of color in the city was Maria Weston, the wife of the well-established free mulatto machinist Anthony Weston. She owned fourteen slaves and real estate valued at $40,075. William McKinlay, the free mulatto tailor, possessed real estate worth more than $25,000, though no slaves. The wood merchant Richard E. Dereef owned fourteen slaves and real property worth $23,000; his brother and business partner Joseph Dereef owned six slaves and $16,000 worth of real estate. Jacob Weston, a free mulatto tailor who lived on Coming Street next door to Henry Ellison's mother-in-law Mrs. Jeanette

Bonneau, had two slaves and real property worth $11,600. Jacob Weston's brother and business partner, Samuel, owned one slave and real estate valued at $9,300. Few individuals were so prosperous, however. Only twelve free Afro-Americans in the city owned real estate worth more than $9,000.[18] In fact, most of the city's free mulatto aristocracy owned less than James D. Johnson.

What distinguished Charleston's free mulatto elite from poor free Negroes was the ownership of enough property to provide a modicum of independence and security. Like James D. Johnson, they owned their homes and many of them also owned their workshops. Yet homeowners made up just one-quarter of the city's free colored population.[19] All the rest rented, and eight out of ten of them had white landlords.[20] If the value of one of Johnson's two houses ($2,000) is taken as a rough measure of the wealth required for a free person of color to have the degree of independence and security enjoyed by Johnson, then 117 individuals had the requisite wealth, and two-thirds of them owned less than Johnson.[21]

Slaveownership was another mark of membership in the free mulatto aristocracy. While slaveowners were spread across the economic spectrum of the free colored community, they were concentrated near the top. In 1860 almost half of the free Afro-Americans with real estate worth $2,000 or more owned slaves, over five times the proportion of slaveowners among those with less real estate. Among individuals like James D. Johnson, who owned at least $4,000 in real estate, three of every four were slaveholders. Altogether, fifty-five persons owned at least $2,000 worth of real estate and at least one slave.[22] They comprised the core of Charleston's free colored aristocracy. They made up only about 8 percent of the city's free colored population, but they owned half of all the real estate and slaves owned by free Negroes.

Some persons with less real estate or no slaves certainly belonged to the aristocracy. Jeanette Bonneau, for example, was without question a member of the elite, as were Robert Houston and William McKinlay. Neither Houston nor McKinlay owned a slave, however, and although Mrs. Bonneau owned one slave, she had only $1,000 worth of real estate. If the boundaries of the free colored aristocracy are expanded to include these persons and others with at least $2,000 worth of real estate *or* one slave, then about one free Afro-American in six belonged to the group. Collectively they owned all slaves and three-quarters of the real estate possessed by the city's free Negroes. Counting their family members, they numbered around 500, or barely 3 percent of the city's Afro-American population.

In some respects it seems inappropriate to call these individuals aristocrats, even by antebellum standards. They had no landed estates or ancestral country seats. Instead of ladies and gentlemen of leisure, they were skilled workers, seamstresses and tailors, mantua makers and carpenters, who worked hard day in and day out. Their wealth did not even begin to match that of Charleston's white elite. In 1860, for example, the average wealth of the white planters in the city was about $54,000, while the average wealth of the top free persons of color was less than a tenth as much. One white Charlestonian in five had real and personal property worth $10,000 or more, compared to one free Afro-American Charlestonian in one hundred. Although free persons of color made up 15 percent of the free population of the city, they owned only one percent of the city's total wealth.[23] Compared to white Charlestonians, members of the free mulatto elite were merely the most prosperous fraction of the free Negro working class.

Their prosperity nonetheless gave them a choice about living in the South. All free people of color had the choice, but only the elite could liquidate their assets in Charleston and cushion a move to reestablish themselves in the North, in Canada, or someplace else where slavery did not exist. A few did leave, like James M. Johnson's brother Charley. But most of those who left were not among the free colored elite or even, like Charley, on its margins. To the free mulatto elite, the future was in Charleston. They could afford to leave, but they chose to stay.

For aristocratic free mulattoes Charleston was home in a sense that went beyond the houses they owned and the jobs they had. The concentration of free people of color in the city made possible a community that sustained them. The fellowship of extended families and of a broad network of friends and acquaintances in church groups, benevolent societies, and other voluntary organizations provided Charleston's free people of color an experience unequaled elsewhere in the state or even in the Deep South outside New Orleans. As much as ownership of real estate and slaves, the community gave the free mulatto elite a sense of belonging in the city. Just as the Ellisons had carved out a niche in Stateburg society, Charleston's free colored leaders had built a small world that was part of, yet separate from, the larger society of whites and blacks. In the years since the American Revolution, free people of color in Charleston had wedged their brown world between the freedom of whites and the slavery of blacks. All the inhabitants of this territory possessed free status. But the wealth, education, and respectability of the leading free mulatto families set them apart from other free Negroes and conferred on them the status of aristocrats of a degraded race, the top of the bottom.

FREE Negroes had lived in Charleston since the city was founded in 1683. They accompanied the early white settlers in South Carolina who came from Barbados, bringing with them a Caribbean tolerance for miscegenation and for free mulattoes as a valuable intermediate class in a slave society.[24] But throughout the eighteenth century the number of free Negroes remained too small to form such a class. When the first federal census was taken in 1790 only 586 free people of color resided in Charleston, less than 4 percent of the city's total population of 16,359. Within the next twenty years the number of free Afro-Americans in the city grew rapidly to 1,472. Although they still made up only 6 percent of the city's total inhabitants in 1810, they were numerous enough to create a free colored community. If all the free people of color in the city in 1810 had resided in a town of their own, it would have been bigger than every town in the state except Charleston and Columbia.

After 1810, as the postrevolutionary manumissions dwindled, the free Negro population of Charleston grew more slowly. By 1830 it had reached 2,107. In the next thirty years the number of free Afro-American Charlestonians continued to increase, though more slowly than ever. In 1860 the 3,237 free people of color in the city made up 8 percent of the population. But, because the slave population of the city had declined since 1830, free people of color made up a larger fraction of the city's Afro-Americans than at any previous time in the city's history. In 1860 free people of color comprised 19 percent of the city's Negro population, compared to 12 percent in 1830 and 7 percent in 1790.[25] Even in 1860 Charleston's free Afro-Americans still outnumbered the population of every town in the state but Columbia and Charleston. More than ever, free people of color in Charleston had the makings of an intermediate class.

Whites like Christopher Memminger and Alfred Huger valued the sizable intermediate class of free Negroes because it protected dominant whites from the potential for slave insurrection and insulated them from the political demands of white mechanics. Charleston's leading free mulattoes understood this reasoning and tried constantly to reinforce it by exemplary behavior. However, the concentration of free Negroes in the city had an additional, quite different meaning for the free mulatto aristocracy. Evidence of that meaning surfaced repeatedly during the antebellum years but never more clearly than in the way the free mulatto aristocracy referred to themselves. When Robert Houston thanked Christopher Memminger for defending free people of color in the state legislature in 1859, James M. Johnson wrote Henry that Houston spoke "in behalf of our people."[26] The term "our people" recurs in Johnson's letters and in other self-references by the city's leading free mulattoes and expresses something of what it meant to belong to an intermediate class. Free mulattoes were separate from both whites and blacks. Furthermore, free mulattoes identified with each other; they referred to each other not as "a" people but as "our" people. And, rather than being a degraded caste, a degenerate racial hybrid, or a random aggregation of individuals, free mulattoes were a "people" who, despite their individual differences, shared a common identity, a common fate, and a common humanity. "Our people" also captures the peculiar sense in which members of Charleston's free mulatto elite saw themselves as an integral part of the city's society, and yet apart from it. They were outcasts who, paradoxically, belonged. Imbedded in the city's society of whites and blacks was their brown society with a life very much its own.

Kinship was the sinew of Charleston's free brown society. Intermarriage linked free mulatto families into a cousinry that rivaled that of the white aristocracy in its density and complexity. The shortage of reliable records makes it impossible to sort out all the interconnections, but Henry and Reuben Ellison's marriages to the daughters of Thomas S. Bonneau illustrate the general pattern.[27] Through their marriages to Mary Elizabeth and Harriett A. Bonneau, Henry and Reuben became brothers-in-law to the five other Bonneau sisters and kinfolk to their husbands and their husbands' families. Thus the outer fringes of the Ellison family circle included the prominent Weston family (through the marriages of Sarah Ann Bonneau to the free mulatto tailor Jacob Weston and of Louisa Potter Bonneau to the free mulatto machinist John Furman Weston) and the equally well known Holloway family (by the marriage of Frances Pinckney Bonneau to Richard Holloway, Jr.). In addition, the Ellisons were kin to the families of the free mulatto tailor James Johnston (through his marriage to Eliza Bonneau) and of the free mulatto butcher James Wilson (via his marriage to Martha S. Bonneau). Simply by their relationship to Richard Holloway, Jr., the Ellisons counted his eleven brothers and their wives among their distant kin. Every member of the free mulatto aristocracy was not kin to the Ellisons, but enough of them were to give the term "our people" a distinctly familial cast.

The high rate of intermarriage reflected the relatively small number of eligible free mulattoes and their sense of themselves as a separate group. In general, free mulatto men refused to consider any of the thousands of slave women in Charleston as potential spouses. Color consciousness was part of the reason, for about 80 percent of the slave women in the city were black. However, color was not the only consideration, and probably not the most important one. In 1860 Charleston District contained almost as many mulatto slave women as mulatto free women.[28] Few free mulatto men selected brown slave women as wives for the very practical reason that, had they done so, their children would have been slaves.[29] Had a shortage of free mulatto women existed, unmarried free mulatto men might have overcome their aversion to slave wives. However, just the opposite was the case. In 1860 free Afro-

American women in Charleston outnumbered men more than three to two.[30] Henry Ellison's unhurried survey of young free mulatto women in Charleston in the late 1850s was not a luxury reserved to a man who was probably the state's most eligible free mulatto widower. Free Afro-American men were in a position to be choosy. Their choices indicated their desire to separate themselves from slaves.

The sexual imbalance made it more difficult for free Afro-American women to keep their distance from slaves. About four out of ten free Negro women in Charleston in 1860 could not expect to find husbands among the city's free Negro men. A good many of them had to choose between remaining unmarried and accepting a slave husband. Although female slaves in Charleston outnumbered males, the sex ratio was much nearer parity than it was for free people of color. In 1860 there were 89 slave males for every 100 slave females.[31] Slave men were not only available, but they also presumably saw the attraction of a free colored wife who could give birth to free children. For a slave man in South Carolina after 1820, marriage to a free woman of color represented the last crack in the doorway to freedom; the man could not become free and his marriage had no legal standing, but his children could be free. Precisely how many free women of color in Charleston took slave husbands is impossible to say, but the 1860 census figures suggest the number was not small.

Women headed just over half of all the free colored households in Charleston, and virtually none of these households had a coresiding spouse.[32] Most of them did, however, have children.[33] Even if one makes the most generous assumptions about the mortality rates among free men of color or the likelihood that men might be temporarily working away from home, it is certain that many of these children did not have free colored fathers. Since every child in households headed by free black women was listed as black, their fathers were not white, if the racial evidence in the census can be given credence.[34] Instead, it is likely that many of these free black women were wives of slave men, most of them black. Certainly the women's economic status did not elevate them much above slaves. Free black women who headed households were the poorest of the poor. Their mean wealth was only $155, and more than nine out of ten had no wealth at all. They were at the bottom of free Afro-American society in Charleston intermingled with slaves.

Free mulatto women were often in the same position as free black women. Virtually none of the households headed by light-skinned free women had a coresiding spouse, yet over half had children.[35] Many of the fathers of these children were slaves. Some of the other fathers were probably white men. Certainly more than a few white men kept free colored mistresses in the city. Although the practice did not have the sanction it received in New Orleans, it was common enough and was tolerated so long as it was not flaunted.[36] It was one reason for the sexual imbalance among free Negroes in Charleston. Up to the age of sexual maturity free colored females were only slightly more numerous than free colored males. Beginning about age fifteen, free colored women outnumbered men almost three to two.[37] Presumably a fair number of the "excess" women in the city were concubines of white men. Although many of the free mulatto mothers who headed households had children fathered by slave men, enough of them were concubines of white men to pull unmarried free mulatto women as a group in the opposite direction from free black women. Even though nearly nine out of ten free mulatto women who headed households were propertyless like their counterparts among free black women, unmarried free mulatto women were more likely to be separated from slaves and intermingled with whites. Occupying a stratum near the bottom of the city's free colored community, free mulatto women who headed households nonetheless composed a zone in which the distance from slaves began to increase.

Higher up, in the strata occupied by free Afro-American men who headed households, the distance became almost unbridgeable. Male-headed households were almost the mirror image of female-headed households. More than two-thirds of them had coresiding spouses.[38] Furthermore, nine out of ten of the male-headed households that contained children also contained the children's mothers, while only 4 percent of the female-headed households with children had both parents present. Free men of color clearly opted to marry free women, to have free children, and in that way to set themselves apart from slaves. This was as true of black men as mulatto men. The structure of the households headed by black men was identical to those of mulatto men, with one crucial exception that reflects the significance of color as a marker of one's distance from slavery. More than nine out of ten of the coresiding spouses of mulatto men were mulattoes, according to the census.[39] Since about a quarter of the free Negro women in Charleston were black, these men clearly avoided black women in selecting a wife. Among the households headed by black men the color consciousness was equally acute, according to the census. More than eight out of ten (83 percent) of the spouses of black men were black. Whether free black men had difficulty wooing free mulatto women or instead preferred black woman as wives is impossible to determine.[40] Even if the census data are only a rough guide to the social practices of Charleston's free people of color, it seems clear that free mulattoes sought to set themselves apart not only from slaves but from blacks. The bonds of kinship tended to encircle free people of approximately the same hue.

Color also signified economic distance from slavery. In Charleston, as in the countryside, mulattoes were better off than blacks. The mean wealth of free mulatto women who headed households was $427, almost three times greater than that of free black women, and about the same as the margin that separated rural free mulatto and free black women.[41] The mean wealth of free mulatto men was nearly half again larger than that of free black men, but both groups of men in Charleston were more prosperous than their counterparts in the country. In the city free mulatto men had a mean wealth of $1,107, twice that of rural free mulatto men ($549); the average wealth of free black men in the city was $770, more than twice that of those in the country ($283). Although no free person of color in South Carolina knew these figures, their meaning was clear enough to virtually everyone. Even though almost two-thirds of free Negro men in Charleston were propertyless in 1860, the other third bathed in the glow of prosperity compared to their country cousins. A neatly dressed, well-spoken, well-mannered free Negro was assumed to be from Charleston, where free men of color tended to be tradesmen rather than farm laborers. The easily visible economic difference between urban and rural men of the same color was reproduced between mulatto and black men in the city. Color counted, especially in Charleston. The association of modest prosperity with light skin reinforced the significance of skin color as an index of distance from slavery. In Charleston, the color of a free person's skin suggested not only ancestry but also relative economic security, and both free mulattoes and free blacks understood the code.

Color consciousness was so acute in Charleston that free mulattoes and free blacks constituted two nearly separate communities. No rigid wall stood between the two communities, but members of each group acted in many ways as if one did. The keen awareness of color reflected in the selection of marriage partners extended to almost every voluntary association among free people of color in the city. The mutual-aid societies founded by free Afro-American men are prime examples.

IN 1790 five men who declared themselves "free brown men, natives of the city of Charleston" organized the Brown Fellowship Society, the most prestigious mulatto organization in the city.[42] The Society was limited to fifty members who were required to pay an initiation fee of fifty dollars plus monthly dues. The contributions supported payments of not less than $1.50 a week for members who became too ill to work and, if a member should die, a decent funeral and burial in the Society's cemetery. If a member's widow and orphans were indigent, the Society would provide an annual stipend of sixty dollars. The Society also committed itself to extend "needful assistance" to up to five "poor colored" orphans or adults.[43] But self-help, not charity, was the primary purpose of the Society. Membership was reserved for the leading free mulattoes in the city.

The roster of the Brown Fellowship Society reads as if it were the Ellisons' address book. Thomas S. Bonneau, Henry and Reuben Ellison's father-in-law, joined the Society in 1816; John Mishaw, William, Jr.'s father-in-law, joined a year later. The Westons, the Dereefs, the Holloways, the Sasportases, the Kinlochs, William McKinlay, Robert Houston, and many other of the Ellisons' friends and relatives in Charleston belonged. Since the Ellisons did not live in the city, they could not join the organization, and it appears that neither James M. Johnson nor his father ever became members.[44] The Brown Fellows were the elite of what Johnson called "our people," and they excluded from their society all free blacks. A rule adopted in 1828 required each applicant for membership to be sponsored by two members who had to declare in writing "the FACT, that said applicants are Free persons."[45] Nothing in the rule book prohibited black members, but the unwritten rule was applied uniformly. Every member whose race can be identified was a mulatto.[46]

In 1843 free black men formed their own organization, the Humane Brotherhood. Its rules limited membership to no more than 35 "respectable Free Dark Men."[47] Their interpretation of "Dark" was flexible enough to admit several men who were listed in the federal census as mulattoes, but the majority of members were black.[48] The Humane Brotherhood had the same purposes as the Brown Fellowship Society. It provided sick benefits, burial expenses, and an annuity for widows and orphans of deceased members. Since members of the Humane Brotherhood had only a fraction of the wealth of the mulatto elite, their annuity for widows was twelve dollars, a fifth that of the Brown Fellowship Society.[49] Nonetheless, like the Brown Fellowship Society, the Humane Brotherhood purchased and maintained a burial ground for its members. The cemeteries of the two societies stood side by side on Pitt Street, separated by a sturdy fence.[50]

That fence symbolized the color barrier than cut through Charleston's free colored society. Like other fences, it was not impenetrable. Free blacks and free mulattoes knew one another, talked to one another, and did business with one another. John Mishaw even managed to belong to both the Humane Brotherhood and the Brown Fellowship Society at the same time, the only person ever to do so.[51] On the whole, however, free mulattoes and free blacks did not socialize with one another, and they rarely married one another. The care with which free mulattoes policed the color barrier is illustrated in the minutes of another free mulatto organization in the city, the Friendly Moralist Society.

Founded in 1838, the Friendly Moralist Society required that a prospective member be certified by three existing members as "a bona fide free brown man; over the age of eighteen; of moral character, and of good standing in the community."[52] This requirement was backed by a strict penalty: "Should it be charged and proven that any member is not a bona fide free brown man, he shall immediately be expelled; and each of his recommenders shall be fined two dollars."[53] The Friendly Moralists took these rules seriously. In 1844, for example, member Robert Mishaw challenged the membership application of Richard Gregory with the claim that the "gentleman having united with a Society [of] Black men makes himself a Black Man." Job Bass, the president of the Society and one of the members recommending Gregory, disagreed. Bass argued that mixed ancestry was the sole basis of mulatto status. Even "if the gentleman were to be exposed to the schorching [sic] rays of the sun on the shores of Africa," Bass declared, "he would still be A Brown Man." Black skin and "the fact of his being associated with Black men could never make him a Black Man."[54] Despite Bass's argument, a slight majority of the Friendly Moralists evidently shared Mishaw's doubts that a *bona fide* free brown man would voluntarily associate with free blacks, and they rejected Gregory's application.[55] The Society's rigid insistence on unimpeachable racial qualifications surfaced again four years later when Edward Logan, a member of the Humane Brotherhood, applied for membership. Friendly Moralist Michael J. Eggart argued that Logan was "not eligible to membership being a black man." When another member demanded that Eggart define "the word brown," Eggart stated the iron-clad rule of ancestry. To be brown "the individual must be [a] descendent of brown parent, or white amalgamated with black."[56] A heated debate of Logan's candidacy stretched over several meetings, and finally the members denied him admission.

The debate showed that Eggart's definition of "brown" was not universally shared, even by the free mulattoes in the Society. However, the time and energy the Friendly Moralists spent screening the racial credentials of prospective members signify that all agreed it was of the utmost importance to determine whether a candidate was a mulatto or not. In theory, one drop of white blood made a man brown and eligible for membership. In practice, ancestry was difficult to prove, and an applicant's claim of mixed ancestry could be outweighed by skin color or personal associates. These factors made the definition of "brown" debatable, but the Friendly Moralists' uniformly mulatto membership proves that the debates were always settled by keeping blacks at arm's length.[57]

The membership policies of the Friendly Moralist and Brown Fellowship societies, like the selection of free mulatto wives by free mulatto men, grew out of a widely shared sense of a separate mulatto identity. That sense underlay the term "our people" and infused it with social significance, identifying free mulattoes as the intermediate class between slavery and freedom and between blacks and whites. The most probing analysis of mulatto identity in the slave South is contained in a recently discovered speech Michael Eggart gave to the Friendly Moralist Society in 1848.

Free mulattoes inhabited "a middle ground," Eggart declared, a social territory bounded on one side by "the prejudice of the white man" and on the other by "the deeper hate of our more sable brethren."[58] New racial theories held that mulattoes were weakened hybrids, "excrescencies, . . . superfluous and monstrous productions . . . [who] draw an unwelcome existence from their Originals." According to these theories, Eggart pointed out, "utter extinction seems to bee our inevitable doom." By natural selection, "the Whirlpool which threatens to swallow us up entirely," free mulattoes' middle ground would disappear. However, Eggart asserted, such views were wrong; "excrescencies have no living in themselves. . . . But ours is gods own image. [I]n our nostrals is his breath. [O]ur capacities mental and physical are as good as either of the races." Free mulattoes were an equal race, Eggart proclaimed, neither inferior to whites nor superior to blacks. Their racial identity should become the basis of group solidarity, for only then could the middle ground be secure. The pressure of white prejudice and black hatred was unrelenting. It threatened to eliminate the middle ground by social and political, rather than natural, means. "[L]ike ancient Israel we can lay claim to no spot on Earth," Eggart said; "the position of our people wherever they are to bee found . . . [is] hemmed in by unsinking prejudice on the one hand, and by foul hate on the other, whither shall we fly, no spot on earth where the colored man is to bee found is clear of it." Inescapably, free mulattoes existed on a middle ground that constantly seemed to shrink.

The only security, Eggart announced, lay in mulatto solidarity. "[T]heir is naught that we lack as A people but A unanimity of sentiment A thousand times greater than it now is," he said.[59] Mulattoes had to confront their "all absorbing" dilemma as a people, using their racial identity as a source of strength to protect their tenuous social position. First, free mulattoes had to realize that they depended on each other, that no progress would be made "untill all of us have advanced in the great art of looking beyond ourselves and those immediately connected with us, to the welfare of our people generally." Charity toward free mulattoes less fortunate than the young tradesmen in the Friendly Moralist Society was a step in the right direction, Eggart argued, but it was insufficient. A community-wide education program promised to promote mulatto solidarity and to stabilize the boundaries of the middle ground. Education "is our life our sun our shield," Eggart proclaimed. "Withdraw from us the bright rays it shed around and worse than Agean [*sic*] darkness will encompass us, [for] what but Education raises us Above the level of the slaves." In Charleston, "The ignorant and degraded are taken as the Representatives of our people," Eggart observed. If the entire free mulatto community in the city "would bee enlightened by the power of Education how much more vived [*sic*] how much brighter would the line of seperation bee between us and the slaves." Eggart believed that the brighter line of separation would be doubly valuable. Free mulattoes would not only be distinguished from slaves, but also the line separating the two "would bee so bright that it would Eventually triump [*sic*] over the prejudice of the white man." Meanwhile, free mulatto organizations like the Friendly Moralist Society and the Brown Fellowship Society could "add bone and sinew to our strength as A people" by cooperating to raise money to pay a teacher for all the mulatto children in the city. Eggart acknowledged that his proposal was expensive and unprecedented. Nevertheless, it was justified. "As far as my inexperience can perceive this is the only means by which we can dispel the heavy cloud that hangs upon our political horizon. Knowledge is power, it is A power not to bee limited, but can bee brought to bear against any Obstacles, or surmount any difficulty[.] Let us seek diligently to obtain it ourselves, and by every means in our reach to dispence it to every one bearing our mark upon their foreheads."

Free mulattoes in Charleston never enacted Eggart's ambitious plan, but not because they considered his ideas bizarre. Eggart spoke from within the uppermost reaches of the free mulatto aristocracy. At the time of his address to the Friendly Moralists he was twenty-six years old, a wheelwright, and the husband of Joanna Dereef, the eldest daughter of the Johnsons' and Ellisons' friend Richard E. Dereef, in whose household Eggart and his young wife lived.[60] Shortly after Eggart's speech the Friendly Moralists elected him to the vice-presidency of the society, and he later advanced to the Brown Fellowship Society and served as an officer.[61] Eggart's continued high standing among the city's mulatto elite suggests that he shared their outlook, reflected their anxieties, and echoed their strategies for survival.

Eggart's educational plan was a radical extension of the general political perspective of the city's free mulatto leaders. Nothing in Eggart's proposal attempted to reduce blacks' resentment of free mulattoes' snobbery; instead, education would sharpen the distinction between mulattoes and blacks and increase blacks' hostility to mulattoes and their pretensions. Eggart believed mulattoes should turn away from blacks toward whites. Eggart's scheme embodied the mulattoes' conventional faith that some of their best friends were white, that white prejudice against mulattoes could be overcome by empirical evidence of an educated free mulatto community, that whites could ultimately recognize mulattoes as a separate, distinctive, and worthy people. Eggart deviated from widely shared views only in the depth of his anxiety. The Friendly Moralist and Brown Fellowship societies did not take up Eggart's plan partly because they had enough to do simply attending to their routine business. But the more fundamental reason was their complacency. Eggart asked the city's free mulatto aristocrats to doubt what they had staked their lives on, that their skilled crafts, their property, their brown color, and their white friends provided them with sufficient security. Having achieved elite status in Charleston, they were confident that the tiny sliver of middle ground they occupied was shielded and secure. Despite Eggart's plea, Charleston's free mulatto leaders continued to think of themselves, their families, and their closest friends—rather than all free mulattoes—as "our people."[62]

OTHER free people of color in Charleston shared Eggart's anxieties, but they came to different conclusions. Unlike Eggart, they found the middle ground in Charleston intolerable. Just a month before Eggart's speech to the Friendly Moralists, a group of forty-five free Afro-Americans departed from Charleston on the brig *Colonel Howard,* bound for Liberia under the auspices of the American Colonization Society.[63] Some of these men had emigrated to the North a few years earlier, but, they told an agent of the Colonization Society, "they found themselves so depressed and despised and crowded out of employment, and so much less respected than they had been in Charleston, that they could not endure it, but returned to their old homes, quite satisfied with their trial of freedom in a free State, and much prefering [*sic*], as the least of two evils, such freedom as they can enjoy in a slave State."[64] After a time, however, their limited freedom in Charleston proved unsatisfactory, and they concluded "that in this country they can never possess those rights and privileges which will make them men."[65] They hoped Liberia would prove more hospitable.

Eggart reminded the Friendly Moralists of the departure of this group, noting that "Many of our people are now on their way to the Liberian Republic, anticipating that liberty which is to bee desired by every man."[66] Eggart warned that they were bound to be disappoinnted, and, as an example of what they should expect, he referred to a recent massacre of mulattoes by blacks in Haiti.[67] Despite such risks, scores of free Afro-Americans emigrated from South Carolina to Liberia at mid-century. Between May 1848 and November 1852, 238 free people of color left Charleston for Liberia, the largest continent of immigrants to Africa ever to leave the state.[68] They too saw the thunder clouds Eggart noted on the horizon, and they decided to run before the storm.

A few members of the free mulatto elite succumbed to the appeal of emigration. Both the Brown Fellowship and Friendly Moralist societies provided for a partial refund of accrued benefits to members who left the state.[69] The minutes of the Friendly Moralist Society document requests for refunds by several members who were leaving, evidently bound for New York, Boston, Toronto, or other cities in the free states and in Canada.[70] Although Charley Johnson's move to Toronto seems to have had something to do with his health, his decision may have been colored by favorable reports of the racial climate in Canada sent back by several of his Charleston friends who preceeded him.[71] Friendly Moralist Edward Holloway announced his intention to leave Charleston in 1846, and, after a prolonged stay in the North, he wrote from New York in 1857 to one of his many brothers who had remained behind in Charleston. "Emmigration [sic] seems to be the leading topic of conversation & discussion among the Colored residents of the City of New York," he reported. "As a people there is a manifestation of considerable anxiety and dissatisfaction with matters and things in general. There seems to be a kind of reaction in the minds of the knowing ones, and every body seriously considers there [sic] present position and future prospects. The general conclusion is that this is not our abiding home." Holloway admitted that because of the "general *malady*" he had "contracted the contagion." In the United States he could never attain "political equality"; yet, he wrote his brother, "my mind aspires for greater attainment and I feel that the Day is not far distant when I shall enjoy the full fruition of Political Intellectual and Physical *Manhood.*" When that day arrived, Holloway did not expect to find himself in Liberia or Canada but in Jamaica, "that *promised land.*" Jamaica offered "Social & Political Equality," Holloway asserted, and he urged his brother to announce among his friends in Charleston, "Let *Emmigration* [sic] be the *Watchwords.*"[72]

The Johnsons and the Ellisons certainly knew about conditions in Canada from their contact with Charley Johnson. Charley's wife Gabriella made periodic visits back to Charleston and William Ellison Jr. visited Charley in Toronto at least once.[73] From their other friends and relatives in Charles-

ton they doubtless received word of the experiences of emigrants to Liberia and elsewhere. In May 1860 they heard directly
from an emigrant to Jamaica, a free man of color named Jack
Thomas who had been their neighbor in Stateburg until he
left in 1843. Thomas's letter was anything but encouraging. "I
wish I was back home," he wrote, ". . . it seems as there has
been a curse upon us ever since we left home." Only two years
after leaving Stateburg with his family he "completely Failed."
They then moved to Panama, where he, his brother, and his
father worked as overseers for the Panama Railroad Company. Within the space of a few months his son and his brother
died, his father suffered an injury that disabled him permanently, and Thomas himself had only his work as a barber to
support the remnants of his family. "You see the whole Bur-
then is thrown upon my Shoulders, and being in a country
like this where every man is for himself, I find it *awfully hard*
to get along," Thomas wrote, obviously hoping to touch the
Ellisons' sympathy and pocketbook.[74] Even without letters
like Thomas's, the prospect of emigration seldom tempted
the Ellisons and their peers among Charleston's free mulatto
elite.

Nevertheless, the emigrants represented one response to the
chronic tensions of life on the middle ground, tensions that
most of the free mulatto elite had learned to live with. The
tensions inherent in their intermediate position came from
forces that tugged in opposite directions. As Michael Eggart
emphasized, "our people" had to separate themselves from
slaves as much as possible in order to avoid the degradation
associated with slave status and black skin. Yet the more they
set themselves apart from slaves by owning property, making
contracts, and having free families, the closer they came to a
hazardous equality with the status of whites. They had to make
concessions to white prejudice, to reassure whites that they
were staying in their place. But every concession, every failure
to assert their freedom to the full, not only kept them safely
below whites but also narrowed their distance from slaves.
All the character traits they employed to elevate themselves
above slaves had to be repressed from their fullest expression.
Every time they refused to challenge white prejudice, they
assumed a racial identity that hinted of slavery, an identity

they found less than flattering. But only if they assumed that identity would whites allow them to exercise their freedom. To survive on the middle ground, free people of color had to affirm the freedom they shared with whites and qualify it because of the racial ancestry they shared with slaves, a demanding and frustrating assignment.

Members of the free mulatto elite carefully avoided pushing their freedom too far, but they did not confuse what was necessary with what was just. James M. Johnson maintained this distinction when he wrote Henry Ellison about the stepped-up police surveillance in Charleston during the Democratic convention, "if you have lost the Rights you ought to find solace in making a Retreat from the Heat."[75] This casual, almost flippant sentence captured the belief of Johnson and his friends that they had "Rights," not privileges; that when whites prevented them from exercising their rights, they "ought to" (not "would" or "could") "find solace in making a Retreat"; that by withdrawing from confrontation they retreated rather than surrendered; that their retreat was a tactic to be invoked for temporary protection rather than a prelude to defeat. The tone of Johnson's remark expresses the free mulatto elite's confidence that, when the searchlight of white scrutiny turned in their direction, they could nimbly duck into the shadows.

The rights of free people of color represented the contested terrain of the middle ground. Free Afro-Americans in Charleston asserted their rights when they could and retreated when they had to. They played an active part in shaping the upper boundary of their freedom, in defining the equilibrium between what they were willing to risk and what whites were willing to tolerate. In 1791 a group of Charleston free Negroes went so far as to petition the legislature, pointing out that they had been counted as citizens in the apportionment of South Carolina's representation in Congress and that "they have at all times since the Independence of the United States contributed and do now contribute to the support of the Government by chearfully [*sic*] paying their Taxes proportionable to the Property with others who have been during such period, and are now in full enjoyment of the Rights and Immunities of Citizens and Inhabitants of a Free Independent State."[76] They made clear that they did not "presume to hope that they shall be put on an equal footing with the Free white citizens of the State" and asked merely to be allowed to testify against whites in court and to be tried in the same courts as whites, rather than in the magistrate's courts that dealt exclusively with slaves.[77] Despite the modest request, the legislature ignored the petition, and a few years later Charleston vigilantes harassed at least one of the petitioners. Before 1865, free people of color in South Carolina never came any closer to formal political participation. Instead, they engaged in the politics of daily life.

IN countless ways Charleston's free Afro-Americans asserted their autonomy and self-reliance. By maintaining their free-dom and passing it along to the next generation they took care of the essentials themselves. By practicing skilled trades, by accumulating property, and by acquiring an education, free people of color made a mockery of their supposed genetic handicaps. So long as they stayed in Charleston (or anywhere else in the United States for that matter) they had no alter-native to depending on the white majority for customers and for the indifference that allowed them space to live. But on all the matters of life in which they had a choice, they typically turned toward each other, decreasing their dependence on whites as much as practicable and quietly making the political statement that they were human and responsible.

In 1803 Thomas S. Bonneau and several other members of the Brown Fellowship Society organized the Minors' Moral-ist Society to support and educate free colored orphans.[78] The Christian Benevolent Society, founded in 1839, distributed aid to sick, impoverished free people of color; in the 1850s its executive committee included James D. Johnson, Jacob Wes-ton, Robert Houston, Joseph Dereef, Malcolm Brown, and other free mulatto leaders.[79] These organizations reinforced the associations of kinship and neighborhood and gave a tan-gible reality to the notion of community. However, their lim-ited resources did not reach very far into the masses of Charleston's poor free people of color. In the seventeen years between 1839 and 1856 the Christian Benevolent Society aided seventy individuals and spent a total of $1,228, an average of four persons a year and less than $18 per person.[80] Although this aid did little to relieve the poor, it indicated that the city's free colored elite did not entirely cut themselves off from the rest of the free colored population. Furthermore, even by providing limited charity, the free mulatto leaders demonstrated that poor free people of color need not depend exclusively on whites, that they could turn instead to "our people."

Education, Michael Eggart emphasized, distinguished the free colored elite from slaves. Free colored children not only had to learn to read, write, and calculate, but they had to be taught about their unique social position. Their education occurred at home, in workshops, and on the streets. But some of it occurred in classrooms of private schools directed by free mulatto teachers. Thomas S. Bonneau headed a school that taught children of the free mulatto aristocracy between 1803 and his death in 1831.[81] Exactly how Bonneau acquired his own education is unknown. Possibly he was educated by his father, a French Huguenot who settled at Port Royal in the eighteenth century.[82] In any case, Bonneau's school served as an important cultural institution of the free mulatto elite. Bonneau put his students in touch with the wider world of learning and extended their horizons beyond the confinement of Charleston. Even more important, his students came to know each other, to see themselves as the heirs to the middle ground occupied by their parents. The influence of Bonneau's school reached throughout the antebellum period, since Bonneau taught the teachers of the succeeding generations. William McKinlay and Frederick Sasportas were among his students and later helped with the school. After Bonneau's death another student, Daniel Payne, headed his own school, where he taught, among fifty other children of the free mulatto elite, Michael Eggart and three of Bonneau's daughters. By the 1850s free mulatto children in Charleston were taught by Bonneau's youngest daughter, Francis Pinckney (Bonneau) Holloway, and by Samuel and Edward Beard.[83] In these schools free colored children learned that education anchored their freedom, that it allowed them to judge things for themselves, and that free people of color did not need whites to teach them these lessons.

The schools reinforced one of the central cultural assumptions of Charleston's free mulatto aristocracy. The schools existed, teachers taught, children learned, but after 1834 it was all against the law. The continued operation of the schools, like so much else in the lives of the city's free Afro-Americans, demonstrated that the middle ground was a twilight zone in which illegal customary practices were tolerated so long as they remained only half-visible, and apparently harmless. The rules set by whites could change suddenly and unexpectedly, as Daniel Payne and his students knew very well. In the summer of 1834 Payne sent Michael Eggart and two of his other students to the plantation of Charleston alderman Lionel Kennedy, where they were to obtain from Kennedy's slaves a certain poisonous snake for zoological study. Kennedy discovered the boys, quizzed them about their errand and Payne's curriculum, and, although there was nothing subversive about either, became alarmed, probably remembering the Denmark Vesey conspiracy he had witnessed twelve years earlier. Under pressure from Kennedy and others in Charleston, the legislature passed the 1834 law, and Payne fled Charleston fearing for his life.[84]

Although Payne did not return to the city during the antebellum years, not long after he left Charleston tensions relaxed, and free colored schools once again held classes just as before. This episode, like so many others, displayed the significance of maintaining a sharp distinction between public and private life. So long as the schools remained in the subterranean private world of the city's free people of color, they were tolerated. Once they were exposed to full public view, they became subject to the merciless force of the law and were temporarily rooted out, only to spring up again in the privacy of free colored homes and shops. Whites allowed the schools to continue so long as they were satisfied that what occurred in them was completely above reproach. No fools, the teachers in free colored schools fully conformed to these expectations. Yet they taught their students something that might have aroused white concern had whites given it much thought: public behavior had to comply rigidly with white assumptions about racial order and with the law; private life was another matter, more relaxed, more flexible, and more free, though never without risk.

This lesson was the great open secret about life on the middle ground. It accounted for both the rigidity of public life and the pleasant informality of private life. Even the wealthiest and most reputable free persons of color had to observe the niceties of racial etiquette in public. Late in 1860 the Charleston correspondent of the New York *Tribune* reported that although Richard E. Dereef was wealthy, educated, and respected, as were his sons and daughters, "if one of those daughters wears a vail [*sic*] over her face, the first policeman will strip it off, for that is only a privilege accorded to the white girl, with no negro blood in her veins."[85] If Dereef himself were out after the curfew, he could be clapped in jail and held until his white guardian came to free him. Needless to say, Dereef and his children understood the rules and followed them. Yet it was easy to overstep the boundary both because some whites took offense at what others ignored and because conforming to white prejudice was humiliating. James M. Johnson wrote Henry Ellison about a free man of color named Hare who, Johnson felt, foolishly called attention to himself in Kingsville, a small town about seventy miles northwest of Charleston. Hare claimed to be a white man and boasted that Maryland was an abolition state.[86] His remarks provoked a white factor from Maryland named Cole who interrogated him, discovered he was a free Negro, and then stripped off his shirt and "gave him the *limit* of the *law,* 'well filled, pressed down and shaken together,' upon his bare back."[87] In public, prudent free mulattoes did not trespass on whites' assumptions about proper racial behavior.

Charleston's free mulattoes had their own expectations about racial propriety, and they insisted on observing them. When an agent of the Colonization Society attended a large Methodist church in Charleston in 1847, he found it "very singular, indeed, . . . that the *blacks* and the *mulattoes* did not sit together." Whites occupied the main floor of the sanctuary, blacks filled two-thirds of the large circular gallery, and the other third "was occupied exclusively by mulattoes." The agent was informed that the mulattoes "utterly refused to sit promiscuously with the blacks; and that, in all the relations in life, they maintain the same dignified reserve; that the two classes are as totally distinct as it is possible for them to be."[88] Free mulattoes' stiff-necked refusal to associate with blacks caught the attention of many other observers. The color barrier within free Afro-American society seemed remarkable to most whites because the distinction between mulattoes and blacks appeared to them a fine point, almost comically trivial. Negroes, after all, were Negroes. White attitudes reflected not only their racial prejudice but their failure to understand the significance of the color consciousness of free mulattoes. Scrupulous observance of the distinction between brown and black allowed free mulattoes to make the middle ground visible, to reproduce in all the activities of daily life their separateness from blacks. Free mulattoes' racial rituals represented their attempts to shape social reality to their sense of themselves as an intermediate class, to give repeated public demonstrations that their social niche had clear racial boundaries and that their racial niche had equally crisp social limits. Free mulattoes' discrimination against blacks was their way of staking claim to the middle ground.

Unlike social space, geographical space was not rigidly stratified by color. Whites, mulattoes, and blacks lived in a mosaic throughout the city.[89] The wealthiest whites who lived along the hushed, shaded streets south of Broad, nearest the refreshing breezes from the sea, typically had their slaves living in the house or in a separate building nearby in the yard. Few free people of color could afford to live in the expensive neighborhood of rice planters, commission merchants, lawyers, and bankers, and the same was true of most whites. They lived farther north on the Charleston peninsula, where housing was cheaper. Almost two-thirds of the free Afro-Americans in the city lived in the upper wards north of Calhoun Street, the old boundary between the city proper and the Neck.[90] In every ward they were far outnumbered by both whites and slaves who lived adjacent to them, across the street from them, and on the alley behind them. Nonetheless, the free colored population had a vaguely defined center in the city, clustered around Coming Street. More free Afro-Americans lived on Coming than on any other street in the city.[91] In addition, the free colored residents of Coming Street included such prominent persons as William McKinlay, Jacob Weston, Mrs. Jeanette Bonneau, and James D. Johnson. Even on Coming, however, free people of color were by no means dominant; slaves outnumbered them two to one, whites three to one. But, as in the Methodist church visited by the Colonization Society agent, whites, mulattoes, and blacks who inhabited the same space were careful to partition it by color and class.

AFTER the family, the church was the most important cultural institution of Charleston's free Afro-Americans. Its significance stemmed in large measure from the fact that, unlike the family, it was not the exclusive domain of free people of color. In church free people of color performed the most visible and the most profound rituals of the middle ground. In church the public and private worlds of free mulattoes intersected in a space they shared with blacks and whites, congregated on the common ground of their mortality. Baptisms and confirmations, marriages and funerals celebrated intimate events of family life in an interracial, multi-class community. Free people of color participated fully in congregational life, sponsoring baptisms, standing up at marriages, and serving as pallbearers at funerals. Their participation in these rites was almost as rigidly stratified as the seating in the galleries. On the whole, they looked after their own, ushering each other along the passages of Christian piety. Thereby they affirmed their identification with each other and their collective responsibility. They declared in public the human completeness they otherwise had to keep private.

Like the Ellisons, most members of Charleston's free colored aristocracy attended the Episcopal church.[92] The parish register of St. Philip's church, where some of the city's most aristocratic whites worshiped, reads like a social directory of the free mulatto elite.[93] Mr. and Mrs. Thomas S. Bonneau took an especially active part in the life of the congregation, baptizing their children, sponsoring the baptisms of others. Free colored parishioners of St. Philip's founded the Brown Fellowship Society, and its membership continued to be dominated by Episcopalians. Free people of color worshiped also at St. Michael's, St. Mark's, St. John's, St. Luke's, St. Paul's, and Grace Episcopal, whose congregation included the Johnsons and other prominent free mulatto families.

James M. Johnson attended Grace regularly while he was

in Charleston, and from time to time he visited other congregations. Church was a focal point of his social, intellectual, and spiritual life. He noted who appeared in church with whom, and he kept tabs on visiting ministers and missionaries. He observed the Episcopal bishop of South Carolina, Thomas Frederick Davis, as he stopped through Charleston on his way to Philadelphia for surgery to correct his cataracts.[94] Johnson took a special interest in Bishop Davis because he lived in Camden and was known to the Ellisons, having confirmed one of their slaves a few years earlier at Holy Cross in Stateburg.[95] Johnson also participated in prayer meetings, listened to sermons, and enjoyed hymn singings. Religious activities were as meaningful to Johnson as they were pleasant. Johnson's faith, like that of other Episcopalians, was not of the straight-laced, hard-shell variety—consider the oyster and champagne refreshments he and Eliza Ann had imbibed at a recent wedding. While worldly, his faith was genuine and deep. When his sister, the new wife of his stepson John Buckner, died suddenly and unexpectedly, Johnson was certain that she would receive God's "condescending Love & Mercy" and that her soul would be saved. Her death was the "will of God & we dare not murmur. He doeth what seemeth good in his sight," Johnson wrote Henry, adding that at the very hour of her death he had been listening to a sermon on the scriptures in St. Mark that warned, "But of that day and *that* hour knoweth no man, no, not the angels which are in heaven, neither the Son, but the Father."[96]

Johnson's religious reflections extended beyond the deathbed to other practical issues of daily life. He advised Henry, in his search for a new wife, to look not just for "beauty & form" but also for "a kind & gentle disposition & a loving Heart. And where is this to be found but in the Christian Ladies."[97] When the Diocesan Convention of South Carolina assembled in Charleston in May, Johnson went to the early morning prayer meeting at Grace and later sat in on at least one of the convention sessions. Loyal to his Stateburg home and his membership at Holy Cross, he appreciated the defense of upcountry dioceses made by one delegate in response to the sarcastic complaint of a low-country man about plans to hold the next convention in the remote back-country village of Abbeville.[98] But what riveted Johnson to his seat was an intense controversy over slave marriages. "I had no time to stay," Johnson wrote Henry, "but when Col P[hillips] got the floor I could not get away."[99]

Col. John Phillips, a delegate from the low-country Christ Church Parish, attacked a proposal before the convention drafted by a committee headed by Christopher G. Memminger. Memminger's committee had been appointed by the 1858 convention to consider "under what circumstances a clergyman may unite slaves in marriage."[100] The question arose frequently when a slave husband and wife were separated by sale: although the two might be hundreds of miles apart and have no hope of ever being reunited, were they still married? Could they take a new spouse? Could an Episcopal minister officiate at the new wedding? The highly controversial report of the Memminger committee answered "yes" to the last two questions, for reasons Col. Phillips and others found alarming. The report declared that "the relation of husband and wife is of divine institution, and the duties which appertain to it are of universal obligation, and bind with the same force the master and the slave." This meant that it was "the duty of every Christian master" not to "infringe the Divine injunction forbidding the separation of husband and wife." When an involuntary separation of slave husband and wife did occur, the report recommended, the slaves were "entitled to sympathy and consideration" and should be allowed to remarry under the auspices of the church. The master who separated them did not "recognize the force of Christian obligation," the report concluded, "and is responsible to God for disregarding his commands."[101]

Phillips and other opponents of the report took issue not with the humane consideration of the predicament of slaves but with the judgment against masters. The opponents agreed that the Christian master should honor the marriage bond between slaves, "and in this, as in all other respects, to govern his slaves in strict conformity to the laws of God." However, they argued, "the evil of separating husband and wife, arises not necessarily from the institution of domestic slavery, but like all other evils incident to every form of human society, is the result of the fallen condition of man."[102] Essentially, the debate turned on whether the church should consider a master who separated a slave husband and wife merely another predictable descendant of Adam, and forgive him, or whether such a master should be condemned. The convention could not decide the question and tabled Memminger's report.

What arguments Johnson found compelling cannot be deciphered from his brief remarks to Henry. His warm feelings toward Memminger might have inclined him toward the report, but if so, he did not hint of it in his letters to Henry. The most reasonable speculation may be that Johnson did not have a firm position on the issue, that he was captivated by the debate not because he identified with either side but because he considered the question important and difficult: what *was* a Christian master to do? Although Johnson himself did not own slaves, his father and his father-in-law did, and he lived and worked among them in Stateburg and in Charleston. If he harbored any special solicitude toward them, no record of it has survived. Instead, surviving evidence suggests that Johnson identified with slaves no more than the typical master, white or Negro.

When Bishop John Payne, a white Episcopal missionary on the west coast of Africa, visited Charleston in January 1860, Johnson went twice to hear his "interesting accounts of his Mission." The second time Payne sang " 'There is a happy land' translated in the native dialect as sung by them. It was beautiful," Johnson told Henry.[103] Johnson said nothing that suggested the native dialect was in any way part of his heritage, nothing that suggested he had reservations about what Bishop Payne referred to as "that mysterious Providence which had brought so many millions of its [Africa's] natives to our shore, fused their several hundred different dialects into one language, and enlightened very many with the knowledge of the saving grace of Christ. . . . "[104] Instead, Johnson's attitude toward Bishop Payne's African mission seemed to grow out of his general support of church missions. He expressed equal or greater interest in the work of J. Lloyd Breck, a white Episcopal missionary to the Chippewa Indians in Minnesota.[105] Although the sparse evidence is not conclusive, it suggests that Johnson recognized no racial brotherhood with slaves but only a human kinship that included Indians and whites as well.

Free colored Methodists infused the notion of human kinship with a vitality that manifested itself a good deal closer to home. Prominent free men of color like Richard Holloway and Samuel Weston were Methodist class leaders, directing the worship of small groups of free men of color in church and exhorting slaves in Charleston and on plantations throughout the low country to follow Jesus.[106] Thousands of slaves and free blacks responded, swelling Methodist ranks to many times the size of the thin columns of Episcopalians.[107] The success of the Methodists, their decentralized congregational structure, and their comparatively democratic concern for human souls of all colors and classes gave their religious message a political volatility lacking among the Episcopalians. Few people in Charleston could forget that just five years before the Denmark Vesey conspiracy thousands of black Methodists had withdrawn from the white-controlled church and set up their own African Methodist Episcopal Church, which thrived despite efforts by Charleston authorities to suppress it.[108] When the Vesey investigation turned up evidence implicating the church as a center of insurrectionary organizing, the city council ordered it to be turned into a pile of rubble.[109] Although black Charlestonians continued to throng Methodist churches after 1822, whites maintained control of the pulpit and the policies. That did not prevent disputes from arising when, for example, black Methodists refused to relinquish their seats in a crowded sanctuary to their white brethren.[110] White Methodists were no less insistent than Episcopalians that when God's grace exceeded the seating capacity of the church, God intended Negroes to obey His will and stand in the back.

In both Episcopal and Methodist churches, Charleston's free people of color joined other worshipers in affirming the theological truth of the common humanity of all peoples. That affirmation helped undercut any tendency of free Afro-Americans to identify with slaves, to recognize in their shared ancestry any special bonds of kinship or loyalty. Christian theology suppressed racial identification and squelched racial politics by asserting that Charleston's free people of color were as much kin to whites as to slaves, that their temporal loyalties encompassed the entire community of Christian believers of all colors and statuses, that the crucial question of power had less to do with relations among men in this world than with the relation between each Christian and the Lord. In their faith as in so many other ways, Charleston's free Negroes were similar to most other Americans, who struggled along, not at war with the world but trying to make the most of it as it was given to them, trying to make do, all the while casting an anxious glance forward at death and the promise of eternal life.

AFTER the busy winter and spring months of 1860 in Charleston, James M. Johnson longed to return to Stateburg to visit his wife and enjoy the company of the other Ellisons. His father hoped to accompany him to the upcountry and say goodbye to the Ellisons before leaving on his trip to Canada. Illness delayed the elder Johnson's trip to Stateburg until midsummer, and he refused to take off for Canada until he could get rid of what his son called "his pest," a very expensive gun he was trying to sell in the city.[111] Around the first of August both Johnsons came back to Charleston from Stateburg and made preparations for James D.'s departure to Toronto. Shortly before he left, the old man wrote Henry to thank him and William for a gift that had arrived by express, though the "delay has fermented the preserves & rashness has spilt the Honey & with the spoiling of the grapes it was a pickle pie." He could not resist crowing to Henry, "By the way, My Worthy Friend, before I got yours I had sold my gun for $1000 less some $100 for expenses. It is said to be the best sale had in that Market & the Broker Wagers a Fine Over Coat if it is demurred to. Say no more about bad speculating until you hear she is on hand again."[112] Buoyed by his shrewdness, the elder Johnson sailed for Canada in the highest spirits, while his son took the train back to Stateburg for a few quiet August weeks in the High Hills.

VII

Masters or Slaves

ON August 7, 1860, James Drayton Johnson steamed out of Charleston harbor bound for Boston, home of William Lloyd Garrison, Wendell Phillips, Charles Sumner, and so many others considered abolitionist fanatics by white South Carolinians. Johnson arrived in Boston a week later and left the ship to get a haircut and shave. As luck would have it, he encountered a neighbor from Charleston, a free man of color named Henry Lee. Lee told Johnson not to tarry, since the ship he was planning to take from Boston to Portland, Maine, was set to leave that evening. Johnson made it back to the ship in time for the trip to Portland, where he transferred to the Grand Trunk Railroad for the overland journey to Toronto, crossing over the St. Lawrence River into Canada on the recently completed mile-long Victoria Bridge, just below Montreal.[1] He pronounced the bridge "of its kind the grandest structure in the world," and it was a fitting introduction to the wonders of Canada.[2] "It is scarcely possible for me to give you an idea of all that I have seen since I left home," Johnson wrote Henry Ellison.[3] His letters to Henry and to his son James bubbled with a tourist's wonderment. "Father . . . is enjoying the sights with a zest," James M. told Henry.[4]

Johnson arrived in Toronto on August 17, and soon afterward his son Charley took him to see Niagara Falls. He walked across the Niagara suspension bridge, and, while standing some 245 feet above the rapids, he "saw two men . . . walk across the River Niaggara on a rope[, one] take a cooking stove on his back[,] place it on the rope[,] make a fire and then cook eggs."[5] Rivaling the daredevils' precarious breakfast were the amazements of the city of Toronto. "I have seen this city lit up with gas representing all the varied forms which it were possible for the most fertile imagination to depict," he wrote Henry. When the Prince of Wales passed through Toronto, Johnson saw "the streets lined with thousands and tens of thousands, and . . . heard 5000 children sing 'God save the Queen.' " The city went all out to honor the prince; "riches of the most magnificent description [were] towering over the streets," which had "the appearance of a flower garden." Johnson actually saw the prince, "the apparent heir to the Throne of England," but the glitter of royalty did not dim his fascination with everyday life in the city. He admired Toronto's "magnifficent [*sic*] buildings" and noted that "all colors and classes obtain admission to them." People in Toronto were "apparently happy," Johnson observed, "but I have not seen much money. It seems a scarce article." To Johnson, fresh from selling a thousand-dollar gun in Charleston, that was a major drawback to Canada. "This is to my mind a poor country," Johnson declared, "but some persons are living in it"— barely, he seemed to imply.

Struggling to make a living as a tailor, his son Charley had recently rented a two-story brick house in St. John's Ward, the section of the city that contained the most people from the United States, among them several dozen Afro-Americans.[6] Charley had been in Toronto for almost two years, and, although he had kept busy, he had little to show for it. Toronto needed tailors; in August, Lawson's at the Sign of the Elephant on King Street wanted to hire fifty tailors, and other firms advertised similar openings, including D. Sutherland, a firm near Charley's house.[7] But Charley may have been trying to compete with these large, better-capitalized merchant tailors. If so, he failed. He hired journeymen, but he had a hard time collecting his bills, even those still outstanding from his days in Charleston. In November 1859 his brother James had diplomatically mentioned to Henry that if his father, William Ellison, "saw fit to assist him [Charley] pecuniarily . . . I am confident it would be cordially accepted &, if necessary, would guarantee to protect him from loss in the premises."[8] For whatever reason, the elder Ellison evidently did not see fit, though Henry did what he could to help by ordering an overcoat and some other clothing from Charley, then waited through the cold winter months in Stateburg while the order slowly made its way to the upcountry, arriving just in time for spring.[9] In May, James appealed to Henry once again, noting that Charley "is going to church, become a Teetotaller, & is happy in his new and enlarged House." To these hints that Charley had changed some bad habits James added, "He only wants a heavier stock & that cannot be had without Money, which you know is scarce; can't you lend a helping hand. You will not lose it," a suggestion that probably left Henry cool.[10] In any case, Charley's experience gave his father little reason to doubt his impression that in Toronto, "Every body is getting along, though by appearances slowly."[11] When Charley filled out a Canadian census form in January 1861 he noted that the total value of his personal and real estate amounted to $200.[12]

While his son's finances may have troubled James D. Johnson, he clearly enjoyed the reunion with Charley, his daughter-in-law Gabriella, and his granddaughter Charlotte. Although he was away from his wife and friends in South Carolina, Johnson was still in the midst of his family and others in the Toronto colony of "our people." Gabriella and Charlotte took him on picnics. Old friends from Charleston's free colored community entertained him with visits to a church "Love Feast" and to "class meetings."[13] He reported to Henry that one of their free colored acquaintances from Charleston had "taken his third wife, a large blustering looking English girl."[14] Despite the pleasure of renewing old friendships, visiting his family, and seeing the exhilarating sights, Johnson wrote Henry that he "yearned for my home."

Johnson was not merely homesick. A recent letter from his son James in Charleston made him "doubt the propriety of my return" to South Carolina.[15] Indeed, he wrote Henry, "I regret to learn through James that things looks so dark and gloomy at home." The bad news from Charleston made him worry that he would never be able to get back into South Carolina, that the law prohibiting the reentry of free persons of color who had left the state would be strictly enforced. Whites in Charleston might see his trip to Boston, Portland, and Toronto as proof of their claims that free persons of color could serve as abolitionist emissaries and refuse to allow him to return to his home. If he violated the law and slipped into the city, he could be punished with enslavement, the prescribed punishment. Johnson was "anxious," partly because he had brought along Henry's trunk and wondered how he would get it back to him, but mostly because he left behind in Charleston his wife, "the one I most dearly loved and cared for." The news from Charleston ended his carefree retirement trip with an aching worry. "I cannot describe my feeling," he confided to Henry; "I am really comfortable and yet from the pressure which may occur by a return I am miserable."

JAMES MARSH JOHNSON may have heard the bad news from Charleston shortly after he arrived back in Stateburg. On August 9 the Charleston *Courier* printed a brief notice that the city treasurer had sold three or four hundred slave badges in the last two or three days. The *Courier* explained that sixty or seventy Negroes had been arrested by the police for working out without the badges required by city law. When their cases came before the mayor's court, presided over by Mayor Charles Macbeth, most of them argued that they were free people of color, not slaves, and that the badge law did not apply to them. However, the *Courier* pointed out, state law forbade emancipation after 1822 (the correct date was 1820). Some masters ignored the law and manumitted their slaves anyway, without providing the legal protection of an ownership in trust. "The announcement by the Mayor that such negros were not free, created considerable commotion among those outside [the courtroom] who were similarly situated as the parties arrested," and, the *Courier* concluded, "The rush to the Treasurer's office for badges, has, in consequence, been unusually large."[16]

Johnson may have read this item in the *Courier* as early as Friday, August 10, three days after the Tuesday his father left for Canada and he had returned to the High Hills. Johnson's earlier letters from Charleston make clear that the Ellisons often saw the city newspapers. Even if Johnson and the Ellisons did notice the report, it may not have aroused much concern. Essentially, the report only said that the crackdown against slaves and free people of color that had been going on since early spring was continuing, though at a new level of intensity. Johnson had expressed no anxiety about the crackdown; it did not threaten to impinge on the free mulatto aristocracy. Nothing in the *Courier* item indicated that people like Johnson and the Ellisons had anything to worry about. Their freedom was legally sound. Nobody suspected them of belonging in that no-man's land of quasi-freedom recently inhabited by the unfortunates whom Mayor Macbeth had pushed back across the line into slavery.

Whether Johnson and the Ellisons saw it or not, the eight-sentence item in the *Courier* contained an ominous warning that the political winds had shifted, that "our people" were no longer sheltered from the full force of white repression. In Charleston, what had begun as a routine crackdown on violations of the slave badge law had turned into an all-out assault on free Negroes. The brief announcement signaled the outbreak of a crisis of survival, a crisis the free colored aristocracy had been confident would never come. As never before, they confronted a threat to freedom itself. Although the term did not acquire meaning for another seventy-eight years, the eve of James D. Johnson's departure for Canada and his son's visit to Stateburg amounted to an antebellum *Krystalnacht*.

James M. Johnson returned to Charleston no later than August 19, less than two weeks after he left. On the train back to Charleston he heard that petitions were being circulated among upcountry legislators demanding that a law be passed to sell into slavery rural free Negroes "who are considered worthless, prior to passing a Law for the removal of the Body," the entire free colored population. Supporters of the petition alleged that free Negroes in the country were "equal to Bears at stealing corn," Johnson wrote Henry, adding sardonically that the current short supply of corn would be used as an excuse to enslave free Negroes "as How to make a larger crop next year."[17] The conversation on the train indicated that the assault was not confined to the city.

On Sunday evening, the nineteenth, soon after he arrived in Charleston, Johnson went to Joseph Dereef's house, where he learned alarming details about the crisis. The next day he sent Henry a full report, the first of six letters he sent to the Ellisons during the next eight weeks, chronicling the enslavement crisis in Charleston. The first sentence of his letter on August 20 suggests that he and the Ellisons had caught wind of the crisis while he was still in Stateburg, since it contains no introductory phrase, no clause explaining that things had unexpectedly taken a nasty turn. Instead, Johnson wrote as if the Ellisons already knew that a crisis existed, and he compressed into a few words its portent for the free mulatto elite: "Since my absence the agitation has been so great as to cause many to leave who were liable to the law of 1822 & the panic has reached those whom that law cannot affect."[18] The full meaning of those last ten words was not lost on the Ellisons. They, like most of their free mulatto friends in Charleston, had no reason to fear strict legal tests of their freedom. Yet just such people, their kinfolk and acquaintances in Charleston, were panic-stricken.

Johnson's reference to the law of 1822 reflects the widespread confusion among both Afro-Americans and whites about the precise legal basis of the crisis. What Johnson, the *Courier,* and evidently even Mayor Macbeth meant by the law of 1822 was the prohibition of manumission that was enacted in 1820. To pass the test of this law, free persons of color had to have documentary proof that their freedom antedated 1820, or that their mothers' did. William Ellison had prepared for such an eventuality in 1838 when he created a record of the birthdates of his children with the clerk of court in Sumter. Few free people of color were as meticulous about documenting the legal basis of their freedom. Those who were freeborn or freed before 1820 knew they were free, their white friends knew they were free, they paid the state capitation tax on free Negroes and, if they lived in Charleston, the special city levies on free persons of color. Capitation tax receipts, listing in the Charleston Free Negro Tax Books, and common knowledge had always been sufficient proof of their freedom, on the few occasions when proof was demanded.

During the first week in August, when Charleston police rounded up Negroes who claimed to be free and who rested their claims on the usual proofs, Mayor Macbeth evidently began to insist on strict adherence to the legal requirement of proof of either free birth or manumission before 1820. Macbeth enforced what the law assumed—that a Negro who lacked irrefutable proof of freedom was a slave. During the enslave-ment crisis in Charleston the informal personal relationships with whites that had previously shielded free persons of color turned into a dangerous legal trap. To avoid enslavement, each free Afro-American in Charleston needed certain specific legal documents, documents that many Afro-Americans who were legally free and whose freedom was recognized by influ-ential whites had simply never troubled themselves to obtain because everyone who counted *knew* they were free. In August, the personalism that had shielded the freedom of the mulatto elite proved to be almost worthless to hundreds of free Afro-Americans.

Johnson cited a poignant example in his first letter to Henry. He told of a free woman of color who came to Joseph Dereef for help. Dereef knew the woman's grandmother "to be Bona fide," that is, legally free; "& [he] knew her mother also, when she had this child." The woman came to Dereef because she had no documentary proof of the free status of her mother or her grandmother, and Dereef was "the only person that knew her origin that she could refer to." Dereef, however, "could not relieve her"; as a free man of color he could not give sworn testimony in her behalf. His knowledge of her birth to a freeborn Negro woman had no legal value. Under normal circumstances, his wealth and respectability might have given his testimony weight even though he was not under oath. But under normal circumstances the free woman of color who came to him did not need his testimony. Mayor Macbeth demanded compliance with the letter of the law, which meant Dereef's word could not protect this legitimately free woman from enslavement. By a strict interpretation of the law, through no fault of her own, her freedom vanished. Dereef "seems to be more oppressed than any one I have spoken with," John-son wrote Henry.[19]

The woman who came to Dereef was by no means the only free person of color who could not document free status. "[T]here are numbers in the same dilemma," Johnson wrote. It is easy to imagine why. For that freeborn woman and oth-ers like her, the relevant document was not something they were likely ever to have possessed but a document that belonged to their mothers, or, in the woman's case, to her grandmother. Assuming that a statement of the grandmother's manumission existed at one time, that document had probably been created from forty to sixty years earlier and, in the intervening years, may have been misplaced, forgotten, or destroyed. Furthermore, any white person who could supply iron-clad testimony in Charleston in 1860 that the grandmother was indeed legally free in 1800 or even 1820 was likely to be hard to find. Freeborn Afro-Americans probably had the most questionable credentials. Individuals born after 1820, who composed the large majority, could not possibly have been legally manumitted. The legal presumption that they were slaves was supported by their age and had to be overruled by proof of the free status of their mothers. By 1860 many of their mothers were dead and many of the survivors had no record of free status that would withstand strict legal scrutiny. The birthright of freeborns that in the past had been their lifeline to freedom, extending across as many as three generations, now dragged them back into bondage. "It is such cases that awaken sympathy," Johnson said.[20]

Johnson's statement implies that other cases failed to awaken his sympathy. Presumably he had in mind the hundreds of Afro-Americans who had no legitimate claim to free status, slaves who had managed to turn their masters' loose supervision into *de facto* freedom. The police had been picking up such persons since the beginning of the spring crackdown, and Johnson had never uttered a word of sympathy for them. They probably predominated among the three or four hundred Negroes who, according to the *Courier,* rushed to acquire slave badges as soon as it became clear the mayor would no longer recognize their freedom. Johnson expressed his amazement that the crisis was so severe that "persons who for 30 yrs have been paying capitation Tax & one of 35 yrs . . . have to go back to bondage & take out their Badges."[21] Their hurry to embrace slave status came from desperation. They knew their freedom had no legal basis, that it existed only in the interstices of slavery in the city, in the opportunity to live and work away from their masters. By quickly taking out badges as slaves, they protected the few advantages they had. They retained the masters who had allowed them to pass themselves off as free, possibly without even being aware they had done so. By ratifying their slave status with their existing masters, they avoided being seized by the police and sold to the highest bidder. Buying badges was also safer than trying to run away; a master who failed to get his share of weekly wages would eventually set out to retrieve his valuable property and, if he succeeded, would be certain to tighten the bonds of servitude or sell the runaway. For slaves who had passed as free, wearing slave badges once again promised to change their lives far less than any other option they had. Perhaps Johnson had little sympathy for them because they had been living beyond their legal means and—worst of all—because their efforts had bought trouble for freeborn and legally freed persons of color.

Characteristically, when Johnson mentioned the fate of the masses of free Negroes he assumed the viewpoint of the free mulatto elite. He mentioned to Henry that slaves who belonged to the Dereefs had been forced to take out badges. But rather than commiserating with the freshly minted slaves, he sympathized with the Dereefs, who "have had to pay some $80 fines, for Servts without Badges."[22] Johnson's attitude was the product of years of daily practice in remaining aloof from free blacks and slaves. Yet the pressure of the enslavement crisis was rapidly making that attitude anachronistic. Distinctions between brown and black and between freedom and slavery, distinctions that framed the outlook of "our people," were beginning to blur. The law and white politics conspired to pull the middle ground out from under the free mulatto aristocracy and to push them backward toward slavery.

AFRO-AMERICANS who could prove their free status, whether they were freeborn like James M. Johnson or legally freed like William Ellison, could still become entangled in laws that threatened them with slavery. The state law of 1822 required that every free man of color have a white guardian, duly registered with the clerk of court. The penalty for noncompliance was enslavement. The constant reference to the law of 1822 during the enslavement crisis in Charleston suggests this provision may have been invoked against many free Negro men who neglected to obtain a white guardian, who failed to register the guardianship properly, who lost the necessary legal documents, or whose guardian had died, moved, or no longer accepted his legal role. Freeborn men were especially vulnerable to this law, since they were the most likely to overlook it, either out of ignorance or because they did not imagine that they would ever be challenged about it. Henry Ellison and William Ellison Jr. never registered with a white guardian in Sumter up to 1842, when the extant records end, long after they were required by law to register.[23] Presumably they assumed that Dr. Anderson was their guardian as much as he was their father's. Although Dr. Anderson probably considered himself the guardian of all the Ellisons, the law did not recognize such casual extensions of guardianship unless the presiding judge happened to be in the mood to waive the technicalities, as Charleston's Mayor Macbeth obviously was not. James M. Johnson surely had a white guardian, but no record of the arrangement has survived. However, it is likely that many other free men of color in Charleston were, in Johnson's phrase, "liable to the law of 1822" because they had failed to cement a legal relationship as the ward of a white man. In the absence of a white guardian they became subject to a white master.

Another legal trap door into slavery hinged on the trusteeships used by masters who wanted to manumit a slave after 1820. Individuals like William Ellison's daughter Maria were slaves belonging to trustees who, according to the terms of the trust, allowed them to live as if they were free persons. In Charleston such persons now had to take out badges as slaves, regardless of the trust. Furthermore, if the trustee had died without providing for the transference of the trust to an heir, the slave held in trust lacked a master and could be seized and held as a slave by any white person or confiscated by the police and sold at public auction. Maria (Ellison) Jacobs was in precisely this situation in Winnsboro; her trustee, William McCreight, the white gin maker with whom her father had apprenticed more than a half-century earlier, had died in 1859.[24] If Maria had lived in Charleston in 1860, she might well have been among the many others like her who had to buy slave badges. When William Ellison heard about the Charleston crisis from Johnson's letters to Henry, he surely thought of Maria, but Johnson himself never referred to her or even hinted

that he was aware of her existence, much less her vulnerability.

Even more vulnerable were individuals who had been manumitted by their masters after 1820 without the provision of
an owner in trust. They were free in the sense that their legal
master had renounced ownership of them, but the law considered them slaves without masters. Charleston was a mecca
for such individuals, since the absence of a master could easily
be obscured in the anonymity and bustle of the city. Their
numbers included the Westons, one of the most prominent
free mulatto families in the city. Anthony Weston, the patriarch of the family, was in some ways the William Ellison of
the low country. Born a slave in 1791, Toney—as he was then
called—belonged to the wealthy rice planter Plowden Weston. By about 1810, the mills near Georgetown that hulled
and processed Weston's rice were built and maintained by
Toney, who had become an expert mechanic. Weston owned
140 slaves, but he singled out Toney for special attention,
giving him gifts from time to time and allowing him to control his own time for about half of each year.[25] When Weston
died in 1827, his will provided that "in consideration of the
good conduct and faithful Valuable services of my Mulatto
man Toney, by Trade a Millwright," Toney was to be allowed
to continue the privilege of controlling half his time for six
years, while he trained other Weston slaves to take his place,
and then be given all his time and, if possible, emancipated—
a boon Weston gave to only two other slaves, both house
servants who had given him exemplary attention.[26] The terms
of Weston's will made Toney—now Anthony—a free man by
1833, and he employed his freedom and his skills to amass
more wealth than any other free man of color in Charleston.

Although the scanty evidence makes it impossible to unravel
the details of Anthony's career as a free man of color, it appears
that he married one of Plowden Weston's Charleston house
servants, a woman named Maria, possibly buying her freedom with his earnings from his millwright's shop in Charleston, as he evidently did the freedom of two other Weston
slaves, Samuel and Jacob, who were apparently his brothers.[27] By 1860 Anthony Weston still did thriving business as
a millwright in his shop on Calhoun Street, and he had accu-

mulated real estate worth $40,075 and fourteen slaves, all held by his wife, apparently because her legal claim to freedom was stronger than his.[28] Although Plowden Weston's heirs and many other white Charlestonians considered Anthony Weston a remarkably successful free man, legally he had no right to property of any kind, since he was still a slave. Unlike the slaves with lax masters who hurried to the city treasurer's office in the August crisis to take out their badges, Anthony Weston and other slaves without masters waited for the knock on the door that would prove to be the Charleston police, who—James M. Johnson wrote Henry—"have declared their intention not to leave one [free colored] family uncalled upon." They waited, and they worried. "It is beyond doubt that it will kill many," Johnson predicted; "It is like the heat of this summer conceded to be the hottest & most deadly assault ever made upon this class, & animal, like vegetable life, must wither & die from the shock."[29]

Johnson's imagery was justified, considering what it meant for a free person of color to cross the line into slavery. First of all, the person lost all property he or she may have owned. Since the pertinent Charleston court records have vanished, it is impossible to determine exactly how authorities disposed of the property of those enslaved. The law allowed Mayor Macbeth and the other magistrates of his court to confiscate the property and keep it for the city and the state, or, if they chose, auction it off to the general public. The magistrates had the same options with their new human property. Of all the categories of free Afro-Americans who were being swept up in the police dragnet, only slaves whose masters had allowed them *de facto* freedom could predict who their owners would be. Freeborn Negroes who could not document their mothers' freedom, legally freed persons who lacked the necessary documents, free men of color who had failed to obtain guardians, slaves held in trust and allowed to live as free persons by trustees who were no longer accessible, and slaves who had been manumitted illegally by their masters without the provision of a trustee—all of these individuals lacked the one thing the law required a slave to have: a master. They had no way to know who would become their owner. Initially, the magistrates themselves seized the new slaves. "The magistrates boast of the good it has done them & Trusted that they did not know they were so rich," Johnson noted. "Slaves have come by magic," he added bitterly; "It is evident that the movement is intended for their [the magistrates'] emolument." To the magistrates' new slaves, Johnson declared, "it must prove the Death of many & the loss of earthly goods, the hard earnings of a life time, to others."[30] But the most important loss was free status.

When free persons of color were forced by the mayor's court to enter slavery by taking out a slave badge, they instantly lost all control over their lives. Any contracts they had been party to were now void. Any legal suits they had begun were now ended. They had to go where their masters told them, do what their masters ordered them to do when their masters ordered them to do it. But perhaps the most horrible repercussion of slave status was its effect on the families of the new slaves. The moment any free woman of color became legally recognized as a slave, her children also became slaves, as did their children, if they had any. The enslavement of each free woman of color had a sickening domino effect among her descendants. Individuals like the freeborn woman who came to Joseph Dereef pleading for help probably had never dreamed that they might personally experience the nightmare of slavery. Now she, her siblings, and her children were stalked by the specter of slavery in the guise of the Charleston police. If she lost her freedom, all the others were in jeopardy.

Johnson did not mention the name of the woman who appealed to Dereef, or name many of the 700 or so other Afro-Americans who had to comply.[31] But he did tell Henry the names of a few of the persons who were being terrorized by the police and the mayor. William Fordham, a middle-aged free colored barber, "had to comply with the Law," Johnson noted.[32] He also observed "Mr Jon Lee going down to Stmr to get off Demar's wife & *Matthews children.*"[33] Samuel Demar was a free man of color who paid taxes on real estate worth $2,000 and two slaves, one of whom may well have been his wife.[34] The "Matthews" Johnson referred to was probably John B. Mathews, a fifty-year-old mulatto tailor who owned real estate worth $5,000 and one slave, a woman about his age who was most likely his wife.[35] If these inferences are correct, Jon Lee's errand was urgent. Mathews's children, Elizabeth, Matilda, Harriet, and C. Pinckney, would lose the free status they had registered in the 1860 census unless they got out of Charleston before the police discovered them. Demar's wife, who may well have been living as a free woman, probably confronted a similar fate if she stayed in the city. Being escorted to the steamer by Jon Lee, the well-known free colored steward of the Charleston Club—a popular watering hole of the city's white chivalry—may have meant nothing more than that Samuel Demar and John Mathews happened to be out of town when the crisis struck. Or, Lee may have been exploiting his privilege to travel freely in and out of the state to procure supplies for the Charleston Club as a convenient cover for getting the dependents of two of his free colored friends on an outbound steamer without raising suspicions.[36]

Demar's wife and Mathews's children joined many other free Afro-Americans who tried to stay one jump ahead of the Charleston police. "Those who are now hunted down have divined what is to be done with them & before their destiny is sealed by an amendment [which could prevent them from escaping] are wisely leaving by every Steamer & Railroad too. The [Philadelphia steamer] Keystone State takes out several today," Johnson wrote on August 20.[37] A week later he mentioned that Edward Beard "has closed his school & is about to leave before he is pounced upon."[38] A week after that he reported that the "tide of emigration has not stopped."[39]

The August refugees were Afro-Americans whose freedom was least secure. Those with the weakest claims to free status left immediately, probably without having time to make arrangements for settling their affairs in Charleston or for sending word of their departure ahead to their destination. Others who felt safe enough to stay a few extra days in the city had a little more time to close down their businesses, collect accounts outstanding, consult with relatives and friends, find someone to manage or to sell any real estate they might have, and decide where they should go—luxuries the first wave of emigrants had no time to indulge in. But even with an extra week or two in Charleston, emigrants had difficulty winding up their affairs. In August many white Charlestonians left the city, seeking relief from the oppressive heat and the business doldrums. Free colored tailors and seamstresses who were about to emigrate had no way to collect from the vacationing whites. Whites probably did not rush to pay their accounts with the departing free Negroes; they knew why the emigrants were leaving, and they could recognize a windfall when they saw one. The emigrants themselves had little leverage. Standing on the edge of slavery, they were hardly in a strong position to collect wages or to sell their real estate. In addition, the large number of emigrants who put their property up for sale at about the same time saturated the market, depressed the price, and further weakened their bargaining power. Johnson told Henry that "you can see Hand bills on property held by cold. [colored] people in every quarter [of the city], which will have the effect of depreciation."[40] Despite these heavy disadvantages, emigration was preferable to slavery. Johnson reported that the emigrants' white "friends and counsellors tell them to leave. The time is at hand when none may remain but them [whites] and their slaves." The free colored emigrants agreed with the advice "as they are to be embraced in the latter."[41]

Some Afro-Americans whose freedom was questionable felt secure enough to file a court challenge to their enslavement. Johnson wrote, "Of the many hundred[,] perhaps [a] thousand cases before the court represented by Lawyers & Gentlemen of standing, but one or two have stood suit & they are for persons lately freed."[42] Johnson did not mention the outcome of those one or two cases, but since persons recently manumitted had the weakest claim to freedom, those cases could not serve as indicators of how the hundreds of other, more difficult cases might be decided. The legal records and court documents that contained information about the cases no longer exist, making it necessary to conjecture about the legal issues.[43] Clever lawyers probably found dozens of technical and material arguments that could be constructed into a defense of the free status of a certain Afro-American, but a central issue in many of the cases must have been the difficult question of whether an individual master's will was supreme over the law of the state. If a master had manumitted a slave by provision of his will, duly approved and registered with

the proper legal bodies, could the state law of 1820 prohibiting such manumissions overrule the master's intent expressed
in a document with the authority that, in the law, comes nearest to reverence? There is no way to know how this question
was resolved in the hundreds of cases before the courts or
even whether the cases ever came to trial. Only a week after
writing Henry about the lawsuits, Johnson noted, "Nothing
more is heard of the suits."[44] It may well be that the main
purpose of the suits was not to resolve the question of freedom but to complicate it, and thus buy time to maneuver, to
decide what to do, to see if the crisis would pass, to allow
things to return to normal.

THAT things always returned to normal had become an article of faith among Charleston's free mulatto aristocracy. Even
after the Denmark Vesey conspiracy, when a gallows with
twenty-two nooses stood on the edge of town, the city had
relaxed. Free people of color were permitted to carry on their
daily lives more or less as always. During the decades since
1822, political and racial tensions had surged several times,
usually accompanied by an attack against slaves and free persons of color. However, as in the most recent crackdown that
began in the spring of 1860, members of the free mulatto elite
were only slightly affected. Like James M. Johnson, they continued their daily routine with little variation, except perhaps
an extra measure of wariness about inadvertent transgressions
of municipal regulations and racial etiquette.

The August enslavement crisis, like the numerous assaults
of the past, hardly touched the free mulatto elite. Their freedom had a solid legal foundation. Only a few of them and
their family members straddled the line between slavery and
freedom and needed to hurry out of the city to escape the
police. Nonetheless, the enslavement crisis—unlike every other
episode of racial repression—caused a fundamental transfor-
mation in the outlook of the free mulatto aristocracy. Their
faith that things would return to normal became a conviction
that things would never be the same.

Although existing laws did not challenge the free status of
the Ellisons' mulatto friends in Charleston, the August
enslavement crisis drastically affected their everyday lives. Acts

of racial harassment became more frequent and more threatening. A free man of color named James Hicks, a nurse who was about fifty years old, "had his watch & chain taken from him in a Mob raised in Market St.," Johnson reported to Henry.[45] Whites in the mob evidently considered Hicks's fashionable attire an act of insolence and racial insubordination—a watch and chain were the proper accouterments of white folk. Yet William Ellison owned a gold watch, and James D. Johnson, the cagey speculator on a thousand-dollar gun, probably did too, as did many of the other prosperous free men of color in the city.

Dangerous and humiliating racial incidents were not confined to the busy public markets. Johnson told Henry about a young free man of color named James Glover who "was taken to the Guard House at the instance of Dr [Henry W.] Dessausure for standing in a Drug store with his Hat on."[46] DeSaussure would have been within his rights to beat Glover for this act of insolence, but he exercised restraint and sent him to jail instead, where he would appear before Mayor Macbeth accused of a crime punishable by whipping and imprisonment. In June, a free man of color received thirteen paddles and ten days in jail for insolence.[47] Glover was luckier. His white guardian argued before the mayor's court that "an excuse for his rushing into a drug store with his hat on [was] That any servant would be in a hurry when he had a distance to go & it was late & he without a pass."[48] In other words, Glover's guardian claimed that far from being insolent, Glover was hurrying to comply with the city curfew for Negroes; since he did not have written permission to be on the streets after curfew, he was so eager to complete his errand and obey the law that he forgot about his hat. Whether the guardian's story was true or not, "Glover was let off with a Fine of $5," and Johnson believed that the story "saved his paddles."[49]

Racial violence flashed through the supercharged atmosphere in Charleston. Louisa Thompson, a free mulatto washerwoman, was sentenced by the mayor to five paddles and five days in jail for "striking a [white] Lady."[50] Exactly what Thompson was accused of doing may have ranged anywhere from actually assaulting a white woman to defending herself from assault, and an act approaching the latter is more likely, given the comparatively light sentence. After Louisa Thompson had been sentenced, her brother, William Thompson, a young free mulatto laborer, appeared before the mayor's court and "claimed White Laws," Johnson explained. Even under normal circumstances William's assertion would have been risky; in the context of the enslavement crisis it was explosive. He claimed that Louisa was not a free person of color but white, that she should not be judged by the special laws applying only to free Negroes. Had his claim been sustained, one consequence would probably have been that an argument could be made that Louisa's "striking against a Lady" was justifiable. Numerous other consequences would follow, including being able to testify in court, under oath, against whites, and to escape all the other legal restrictions that applied exclusively to free people of color. According to Johnson, William's bold claim convinced the court to omit Louisa's paddles, though the jail sentence was imposed. But that was not the end of the case. "[B]y way of balancing the acct her Brother was ferreted out at his House & beat by Police Officers for presuming to say [that] she was as white as those who arrested [her]." Undaunted, William complained to Police Chief H. L. Bass, who "took the officers aside" and sent William home. "He may look to be redressed with another Walloping," Johnson predicted.

Free mulattoes like Johnson and his friends shunned the brazen claims of William Thompson, probably considering them foolhardy and provocative. Under normal circumstances the acts of a man like Thompson did not implicate the free mulatto elite. Now, however, they tarnished the reputation of one of the city's leading free mulatto families. Near the end of August, Hannah Weston, the twenty-five-year-old daughter of the well-known free mulatto tailor Samuel Weston, was enjoying the sea breezes on Sullivan's Island along with hundreds of other Charlestonians when a white person noticed she had a wounded hand and asked her if the whipping she had received at the mayor's court had caused the wound. She had been mistaken for Louisa Thompson. The erroneous rumor of her transgression and her punishment "was getting credence among the whites," Johnson told Henry.[51]

Samuel Weston "thought it best to stop" the rumor.[52] He took the most direct and daring path. He "called on Mayor McBeth to get him to certify to the falsity of a Report that one of the Miss Westons had undergone punishment for insolence to a Lady." To stand before the mayor in the midst of the enslavement crisis and demand that he correct a rumor took audacity, for Weston had been freed after 1820 and was subject to the law that was sending refugees streaming from the city. The mayor told Weston "he must break the first fellow's head" that repeated the rumor, and he arranged to have the *Courier* print a notice saying the rumor that "a female member of the family of either *Anthony* or *Samuel Weston* had offered some violence to a lady in the street" was "entirely untrue and without foundation."[53] Furthermore, the *Courier* declared, "These *Westons* are very respectable colored persons and esteemed in the community for their character and deportment at all times."[54]

Far from claiming white laws, Samuel Weston protected himself and his family with the traditional defenses of the free mulatto elite: cool nerves, a steely confidence, an insider's knowledge of how to make the system work, and powerful white friends. Weston probably had never before exerted his influence in just this way. It is a measure of his sense of the crisis that he did not wait for the rumor to die out or try to counter it by going to white intermediaries who would, in time, spread the truth. Instead, he put his prestige and his freedom on the line and insisted that the mayor squelch the rumor, not just within his social circle of white planters, lawyers, and politicians but by public denial in the *Courier*. Weston's success illustrates the influence the most respectable free mulattoes could still exert. That Weston felt it necessary to demand a public endorsement of his respectability illustrates the unprecedented pressure the enslavement crisis exerted on the free mulatto aristocracy.

In the past Charleston's free people of color had traveled freely, returning home safely after trips to Philadelphia, New York, Boston, and elsewhere outside the slave states. On the whole, they had enjoyed an exemption from the state law that prohibited any free person of color who left South Carolina from reentering the state, with enslavement awaiting violators. Periodically the law had been strictly enforced. Jehu Jones, a free man of color who ran a hotel in Charleston that the white aristocracy regarded as the best in the city—where Stateburg's Richard Singleton, for example, ran up some impressive bills—was not allowed to bring his family back into the city after they left in 1823 planning to emigrate to Liberia.[55] Although Jones petitioned the state legislature for an exemption and marshaled support from prominent whites, his petition was denied, the apparent victim of his apostasy.[56] If the law had been applied to the rest of the free mulatto elite as it had to Jones, their frequent trips out of the state would have long since turned nearly all of them into slaves or exiles. That was precisely what the enslavement crisis threatened to do.

Moses Levy, an old white man, a former Charleston policeman, and self-professed 'Gentleman," lived on Tradd Street just opposite Adger's wharves where the New York steamers docked.[57] Levy spent some of his time watching passengers disembark, and he was fed up with what he saw. During the crisis he told authorities that he had seen a free man of color illegally reenter the city from one of the New York ships. Levy remarked, according to James M. Johnson, that his son Edwin, a sergeant in the city police, "would put a stop to the practice, it was too common with females especially. Several were seen promenading on Broadway & then they would return here as coolly as whites."[58] That was Levy's real complaint; the crisis gave him an occasion to put such uppity free Negroes back in their place.

The man Levy reported turned out to be Joseph Noisette, a thirty-year-old farmer who lived on the outskirts of the city. Johnson told Henry that Noisette had left Charleston the first of August, pursued not by the police but by his creditors and his wife. Now, after what Johnson called his "child's play," Noisette tried to slip back into Charleston, evidently unaware of the simmering crisis.[59] The captain of the steamer had initially refused to take him aboard in New York, since a person who aided a free person of color to reenter the state was subject to a $1,000 fine and up to six months' imprisonment. Noisette begged two white friends from Charleston to intercede with the captain in his behalf. They talked the captain into letting Noisette come aboard, and then, Johnson noted, Noisette "foolishly secreted himself & when the Captn found it out, he got so vexed he confined him and handed him over to Levy on arrival." The captain, knowing the racial climate in Charleston, had no intention of cooperating with Noisette's surreptitious behavior. Despite the intercession of influential Charleston whites, the captain refused to risk antagonizing the city's authorities. Evidently the captain was willing to allow Noisette to walk down the ramp to Adger's North Wharf just like hundreds of other free people had done before. But by hiding away, Noisette implicated the captain and landed himself in jail. Johnson wrote Henry that Noisette only avoided the penalty prescribed by law by having a white lawyer argue before the magistrates' court that he was in fact a slave. No law prohibited slaves from leaving the state and returning. Slaves had to be allowed to go where their masters' sent them. Thus Noisette avoided formal enslavement by voluntarily pleading that he was already a slave.

Normally, the escapades of a ne'er-do-well like Noisette would have been no cause for alarm among the free mulatto elite. During the August crisis, however, Noisette's case illustrated the erosion of the traditional perquisites of the respectable free people of color. Levy would turn in free Negroes who returned from out of state; steamship captains were aware of the crisis and the law and were determined to avoid becoming entangled in either; influential Charleston whites like the men who had convinced the captain to take a chance on Noisette—one of whom was an Adger, one of the Ellison's white friends of long standing—were not influential enough to keep the captain from handing Noisette over to the police or to arrange a settlement of the case that preserved his freedom. The experiences of other free Afro-Americans proved that more than Noisette's irresponsibility lay behind these disturbing developments.

In his first letter describing the enslavement crisis, Johnson told Henry of a free woman of color who had left Charleston for a vacation in the North. She arranged for a slave who was passing as a free person to take care of her home while she was away. When the crisis broke, a Charleston lawyer, a white man who was a close friend of the vacationing woman, said the servant she had hired "must have a Badge & the Lady who he will do any thing for, must make up her mind to stay [in the North], as no mortal man will be allowed to return."[60] Even a lawyer who was the woman's trusted friend and who was willing to resort to every legal subterfuge to help her had concluded that, under the circumstances, her only alternative was exile. In fact, even going into exile had become problematic. Johnson notified Henry that "Among those leaving by N Y strm was a white cold. [colored] woman who with her children was put ashore." The steamer captain had evidently decided she and her children might possibly be slaves, which would make him an accomplice to slave runaways, a capital offense in South Carolina. The woman was put ashore at the last minute, after her baggage had been stowed, and the captain promised to take care of it for her after he got to New York. Incongruously, once the woman was back in the city, "She was not arrested at all," Johnson reported, confirming the unpredictable whims by which the crisis was visited upon the most respectable free people of color, even when they were white.

As early as August 20 several of the pillars of Charleston's free mulatto community had concluded that they had to subject themselves to the same risks as the white woman of color. Johnson relayed to Stateburg the judgment of John Lee that "It is plain now all must go & his Brother is of the same opinion. *Great change.*"[61] At night Lee tended bar at the Charleston Club while his brother marked billiard scores, both of them privy to the conversations of Charleston's white gentry.[62] The informed opinion of the Lees, a family who had lived in Charleston since well before the American Revolution, deserved careful consideration. Their conclusion that "all must go" commanded the respect, though not the immediate concurrence, of the entire free mulatto community. The free mulatto tailor John Veree "has made up his mind to leave," Johnson told Henry.[63] "Do acquaint your Father of the state of feeling," Johnson said. The crisis was confined to Charleston for the time being, but it was based on "a State law" that applied equally to Stateburg. "[T]o use the expression of those who have the matter in hands," Johnson announced, anticipating the argument most likely to carry weight with William

Ellison, " 'What is to come will be worse.' When that comes every property holder will be glad to take what he can get (irrespective of value) for his property." Johnson notified the Ellisons that, in the considered judgment of their Charleston friends, "this is the beginning. The next session [of the legislature] will wind up the affairs of every free cold. [colored] man & they will be made to leave."

Johnson considered these views important and believed the Ellisons should be acquainted with them, but he was not fully persuaded by them. While other free people of color were taking out badges as slaves and scrambling to stay away from the police, his life remained fairly normal. He gossiped with a white planter from Sumter who said he had "a Brag Cotton Crop" waiting at home while he enjoyed a stay at Summerville, where "they have parties every night, & live as well as in the City."[64] Johnson kept track of Mary, Abby, and Jessie Dereef, the eligible daughters of Joseph Dereef, and playfully told Henry, "They are eager to leave & if you know of a worthy fellow who feels like emigrating you can recommend him. So [long] as they are in good company it dont matter if they are bound to the State of Matrimony. . . . " Despite the grim news of emigration, white mobs in the streets, and white policemen on the rampage, Johnson told Henry he should come down to Charleston. "If you dont come soon you wont find that number of Ladies to select from you enumerated not long since. They are juicing down (reducing) very fast."

Within a week of writing those words, some of the bounce left Johnson's step. None of his letters over the next month and a half renewed Henry's invitation to Charleston. When he wrote Stateburg on August 28, the strain of coming to terms with events in the city had begun to take its toll. "We are not very well. The heat is oppressive," he said, before reporting the latest news and explaining his thoughts.[65] "The stir has subsided, but arrests are still made & the people are leaving." However, he cautioned, as if in response to a statement Henry had made in his first letter since hearing from Johnson about the crisis, "It is vain for us to hope that if it is not the *will* of God he will not permit it." Johnson pointed out that although God was just, "on earth wicked rule prevails" because men are "free agents," free to obey His will or to ignore it. It was a mistake to interpret the enslavement crisis as an unfathomable intervention by the Almighty. "I very much doubt that He wills or sanctions unrighteous acts," Johnson confided to Henry, "although in answer to prayer He often overthrows them and converts them into an engine of good provided we will act in accordance with his will as suggested by His Spirit & not supinely wait for the working of a miracle by having a Chariot let down to convey us away." The crucial theological truth for Johnson was contained in his "provided" clause. Quiescence and passivity while waiting for the miraculous heavenly chariot that would whisk Christians away from their earthly troubles were not what God expected from the faithful. Instead, he expected them to exercise their freedom to combat wickedness. God would help, provided they helped themselves.

THE behavior of the white friends of Charleston's free mulattoes reinforced Johnson's theology. Nothing during the enslavement crisis did more to upset the equilibrium of the free mulatto aristocracy than their discovery of the limits of their highly valued friendships with whites. The discovery was painful because it made clear how little reciprocity had existed in the personal relationships with whites that free mulattoes had nurtured for so many years. Worse, the discovery was unnerving because free mulattoes depended on influential whites to shield them from the law and to protect them from their enemies among upcountry farmers and white mechanics in Charleston. Powerful whites allowed them to exercise their freedom within limits set by racial prejudice and social respectability rather than the law. The actions of their white friends left Charleston's free mulattoes feeling betrayed, abandoned, and—worst of all—dangerously exposed. Although few leading free mulattoes personally faced the choice of buying slave badges or rushing from the state during the August crisis, the fact that any free Negro had to face those choices, that the crisis had been allowed to occur, was profoundly alarming for the free mulatto elite. As never before they had to reconsider the security of their freedom. Their recent experience brought home what they had always known. Despite all they could do for themselves, they could not defend their freedom alone.

The enslavement crisis sprang unexpectedly from the white mechanics' campaign against slave competition. Records that would make it possible to reconstruct the precise sequence of events do not exist. In fact, until Johnson's letters to the Ellisons came to light, the Charleston enslavement crisis had entirely escaped historians' notice. White politicians did not make speeches about it, local newspapers did not print accounts of it, and the free people of color directly affected by it left no records that found their way into the hands of historians. Nonetheless, bits and pieces of evidence, like the *Courier*'s brief account of the rush for slave badges, corroborate Johnson's reports and erase all doubts about the historical reality of the crisis. Most likely, the crisis was not a premeditated intensification of the months-long campaign against slaves who hired out without badges and free Negroes who failed to pay their capitation taxes. Instead, it appears to have developed somewhat inadvertently out of the routines that had been followed dozens of times during the crackdown.

During May, June, and July, as the Charleston police picked up Negroes they suspected of being in violation of the city badge law and brought them before the Mayor's Court, a good many of the suspects probably declared that they did not need a slave badge because they were free. They proved it by their capitation tax receipt and by pointing to their name in the Free Negro Tax Book. Sometime in late July or early August, after having acceded to this defense again and again, Mayor Macbeth searched out the legal particulars required to prove free status. What prompted him to turn to his law books is unknown. Most likely, the police, their informants, or the mayor himself had simply seen one too many Afro-Americans they knew for certain to have been illegally manumitted or not manumitted at all evade prosecution by conforming to the very rules set by the prosecutors. It had to be frustrating for city authorities. The mayor had come into office pledged to enforce the laws strictly and to keep the city's Negroes in line, promises he had kept by overseeing the crackdown since early in the spring of 1860. He may have been reminded of his promise by a letter that appeared in the *Courier* on August 4, complaining of "negro huts" inhabited by slaves who hired their own time, and urging the city "by every *moral* and *pecuniary* consideration, to *enforce* their Ordinance which expressly legislates against this crying evil."[66] He had a healthy respect for the electoral clout of the city's white mechanics, and he knew that anything he could do to reduce slave competition, or to give the appearance of reducing it, would receive the enthusiastic support of white workingmen. Demanding that Negroes' assertions of free status meet the most rigorous legal standards promised to build political capital for Macbeth without making any important enemies. Who could object to forcing Negroes to obey the law?

Macbeth's timing, though probably unintentional, could not have been more propitious. Although the number of white mechanics had grown as the number of slaves in the city diminished, the city never had a larger proportion of white workingmen than in August, when nearly every white person who had the money escaped the stultifying heat of the city and the accompanying risks of deadly disease. It is a measure of Macbeth's dedication to his job as mayor that he stayed in town during August. A prosperous attorney, the owner of a fine house at the corner of Legare and Gibbes, ten slaves, and two carriages, Macbeth came from the social class that typically spent August on the sea islands or in the North.[67] He also came from the social class that contained many of the friends of Charleston's free mulattoes.

At first, James M. Johnson took the view that influential whites had not abandoned their Afro-American friends but had instead been overpowered by white workingmen. "The higher class is quite incensed" about the mayor's actions, Johnson wrote Henry on August 20, "but it is too late. The power is into other hands & when they have got rid of the cold. [colored] population they will try to make them [the higher class] subordinate."[68] Johnson correctly diagnosed the social origins of the impetus behind the enslavement crisis and the mixture of class and racial animosity that fueled it. But his initial belief that the "higher class" was powerless to halt the crisis was undercut by the disturbing reluctance of many leading whites to step forward to defend their free colored friends. Likewise, Johnson's optimism that, for the most part, he and his friends would remain untouched, was tested every day. He told Henry the police had not yet come to Coming Street, but when they knocked—as he expected they would—he had no fear of being arrested. "I am glad I am here," he said, "for the many reports with the startling facts require some one in every house to allay the excitement."

One of the startling facts that became clear in the next eight days was that most individual white men who had served as guardians or trustees of free persons of color succumbed to the balance of political power in the city and simply went along with the police and the mayor. Rather than protecting their free Negro wards, they cooperated in hustling them along into servitude. Johnson noted, however, that Col. William Whaley, a wealthy white attorney, said "he will stand a law-suit before complying."[69] In other words, Whaley evidently insisted that he would refuse to cooperate with the mayor until he had obtained a judgment from a higher court that forced him to allow the mayor's capricious, though legal, interpretation of the credentials of free status to overrule Whaley's own legal authority as either trustee or guardian of a certain free person of color. Regrettably, Johnson reported, Whaley was an exception; "the majority [of white men in Whaley's position] has succumbed." In fact, the white trust-ees who actually owned the slaves who had been living as free persons would not even pay for the slave badges those per-sons now had to buy. "The money has to come out of the purses of those held in Trust," Johnson wrote.

Johnson emphasized the capitulation of most whites by cit-ing the examples of two other white men like Whaley who refused to go along. General John Schnierle, a neighbor of Johnson's, appealed to an older code than the law. Johnson said that Schnierle "placed himself in the stead of a Man he holds & defied them [the police] to touch him. He would beat the one to Death who did."[70] Although the threat may not have been physically intimidating to Charleston police-men, it probably made them pause nonetheless. Schnierle was a wealthy white man, the owner of nineteen slaves, a general in the militia, and a former mayor with a large following. Thomas Webb, a white factor and commission merchant who also lived near Johnson, stood up against the police bullies who had beat William Thompson, the young free mulatto laborer who claimed his sister Louisa was white and should be tried by white laws. In the presence of the policeman who had roughed up Thompson and other free Negro men at Thompson's house, Webb told one of the free men of color who had been beaten to "take a stick & beat the first fellow that entered his House & the Mayor too & he [Webb] would take the consequences."[71] Johnson reported that when Thompson had been attacked he had two white men with him, "but they were not of the Webb stamp." If only there were a few more white men of Webb's sort, Johnson declared, the police "would get their deserts [sic]." But such white men were in short supply.

Far more typical were the white men who refused to pay for the badges of the slaves they held in trust, or men like Col. Robert W. Seymour, a prosperous white attorney whom Johnson saw standing "in front of our House speaking to an Irish carter on the subject & [who] pointed to No. 7 & 9 as being up for sale."[72] In Johnson's eyes, avaricious men like Seymour and the Irish carter could hardly wait to snap up the real estate bargains made available by the rapid departure of free colored emigrants. In fact, Johnson's houses at 7 and 9 Coming Street had been put up for sale before James D. Johnson left for Toronto, before the enslavement crisis began. Now their market value was sinking in the flood of property that was a byproduct of the crisis. Yet not for the reason that Seymour and the carter believed, not because the Johnsons were slaves. In the conversation of Seymour and the carter Johnson saw the common white failure to recognize any distinction between the free mulatto elite and other Negroes.

Gratifying as it was for most whites to see free Negroes leaving the city and others enter the ranks of slaves, the rapid emigration from the city surprised the mayor's white supporters. Unexpectedly, the relentless pressure from the police created sympathy for free Negroes that the mayor's allies did not welcome. "Our friends sympathise & express indignation which has checked it," Johnson wrote Henry on August 28, "but they are not in power & cant put down the majority."[73] The mayor's supporters among the white workingmen—"the originators," Johnson called them—began to call on him to back off. They "blame the Mayor for being so rash," Johnson said; "They say All [free people of color] must leave but they did not want them ran off thus." The white mechanics sensed among all whites in Charleston a strong racial sympathy for their desire to eliminate free Negroes. But the workingmen did not want free people of color to be dealt with so harshly that it engendered sympathy for the sufferers and undermined the possibility of white consensus on the desirability of getting rid of these anomalous Negroes. White friends of free persons of color expressed their sympathy and indignation as Johnson said, but most of them also felt an undertow of allegiance to the racial arguments of the mechanics. As Johnson and his free mulatto friends were coming to realize, that undertow was almost irresistible. Although the immediate crisis in Charleston subsided by the first of September, it was part of a deeper political crisis that gripped the entire nation. The friends of Charleston's free people of color believed that now as never before white Southerners had to stand together. Personal relationships with respectable free Negroes had to be balanced against the compelling political need for white unity.

The enslavement crisis in Charleston did indeed subside. The police, after making an unprecedented ninety-three arrests in August for slaves working out without badges, made two such arrests in September, six in October, four in November, and only one in December.[74] Arrests of free people of color for nonpayment of capitation taxes declined as dramatically, from fifteen in August to zero in September and October, one in November, and another in December. However, racial tensions in the city remained at a high pitch. Johnson told Henry that the mayor sentenced a slave man to a paddling for an argument with another slave, and the white doctor who treated the "posterior" of the paddled slave said the argument "should have been settled by their owners, the police had nothing to do with it."[75] One of the masters was absent, but the other did not "expect his servt to be dealt with so." Johnson observed that the "Mayor is getting a reputation," even among white slaveowners. If the mayor's zeal annoyed white masters, free people of color suffered no illusions that the ebbing of the enslavement crisis meant that things had returned to normal. When Johnson noted on August 28 that the "stir has subsided," he added in the next breath, "but arrests are still made & the people are leaving."[76] He needled Henry about emigrating with one of the young Dereef girls. "They wont leave before their Father except entrusted to better hands. He is not disposed to move quickly enough for them." Six days later he reported that the "tide of emigration has not stopped."[77]

With one eye on the departing emigrants, Johnson continued his daily routine. On September 2 he even appeared in court, though not because he had been arrested. Federal District Judge Andrew Gordon Magrath, the highest-ranking federal official in the state, invited Johnson into his chambers to take his measurements for a new suit he wanted Johnson to make for him.[78] Johnson hoped to go up to Stateburg on September 6 to get some relief from the unrelenting strain of the last three weeks in the city and to talk over the alarming developments with the Ellisons. On September 5 his young sister, who had recently married his stepson John Buckner, died in Stateburg, but Johnson could not get out of town.[79] Sickness began to plague the city, and Johnson feared the consequences of a brief trip to the upcountry. He told Henry that "persons who have been absent only in the country & returned [to the city] have been taken down with Typhoid & Broken bone Fever which is prevalent." Johnson worried that his wife Eliza Ann would hear of the epidemic and become unnecessarily anxious about his well-being. "I think the city is healthy if persons would not be excited & travel to & fro to agitate the Bile which originates in Bilious [fever] and is apt to terminate in Typhoid," he told Henry, adding that he followed these and other precautions to make certain his system was "not susceptible to contagion & for the rest I trust in an All Wise Providence."

In effect, Johnson was trapped in Charleston. The sickness spreading through the city was actually the dreaded yellow fever. Although the attack was less virulent than the catastrophic epidemic of 1858, Johnson watched the disease claim the lives of several of his acquaintances during September and October, though he remained healthy. Late in September he wrote Henry, "I need a furlough," but the continued illness of John Hoff, one of the free mulatto tailors who worked in his shop, kept him from getting away.[80] Business at the shop was "getting brisk," and Johnson stayed busy.[81] Yet his income was not growing accordingly, possibly because the racial stresses in the city made it imprudent to press whites too hard about their bills. "We find it impracticable to collect any dues to carry . . . on [business] & have to resort to credit," he mentioned to Henry.

Johnson's biggest concern during September and October was neither the tailor shop nor how he could get out of the city, but how he could get his father back in. When a free man of color named Samuel Oakes left Charleston for Toronto in the midst of the enslavement crisis, Johnson asked him to take a letter for Charley, in which he told him the "unpleasant news." He intended the letter to allow Charley to judge the severity of the crisis for himself and to have the opinion of his brother to compare with the account Oakes was sure to give him. Although Johnson had "not intended [the letter] for Father's ears," it accidentally fell into his hands just before he planned to leave Toronto for Charleston.[82] As the elder Johnson wrote Henry, his son's letter conveyed the news that "things looks so dark and gloomy at home" and made him feel "miserable" about the "pressure that may occur by a return" to Charleston.[83] Both James M. and Henry wrote Toronto and tried to reassure James D. "I wrote that I apprehended no difficulty," James M. told Henry.[84] He reminded his father that rumors about free men of color being arrested for trying to reenter the state had existed in the past, and prominent free mulattoes like William McKinlay and Robert Howard had still managed to squeeze in unmolested. He told his father he would enjoy the same special treatment. "I hope this will (with your cogent reasoning) quiet his fears & have him forthcoming," James M. wrote Henry.

The letters evidently convinced James D. to take the risk of coming home. He left Toronto for New York on October 8.[85] A bit of evidence suggests that he may have met in Toronto or New York an old friend from Charleston, a white man named H. R. Harrals, and made the trip in his company. For more than twenty years Harrals had run a hardware store and saddlery in Charleston, and he lived within two blocks of Johnson's houses on Coming Street.[86] If he did travel with Harrals, the white man might possibly have eased Johnson's way into the city, passing the vigilant police with a friendly, knowing nod. But he may have returned to the city alone. In any case, one way or another he made it back into Charleston safely, just as his son had predicted. By the end of October, and maybe earlier, he was back home at 7 Coming Street. It was still possible for a free mulatto man of his stature and respectability to slip unobtrusively back into the city.

On October 16, about the time his father got back in the city, James M. Johnson returned to Stateburg to recuperate from his strife-filled stay in Charleston. In the next few weeks he and the Ellisons had to sort out what the enslavement crisis meant for them, what—if anything—they should do about it. In those quiet, confidential conversations at "Wisdom Hall" in the fall of 1860, Johnson and the Ellisons confronted decisions that as late as mid-August had seemed reserved for other free Negroes. Now, as the foundations of their freedom began to crumble beneath them, they had to decide how to protect themselves not from intimidation or arrest but from slavery. They had to think the unthinkable.

THREE separate but interrelated political campaigns influenced the Ellisons' deliberations. The national campaign for the presidency had been under way since late in the spring. The four-way race reflected both the political fragmentation caused by slavery and the consensus that the integrity of the Union depended on the outcome of the election. Each of the four presidential candidates argued that his position on slavery was the only way to preserve the Union: the Republican Abraham Lincoln promised to protect slavery where it existed but to prevent its expansion into new federal territories; the Southern Rights Democrat John C. Breckinridge pledged to protect slavery everywhere in the federal domain; the National Democrat Stephen A. Douglas was willing to allow settlers in the territories, rather than Congress, decide whether to tolerate slavery in their midst; and the Constitutional Unionist John Bell hoped a vow to uphold the Constitution and the Union was sufficient to calm anxieties about the vexing subject of slavery. Behind each of these positions lurked the possibility that, if it was not endorsed by the electorate, the South might make good its threat to secede.

Imbedded in the presidential electioneering was a second

campaign by a small, determined, and growing number of secessionists in the South. By mid-September it had become fairly clear that Lincoln would carry enough free states to win the November election.[87] As a result, the last few months of the presidential campaign in the South had less to do with choosing a president than with deciding what to do after the president had been chosen. Secessionists seized the opportunity to confront voters and politicians throughout the South with the question of how slavery could be preserved in a Union with a Republican president elected without a single electoral vote from the South. The only way to remain true to everything the South had always stood for, they argued, was to secede. Election day, November 6, confirmed Lincoln's victory; even if only one of Lincoln's opponents had received the vote of every single Southerner, Lincoln still would have won. Lincoln's election gave disunionists the upper hand as the campaign for secession became more formal. State after state in the South scheduled elections to choose delegates to conventions that would decide whether to leave the Union.

In South Carolina, which had a reputation as a bastion of knee-jerk secessionism, disunion had been debated for decades.[88] In one form or another the issue surfaced in virtually every political contest in the state since the 1820s. During the late summer and early fall of 1860 it served as the political touchstone of candidates for election to the state legislature. The legislative race, culminating on October 6—a month before Lincoln's election and the start of the formal campaign for the secession convention—presented South Carolina voters with the issues of the other two campaigns. The new legislature would choose the electors who would cast the state's presidential electoral votes, and it would have the choice of calling a convention to consider secession. While intensely local, the campaign for the legislature confronted voters with questions of momentous national significance. As South Carolinians thought about the proper response to the anticipated election of a Republican president, they agreed on one point. At this moment of political crisis, unity was essential. Political debate in South Carolina, though heated, had always been confined within a narrow range that allowed only one opinion on the defense of slavery. In the fall and winter of 1860 that range narrowed even more. Every white person needed to stand together to defend themselves and their institutions from the aggressive "Black Republicans" in the North, secessionists declared. Even those who had their doubts about secession had no reservations about the wisdom of unity.

The necessity of a united front among white South Carolinians strengthened the political hand of Charleston's white workingmen, and they knew it. They tried to exploit the fresh opportunity the sectional crisis gave them by seeking from ruling-class planters concessions that, they argued, were necessary to cement their loyalty. Having failed repeatedly to overcome the resistance of slaveowners to any tampering with the system of slave hiring, the mechanics directed their attack toward free Negroes. The August enslavement crisis represented the opening barrage of the battle they intended to win in the state legislature. Allied with upcountry farmers, they sought new laws that would confront every free person of color in the state with choices that the August crisis confined to Charleston: exile or enslavement. White workingmen hoped to press their new advantage to remove free Negroes from the labor market and to make the line between freedom and slavery coincide perfectly with the line between whites and Negroes.

James M. Eason led the mechanics' campaign. With his brother Thomas, Eason ran a large foundry on a four-acre site at the corner of Columbus and Nassau streets on the edge of the city, near the South Carolina Railroad yards, not far from Joseph Dereef's house. The foundry was established in the 1830s by Thomas Dotterer, who built the first locomotive for the South Carolina Railroad. Eason was evidently Dotterer's brother-in-law, and he probably received his training as a machinist in the foundry. After Dotterer's death, Eason took over the foundry and built it into one of the largest firms in the city. He employed eighty men who manufactured a wide variety of heavy machines, including steam engines, pumps, threshing machines, rice mills, sawmills, grist mills, sugar mills, and cotton presses. By 1860, when he was forty years old, Eason had done well. He paid city taxes on real estate worth $14,500 and six slaves of his own, plus another twelve slaves and $12,000 worth of real estate (the foundry) jointly owned with his brother.[89]

A proud, successful, ambitious man, Eason took on tasks others considered too difficult. He built the huge steam dredge that had recently deepened the channel in the Charleston harbor. In the middle of August 1860 his shop was busy making castings for bridge construction on the Blue Ridge Railroad, a project so challenging that several Northern foundries had refused to accept it. Although he expected to lose money on the contract, Eason undertook the project because he was eager to demonstrate the skill of his shop in particular and of Charleston mechanics in general. A reporter from the *Courier* who visited the foundry in the midst of the August enslavement crisis wrote that the "great effort" of Eason and his brother was "to build up an entirely Southern manufacturing establishment[,] to raise their own workmen, and to be independent of Northern Foundries."[90] The reporter was informed that the "chief difficulty" Eason faced was "a mistaken public sentiment that Charleston could not manufacture the machinery required for Southern enterprise." Eason promised to make anything from a locomotive to a bolt, inspiring the reporter to predict that the "determined spirit and enterprise of our mechanics" would soon allow Charlestonians "to boast of having all their machinery manufactured on the spot."

That boast carried increasing political weight as the likelihood of secession loomed ever larger. Eason was just as conscious of the political clout of Charleston's white workingmen as he was of their skills as craftsmen. To be independent, the South needed loyal white mechanics. That the *Courier* and polite society in Charleston were as aware of that need as Eason is reflected in the lengthy report about his foundry printed in the newspaper, one of a series of articles that ran from August 17 through September 12.[91] The articles gave detailed accounts of four other large foundries, a woodworking business, a steam sawmill, a railroad car manufacturing concern, a carriage manufactory, and an umbrella factory. The articles were designed to illustrate, the *Courier* said, "that our merchants and citizens, generally, should feel a proper interest, and give a proper encouragement to home industry, to develop the abilities and resources of Charleston mechanics. . . ."[92]

That the readers of the *Courier* needed a guided tour through the shops of leading Charleston mechanics suggests the distance that separated the city's merchants, lawyers, bankers, and planters from its white working class. That the workshops of the mechanics were considered newsworthy suggests the new-found importance of developing "a proper interest" in the affairs of white workingmen. The reports also suggest the awkwardness for Charleston chivalry of trying to express "a proper interest" in white workingmen. The vast majority of the city's white mechanics owned neither slaves nor real estate. Many of them worked in direct competition with slaves and in direct conflict with the interests of the slaves' owners. What concessions could be granted by white masters that would guarantee the political loyalty of white mechanics? Eason and his allies among the white workingmen hammered at that question while the Ellisons, the Johnsons, and the rest of Charleston's free mulatto elite watched their own predicament turn from bad to worse.

Like virtually all the other candidates for the state legislature, Eason campaigned as a secessionist.[93] Unlike all but two or three other candidates, he actively courted white workingmen. His closest ally among the candidates was Henry T. Peake, the superintendent of the sprawling shops of the South Carolina Railroad, a self-made man who presented himself to "Mechanics–Working Men–Merchants . . . [as] the friend of the laboring man and the benefactor of the poor."[94] Another candidate who appealed for the votes of mechanics was George Coffin, a factor who directed the relief operations during the disastrous yellow fever epidemic of 1858.[95] But Eason was the acknowledged leader, and he focused his campaign less on the universally detested Black Republicans than on the free Negroes in Charleston.

One of Eason's supporters, "one devoted to the interest of the working classes (being himself one of them)," urged white workingmen to vote for Eason and Peake since they alone could be trusted "whenever questions arise in which their rights and interests come in conflict with *free* negros—negros free in *fact,* but held by *trustees,* and slaves hiring their own time— plague spots in this community, affecting pecuniarily and socially only working men." Only mechanics "suffered" from this competition, and only they would take the steps necessary to end it. They would put mechanics on an equal footing with all other professions, to which Negroes were denied access. In past elections mechanics heard from candidates about the dignity of labor and "such *clap trap,*" but the protection from competition with free Negroes offered by these men turned out to be the kind that "vultures give to lambs," since legislators who had never been mechanics were more concerned "with the rights of this privileged class of negros."[96] A second Eason advocate put the issue in terms many white workingmen in Charleston could instantly appreciate. He asked if "any *white mechanic* ever felt this dignity of labor when[,] unsuccessful in estimating for a job, he finds that it has been awarded to one of our *very respectable free persons of color* . . . thus adding to his disappointment [at losing the contract], the mortification of feeling that this *dignity of labor places him alone* on the same level with this highly valued and privileged class of negros."[97]

Such arguments, repeated again and again in the city's workshops, grog shops, and groceries, did their work. On election day, October 8, voters turned out in droves, and Eason, Peake, and Coffin won easily. Eason compiled the third highest number of votes among the thirty-six candidates.[98] Only once in the last thirty years (in 1856) had as many Charlestonians voted for state legislators, and Eason's 2,167 votes topped every leading vote-getter in all those elections (again, save 1856).[99] Eason received 234 more votes than the secessionist fire-eater Robert Barnwell Rhett, Jr., 634 more votes than Richard Yeadon, the editor of the *Courier,* and 846 more votes than the secessionist activist and organizer Robert N. Gourdin.[100] Predictably, Eason polled his heaviest majorities in the predominantly working-class upper wards of the city. Eason had a mandate that his colleagues in the legislature could not ignore.

Neither could South Carolina's free mulatto tradesmen. Previously, white workingmen had aimed their attack at the slaves and free Negroes who competed mostly with white laborers. Now, Eason was expanding the assault and focusing it on the free mulatto elite, on men like Anthony Weston who competed with white mechanics like James Eason. When James M. Johnson returned to Stateburg in mid-October, he carried with him news of Eason's campaign and the mounting forces behind it. Exactly how the Ellisons reacted to the news that skilled master craftsmen like themselves were now the targets of white mechanics is unknown. Combined with the events of the August enslavement crisis and the *"Great Change"* among their free mulatto friends in Charleston who now believed emigration was mandatory, the new campaign of the white workingmen could not have been heartening.[101] Neither ownership of slaves nor mastery of a craft promised to insulate the Ellisons from grave threats to their freedom. Like the free mulatto elite in Charleston, the Ellisons were being stripped of their distinctive identity as prosperous, respectable, slaveowning craftsmen and recognized simply as Negroes, all of whom—whites generally agreed—were fit only for slavery. Although the details of the Ellisons' deliberations during the last two weeks of October are forever lost, there is no question about what they decided.

ON October 28 or 29, William Ellison Jr. left Stateburg with at least two and possibly all three of his children, his son William John, 14, and his two daughters, Elizabeth Anna, about 12, and Henrietta Inglis, about 10. On the afternoon of the twenty-ninth, they visited James D. Johnson, the Westons, and other friends in the city. But William had not come to Charleston to make social calls. He came to send his children out of the state, beyond the reach of any new oppressions the South Carolina legislature might design for them. That morning he had gone to the North Atlantic Wharf to buy passage for his children aboard the Philadelphia steamer scheduled to depart Tuesday afternoon. "I tried every plan and made every effort to get them off on board of the Keystone State," William wrote Henry, "but the agents [Thomas S. and Thomas G. Budd] took a stand and would not deviate although [the Ellisons' factors] Messrs Adams & Frost interested themselves much to effect a passage."[102]

The Budds' caution was understandable. If they allowed a free person of color to leave aboard the steamer and the person turned out to be a slave, the Budds were guilty of aiding a slave to run away, a crime punishable by death without benefit of clergy. A young white porter from the New York steamer *Marion* had been convicted of just such a crime in January

1860, and he was still in jail in October, awaiting execution.[103] If, as the Budds insisted, William had allowed his children to be claimed as the slaves of some white person, the Budds would not be culpable, since masters could take their slaves any place they desired. William reminded Henry that if he had agreed to the Budds' scheme, "Then of course they [his children] cannot get a state room."[104] Although Captain Marshman "very kindly offered to take care of" William's children if he would claim they were slaves, "I would not agree to send them as slaves when they are not," William wrote Henry, "and besides they might not be taken care of."

Indeed, had William allowed some white passenger to pose as the master of his children, nothing could have prevented the person from treating them as his slaves, even selling them. After all, the custom house records would document that they were his slaves. This one incident dramatizes why the Ellisons and the rest of the free mulatto elite realized they faced a crisis of survival. Here was the son of the wealthiest free person of color in the state—a planter who owned dozens of slaves, a gin maker who had faithfully served the white planters of Sumter and surrounding districts for more than forty years, an Episcopalian—and the only way he could buy a ticket for his children to go to Philadelphia was to attest that they were slaves. Even the intervention of white factors who had handled his family's business for decades, respected white Charlestonians who could testify to everything about the Ellisons that distinguished them from slaves, was to no avail. To his horror, William discovered that the only thing about the Ellisons that mattered to sensible white men like the Budds was that the Ellisons were Negroes.

Failing to get his children on the Philadelphia steamer as free persons, William went to Adger's wharf, where the New York steamer *Marion* was scheduled to leave two days later. When the ship pulled out of Charleston harbor at 7:00 A.M. on October 31, William's children were aboard, but not as slaves. "They are comfortable provide for," William wrote Henry, "having a state room and I believe a kind capt. which have promise to put them aboard of the cars for Philadelphia under the care of the conductor."[105] For his children to reach their destination, William entrusted them to the steamship captain who would in turn entrust them to some unknown railroad conductor who would oversee their train trip from New York to Philadelphia. While they were on the steamship, the "stewardess has promise to take good care of them. I gave her a trifle so as to incourage her," William said. Even so, William was understandably distraught. "I hope God will be with them and protect them," William wrote. "I am quite worried down."

William's ability to send his children to New York on the *Marion* demonstrates that the free mulatto elite still had room to maneuver in South Carolina. However, that he entrusted his children to the care of white strangers rather than accompanying them himself suggests that the Ellisons had concluded that their manuevering space was small and shrinking. If William had left South Carolina, he might never have been allowed back in. Evidently, he and his family considered that possibility even more dangerous than sending his young children on a long journey alone. But if white South Carolinians had known where William's children were going, they probably would have thrown him and his children in jail and found some pretext to arrest the rest of the Ellisons. William was sending his children to the Lombard Street Primary School, a private school in Philadelphia run by Margaretta Forten, a free Negro schoolteacher and, like her father James Forten, a prominent abolitionist.[106] Unlike the several other schools for free Negro children in Philadelphia, Forten's accepted "boarding scholars."[107] In an abolitionist school in Philadelphia, William Ellison's grandchildren would be safe from the fate that awaited the rest of the family back home in South Carolina. It is difficult to imagine a more secure refuge.

It has proved impossible to discover how the Ellisons learned of Forten's school, how they contacted her, and what they told her of their situation. After William made the arrangements to send his children via New York, he wrote to "Miss Forten" about the change of plans; she was evidently expecting the children to arrive on the *Keystone State*. At the same time, he wrote a free mulatto man named Barquet, who had resided in Charleston for many years but now lived in New York. William apparently asked Barquet to meet the children when they docked in New York and supervise their transfer to the Philadelphia-bound train. "If they get the letter[s] they will be on the lookout for them [the children]," William wrote Henry, adding, "Inform Father and Sister that they are gone."[108]

It is very unlikely that William's children had previously been students at Forten's school. In a small village like Stateburg, word would leak out and whites would give it the most inflammatory interpretation. The Ellisons would not have risked that, just for the sake of a good education for William's children. Nor is it likely that the Ellisons were secretly in sympathy with the Forten's antislavery activities, such as Margaretta's service for many years as secretary of the Philadelphia Female Anti-Slavery Society. And it is difficult to conjure a more implausible friendship than one between the Ellisons and the Fortens. However, they may have had mutual friends or acquaintances. Harriet Forten, Margaretta's sister, married Robert Purvis, himself a prominent Negro abolitionist, whose mother was apparently one of the free people of color near Stateburg known as Turks.[109] Perhaps one of the Benenhalys put William Ellison Jr. in touch with the Fortens. Or possibly an intermediary like Barquet made all the arrangements. Philadelphia's free colored population had no shortage of former South Carolina residents, and one of them may well have helped out. In any case, by sending the children to Forten's school, the Ellisons made a well-informed decision. Their decision revealed that, although they were slaveholders and had never so much as hinted that they had qualms about it, their commitment to slaveholding lacked the ideological fervor of white masters. They were willing to send William Jr.'s children to an abolitionist school if that was what it took to guarantee their freedom. The Ellisons' rock-bottom commitment was not to slavery but to the preservation of their own freedom. During the week before Lincoln's election, honoring that commitment meant sending the grandchildren of one of the South's largest free colored slaveholders to a school run by one of the North's most famous free colored abolitionists.

WHEN news of Lincoln's election reached Charleston at the end of the first week of November, the Charleston *Mercury* triumphantly declared, "The tea has been thrown overboard—the revolution of 1860 has been initiated."[110] Federal judge Andrew Gordon Magrath, James M. Johnson's customer, resigned his office and announced his support for seccession. On November 10, United States Senator James Chesnut Jr. announced his resignation from the Senate. The same day a hurriedly assembled South Carolina legislature authorized the election of delegates to a state convention that would meet December 17 to decide whether the revolutionary tea party should be ratified by a formal vote for secession. One after another the state's leading politicians proclaimed their zeal for disunion. When H. T. Peake returned to the South Carolina Railroad shop after the brief meeting of the legislature, all hands stopped working, the machinery was shut down, the mechanics formed a circle around him, shouted "well done," and gave him nine cheers. He responded with a short explanation of why he had abandoned his loyalty to "this cursed Union."[111] The Virginia secessionist Edmund Ruffin, who seemed to be witnessing the incarnation of his most fervent dreams, watched the South Carolina legislature arrange for the secession convention, then accepted an invitation by John N. Frierson and John S. Richardson, two Sumter District planters, to come to Sumter. Ruffin was met by 150 Sumter Minute Men and escorted to the courthouse, where he spoke to a large meeting called to select candidates for the upcoming election of delegates to the secession convention. Then he hurried off to Charleston to watch, among other festivities, the erection of a ninety-foot "secession pole."[112]

While whites celebrated, free Afro-Americans emigrated. Two hundred Charleston refugees landed in Philadelphia early in November, where some of them talked to newspaper reporters. They said that 780 free persons of color had left Charleston since the enslavement crisis, driven out by the mayor's enforcement of the laws of 1820 and 1822. Like William Ellison's grandchildren, they had managed to escape from Charleston with the help of white friends who arranged to get them aboard steamers to New York. The contingent that arrived in Philadelphia "caused quite a stir in colored circles," one reporter noted.[113] Another observed that "their light complexions and sober behavior have attracted much attention."[114] Among them were carpenters, tailors, masons, shoe-makers, milliners, mantua makers, and nurses, many of them with letters from white Charlestonians testifying to their character and qualifications. The refugees told the reporters that they "have been driven suddenly out of employments by which they gained a living, and are now seeking, under great disadvantages to begin life anew." Although many of them had acquired property in Charleston, "in the haste to get away" they found themselves "compelled to sell at great loss, while of what they leave behind unsold, they fully expect to be cheated." They also had to leave behind family members too old or sick to make the trip. "This compulsory exodus reminds us," wrote the reporter for the New York *Tribune,* "of the revocation of the Edict of Nantz [sic], or the expulsion of the Jews from their European homes."

While free persons of color streamed out of Charleston, city authorities began to put up barriers to the entry of poor white laborers. During the fall and winter a rising tide of transient white workingmen usually came into the city seek-ing jobs moving the annual crop of cotton and rice onto ships bound for Northern and European markets. In mid-Novem-ber, Mayor Macbeth began to enforce a law requiring all ship captains bringing newcomers to the city to post a substantial bond against the possibility that the immigrants might end up needing the city's (threadbare) charity.[115] Charleston-bound New York steamers refused to sell steerage tickets to white workingmen who could not come up with the bond money, and many of those who bluffed their way aboard were sent back North by the vigilant Charleston authorities.[116] City officials, assisted by assorted volunteer vigilance committees, were determined to rid the city of abolitionist sympathizers poisoning the minds of ignorant slaves with fanaticism. One Charlestonian pointed out that "It is well known that our city is at the present time overrun with Abolition emissaries who are disseminating incendiary principles among our negros. . . ." The Charleston police were so ineffective at eliminating these "Northern loiterers about our streets, without apparent occu-pation," that the writer charged they did not even bother to hide their activities.[117]

The anxious search for hidden enemies was an outgrowth

of the feverish preparations for secession under way in Charleston and throughout the state. Minute Men and other military units marched and countermarched through the streets of Charleston. Flags with secession mottoes decorated windows and doorsteps throughout the city.[118] Every red-blooded white Southerner could see that the South must be made strong for the coming test, must be purged of its enemies and cleansed of its impurities, sentiments that James Eason and the white workingmen interpreted as a golden opportunity to "split from our body politic this cantankerous sore [of free Negroes], and stand among our fellow citizens as equals."[119]

Eason and his supporters were not the only ones who wanted a final solution to the free Negro problem. When the legislature reconvened for its regular session on November 26, the Committee on the Colored Population received a bill that proposed to enslave all free persons of color in the state by January 1, 1862, when they would be sold to the highest bidder at a sheriff's auction.[120] In the meantime, the bill would allow free persons of color to enter slavery voluntarily by choosing a white master. The Charleston *Mercury* registered an "emphatic protest" against the bill as "harsh in its policy, wholly unrequired by the public exigencies . . . and remarkably ill-timed."[121] Another Charlestonian attacked the bill with the familiar argument that Charleston's free people of color included many who "have a stake in the welfare of the community, and everything to lose by whatever tends to disturb or overthrow it." He declared these free Negroes "a safe class of people" and denounced the proposed bill as "full of oppression and injustice."[122] Such arguments made sense to the white friends of Charleston's free mulatto elite, but to Eason and the white workingmen, they were the essence of the problem. To white mechanics, the free mulatto tradesmen whom white lawyers, bankers, and merchants defended as the redeeming strength of the free Negro population were instead the very Negroes that required repression.

Eason got himself appointed to the crucial Committee on the Colored Population and presented a bill that struck at the heart of the free mulatto elite. Eason's bill prohibited all free persons of color from "entering into contracts for any mechanical pursuits" and from "carrying on any mechanical business on their own account."[123] Eason's bill would shut down William Ellison's gin shop, Anthony Weston's machine shop, and every other enterprise operated by free colored craftsmen. The bill confronted head-on the customary defense of the free mulatto elite by demanding racial justice for white, not black, mechanics. A Charleston mechanic urged "MECHANICS, WORKING MEN AND ALL WHITE MEN WHO LIVE BY THE SWEAT OF THEIR BROW" to support Eason's bill, since "strong opposition" was expected from "some of those gentleman, who by their calling or profession, are neither subjected to the degradation of such [free Negro] competition, or can feel that the working man has any right to similar protection with themselves against it."[124] Potent beliefs in white equality and black inferiority made Eason's bill irresistible to most white South Carolinians. Governor William H. Gist endorsed the bill in his message to the legislature, declaring that "there must be a distinction between the races, as marked as their different colors, and it must be distinctly and universally understood that the white is the governing race, without an exception, and without regard to disparity of intellect, merit, or acquirements."[125] Although Gist may have intimated that some blacks had better intellects than some whites, his statement touched the nerve of white racism that animated Eason's proposal. The governor was saying that the wealth, the property, the education, the respectability, and the piety of Charleston's free mulatto elite should not restrain the legislature from supporting Eason's bill and putting all Negroes where they belonged, below all whites.

The sectional crisis made racial unity more important than ever before. Part of the reason, "A Master Mechanic" pointed out in the *Courier,* was that "if we ever expect to be independent of the North, it is absolutely necessary that we should elevate the standard of the mechanical arts; and to do which negro *competition* and negro ascendancy must be prohibited."[126] By having to compete with free Negroes, white mechanics were dragged down to the level of blacks, and this caused other whites to consider mechanics "no better" than blacks, an attitude "well calculated to breed discontent and hatred on the part of the white mechanic, and make him an enemy of our institution. . . . " With the passage of Eason's bill, "the condition of the white mechanic would be elevated" and the dangerous division among whites would be sealed by "a close bond of union . . . between the various classes of our citizens, and thus they would be strongly united in support and defence of our Southern Institutions." This volatile mixture of threat and reassurance, of class hostility and racial brotherhood, made the mechanics' bill a litmus of the legislature's willingness to settle the free Negro problem once and for all.

On December 5 Eason's bill was reported out of committee with the recommendation that it pass, with an amendment that prohibited free Negroes from indirectly carrying on any business through a white agent or guardian.[127] In effect, the bill made it impossible for a free person of color to earn a living in South Carolina, except as a wage laborer. Master craftsmen like William Ellison would be reduced to hirelings of white mechanics. The *Courier*'s correspondent in Columbia predicted that Eason's bill would "probably pass both Houses" since, so far as he could gather, most legislators approved it and "mechanical contractors" from Charleston supported it enthusiastically.[128]

Eason's bill confirmed the worst fears of the free mulatto elite, but rather than accepting it as inevitable, they counterattacked. James M. Johnson returned to Charleston during the first week of December, while Eason's bill was in committee. Johnson told Henry that Anthony Weston had a copy of Eason's bill, evidently so free men of color could see with their own eyes what they were up against. Their long-standing friendships with low-country aristocrats paid off when the chairman of the Committee on the Colored Population, John Harleston Read Jr. the representative of Prince George Winyaw, asked for help to defeat Eason's bill. Read asked for "a respectable cold. [colored] man" to bring the city tax book to Columbia.[129] Read planned to use the tax book to document free Negroes' impressive property holdings—including slaves. He apparently wanted to point to the respectable free man of color who delivered the tax book as an example that would persuade upcountry planters that at least some free Negroes deserved protection. Initially, Robert Houston was selected to take the tax book, but since it was Saturday evening, his obligations as sexton at Grace Episcopal Church made it impossible for him to go. John DeLarge, another Grace parishioner, took Houston's place. DeLarge, a forty-year-old free mulatto tailor who lived near Johnson on Coming Street, took the night train to Columbia and gave Read his ammunition.[130]

When Eason heard about Read's strategy, he made "a counter move," Johnson said.[131] Eason rushed back to Charleston, circulated a petition among white mechanics that quickly obtained hundreds of signatures, and hurried back to Columbia to add the final touches to his bill. The petition rehearsed all the mechanics' arguments, but it gave particular emphasis to the need for the law to recognize the mechanics' equality with all other professions, rather than exemplifying the "idea of superiority and inferiority" among whites. "Is it wise to tax the loyalty of the working poor man, by such discriminations to the institution [of slavery] which he is educated to defend, and in the defense of which he is always the foremost?" the petition concluded.[132] Eason himself cinched the argument when he reported his bill to the full legislature. The only purpose of the bill was to prevent free Negroes "from assuming the standard of a master," which rightfully belonged to white master craftsmen. By "allowing free negros to carry on the mechanical trades as masters," the legislature tolerated an injustice among whites and created "a very great tendency to infuse into our slaves coming into contact with them [free Negro master craftsmen], a spirit of dissatisfaction and insubordination, and fastens on his [the slave's] mind the fact that it is only for him to obtain his freedom to be placed as an equal in carrying on any mechanical trade, with the white man."[133] Masters like William Ellison undermined both white equality and slavery, Eason argued, without naming Ellison or any other free Negro. The more abstract the argument, the clearer the principles and the better for a black or white decision.

Inspired by Eason's efforts, Charleston's free mulatto leaders organized "a counter petition," evidently a restatement of the traditional argument that free persons of color were loyal and worthy.[134] John Lee and Jacob Weston circulated the petition among the influential whites who had stood by the free mulatto elite in the past. "They succeeded with the Aristocrats," Johnson wrote Henry. Although the number of signatures was much smaller than on Eason's petition, Jacob Weston told Johnson that "it was signed by the most respectable citisens *[sic]* so that what it lacked in numbers was made up in respectability." Wilmot Gibbes DeSaussure, a prominent East Bay attorney and member of the Charleston legislative delegation, presented the petition to the legislature, Johnson wrote, "as the Petition of Prest. Jas Rose & others in behalf of free persons of color &c."[135] Johnson wrote that the bill giving free Negroes the alternatives of exile before 1862 or slavery afterward would be defeated, but Eason's bill was intended "to accomplish the same result." Having marshaled all their resources, they awaited the decision of the legislature. The fate of Eason's bill and other lesser measures to repress free Negroes, Johnson told Henry on December 7, "is undecided."

Within two weeks it became clear that Eason's bill would not pass, that Charleston free mulattoes had won an important victory. Because crucial records have not survived, the legislative details cannot be fully reconstructed. Several interrelated events appear to have been involved. First, as chairman of the Committee on the Colored Population, John Harleston Read probably controlled when bills from his committee came to the floor of the legislature, and he apparently chose to defend free persons of color from the enslavement bill before considering Eason's proposal. The more drastic enslavement law had a strong appeal to many legislators, but because it was more drastic, it made an easier target for Read and its opponents. On behalf of his committee, Read came out against the enslavement law. He cited the evidence from the Charleston tax book that John DeLarge had delivered to him, pointing out that of the more than a million and a half dollars in taxable wealth owned by free Negroes in Charleston, *"more than three hundred thousand dollars are in slaves."*[136] He repeated the traditional arguments of the Charleston defense of free Negroes and closed with a ringing denunciation of the "injustice and wickedness" of the enslavement law. "Whilst we are battling for our rights, liberties, and institutions," he proclaimed, "can we expect the smiles and counternance [*sic*] of the Arbiter of all events when we make war upon the impotent and unprotected, enslave them against all justice? God forbid that this legislature could tolerate such a sentiment—forbid it, humanity—condemn it, enlightened legislation." Whether or not Read's rhetoric carried the day, his report did; the bill never came to a vote.

Read also probably played an influential role in disposing of Eason's bill. Eason reported the amended bill out of committee on December 14, with a committee recommendation that it pass, which typically insured a full hearing and a favorable vote by the legislature.[137] However, the bill somehow got sidetracked to the Committee on the Judiciary, where it was bottled up and carried over to the next session of the legislature, without ever coming up for consideration.[138] James D. Johnson accurately reported to Henry on December 19 that "The Mechanics Bill is thought to be gone to Old Nick."[139] Most likely, Read and a few other powerful low-country representatives twisted a few arms to keep the bill off the floor of the legislature and safely inside committees they controlled.

Read's successful defense of free persons of color suggests the durability of the personal relationships between influential white men and the free mulatto elite. Shrewd parliamentary tactics and appeals to the legislators' best impulses of justice and humanity saved free Afro-Americans from laws that seemed likely to pass. While Read's tactics were probably more important than his arguments, his words at least reassured free people of color that they had not lost all their white friends, and that their white friends had not lost all their influence. Nonetheless, the major reason the free Negro bills failed to pass was that the legislators had more pressing business preparing the state to reclaim its sovereignty.

The outcome of the December 6 election for delegates to the secession convention was a foregone conclusion. James M. Johnson wrote Henry that the turnout in Charleston was nearly as large as the October legislative election. "I saw a melee at one of the polls between a customer of ours & others," Johnson said, but he added, "I did not wait to see the result."[140] White Charlestonians were edgy and impatient. The secession convention assembled in Columbia December 17, then, fearing a smallpox epidemic, adjourned to Charleston, where on December 20, at 1:15 in the afternoon, it resolved "To dissolve the Union" between South Carolina and the "other States."[141]

Many Charlestonians greeted the secession ordinance with an exuberant celebration. Bands and militia companies paraded through the streets, bonfires made of barrels of rosin turned the central portion of the city into "a perfect blaze of light," while rockets and firecrackers saluted independence, and lanterns adorned the secession pole on Hayne Street.[142] Three days later Johnson wrote Henry that the "demonstrations in honor of Secession are not yet over." Johnson was not misled by the festivities. "It is very diverting, especially to children who do not look to the consequences."[143] While the celebrants failed to consider the consequences, Johnson, the Ellisons, and the rest of the free mulatto elite could think of nothing else.

IN his letter to Henry the day before Christmas Eve, James M. Johnson distilled into one sentence the free mulatto elite's conclusions about the meaning of secession: "Our situation is not only unfortunate but deplorable & it is better to make a sacrifice now than wait to be sacrificed *our selves.*"[144] Events of the last five months had convinced Johnson, the Ellisons, and Charleston's most prominent free mulattoes that there would be no place for them in the newly independent South. Although the enslavement bill and the white mechanics' bill had failed to pass the legislature, Johnson and his friends considered the victory no more than temporary. "One of the bills came up & is postponed," Johnson told Henry. "The others will no doubt lay over until after the adjournment [of the legislature.]" Within the months to come, as the intoxicating diversions that accompanied secession were replaced by workaday routines, the free mulatto elite could forsee that attacks on their freedom would resume. The surge of unity among whites engendered by secession would turn in their direction, and what most whites regarded as the anomaly of freedom for Negroes in a slave society would offer a perfect opportunity to impose rigorous racial logic. Freedom would be restricted to whites, and every person of color would be

made a slave. Rather than sacrifice their freedom, the Ellisons, the Johnsons, and their Charleston friends decided to
sacrifice everything they had built for themselves in South
Carolina and emigrate.

"As it regards Emigration your humble Servt is on the alert
with the whole of our people who are debating where to go,"
the elder Johnson wrote Henry.[145] In the few months since
the August enslavement crisis the debate had changed from
whether to where to emigrate, and it now involved "the whole
of our people." Where to go was a momentous question. As
Michael Eggart pointed out in 1848, a promised land for free
mulattoes did not exist on the face of the earth. Everywhere,
free mulattoes encountered white prejudice and black hatred,
but now, only in the slave South did they confront the likelihood of slavery. That closed the debate on whether to emigrate. As James M. Johnson wrote Henry, "it is now a fixed
fact that we must go." Even Samuel Weston, Johnson said,
who "never had the first notion [of emigrating] before," now
declared impatiently, " 'There has been too *much* deliberation
already,' " an opinion shared by his brother Jacob Weston.[146]

William Ellison and his friends among the free people of
color in Sumter agreed. During November, after Ellison's
grandchildren had departed for Forten's school in Philadel-
phis, while the secession campaign was under way throughout the state and the legislature prepared to take up the free
Negro bills, Ellison began to consider where he should take
his family. In his sober, conservative way, he did not want to
rush. He wanted to know about the alternatives, and he wanted
to cooperate with his friends in Charleston. When James M.
Johnson returned to the city early in December, Ellison asked
him to communicate to Charleston's free mulatto leaders his
financial support for scouting out possible destinations. Johnson reported back to Henry that, "I have pledged the Stateburgians, Your Father especially, as he directed me to do so,
to a movement on foot to send out 2 persons to select a place
or report on certain places where the people may emigrate.
. . . "[147] The Ellisons and their friends among Charleston's
free mulatto elite evidently hoped that by agreeing on a destination they would be able to continue to depend upon each
other as they reassembled their lives in their new home. Once

the scouts had returned and "our people" had fresh news of possible destinations, they would have to make the difficult decision. "I hope it will meet the sanction & support of us all," Johnson said.

None of the possible destinations was very attractive. Conditions in the free states were better only in the sense that slavery did not exist. White prejudice was so virulent that Northern free Negroes were themselves emigrating, as the newspapers informed South Carolinians. Furthermore, in the North free colored trademen would compete with white workingmen who were more numerous, better organized, and more powerful than in Charleston. The chances of gaining a foothold were slim, and the chances of losing out to whites good. While a Negro tailor like James M. Johnson might be able to survive in Philadelphia, New York, or Boston, he faced low wages and bouts of unemployment before he could hope to build up the capital and clientele required to become established and prosperous. Yet a tailor could at least employ the skills he had developed over the years. What was a cotton gin maker to do in the North? For William Ellison and his sons, going north meant abandoning the trade they had mastered. They could survive as general blacksmiths and perhaps in time retrain themselves to repair steam engines and threshing equipment rather than cotton gins. But prospects for a seventy-year-old man and his middle-aged sons were lean at best. How long would it take to build a blacksmith business in a small village in Pennsylvania, say, that would provide the income and stability of the shop in Stateburg? And where were the Pennsylvania (or New York or Massachusetts) villagers who wanted a Negro blacksmith and his family to settle among them?

Because the disadvantages of the free states extended to Canada, South Carolina's free mulattoes looked south. "The majority [of our people] are in favor of Hayti," James D. Johnson reported to Henry in mid-December.[148] The Haitian government actively encouraged Afro-Americans to settle on the island. The government promised immigrants a homestead, agricultural tools, and food and shelter until they managed to provide for themselves. The government hired the American abolitionist James Redpath as the General Agent of Immigration to Haiti, and Redpath tirelessly spread the word that in Haiti, as nowhere else, Afro-Americans would find their homeland. The Charleston refugees who arrived in Philadelphia early in November had hardly touched the dock before Redpath dispatched one of his agents, Reverend Theodore Hollin, to recruit them.[149] Hollin gave several lectures to the Afro-Americans of Philadelphia, detailing the attractions of Haiti and, a newspaper reporter noted, giving "a glowing account of the prosperity of the island."[150] Redpath himself argued that unless Afro-Americans emigrated they faced *"annihilation."* He declared that "Pride of race, self-respect, social ambition, parental love, the madness of the South, and the meanness of the North, the inhumanity of the Union, and the inclemency of Canada—all say to the Black and the man of color, Seek elsewhere a home and a nationality."[151] Where else but in Haiti, of course. Redpath expected Haiti to reap the harvest of tens of thousands of free colored emigrants who were being driven out of the South. In contrast to Africa, he wrote a cotton merchant in England, Haiti was "a civilized country, healthy and fruitful, inhabited by men of African descent who have the proved ambition to create a Black England in the West."[152] Despite these glorious visions, Redpath's enthusiasm played to a skeptical audience. Charleston's free mulatto elite could not forget Haiti's dismal record of racial atrocities. The black nation offered free mulattoes an escape from white racism, but little relief from, and perhaps an intensification of, black hostility. Still, compared to South Carolina in December 1860, many free people of color thought Haiti looked good.

James D. Johnson told Henry on December 19 that "Some few [free persons of color] are leaving here by each Steamer." Johnson expected to join them once the debate about where to go had been settled. "Dont suppose I will be the last [to go] because I have replaced a missing tree. I only want to beautify the exterior [of 7 and 9 Coming Street] so as to attract Capitalists."[153] Johnson's statement exemplifies the practical problems that preceded emigration. The debate about where to go involved weighing one unknown against another, predicting imponderables. To prepare to go involved dozens of decisions about matters that could not have been more concrete. Johnson knew what his houses were worth, and failing to get it after months of trying, he invested in a new tree that he hoped would help attract a buyer. He was ready to emigrate, but he was not about to sell his property at a giveaway price. Yet without selling it, how could he reestablish himself after he emigrated? Johnson's real estate was his major asset. It represented his lifetime savings, and he had to liquidate it if he hoped to support himself after emigration in anything like the modest style to which he had become accustomed in Charleston.

His houses were only the beginning of the matters that had to be settled. He needed to sell his slaves, to pay his bills, to collect the outstanding accounts of his many white customers, and all this at Christmastime, just as the year's crop was moving to market, while white men drilled with their militia companies and vowed to defend Southern honor. Collecting debts in normal times was hard enough; in December 1860 it was difficult to get the attention, much less the money, of delinquent whites. Johnson and the rest of Charleston's free mulatto elite had to decide when they had collected all they were likely to get, when their houses had attracted the highest bid they could expect, decisions that required them to balance the risks of delaying emigration against the financial losses they would incur. Others must have said to themselves again and again what James M. Johnson wrote to Henry—"it is better to make a sacrifice now than wait to be sacrificed *our selves*"—but how much of a sacrifice should they make?[154] Was it foolish to sacrifice everything? Or was it foolish not to?

For William Ellison such questions were even more perplexing. In a matter of a few weeks, or at the most a month or two, he needed to find a buyer for nearly 900 acres of land, more than threescore of slaves, a gin shop and assorted paraphernalia, and "Wisdom Hall" and "Drayton Hall." The buyer needed to come up with fifty or sixty thousand dollars on short notice, unless Ellison wanted to walk away from a debt he could probably never hope to make good. Where was such a buyer to be found? Ellison could not put up a "For Sale" sign. If he advertised his decision to emigrate, he would not only depress the price he hoped to obtain, but he would also risk the wrath of local whites. In effect, he would be telling them that he did not trust them or their neighbors or their countrymen, fighting words to Southern gentlemen in normal times. Ellison somehow had to pass the word quietly that his place was for sale, without announcing—or probably even whispering—why. He could not afford to hint at the truth— that after more than forty years of effort as a free man, a master gin maker, a planter, and a slaveholder, he found himself subject to the degradation and contempt he had tried to avoid by changing his name in 1820 and by his exemplary behavior ever since. His life was on the verge of coming full circle: from April Ellison, slave, to William Ellison, free man of color, to William Ellison, slave. We do not know what Ellison thought on Christmas Eve of 1860. We do know that he had concluded that the haven he had built in Stateburg was no longer safe, that all his effort had bought him the freedom to emigrate. How, when, and where the Ellisons discussed with James M. Johnson, who returned to Stateburg on Christmas Day, to "confer freely."[155]

VIII

Harvest the Wind

D URING the evening of the day after Christmas, 1860, United States Major Robert Anderson surprised South Carolinians by evacuating his indefensible garrison at Fort Moultrie on Sullivan's Island and occupying Fort Sumter in the middle of Charleston harbor. Anderson's refusal to surrender Sumter received the endorsement of the Buchanan administration and set the stage for the next four months of threats and counterthreats as politicians shuttled back and forth between Charleston, Washington, Montgomery, and Richmond. From December 26, 1860, to April 12, 1861, the eyes of the nation focused on Charleston and the impasse at Fort Sumter. By February, Georgia, Alabama, Mississippi, Louisiana, Florida, and Texas had followed South Carolina out of the Union and into the Confederacy. These were exciting, heady times for Southern politicians, abandoning an old government and staking claims to a new one. Leaders on both sides bluffed and postured, stood firm and retreated, skirmished and advanced, contesting the very existence of the Union, and all without shedding a drop of blood. The drama at Fort Sumter orchestrated these national themes on the small stage of Charleston harbor, and everybody watched, not quite certain what would happen if the play spilled over the footlights and engulfed the audience, as it seemed about to do, and did on April 12, when Confederate batteries opened fire on the fort.[1]

For Charleston's polite society, the crisis at Sumter made an ideal drawing-room war. "This rebellion differs from all others," one Charlestonian boasted, "in having spread through society from above, and not from below, from the gentlemen of society and not from the rabble."[2] Conversations had never before sparkled with quite as much high-minded patriotism, dinner parties had seldom savored such choice rumors, and few balls had previously been graced with such a dazzling array of uniformed officers. Mary Boykin Chesnut, wife of former Senator, now Colonel, James Chesnut Jr. reveled in the excitement. "What a dear, delightful place Charleston is," she wrote in late March 1861. "So many pleasant people, so much good talk. . . . " A few days later she remarked, "the atmosphere is phosphorescent." On the evening before the firing on Fort Sumter, she dined with friends and pronounced it "the merriest, maddest dinner we have had yet. Men were more audaciously wise and witty."[3] In no other four-month period after secession would spirits be so effervescent, politics so glamorous, and war so painless. For the South Carolina chivalry, these were the best months of their lives.

The political and military commotion in Charleston was bad for business, however. Shortly after Lincoln's election, Charleston's nine banks refused to discount the notes of the city's merchants, many of them due to Northern suppliers. By late November Charleston merchants complained publicly of the "money pressure" created by the misguided policy of the cautious banks, or, as one merchant called them, "pecuniary synagogues."[4] Merchant spokesmen called for the suspension of specie payments to provide relief, and by November 30 all banks in the city complied.[5] Three bank presidents signed a letter in the *Mercury* promising to resume specie payments "as soon as our political difficulties are adjusted, and the course of trade [is] again allowed to flow in its ordinary channels."[6] Events of the next few weeks made clear that time would not come soon. Early in December the correspondent of the New York *Tribune* reported "much financial distress among the mass of people," especially among the several hundred unemployed workingmen.[7] Merchants were also hard-pressed. "All kinds of property, save cotton, have gone down fifty percent," the *Tribune* noted in mid-December.[8] Shortly after Major Anderson occupied Fort Sumter, the Charleston correspondent of the Philadelphia *Inquirer* wrote that, with the exception of the cotton trade, "every class of business has been paralyzed."[9] At the beginning of the new year the *Tribune* reporter said, "There is almost a total suspension of business . . . there is no collection of debts, credit is collapsed, property is without sale or value; the avenues of trade are closed up; and the prospect is darkening every hour."[10] When the merchant ship *Star of the West* appeared off the Charleston bar on January 9 in an attempt to bring supplies to Anderson's garrison at Fort Sumter, Citadel cadets began the barrage that repulsed the ship and raised the excitement in Charleston to such a pitch that, the *Tribune* reported, "All business is suspended."[11]

The fortification of Charleston slowed shipping to a trickle. To prevent another attempt to supply Fort Sumter, authorities loaded the hulks of four old ships with granite and on January 11 sank them in the channels across the bar at the entrance to Charleston harbor, leaving only Maffitt's Channel open to shipping.[12] The channel nearly paralleled Sullivan's Island, within easy range of the batteries along the shore, whose crews did not hesitate to fire warning shots across the bows of merchant steamers.[13] The blocked channels diverted most vessels to Savannah, and the exuberant firing on ships creeping into Charleston made businessmen understandably skittish. Freight rates went up 50 percent, and the price of cargo insurance became "prohibitive."[14] The restriction of shipping began to pinch the cotton market by late January. In February a cotton factor told the *Tribune* reporter his business was ruined and that he was having trouble paying for his family's food.[15] Business did not improve in March and April, and after April 12 much of what had been business as usual became trading with the enemy, and ceased altogether.

For free people of color planning to emigrate, the business paralysis made it difficult to liquidate property, and the constriction of shipping made escape problematic. South Carolina authorities commandeered the New York steamer *Marion* to help protect the harbor when the *Star of the West* approached, then cleared the ship a few days later to resume its normal course to New York. As the *Marion* lay off Fort Sumter waiting out a storm, two Charleston officers boarded and seized H. T. Graddick, a free man of color who was attempting to emigrate with his wife and mother. Graddick was an experienced harbor pilot who had just quit his job, and South Carolina officials feared that he would make his services available to guide some Northern ship into Charleston waters. Although Graddick denied the charges, officials also removed his wife and mother from the steamer before allowing it to go on to New York. Twenty-three other free persons of color were on board; forty others were ready to leave the city at the time the *Marion* was seized to pursue the *Star of the West* but now were "unable to get away by reason of the turn of affairs," the passengers said.[16]

The refugees aboard the *Marion* were mostly free colored mechanics and their families, "whose destination is someplace where Slavery is not recognized, and confiscation is not to be feared," they told a reporter in New York.[17] They explained the attempts in the legislature to enslave them, to prevent them from working at their trades, and even to forbid them from riding in a carriage. Coming on top of the August enslavement crisis and all the normal restrictions on free Negroes, which the refugees recounted, the new proposals made free people of color "fearful that their liberty may be taken away at any moment; so that all of them who have money at hand are leaving." Another group of twenty free colored refugees had arrived aboard the *Marion* late in December, and the January emigrants said, "this is merely a beginning, and . . . all the intelligent free colored people are rapidly coming to the conclusion that safety is to be found only in getting entirely out of the reach of the Slave Power." The December exiles had already departed for Haiti, and most of the January exiles planned to follow them.

As late as the middle of March free people of color were still able to get out of Charleston. The *Tribune* correspondent wrote that "free blacks continue to leave in large numbers, and cases of great hardship continue to occur."[18] A month earlier the reporter estimated that about 2,000 free people of color had left Charleston since the start of the new year, many experiencing "extreme hardship."[19] The narrow escape route through Charleston harbor closed for good on April 12. After the firing on Fort Sumter, the risks of escape included running the federal blockade and crossing enemy lines.

The Ellisons and the Johnsons did not carry out their plans

to emigrate. No document survives that explains their reasoning while they watched the events of January, February, March, and April from the family compound in Stateburg. Most likely, the depreciation of property, the business standstill, and the shortage of cash and credit faced William Ellison with the prospect of simply walking away from everything he had built, a sacrifice he could not bring himself to make. It appears that Ellison's property trapped him in South Carolina. At least, the Charleston refugees provide evidence that the more assets a free person of color possessed, the less likely the person was to emigrate.

Except for the newspaper reports, free Afro-American refugees left no records of their flight, making it impossible to reconstruct a clear profile of those who left. A rough group portrait of the refugees can be pieced together, however, by comparing lists of free persons of color present in Charleston in 1860 with the names in the 1862 Charleston Free Negro Tax Book. Although this comparison is far from perfect, it makes clear that few members of the free mulatto elite were among the refugees.[20] Of well over 1,000 refugees, the vast majority were poor free Negroes who had little to leave behind in the city. Missing from the city in 1862 were 113 individuals who in 1860 had paid municipal taxes; 94 of them (83 percent) owned less than $2,000 worth of real estate. In contrast, of the 117 members of the free mulatto elite who paid real estate taxes on property worth $2,000 or more in 1860, 108 (92 percent) were still present in the city in 1862. Almost as many of the free colored slaveholders (106 out of 131) remained in Charleston. Those who emigrated were, as the newspapers reported, predominately poor free colored tradesmen and their families. Most of them were carpenters, but carters, draymen, painters, bakers, millwrights, tailors, laborers, and upholsterers also left, as did lesser numbers of other craftsmen. For these men and their families, the decision to emigrate was easier than for the Ellisons, the Johnsons, and other prosperous free Negroes simply because freedom was just about their only possession. Despite the decision of the Ellisons and all their Charleston friends to emigrate, they could not break their bonds to their property in the few months they had to escape. By default, they mortgaged their freedom to their wealth. After April 12, all they could do was hope for the best.

Well before then, many members of the free mulatto elite had taken steps to try to guarantee that the best would not be as bad as they feared. On January 10, the day after the *Star of the West* was turned back, thirty-seven leading free men of color from Charleston sent a memorial to Thomas J. Gantt, the clerk of the Court of Appeals, who lived on Coming Street just above Calhoun.[21] The same day, twenty-three free colored leaders in Columbia sent an identical memorial to J. H. Boatwright, the Mayor of Columbia, and another memorial was sent to Governor Francis W. Pickens by twenty-three of Charleston's most prominent free mulattoes.[22] Among the signatures on the memorial to Gantt were those of John Lee, Jacob Weston, Frederick Sasportas, Richard Holloway and his sons, and James Johnston (not Johnson). The memorial to the governor came from the likes of William McKinlay, Robert Howard, Richard E. Dereef, Joseph Dereef, and Anthony Weston. Neither the Ellisons nor the Johnsons signed the memorials, but virtually all their Charleston friends did. The memorials represented a carefully coordinated attempt by the free mulatto elite to stake their claim to what was left of the middle ground.

The memorials wrapped the free mulatto elite in the flag of the white race. "We are by birth citizens of South Carolina— In our veins flows the blood of the white race[,] in some half[,] in others much more than half white blood."[23] White South Carolina nativity was the strongest possible claim to legitimacy. The memorialists reinforced it with a pledge of dependence and loyalty. "Our attachments are with you, our hopes of safety & protection from you. Our allegiance is due to *So. Ca.* and in her defence, we are willing to offer up our lives, and all that is dear to us."[24] This promise to die for South Carolina was qualified by requesting Gantt to offer the Charleston group to the governor for "any service where we can be most useful," with two significant restraints: that if the men were ordered away from Charleston, the state would provide for their wives and children; and that the men themselves be subject only to such orders as met the approval of Gantt, a neighbor of William McKinlay, Jacob Weston, and other free mulatto leaders.[25] It was surely no oversight that the Charleston memorialists, unlike those in Columbia, did not send their letter to the mayor, Charles Macbeth. In effect, they asked to be placed under the orders of a white man they knew and trusted, with a stronger promise than any white volunteers received: that their families would be protected. The memorial to Governor Pickens was equally circumspect. The signatories, "Free Men of the City of Charleston," offered "to be placed or occupy any position" the governor designated, and professed their readiness "whenever called upon to assist in preparing the State a defence, against any action which may be brought against her."[26] Governor Pickens's response was predictable; he refused the offer and told them he would come to them only as "a last resort."[27]

As a ploy, the memorials were a master stroke. Two weeks earlier many of the memorialists had resolved to leave South Carolina as soon as possible. During the last few days they had not changed their minds, only their strategy. They resolved to ask for what they knew they could not get as a way of getting what they knew they could not ask for. They needed reassurance that they would be left alone, and to get it they asked to join the flower of white manhood and defend the state. They did not offer their money or their property; they did not request approval of a free colored company; and what they did offer was tied with two important strings. The new strategy grew out of an old commitment, to do whatever was necessary to preserve freedom. The memorialists did not declare their undying loyalty to slavery. But by professing their qualified loyalty to South Carolina, they hoped to reaffirm that old commitment. If their memorials, like their petition against Eason's bill, were intended to do nothing more than buy time, they succeeded until April 12, when time ran out.

Within three weeks of hearing from South Carolina's free mulatto elite, Governor Pickens received word that not all free Negroes were eager to take their stand with the Confederacy. Late in January 1861 James Redpath wrote Pickens, asking him not to destroy a brig Redpath had chartered "for the peaceful purpose of conveying people of color" to Haiti. Redpath explained that almost sixty free persons of color, "nearly all of them natives of South Carolina," were "engaged" to sail on the vessel within weeks. "Many others, I am credibly informed, are preparing to leave your State for Hayti," Redpath said. Since "South Carolina . . . does not desire to retain this class of her people," Redpath asked permission to send an agent to Charleston to arrange for the emigrants to depart directly for Haiti, rather than having to go first to New York.[28] If Governor Pickens replied, his remarks have not survived. But there is no uncertainty about his refusal to allow an agent of the abolitionist Redpath to come into Charleston, if indeed Redpath had an agent foolhardy enough to undertake the assignment. Even without an agent, Charleston's free Afro-Americans were still struggling to get passage out of the city bound for free soil.

Free men of color who lacked the social standing to address the governor but who had decided to make the best of their situation offered their labor to help with fortifications around the city. Early in January a group of 150 "able-bodied free colored men" offered to work without pay on the breast-works being constructed along the coast.[29] Slaves too were hard at work erecting batteries, but they were not the only ones. The correspondent of the New York *Tribune* noted that the white chivalry had to set aside their muskets and swords and grapple with "the spade and the wheelbarrow." On the fortifications, "representatives of Carolina's best blood labor side by side with the blackest slave," the correspondent observed, savoring the irony.[30] When the correspondent inquired among Negroes about their reasons for volunteering, they told him "the inducements were to escape the lash of the owner, and avoid being suspected of disloyalty to their masters." Less than a month before the firing on Fort Sumter, "intelligent colored men" told the *Tribune* correspondent that they "are looking, as indeed all their race are, to this struggle as the beginning of that end which shall secure to them the possession of their dearest rights."[31]

WHEN the Civil War erupted in Charleston harbor, William Ellison was seventy years old. Born a slave in the spanking new American republic, he was now a free man in a government that celebrated a new birth of slavery. His Confederate experience was brief, however. On August 5 his white guardian and family physician Dr. W. W. Anderson began to make frequent visits to "Wisdom Hall." After November 2 Dr. Anderson came to see the elderly ginwright almost daily.[32] On December 5, 1861, William Ellison died.[33] Following a funeral service at Holy Cross the next day, his family laid him to rest alongside his wife Matilda, who had died eleven years earlier.[34] From Charleston, James D. Johnson expressed to Henry "feelings of the Deepest condolences in your recent affliction in the loss of my Esteemed friend your father." Johnson said he was "in hopes of seeing your Dear Father before he breathed his last in this world, but alas! little did I think that I would have been deprived of the pleasure."[35] Johnson and his wife Delia were aggrieved by Ellison's death, but they did not make the trip to Stateburg because of the crisis in the low country. Early in November federal forces captured Port Royal, less than fifty miles south of Charleston, where they established a permanent Union stronghold on the coast.[36] Charlestonians expected an attack on the city at any minute. The panic was such that Johnson feared his wife might "become distracted" by the additional stress of a visit to the bereaved Ellisons in Stateburg.[37]

William Ellison's tombstone stood first in the first row in the family burying ground. The brief inscription on the stone concluded, "In God we trust."[38] Those words may speak as much for Ellison's survivors as for his own faith in the tender mercies of divine providence. Ellison's faith had never caused him to slacken his efforts in the world. With the patriarch's death, responsibility for the survival of the Ellison family shifted to the shoulders of his children. Faced with their supreme crisis, Henry, William Jr., and Eliza Ann lost the strategist who had plotted the family's course through the antebellum years. The outbreak of war broke the tension of the secession crisis, but it did not relieve the fears of the state's free colored population. The files of the South Carolina legislature bulged with proposals to restrict freedom and even to end it. Anomalous in the antebellum South, free people of color were more of an anomaly in a nation that proclaimed slavery as its cornerstone. No one could predict that public professions of loyalty to the Palmetto State and its institutions would preserve the freedom of Negroes. Under the pressures of war with the North, white Southerners might well decide to rid themselves once and for all of these odd Confederates.

As directed by his will, William Ellison's estate passed into the hands of his three surviving children.[39] Each received the allotted portion, but the estate remained unified.[40] As always, the Ellison family lived and worked together. All three children were appointed executors of their father's property, but Henry, apparently groomed to succeed his father, became chief administrator. Routine legal matters—appearing at the Sumter courthouse, advertising for debts due the estate, appointing appraisers, filing returns of their administration of the property—ground on in the months after William Ellison's death.[41] Other tasks confronting the Ellisons were not as perfunctory.

To sustain what their father had achieved, the Ellisons had to demonstrate perceptions as keen and responses as astute as his. The children had imbibed the lessons of their father's life, but they looked out upon a social and political landscape transformed by war. Lofty political arenas where whites would decide the fate of free people of color were beyond the Ellisons' influence. Their politics lay in the High Hills, in Stateburg. In this familiar territory they encountered the war. Minor, practical exigencies irritated most Southerners. One resident of Sumter recalled that during the war, families who had lived in baronial splendor made dresses from homespun, parched cotton seeds, rye, and sweet potatoes as ersatz coffee, concocted plum cakes not from the customary ginger and jam but from red peppers boiled in watermelon juice, wrote letters with pokeberry ink, and read by the light of lard lamps.[42] These deprivations called forth uncomfortable changes in private life. But the Ellisons could not meet all the challenges they confronted within the privacy of "Wisdom Hall." Every master experienced hazards during the war, but the dilemmas of black masters were unique. To meet them, the Ellisons had to venture out into their community, where their own sagacity or stupidity promised to have direct, immediate, personal consequences for their security.

Cotton was an early casualty of the war. As gin makers, the Ellisons suffered quickly. The secession scare in late 1860 disrupted the normal marketing and financial arrangements planters relied on to dispose of their crop. By the time the bolls began to burst open in 1861, most planters still had unmarketed cotton on hand. The federal naval blockade of rebel ports and the Confederate embargo on shipping cotton outside the South sent cotton production into a tailspin. The cotton harvest plummeted from 4.5 million bales in 1861 to 1.5 million bales in 1862; in 1863, the crop barely reached a half-million bales.[43] As cotton production tumbled, so did the planters' need for gins. The meticulous reports Henry filed as administrator of his father's estate in 1862 show only two gin sales: a fifty-saw gin to a Mr. Young for $100 and a smaller gin to a Mr. Hodge for $66.67. For the duration of the war, the Ellisons neither sold another gin nor advertised to try.

The gin shop was not covered with cobwebs, however. While the brothers stopped building gins, they repaired a few and maintained a strong trade in general blacksmith work. On December 8, 1863, for example, R. M. Durant paid "Henry and William Ellison" $30 for gin repairs.[44] Workers in the Ellisons' shop still mended buggies, shoed horses, crafted wagon wheels, forged nuts and bolts, and fashioned tongues for wagons and carts. The list of customers during the war included most of the names on antebellum accounts—Lenoir, Richardson, Anderson, Frierson, Reynolds, Cantey, Spann, Moore, Moody, Sumter, Singleton—but now the familiar names often followed titles of military rank. The stagnant gin business reduced the income from the shop, but, fortunately for the Ellisons, their survival did not hinge on black-smithing.

Before the war, cotton surpassed the gin shop as William Ellison's chief source of income. But the war strangled the Ellisons' cotton production just as it did other planters'. In July 1862 Henry and William received $494.24 from the sale of fifteen bales, no doubt part of the 100 bales their father had in storage when he died. In April 1863 the brothers sold their last cotton of the war for $868.14. Like most Confederate states, South Carolina limited the number of acres a planter could legally seed in cotton. Growing cotton in the Confederacy was both unprofitable and dangerous. The duty of every planter, Southern newspapers trumpeted, required them to grow food for The Cause in fields previously sown with cotton. Planters who stubbornly defended their right to grow what they wished sometimes received unwelcome visits from local committees who came to inquire about the planters' priorities. The Ellisons apparently did not bother to plant even their allotment. They wanted to avoid these nighttime callers.[45]

The Ellisons converted their entire plantation to food production. Almost all planters boosted their acreage of provision crops, but few matched the Ellisons' metamorphosis. Before the war they had grown enough corn, sweet potatoes, peas, and beans to make their plantation self-sufficient.[46] Now, however, food production was patriotic, and very profitable. Despite the unprecedented demand for provisions, other planters were either unable or unwilling to convert. They came to the Ellisons' to purchase the food they did not grow themselves. Moreover, as one woman remembered, the hills of western Sumter District "were full of refugees from Charleston."[47] Migrants from the coast often brought their slaves with them, far away from Yankee raiding parties and from the land on which they might otherwise have grown food. They gave the Ellisons additional hungry customers. Early in the war, wagons loaded with food crops rolled from the Ellisons' fields to plantations and farms throughout the High Hills and beyond.

At the Stateburg crossroads, corn became king. Planters who had formerly visited the shop to dicker for gins now came to bargain for grain. L. M. Spann, for example, paid $55 for corn in January 1863. Before the year was out he returned three times to buy several hundred dollars' worth. Many of the Ellisons' sales were large, like Spann's, but some of them were tiny, such as Mr. Master's purchase in June 1863 of one dollar's worth of corn. Large planters and hard-scrabble farmers alike turned to the Ellisons. If corn could sustain the Confederacy, then they were doing their part. Rich and poor could attest to the Ellisons' loyalty. Business was brisk enough to cause the Ellisons to invest $25 in January 1863 for a corn sheller to help them keep up with demand. Peaking in 1863, corn sales brought the Ellisons several thousand dollars during the war.

Just as corn bumped cotton at the beginning of the war, corn was later nudged aside by another food crop—sorghum.

Military events and the disruption of slavery in Louisiana caused sugar production to collapse more rapidly than cotton.[48] Lacking sugar, Southerners with a sweet tooth searched for a substitute. A woman who refugeed with her Manning and Richardson cousins remembered that "Everybody planted sorghum, a kind of sugar cane, the juice of which was pressed out by a small wooden mill in the barnyard, and then boiled in large iron kettles into syrup, and this was the only sweet thing we had. . . ."[49] Crippled by the absence of men to oversee the cultivation of this new crop, home production seldom proved sufficient.[50] The Ellisons nimbly stepped in to supply plenty of sweetener. Although the technical requirements of sorghum production were modest, the Ellisons' skilled slaves made their work force better prepared than any of their neighbors' to produce syrup for sale. The Ellison brothers may also have discovered that syrup made a larger profit than corn. As syrup sales rose, corn gradually declined. The first sale came in September 1863—a mere $7.15—but the following month the Ellisons tallied $600 in sorghum sales. In 1864 they delivered several thousand dollars' worth of their syrup to sugar-starved Sumterians.

The Ellison plantation became a giant general store for agricultural produce. Corn and sorghum were the major crops, but the Ellisons also raised bushels of surplus peas, potatoes, and peanuts. They usually sold these auxiliary crops in small lots, but in the aggregate they returned a sizable income. In addition, the Ellisons grew large crops of fodder for local livestock. They also increased their own production of animals for the marketplace. They sold a few live pigs, small amounts of bacon and lard, and larger quantities of beef. Local residents in need of basic provisions could satisfy their requirements by a trip to the Ellisons'.

Always resourceful, the Ellison brothers discovered still other ways to make money and be of service to the community. When shortages of horses and mules developed, the Ellisons made theirs available for hire. On August 13, 1862, for example, they rented out a mule for a dollar, and the following week, a horse for 75 cents. More often, they hired out their horses and mules harnessed to their wagons and carts. Sometimes the Ellisons themselves did hauling for their neighbors.

They received a few dollars for most hauling jobs, but in August 1864 one individual paid them $120. When the brothers purchased more household or shop goods than they needed—such as leather or cheap cloth—they made the excess available for sale to their white neighbors.

The Ellisons enjoyed the patronage of scores of white neighbors, but by far their best customer was the Confederate government. Seeking to keep a massive army fed, equipped, and in the field, the government needed huge quantities of goods the Ellisons produced. Sumter District's inland location and network of railroad connections made it a center for army stores. Thousands of freight cars loaded with war supplies rolled north on the Camden branch, just a few miles from "Wisdom Hall."[51] The Ellisons' first transaction as army provisioners occurred October 9, 1862, when the brothers received $550 from "Col. S. J. Bradley for corn and fodder sold to the Government." A dozen purchases followed this initial sale, and by the end of the war the government had paid the Ellisons nearly $5,300, mostly for corn and fodder, but also for bacon, corn shucks, cotton, and a horse. A March 1863 impressment law gave Richmond officials authority to take what they needed and pay what they wanted. Planters complained that the government paid only half the going rate, and they haggled and refused to sell.[52] With one exception—when the Ellisons received $700 from a Mr. Coles for a "horse impressed for govt."—the brothers evidently sold voluntarily. Whether they received the market price or only half, they earned a small fortune from the government. They also earned a solid gold reputation as loyal Confederates.

The government may have hired several Ellison "Mechanics." Skilled slaves whom the Ellisons no longer needed in the gin shop, these men earned their masters $444.50 for 1862 and $510.52 for 1863. In each instance the employer paid the hire the following spring. The collapse of the government in the spring of 1865 could explain why the Ellisons showed no income from slave hiring in 1864. But private businesses may also have employed their artisans. Shorthanded manufacturers desperately needed skilled workers, especially when they accepted government contracts. Within a few miles of the Ellison place, private firms entered agreements with the government to cast field guns, make artillery harnesses, and build gun carriages and caissons, all tasks suitable for the Ellisons' slave mechanics.[53]

Whether the Ellisons volunteered their valuable slaves or the government impressed them is not clear, but the evidence suggests voluntary hiring. The brothers received a large sum for slave wages for 1862, the year before impressment became common practice and official Confederate policy. Early in the war the government usually secured slave labor by voluntary contracts with their owners. Field commanders still sometimes impressed slaves and sent them to the South Carolina coast, where they worked under brutal conditions on fortifications.[54] Although the government paid planters for their slaves, the payments were tokens and erratic at that.[55] By promptly and freely hiring out their slaves, the Ellisons received good wages for redundant workers, employed them in the neighborhood, and secured them skilled work. They may also have gained immunity from impressment. Although the Confederate Congress legalized impressment in March 1863, South Carolina allowed planters to sidestep the law until December by paying small fines.[56] No fines appear in the Ellisons' careful accounts. It was not because government agents overlooked the numerous slaves in the High Hills. Jacob Stroyer, a slave on one of the Singleton places, remembered that in 1863 a man went "to different plantations, gathering slaves from their masters to carry off to work on fortifications, and to wait on officers." Stroyer was one of ten slaves impressed from Singleton's plantation.[57] The Ellisons were powerless to resist impressment, but they may have been shrewd enough to escape it.

They had somewhat more leeway in dealing with their High Hills neighbors. For instance, they set the prices they charged for the produce of their plantation. Unfortunately, it is not possible to compare their rates with market prices. Their accounts usually include the item sold, the purchaser's name, and the amount of the total bill, but not the item price or the quantity bought. Furthermore, prices varied sharply from one time and place to another and fluctuated wildly in a single neighborhood within a few days. "Flour was 12$[,] today 25$ a bag," a Columbia woman explained in June 1863, adding "fowls sold yesterday $1 pr pair, were $2.50 not long since."[58] What is clear is that the Ellisons were not hoarders, a charge Southerners increasingly leveled against many white planters. It is unlikely the Ellisons were gougers either. They did not want accusing fingers pointed at them as selfish speculators fattening on their neighbors' miseries. They had no need to extort to make huge profits. Skyrocketing prices assured that anyone who could produce surplus food crops could do well at market rates. Rather than begrudge the Ellisons their profits, the government and the citizens of Sumter District evidently were grateful to have such bountiful providers.

While the income of most cotton planters shriveled to a fraction of its prewar size, the Ellisons' soared. More diverse in their operations than most of their neighbors since the 1830s, they were prepared to take advantage of fresh opportunities. Just how well is revealed in their accounts. From March 1862 through January 1863 the income from their father's estate was pennies less than $2,550. From February 1863 through December 1863 the estate earned just under $7,860. And from January 1864 through December 1864 the Ellisons collected a whopping $12,738.11. Even deducting for roaring inflation, the ledgers show that Henry and William Jr. were their father's sons. In difficult times they proved to be as able and opportunistic as their father in his day. They also did not neglect their social and political flank. They managed the estate with such finesse that it combined patriotism with high profits.

AS producers the Ellisons benefited from wartime shortages, but as consumers they too were victims. Medicine was hard to come by in the Confederate states. In 1862 and 1863 the Ellisons paid $130 for quinine and other drugs, including $2.00 for "whiskey for medicinal purposes." They also bought small quantities of fodder, tallow, wheat, nails, salt peter, and rye, but even small quantities were expensive. When they bought a mare and colt in 1864 they paid $1,800. Three years earlier their most valuable horse was worth $140. The price of salt ballooned during the war. In 1862 alone the Ellisons paid $400 for salt. The following year they reduced their expenditures for salt to $111, and in 1864 they did not spend a dime. They managed to barter their produce for salt from family members in Charleston. "This will acknowledge the receipt of the corn sent for which accept my thanks," Henry's sister-in-law Louisa P. Weston wrote from the city in March 1864. She added her regrets that "I was unsuccessful in getting the salt off to you." She had hoped to send it with one of the Johnsons who was on his way to Stateburg, but signals crossed and she missed the connection. "I however trust God willing to get up there in about 3 or 4 weeks time and if that time will suit, I will bring it up myself."[59] By exchanging upcountry corn for low-country salt, the Ellisons saved cash and helped hard-pressed kinfolk in the city. Although Charleston lay under siege, members of the Ellison family still traveled freely from Stateburg to Charleston and back, maintaining close, mutually beneficial ties.

Family ties could bind in other ways. Henry and William Jr.'s expenses included $200 for "labor done." One of their hired laborers was their nephew, John Buckner. Having received no bequest from his grandfather, Buckner did odd jobs for his uncles. For some carpentry and bill collecting, they paid him $55. But they did not rely on Buckner to collect all the bills due the estate. In 1862 and 1863 the Ellison brothers employed R. Gale "for collecting" and paid him $34. Perhaps he worked territory beyond easy reach of Stateburg, where Buckner lived. Close to home, the Ellisons hired "Sam belonging to the estate of Mr. Waties" for $53.60 and paid Mike $3 for "work done" on the plantation, wages Buckner could have used. He had a wife and a growing brood of small children to support, and he was able and willing to work. His wife Sarah brought in a little income from sewing. In October 1861 she made six items of clothing for James Moody for $6.75, and the following year she earned the same amount for making dresses and jackets for Moody youngsters.[60] Sarah and John Buckner did not reap much of the Ellisons' wartime harvest.

Another family member did not participate fully in the Ellisons' wartime enterprises. In the 1850s James M. Johnson and William Ellison had a shoe business, but the fate of the business after Ellison's death is unclear.[61] It may be that Johnson, who returned to Stateburg on Christmas Day, 1860, and lived in "Drayton Hall" for the duration of the war, simply took over the business, accounting for its absence from the records of William Ellison's estate. Henry and William continued to purchase large quantities of leather, spending almost $350 in 1863 alone. The gin business was nearly defunct, and they needed little leather belting. Perhaps they bought the leather for Johnson to make shoes. One purchase in January 1863 specified "sole leather." However, the Ellisons reported no income from a partnership with Johnson, and they bought shoes elsewhere. In September 1862, for example, they "Paid Caesar Frierson for making 3 pairs of shoes." A year later they paid Capt. John Frierson, presumably Caesar's owner, $70.50 for making shoes. Whether the Ellisons' brother-in-law continued to make shoes cannot be known from the Ellisons' accounts, and no other records have survived. Although Johnson was a close friend of both brothers, the death of William Ellison does not appear to have drawn him any closer to the inner circle of the family's economic life.

The Ellisons' greatest expense was the Confederate government itself. What the government paid the Ellisons with one hand it very nearly took back with the other. Government purchases brought the Ellisons $5,300, while taxes cost them about $5,000, more than one-fifth their total wartime income. Unlike many Southerners, the Ellisons evidently paid without hesitation. Once they even overpaid and received a refund of $150 for "overcharge on income tax." On April 22, 1863, they spent $1,500 cash for Confederate war bonds. They could afford to invest in the government. From March 1862 through December 1864 they had an income of $23,145 and expenditures of $11,857, a tidy profit of more than $11,000. Only blockade runners and similar wily souls did better.

Unfortunately for the Ellisons, most of their profits were in Confederate paper. At war's end they held $1,500 in Confederate bonds, $1,100 in 7.30 Treasury notes, $4,700 in 4 percent certificates, and $1,772.10 in Confederate currency. Investing more than $9,000 in the Confederate cause may seem heedless, but blue-chip investments were hard to find. Moreover, while Confederate investments appear reckless in hindsight, at the time they were prudent politics. What better way to demonstrate faith and commitment than with 7.30 notes: 7 percent paper payable thirty years after victory.

Through their service as provisioners and investors the Ellisons bought protection. Long after the war ended, white South Carolinians forgot little about the late unpleasantness, and the Ellisons' behavior paid dividend after dividend.

Few planter families compiled a better war record than the Ellisons. They more than fulfilled every obligation the government imposed. As soon as the call went out, they quit growing cotton and began producing food crops. They supplied their neighbors and the rebel armies with provisions. They hired out their skilled slaves, apparently for war-related work. They paid all their taxes on time and invested their profits in government notes. Rather than slackers, backsliders, hoarders, or speculators, the Ellisons were model Confederates. All their record lacked was a long list of family members who wore gray. They could not match the military service of their lordly neighbors twenty miles west. "In the Preston & Hampton families, Wade Hampton is the only one not in the field," Oscar Lieber wrote his parents from a Charleston battery six days after the firing on Fort Sumter. He hastened to explain that Wade Hampton's "company has not yet been accepted." Lieber ticked off the family roster: "Col. Preston is a corporal in the Mounted Rifles, Johnny is here in the Sumter Guards, Willie as Lieut. of Regulars in Moultrie. Venable is a Lieut. in the Mounted Rifles. Kit Hampton and Wade Jr and Preston Hampton also. Manning is an aide of Beauregard's; and so it is in almost every family I know of."[62]

According to the law, it could not be so in the Ellison family. People of color were not eligible for military service. In 1861 the South Carolina legislature expressly prohibited Negroes from using firearms.[63] Some Southern states early in the war permitted free colored men to muster into state or local militias, but no state allowed Negroes to serve as regular soldiers. The Confederate government was equally cool to dressing brown and black men in gray, until the final days of the war.[64] Most free men of color who aided the state were pressed into labor batallions by the conscription act of 1862. In Charleston free colored volunteers performed valuable service as firemen. By 1865 they composed the only fire companies in the city. James H. Holloway, a member of the Brown Fellowship

Society, recalled proudly that "members of the Society, not as an organization, but as individuals" saved Charleston from the fires ignited by Union bombardment.[65]

The Ellison family contributed more than a laborer or a fireman. On March 27, 1863, John Wilson Buckner enlisted as a private in the 1st South Carolina Artillery. He was wounded in action on July 12, 1863, at Battery Wagner. He remained in the army, according to his official Confederate military record, until October 19, 1864. Because his "furlough expired," he officially became a deserter.[66] However, his desertion was a technicality because years later he was praised by local whites—who were in a position to have known the truth—as a "faithful soldier."[67] For most free Negroes, even to attempt to join the army was dangerous. When three brothers who were "very dark skinned" and "at the Turpentine business" tried to enter the Camden militia in 1859, a white man objected, claiming "they were not white and had no right to muster." In the fight that ensued, one man was shot.[68] Buckner served in the companies of Capt. P. P. Galliard and Capt. A. H. Boykin, local white men who were acquaintances of Buckner and the other Ellisons.[69] Although everybody knew Buckner was a Negro, personal associations and a sterling family reputation nullified the law and made Buckner an honorary white man as a soldier. Seven Benenhalys also enlisted (and only one returned), but the Turks claimed they were white, and prominent white men from the area defended their assertions.[70] Whatever Buckner's motivation for enlisting—heartfelt loyalty, an itch for adventure, a desire to escape his stingy uncles, or a courageous assertion of manliness—he gave whites an unmistakable confirmation of the Ellisons' political sympathies.

Cagey behavior was routine in the Ellison household, but never more so than during the war. War inflamed age-old fears of slave rebellion. Near Camden, Emma Holmes noted in her diary in October 1862, "It was only a few weeks ago that a plot of insurrection was discovered among the negroes in the upper part of this district—it was very weak and ill-arranged and was confessed by one of them. A number were put in jail and are to be hung this week."[71] War also fueled white suspicions of free Negroes. Vigilantes rode their self-appointed beats, and the state legislature kept an eye on free persons of color.[72] In 1861 the legislature considered a bill calling for the enslavement of free people of color convicted of certain crimes, a renewal of the bill debated in the 1860 session. After lengthy deliberation, the bill passed the lower chamber but failed again in the Senate.[73] When white mechanics in Cheraw asked for relief from slave competition, the legislature responded more positively and granted their request by "prohibiting free Negroes and People of color from carrying on mechanical pursuits" in Cheraw.[74]

The Ellisons must have seen an editorial in the July 1863 Sumter *Tri-Weekly Watchman*. After noting the Charleston *Mercury*'s attack on planters who refused to give up slaves to work on the defenses of Charleston, it asked, "The *free negroes* of the State—what is their number, and why are they not pressed into this service? The conscription forces *white* men into the army, and the law requires the planter to send his slaves to the coast; why then should the *free negro,* the most idle and unprofitable member of the body politic, be excused from all service? . . . In Sumter District alone there are over thirty, liable to road duty, who are abundantly able to make the dirt and timber fly—why are *they* not pressed into service?"[75] Although the editorial was not aimed at the Ellisons, they could not be oblivious to its message. Pejorative stereotypes of free Negroes persisted. As the editorial implied, safety for free persons of color lay in service.

The Ellisons' service was not limited to producing food, paying taxes, hiring out their slaves, and providing a soldier. They also continued as good parishioners at Holy Cross. Each Sunday they joined their white neighbors to hear the rector pray for victory against the Yankees. In June 1863 they arranged baptisms for Tina, Fanny, and Violet, "servants of the Ellison family."[76] The church had difficulty collecting pew assessments from cash-strapped communicants, but the Ellisons paid regularly. Assessments had doubled since the 1840s, and the Ellison family had expanded to two pews. In each of the war years they paid $140 in pew fees. By their attendance, participation, and steady contributions, the Ellisons constantly reconfirmed their reputations as reliable members of the Stateburg community. In April 1863 they went a step further and subscribed $20 to a special fund at High Hills Baptist Church, the sort of generosity any community appreciated.

Good citizenship could not protect them forever. Having survived the dangers posed by the white citizens of Sumter, the soldiers of the Confederacy, and the politicians in Columbia, the Ellisons confronted the destructive armies of General William Tecumseh Sherman. War was slow to reach the South Carolina back country, but in the last winter it arrived as a firestorm. After marching from Atlanta to the sea and capturing Savannah, Sherman pushed his 60,000 soldiers into the "hellhole of secession." He entered Columbia on February 17, 1865, and when he left three days later much of the capital of South Carolina was in ashes. Sherman advanced to Winnsboro, William Ellison's boyhood home, then veered east, crossing the Wateree about thirty miles north of Stateburg.[77] The Ellisons and their neighbors could see the glare of burning buildings in night skies along Sherman's route, and they probably breathed a sigh of relief, thinking they were spared.

Sherman had not forgotten them, however. He ordered Brigadier General Edward E. Potter to march north from Charleston to destroy the railroads and military stores in Sumter District. Burning as they advanced, Potter's 2,700 men entered the town of Sumter in the second week of April. Before smashing the printing presses of the Sumter *Watchman,* which had printed William Ellison's gin advertisements, Potter's men published a declaration of emancipation, then promptly marched west. Bivouacking in Manchester, a railroad center, Potter established his headquarters in Richard Singleton's home. The Yankee general then turned north toward Stateburg and destroyed, among other places along the route, the home of James Caldwell, a patron of James M. Johnson's tailor shop in Charleston. Since "Wisdom Hall" stood less than one hundred yards from the road, the Ellisons must have trembled when a detachment of federal troops entered Stateburg on April 13. The soldiers destroyed several buildings and moved north, advancing as far as Camden. Then they turned back, skirmishing along the way, and passed again through Stateburg on their way to the coast.[78] Within days, the war was over.

The Ellisons survived. Southerners had not enslaved them

and Northerners had not burned them out. The preservation of the Ellisons' freedom did not depend solely on their unique material contributions to the Confederacy. Whites permitted the entire free Negro population to remain free during the war. Their economic contributions, unlike the Ellisons', were negligible. Even their labor was minimal, and often given reluctantly. Nevertheless, in the eyes of whites free Negroes had behaved themselves. They had not become a fifth column for federal forces, instigating slave revolts or sabotaging military operations. Their behavior allowed white people to turn their attention to the powerful enemy without, away from the few thousand suspect free persons of color within. The Ellisons' escape from destruction at the hands of federal troops rested on pure luck. Northern armies occasionally took vengeance on well-known Confederates, but more often their assaults had military rather than political objectives. Still, had Potter's troops known about the wartime activities of the black masters who lived at the crossroads, they might have paused long enough to light a fire.

Like other Confederates, the Ellisons did not escape the consequences of Northern victory. Defeat brought occupation and emancipation. The well-worn title "free person of color" no longer had meaning. Now all people were free. The special status that separated the Ellisons and their friends from the vast majority of Negroes died with the Confederacy. The middle ground between slavery and freedom on which the Ellisons had stood for decades slipped into the past along the new racial fault line created by emancipation. Now, the Ellisons were simply Southern Negroes. What that would mean in the years to come, no one could say. The only certainty in the spring of 1865 was that life in Stateburg would never be the same.

AFTER a bombardment by federal artillery destroyed her family home in Charleston in December 1861, Emma Holmes joined thousands of other low-country whites who fled inland. She spent most of the war in and around Camden, safe from all but the depressing news from the battlefields. When the war reached Camden in March 1865, however, her spunky optimism could no longer withstand the reality of the new order. "Every tie of society seems broken," she declared. Yankees swarmed over the countryside like "locusts," and "vile negro-soldiers" encouraged former slaves "to insult their former masters by every petty way malignity can suggest. . . ." At church, Negroes "were all in the most ludicrous & disgusting tawdry mixture of old finery, aping their betters most nauseatingly. . . ." Respectable whites were in a "constant state of anxiety and alarm," especially since "the poor whites [were] as much suspected as the negroes, for they were equally active in using Yankee license to rob. . . ." In May, friends and family members straggled back to the state, "homeless, penniless, clothesless, with the past an awful quivering wreck, and the future a blank. . . ." Like other whites of her class, Emma Holmes lived a nightmare. "We are (I am quite sure) the *last* of the *race* of South Carolina," she proclaimed. "All talked of emigration somewhere beyond Yankee rule."[79]

Four years earlier, free Negro South Carolinians had contemplated emigration in order to avoid disaster. Now the emigrant's shoe was on a white foot. Just the thought of leaving home made Emma Holmes shudder. "What a living death would exile be, away from all that made life dear." Besides, there were bewildering practical problems. "For married men," she observed, "emigration is easy to plan, but hard to carry out." Money was scarce, and land almost impossible to sell. Transportation was no easier to come by. Consequently, she wrote, "All feel that whatever they might be able to do in the future, for many months at least, they have to sit passively & wait to learn the course to be pursued toward us."[80] For many of the same reasons that the free colored elite had not emigrated in 1861, the white chivalry bided their time in 1865. But they did not let their fate rest solely in the hands of their conquerors and their former slaves. Neither did the Ellisons.

The dust from General Edward Potter's soldiers marching past the crossroads probably announced freedom in the Ellisons' slave quarters. Elsewhere in the South slaves took advantage of the war to step up their campaign of resistance. By the time federal troops arrived, they sometimes could only confirm freedom the slaves had already seized.[81] The circumstances in the Ellisons' quarters at the end of the war are unclear. But compared to white planters, the Ellisons enjoyed certain

advantages in the struggle for mastery. Except for John Buckner, the Ellison men stayed home throughout the war, directly
supervising their slaves. Judging from the profits the Ellisons
piled up, their slaves worked hard, at least through 1864. Records for the first half of 1865 show little production, but it is
impossible to tell if they reflect the disintegration of slavery
or merely the disintegration of careful record keeping.[82]
Whether taken by the slaves or proclaimed by federal troops,
freedom was a reality for all Negroes in the spring of 1865.
The Ellisons had become masters without slaves.

Southern whites predicted that emancipation would result
in race riots, economic decay, and sexual chaos.[83] For the Ellisons, freedmen were unlikely to conjure up the last of this
trilogy of fantasies. Eliza Ann, after all, already slept with a
Negro man. Slavery, moreover, held different meanings for
the Ellisons and for white masters. To whites, slaveholding
was the basis of power—political, social, economic, and racial.
Mastery burrowed into the marrow of their identities. To the
Ellisons, slaveholding was a tool, part of a pragmatic strategy
to prosper and to obtain security in a society hostile to all
people of color. The loss of slaves did not devastate the Ellisons' self-conception. But emancipation was costly, just as it
was for other planters. Assuming the Ellisons' slave force grew
by natural increase during the war and was not reduced by
sales, the family probably owned about eighty slaves at the
moment of emancipation, valued at perhaps $100,000. In
addition to losing slave capital, planters predicted that the
labor of former slaves would be worthless. The Ellisons could
not ignore the prophecies that freed people would not labor
without coercion and that King Cotton was as dead as slavery.

Former masters had no alternative but to test their auguries
and attempt to rebuild with former slaves. Like others, the
Ellisons moved quickly to procure workers. Freed men and
women in 1865 commonly signed contracts under the supervision of agents of the Freedmen's Bureau. Typically the contracts specified that freed people would finish out the year on
their former owner's plantation, usually working for a share
of the crop already in the ground.[84] Fresh from bondage,
freed men and women had no money and were unable to pay

the two-dollar capitation tax assessed by South Carolina. Their
employers often paid their tax, refastening the old links of
dependence. In 1865 the Ellisons paid the capitation tax for
twelve men.[85] Six of the twelve had first names that match
those of slaves William Ellison bequeathed his children in 1861.
Isaac Jenkins, who had carried messages and packages back
and forth from Charleston, was among them.[86] The Ellisons'
white neighbors also paid taxes for freedmen—James M.
Caldwell paid for six, Isaac Lenoir for nine, Isham Moore for
seventeen, and Dr. W. W. Anderson, the son of William Ellison's guardian who had died in 1864, paid for twenty-six.[87]
Several of the twelve men employed by the Ellisons probably
had families, and some of their wives and children may also
have worked in the Ellisons' fields. But the number of freed
people on their plantation was far short of the number of
slaves they had recently owned. If they had employed in 1865
the same slave men they owned in 1860, they would have paid
capitation taxes for at least twenty-five men. Since six of their
twelve laborers in 1865 did not belong to them at the beginning of the war, it appears that the Ellisons did not sign contracts with three-quarters of their former slaves.

Under the contracts of 1865, freed people returned to plantations that operated along familiar lines, too familiar for most
of them. Landlords continued to work Negroes in gangs, to
stand over their work, to limit personal freedom, and sometimes more. One Sumter freedman remembered that when a
white man came into the fields whipping, a former slave ran
into town to report it to the federal provost marshal. He "met
a crowd of other colored people," all of whom had encountered "difficulties with their former owners, and came from
all parts of the country, seeking redress." In December, when
freed people faced the decision of whether to sign on again,
he reported that "Nearly all the slaves [*sic*] left and went out
and made contracts with other landlords."[88]

Denied land of their own, most freedmen had no choice
but to work for white landowners. But they were determined
to end the plantation system. They sought to bury gang labor,
white supervision, and the old slave quarters with slavery. They
demanded to live and work as free people. Whites tried desperately to preserve the routines of slavery and to retain their

authority over the lives of former slaves. Freedom, whites hoped, would mean no more than paying low wages. The struggle between laborers and landlords over the content of freedom resulted in the system of sharecropping. This compromise emerged rapidly after the war. It permitted freed people to live in family cabins on small patches of land and to establish a family economy by working the land themselves, paying their rent with a share of the cotton they grew. For their part, landlords retained some supervision and the crucial control over land and production. Measured against slavery, freed people considered sharecropping a desirable, though far from ideal, form of freedom.[89]

On the Ellison place, the plantation system broke down as it did elsewhere, but sharecroppers did not replace slaves. Hardly anyone replaced slaves. The Ellisons evidently refused to compromise and insisted on hiring farm laborers for wages. Freed people rejected working for wages for white planters because it meant continued white control over their daily labor. They apparently did not find the prospect of wage labor for the Ellisons any more attractive. Furthermore, slave parents who had had their little girls sold away from them may not have been willing to work for the Ellisons under any circumstances. But it was not just the Ellisons' former slaves who stayed away from them. By refusing to adjust to the minimal demands of freed men and women, the Ellisons virtually withdrew from commercial agriculture. They retained all the land they inherited from their father, but they stopped being large farmers. They almost stopped being farmers at all.[90]

The Ellisons managed to contract with a few wage laborers who cultivated just a fraction of their land. They hired too few hands to maintain the old plantation system. Instead, the Ellisons' laborers farmed small, individual plots for subsistence wages. In 1868, for example, incomplete records show that the brothers paid Jack Wade, Monday Davis, Minto, and Jack $71.45 for labor, less than $20 each for the year. Two years later they paid $59.85 to Brutus Rawlinson, Charlotte James, and Joe Black. Some, and perhaps all, of these hired hands lived in cabins on Ellison land. The Ellisons charged rent for the cabins and maybe some garden space. In 1869 their seven renters paid $78.45. Toward hired hands and renters the Ellisons exhibited no more benevolence than their father had shown toward his slaves.

Cotton production resumed after the war, but the Ellisons' fields no longer turned white in the fall. Since they had quit growing cotton during the war, the Ellisons had to buy cotton seed to plant again. In 1866 they paid W. E. Richardson $31.25 and James M. Caldwell $90.00 for seed. The next year they bought a little more seed from L. M. Spann for $40.00. Yet even these modest sums do not convey how precipitously the plantation declined. William Ellison had cultivated 500 acres in 1860, but in 1870 his children had only 118 acres under cultivation. James M. Johnson farmed a tiny plot of 8 acres of Ellison land, John Buckner worked 20 acres, and Henry Ellison 90 acres. Johnson evidently tilled his land by himself. Buckner hired laborers, paying them wages of $250 a year. He probably hired his wife's relatives—Lawrence, Laurendon, and John Benenhaly—all young, illiterate farm hands who lived with him.

Henry's bill for farm labor in 1870 came to $450, about five or six workers at the rate Buckner paid. But Henry may have employed even fewer, and not all of them black. In 1871 he paid A. P. Vinson, a white man, $282.27 for "making [a] crop" for the estate. That same year he also paid ex-slave Minto Spencer $45.00 for "work done in field." Some of Henry's employees lived in cabins near "Wisdom Hall." According to the census, eight black families lived in immediate proximity to the Ellisons. Six of them were headed by illiterate farm laborers, three of whom definitely worked for the Ellisons. Peter Spencer, 49, had a wife and two children; Isaac Jenkins, 30, was married and had one child; and John Wade, 37, had a wife and two youngsters. Three other families—Isabella Spencer, 40, and her two children; Eliza Williams, 22, her six-month-old son, and Ellison Bennett, 21, a farm laborer; and Eliza Goodwyn, 50, and her young son—also may have worked for the Ellisons. Why these individuals worked for wages when most freed people opted for sharecropping is unclear. Some were former slaves of the Ellisons who may have stayed out of an attachment to their old masters or to the neighborhood. Others, especially the women with children and no husbands, may have been unable to do better.

With such a small labor force the Ellisons could not even approach their antebellum production. Their 118 cultivated acres produced only fourteen bales of cotton in 1870. On slightly more than four times that acreage, their father grew almost six times as much cotton. The wartime cornucopia of provision crops had dwindled by 1870 to small quantities of corn, beans, and sweet potatoes. The value of all agricultural produce in 1870 was $1,301. Wages consumed $700 of that sum. The Ellisons' principal source of income since the 1840s was moribund. Approximately 770 acres of the plantation lay fallow—220 acres of "woodland" and 550 acres "unimproved." They had not converted their unimproved acreage into grazing land, since their livestock comprised only two horses, three mules, four milk cows, five head of cattle, and six swine. The High Hills wilderness their slaves had cut back to make a plantation during the antebellum years now began to reclaim the land.

For half a century the gin shop anchored the Ellison family economy. At first glance, it would appear that the shop should have been in an advantageous position after the war. Cotton prices remained high until the early 1870s, and planters with cash, credit, laborers, and the heart to try planted cotton. Production in South Carolina rebounded from wartime lows, reaching 180,000 bales in 1868 and 374,000 in 1872.[91] As always, cotton required gins and ginwrights, and the need in the High Hills was urgent. When Potter's soldiers swept through Sumter District in 1865, they destroyed more than 100 cotton gins.[92] Scattered records show that the Ellison shop was in business in the years immediately after the war, doing both blacksmith and gin work. In August 1866, for example, R. R. Briggs, whose gins Potter's troops had missed, paid the Ellisons $42.25 for repairs. The following year an old customer, Isham Moore, paid them $39.00 for gin repair.[93]

The gin business resumed, but the shop never recovered. Like their fields, the Ellisons' shop required the labor of freedmen. Skilled freedmen were even more difficult than field hands to hold to old routines. Freedom gave artisans fresh opportunities, which they quickly explored. Hundreds of blacksmiths and carpenters fled plantations and crowded into Charleston and other towns, where they tried to build inde-

pendent businesses.[94] Unable to hire their former slave artisans, the Ellisons had to rely on their own labor. Both brothers
were close to fifty years old, and they may not have been eager
to put in long days without skilled assistants to take care of
the heaviest and dirtiest chores. But at age thirty-four in 1865,
John Buckner was in his prime and ready to work. His uncles
Henry and William Jr. retained ownership of the shop, but
they turned over its daily operation to him.

In 1870, for the first time in forty years, just one member of
the Ellison family declared the occupation of gin maker, John
Buckner.[95] However, the gin shop continued to be known as
the Ellison shop, signifying its ownership and reputation. Most
likely, Buckner worked in the shop with one or two other
men. In 1865 he paid the capitation tax for Theodore and
Robert, evidently his employees.[96] Since the men's names do
not appear on the list of William Ellison's slaves, they probably were not former slaves whom the old ginwright had trained
to the trade. Instead, they were apparently unskilled freedmen, the only hands Buckner could hire.

The loss of unskilled labor meant the quantity and quality
of the shop's production declined. In 1869 one of the Moody
family, customers of the Ellisons for more than three decades,
turned to a new blacksmith. The bill Jack Bowen submitted
to the Moodys indicates he was barely literate, probably a
former slave.[97] Nevertheless, he took business away from the
Ellison shop. Bowen was not the only freed blacksmith that
dislodged loyal Ellison customers. In March 1867 a man named
Peterson collected $97 for blacksmith work for Dr. W. W.
Anderson. A year later he received an additional $34.[98]
Although Dr. Anderson continued to do business with the
Ellison brothers, he no longer depended on them for his
blacksmith trade. Without a smoothly functioning team of
skilled workers, the shop could not remain a busy, efficient
place. John Buckner's economic status in 1870—$300 in per-
sonal property and no real estate—reflects the sorry state of
the gin and blacksmith business.[99]

BY 1870 Henry and William Ellison Jr. called themselves
neither farmers nor gin makers. Now they were general merchants.[100] Sometime between the end of the war and 1870 the

brothers built a general store within steps of the gin shop their father had constructed almost fifty years earlier. Although we cannot be certain, it appears the brothers built the store soon after the war ended. Whether they opened the store as a reaction to their difficulty hiring field hands and artisans or whether they had this business in mind before the war ended is not clear. In the months immediately after the war they had to consider the strictures of the South Carolina Black Codes. Among other provisions, the Codes provided that "No person of color shall pursue or practice the art, trade or business of an artisan, mechanic or shopkeeper, or any other trade, employment or business (besides that of husbandry, or that of a servant under a contract for service or labor) on his own account and for his own benefit . . ." without obtaining a license from the judge of the local district court.[101] The Codes required free men of color to apply for a license each year, which involved convincing the judge of their skill and good character and paying a fee of $10 for mechanics or $100 for storekeepers. If whites complained about licensed workers, the licenses could be revoked. However, the Ellison brothers did not need to acquire licenses and accommodate their plans to the Black Codes, since Major General David Sickles, the commanding officer of the Union army in South Carolina, countermanded them early in 1866.[102]

By that time or shortly afterward, the brothers were already beginning to scale back their investment in agriculture. In that year and subsequent years they sold horses and mules. Richard Anderson, a son of their father's guardian, bought a mule in 1866 for $117, and the next year his brother, Dr. W. W. Anderson, bought two for $260. Mules were in short supply, and earnest farmers wanted more, not fewer. At the same time they sold mules, the Ellisons placed sizable orders— $200 in 1867, for example—with Adams and Frost, their old factors in Charleston.[103] Although the records do not indicate what they bought, they probably were adding stock to the shelves of their new store.

Surviving records do not permit us to reconstruct with certainty the reasons the Ellison brothers made this drastic break with their past as planters and gin makers. The exodus of skilled workers from their shop doomed the gin business immediately after the war, and the Ellisons could do little about it. The days of the shop were numbered anyway. Within a decade huge factory-produced gins drove small handmade machines like theirs to the fringes of the market, a development the Ellisons could not have foreseen.[104] They continued to lend their name to the gin shop, but not their full attention. The brothers had a better chance to prevent the collapse of their plantation. Although freed Negro families kept wives and children out of the fields after 1865, creating a general labor shortage, other High Hills planters managed to secure enough labor to keep scrub oak from recapturing their land.[105] The Ellisons do not appear to have tried. By rejecting sharecropping, they forfeited agriculture. Furthermore, it appears that they quit the freedmen before the freedmen quit them. But why?

Everywhere in the South in 1865 planters predicted that emancipation meant agricultural disaster. Their pessimism continued even after cotton production began to rise. "I can see no hope for the South in our time," Dr. Mark Reynolds, a friend and customer of the Ellisons, wrote in February 1870. Economic catastrophe could only be averted, he believed, by attracting a new class of farm laborers—white Europeans "from England if possible."[106] The white gentry perceived farming on a large scale as risky business. The Ellisons had never been much for taking risks. Their principal economic rule was always safety first. Their accustomed conservatism may have dissuaded them from pouring money and energy into agriculture, especially into a sharecropping arrangement that diminished their control and raised the stakes of the gamble. No one knew how the experiment in freed Negro labor would turn out. Those who claimed to know promised utter failure, and even optimists worried.

Race probably influenced the Ellisons' decision to pull out of agriculture. Some whites abandoned planting because they could not stand to negotiate in their own fields with freedmen. They found it demeaning and humiliating to put their signatures on contracts with former slaves, now their legal peers. Formal distinctions between free and unfree vanished. Now, racial and class divisions were all that stood between landlords and tenants, whites and blacks. For the Ellisons, such distinctions may have been uncomfortably fine. Extensive farming would make them economically dependent on freed people, and it would draw their lives closer to large numbers of former slaves. From the time April Ellison moved to Stateburg in 1816, he and his family had distanced themselves from the mass of blacks. Slavery made an effective barrier between the free brown Ellisons and their black slaves. But after the war that barrier lay in rubble. Restoring agriculture with freed Negro labor promised the Ellisons social and economic risks. They chose not to take them.

The Ellisons rejected agriculture because they had an alternative that was both economically and socially attractive. In every way, a general store looked promising. The brothers would not lose status by moving from planting into storekeeping, for they were already businessmen. They had years of experience dealing with customers, ordering supplies, and keeping careful accounts. They already had long-standing business relationships that stretched to factors and suppliers in Charleston. Not even the challenge of economic change was new to them. During the war they had transformed their father's cotton plantation into a vast garden of food crops. As wartime provisioners, they had operated what amounted to a huge grocery for the citizens of the High Hills. And throughout their lives they had honed the skills of pleasing customers, acquiring temperaments that many whites found lacking in themselves.

R. L. Burn, a young white man who opened a general store in Greenville, explained the special qualities required to succeed. "I have nothing to do but sit in the store," he wrote a family member in 1866. "Today may be a right good day for trade but tomorrow will make up for it in dullness," he said. He tried to read or do some writing when things were slow, but "some one is sure to come in and look at something for an hour and then go out without buying or to want a spool of thread[,] a paper of pins or needles or some other little things with a five dollar bill to change before you can sell it to them." He would become "disgusted with the world and sit down to smoke my pipe when in steps some dainty little female and wants a thousand things that you have not got and winds up by saying that she does wish you had your spring goods for she is afraid to buy any thing until she sees what the fashions are going to be." At such times he wished he were "out on a good farm plowing a lazy mule so that I could take my fill of abusing it and so let off some of the steam that will accumulate until you almost burst if you try to suppress it." He concluded, "a store is a great place to study human nature. . . ."[107]

Studying human nature was the Ellisons' stock in trade. They knew the white planters of Sumter District, and that knowledge paid dividends in their new store. With the breakdown of the plantation system and the factorage arrangements that supported it, thousands of small country stores sprang up to provide provisions, credit, and marketing services to hundreds of thousands of back-country sharecroppers. Landlords usually supplied their tenants with land, mules, farm tools, and housing, while country merchants stocked food, clothing, and household items. Merchants advanced goods on credit, taking as collateral a lien on the freedmen's share of the cotton crop.[108] Had the Ellisons been typical country store owners they would have catered to the black freed people in and around Stateburg. But they were not typical.

Accounts for the store have not survived, but it is clear that the Ellison brothers' clientele was white, not black. Old Burrel Moody, a rough-cut white planter with more than 600 acres, was a regular customer in the early 1870s. He bought cheap calico cloth, lye, plug tobacco, brogans, buttons, thread, homespun, pepper, peas, nails, handkerchieves, pots, and pans, a shopping list little different from that of the average sharecropper. The Ellisons may have had a few local black croppers among their customers. But even Moody sometimes bought luxury goods like tea, rye whiskey, and sherry, which were beyond the reach of most freed people.[109] The Ellisons stocked their shelves with items from the top of the line. A white resident of Stateburg recalled that her mother patronized the store at the turn of the century. Her mother told her the store carried an assortment of first-quality products, including fine cloth and fancy tinned goods from Charleston.[110] Rather than becoming furnishing merchants for black tenants, the Ellisons ran a general mercantile establishment for white landlords.

Because they served the quality, the Ellisons did not take liens on their customers' crops. Their patrons paid with cash or personal notes, just as they had for gin and blacksmith work in the old days. In February 1868 Dr. W. W. Anderson paid the Ellison brothers $80 on his account.[111] Occasionally the Ellisons received baled cotton in payment. In January 1874, for example, Burrel Moody paid part of his bill with a cotton bale. The Ellisons promptly returned him $20 to pay his taxes.[112] But the Moody family was often slow to pay. "We write to say to you that we are very much pressed for money to discharge our obligations in Charleston for goods bought there," the Ellisons informed R. J. Moody in October 1876, "and we would be glad if you would Come and See us this Coming week, and let us have the money for your account."[113] Sometimes the Ellisons had to go to court to get the Moodys to settle up. When the inheritors of Burrel Moody's estate failed to make good his debts, the brothers laid their claim before Judge Thomas E. Richardson in Sumter, and three months later they received their money.[114] Many country merchants had cotton gins and presses on their premises that small farmers could use for a price.[115] Although the Ellison brothers still owned the gin shop, nothing suggests they provided ginning services, further evidence of their unusual list of planter customers.

The Ellison brothers' decision to become merchants did not represent a complete break with their past. They changed businesses, not customers. Always, the list of patrons, not the particular trade, was what counted. Wise conservatives, the Ellisons decided to change in order to keep what they had. A store freed them from association with and dependence on freed blacks. Their store required only their labor, and it allowed them to continue to mix with prominent white people. The same whites who had come to buy gins before the war and provisions during the war now came to purchase the special goods the Ellisons freighted up from Charleston.

During the postwar years the leading white families of the High Hills were a little threadbare, as were the Ellisons. Storekeeping could never rival their antebellum income from the gin shop and plantation, most of it produced by their slaves. Storekeeping in the postbellum South came with no guarantee of survival, much less prosperity. Some stores were fly-by-night operations run by no-accounts who were not above buying cotton after dark with no questions asked. But even well-educated, respectable storekeepers could not always make a go of it. After the war, the Ellisons' neighbor Richard Anderson—a former Confederate general—tried his hand at farming, then moved up the road to Camden to open a store. "The business of the Road has fallen off to little of nothing," he reported in June 1873. "We have nothing to do, except fan ourselves and fight the flies—varied occasionally with the highly intellectual employment of twirling our thumbs."[116] Anderson's empty cash register eroded his good humor, and five years later he grimly announced that he was going broke in Camden and thinking of moving to Baltimore.[117]

Inexperience may have contributed to Anderson's failure, but he also faced stiff competition. In 1880 the little town of Camden counted twenty-seven stores.[118] Down the road twenty miles, the Ellisons had the only store in Stateburg. However, they did not have a stranglehold on the neighborhood. Rural merchants who provisioned sharecroppers often gained monopolies because they were the only local source of credit.[119] With a crop lien, merchants came into conflict with landlords, vying for first claim to the sharecroppers' produce.[120] The Ellisons neatly sidestepped this class conflict by avoiding crop liens and extensive trading with black sharecroppers. No landlords depended on the Ellisons for credit to tide them over from season to season. White planters obtained those funds elsewhere, and they shopped at the Stateburg crossroads simply because it was convenient and agreeable. Anytime they found fault with the Ellisons' stock or service, they could take their business to stores in Camden, Sumter, Columbia, or even Charleston. In 1870 Henry mentioned that he kept the store open until 10 o'clock in the evening and sometimes even slept there.[121] The lamp in his window announced that he was ready to sell whenever his customers wanted to buy.

High Hills residents purchased enough to make the Ellisons a success in their new business and to sustain their reputation for good and useful service. The credit ledgers of the R. G. Dun Mercantile Agency chart their achievement. Dun reporters went from county to county investigating businesses. They talked to local people and checked public records to establish as best they could the owners' financial assets. They then sent their estimates of each firm's "pecuniary strength" and "credit rating" to the main office in New York. Reputable merchants wanted a good listing in order to obtain credit from wholesalers.[122] From 1872 to 1880 the Ellisons received twelve ratings. The brief reports assess the economic condition of the business as well as their character and standing in the community.

The first report, filed in November 1872, stated that the Ellisons, once "colored slaveholders," were worth $2,000 to $3,000 and were "very hon[est] upright men." Subsequent reports embroidered these themes, reassuring lenders. In March 1874 the agent observed that the brothers had been "always free and before the war owned 30 slaves, are men of good character, steady, hardworking and industrious." He estimated their worth at $7,000 to $8,000. Three years later the report stated, "Doing well. Honest & industrious. Temperate Reliable & in good credit for business wants." It gave $6,000 as their estimated worth. In February 1878 a verbose investigator wrote, "Have been Free Negroes for most of their lives. Are industrious hardworking men, of good standing[,] always acted honestly & regarded worthy & safe for credit." The last two reports emphasized that the Ellisons were "Men of very good standing. Economical & have accumulated some ppty" and that they were "spoken of highly."[123]

The Ellisons had survived the transition from gin makers and planters to storekeepers. But as the Dun reports reveal, they were no longer wealthy men. The highest estimate of their assets in the 1870s was $8,000. Their father's estate had been worth almost ten times as much. Plumeting land values, a crippled shop, and emancipation made them much poorer. Still, a June 1875 entry in the Dun ledgers describes them as "Rich," a word that says as much about the poverty of the postwar South as about the prosperity of the Ellisons. The standards by which the white community judged Negroes did not undergo a similar decline. If anything, the turbulence of Reconstruction and Redemption made white men more vigilant and unpredictable than ever. Nonetheless, the Ellisons' sterling reputation remained intact. Whites continued to appreciate their hard work and careful habits and to reward them with patronage and respect. The network of relationships that bound the Ellisons and their white neighbors endured, reinforced now by the store. Stateburg remained their sanctuary.

DURING Reconstruction the Republican party became the political sanctuary of the overwhelming majority of South Carolina's Negroes. Ex-slaves flocked to the party of Lincoln after Congress passed the Reconstruction Act of 1867, requiring rebel states to adopt new constitutions that authorized, among other reforms, Negro suffrage. Many well-educated members of the antebellum free mulatto elite also found a home in the Republican party, where they assumed positions of leadership. Several of the Ellisons' Charleston acquaintances—including members of the McKinlay, Sasportas, DeLarge, and Shrewsbury families—sought to exploit the new political dimension of their freedom by reaching down toward freedmen. As Republican leaders, the members of the old free mulatto elite attempted to shape the freedmen's efforts to enhance their formal freedom with rights and privileges previously reserved exclusively for whites. As politicians, mulatto Republicans also hoped to consolidate a position in the new order between white and black that would approximate their old prewar status on the middle ground between slavery and freedom.[124]

One of the delegates to the South Carolina constitutional convention of 1868 that formalized "Black Reconstruction" was Henry Jacobs of Fairfield District, the husband of William Ellison's daughter, Maria, whose legal slavery lasted until the general emancipation. A Republican, Jacobs represented his district in the state legislature between 1868 and 1870.[125] In Sumter District, eleven Negro Republicans either sat in the constitutional convention or served in the state legislature between 1868 and 1876, but only two were, like Jacobs, free before the war.[126] Neither of them was an Ellison.

Political creatures to their toes, the Ellisons had long engaged in the subtle, informal politics of personalism. In 1868 Henry Ellison, William Jr., and John Buckner registered as "colored" voters in the Stateburg election precinct.[127] Enfranchised for the first time, the Ellisons entered a world in which the nuances of personalism became denatured and formalized into a vote. In Sumter District, whites had no more use for neutrality on Reconstruction than they had on slavery before the war, on Yankees during the war, or on carpetbaggers afterward. As new voters, the Ellisons had a simple choice: they could vote with their old white friends or against them. No evidence suggests they hesitated or wavered, even for a moment.

The Republican party offered the Ellisons little but trouble. In South Carolina the party sponsored numerous democratic reforms, including a cautious program of land redistribution.[128] As large landowners, the Ellisons had no desire to share with anyone, white or black. Proposals to promote racial equality held little more attraction for them. Since the 1820s the Ellisons had made every effort to set themselves apart from blacks. They maintained that posture after the war when they shifted from being planters to storekeepers. Each year after 1865, whites made fewer distinctions between black and shades of brown. The mulatto Ellisons were not about to hasten the destruction of their special status by joining hands with ex-slaves in Republican politics.

If the war had severed the Ellisons' associations with High Hills whites, perhaps the family might have been tempted to experiment with new allies. During the war, however, the Ellisons' ties to the Stateburg community became stronger. After Appomattox the Ellisons continued to nurture those customary relationships in their store, at church, and in the neighborhood. But more than ingrained habit and social reflex animated their upward alliances. As always, sober self-interest dictated their actions. Why should they jettison old white allies who still provided economic and personal security? The Ellisons had nothing to gain by turning toward ex-slaves and maverick whites in the Republican party. Instead of trying to bridge the antebellum gap between brown and black, they worked constantly to preserve the antebellum proximity between brown and white. Their politics grew out of time-honored social and economic relationships.

The Ellisons became Democrats. Records of their votes from

one election to the next do not exist, but their political allegiance is beyond doubt. A remarkable document from the turn of the century—the Minute Book and Roll of the Stateburg Democratic Club—reveals choices the Ellisons had made twenty-five years earlier. During the 1890s, when whites lynched to defend white supremacy and defined blackness by the "one-drop rule," when almost all Negroes were disfranchised and thousands fled the state, the Ellisons were ensconced in the local Democratic Club, surrounded by old white friends.[129]

Records for the Stateburg Democratic Club span the years 1890 to 1910 and are crowded with familiar names.[130] Dr. W. W. Anderson and W. M. Lenoir presided over the organization, and Spanns, Sumters, and Reynoldses belonged. In 1890, so did John Buckner and two of his sons, and William Ellison Jr. and his eldest son, William John. Within the next twenty years two more of John Buckner's sons appear on the rolls along with two of the sons of Henry Ellison. The Ellisons' participation in the Stateburg club reflected the Democratic party's policy of permitting county organizations to set their own rules for membership. At the local precinct level, where, historian William J. Cooper Jr. observes, "everyone knew everyone else," membership in the Democratic club "became mandatory for social acceptance."[131] Late in the 1870s some Democrats advocated a straight-out white man's party, but Sumter District whites reminded them that Negroes had rallied "to the support of honesty and home rule" in 1876, when the party redeemed the state from Reconstruction. They urged the straight-out faction to remember that "colored Democrats stood by us in our time of need."[132] Nevertheless, most local organizations had purged Negroes from the party rolls by the early 1890s.[133] The few who remained had to prove that they had indeed voted for Wade Hampton and Redemption in 1876 and had been loyal Democrats ever since.[134] The Ellisons' presence in the Stateburg club at the turn of the century confirms their politics in the 1870s. When John Buckner died in 1895, an obituary in a Sumter newspaper commemorated his loyalty by recalling, "when the war was over he remained true to his friends and was a true and tried democrat."[135]

The conservative strategy William Ellison devised early in

the nineteenth century continued to guide his family into the twentieth. They hugged to the contours of the political and social landscape he had first mapped. After the war, for example, when most Negro parishioners abandoned Holy Cross, the Ellisons stayed put. In 1868 the Ellisons comprised four of Rector Robert Wilson's seven colored communicants, the last remnant of 150 prewar Negro worshipers.[136] As before the war, Holy Cross rectors baptized Ellison children and buried Ellison dead. Yet repetition of familiar rituals did not engender a new passivity on the part of the Ellisons. The old, familiar South changed. Poverty eroded personal associations, race relations became harsher and more rigid, and the elevated status enjoyed by the antebellum free mulatto elite deteriorated. To maintain continuity in their lives, the Ellisons had to be as astute and diligent as their father.

Stateburg remained friendly territory, but Sumter District, like the rest of the South, grew increasingly hostile and dangerous. The words "Strictly a White Man's Paper" were emblazoned on the masthead of the *True Southron,* the newspaper with the largest local circulation. Editorials confirmed the motto. "The intellectual differences between the races are not artificial or imaginary distinctions," the *True Southron* proclaimed in 1881, "but are as marked and real as those which God has stamped upon their physical appearance."[137] The editor's racial opinions made him an advocate of lynching. Some white Southerners denounced the practice, but the *True Southron* editor cautioned against sentimentality. There are "cases in which lynch-law is necessary," he explained. Each lynching "should be judged on its own merit, and condemned or condoned" accordingly. He cited as an example of a good lynching a recent incident in Orangeburg in which a black man was accused of raping a white girl. "Do not abolish the lynch-law," he said. "Let it remain as one of the unwritten statutes of our land. Let its right hand of death be held out over the people."[138]

In the rough, bitter world of the redeemed South, the Ellisons avoided the lynch rope. But the general deterioration of racial civility abraded their reputation and, in one celebrated instance, made their name a term of reproach. In 1880 a longstanding blood feud between the Cash and Shannon families of Camden degenerated into a duel. When William McCreight Shannon saw the "Camden Soliloquies" in the July 9 issue of the Kershaw *Gazette,* he issued a challenge to Bogden Cash, the author of the doggerel. Shannon had served in the state legislature in 1857 and in Kirkwood's Rangers during the war, returning home afterward to succeed his father, Charles John Shannon, as president of the Bank of Camden. The elder Shannon had named his son for William McCreight, the respected ginwright of Winnsboro with whom he had worked in the frontier days of the upcountry. In 1880, Bogden Cash began his slanderous attack on Shannon with

> My Daddy was a Gin Maker
> And worked cheek by jowle,
> With Ellison, a negro,
> ('Tis a secret) by my soul.

Cash's insults also charged Shannon with stealing, swindling, and running from a fight. The two men met in a duel in Darlington County, where Cash killed Shannon. Cash was tried for violation of the anti-dueling laws but acquitted. Said to be the last duel in South Carolina, it was far from the last act of violence. Cash himself was later cut down in a shootout after he had beat to death a sheriff and a bystander.[139]

From Stateburg the Ellisons could hear their name mentioned in the public outcry against the Cash-Shannon duel. Rather than being praised as epitomes of respectability, the Ellisons had become simply Negro workingmen whose color degraded white co-workers. Outside Stateburg, the Ellisons' name tarnished white reputations by association. The Ellisons lived out their lives inside the village, secure in the cocoon that protected them from the meanness that lurked within a few miles of "Wisdom Hall."

THE Ellisons preserved peaceful relations with local white people for the duration of their lives. But in 1870 the Ellison family itself began to disintegrate. After William Ellison's death in 1861 his family had remained a cohesive social and economic unit. The death of his daughter a decade later triggered dissension within the family.

On March 4, 1870, when she was fifty-nine years old, Eliza Ann Ellison Buckner Johnson died. Her family buried her in the family graveyard, and her husband James M. Johnson inscribed on her tombstone, "My Angel Wife, Gone to Rest."[140] William Ellison's will provided that, upon Eliza Ann's death, her share of the estate be passed not to her husband but to her surviving children, William Ellison's blood kin.[141] Eliza Ann's only child was John Buckner, who still lived in "Drayton Hall" along with his second wife Sarah and their four youngsters. When his mother died, Buckner was thirty-nine and almost propertyless. He owned no real estate and valued his personal assets at $300.[142] He evidently appealed to his uncles to divide his grandfather's estate and give him his mother's share. Henry and William Jr., however, refused to relinquish control over the family property.

In February 1871, almost a year after his mother's death, Buckner brought his claim to the probate court in Sumter. He sued his uncles for one-third of William Ellison's estate.[143] He pointed out that he had met the one qualification his grandfather had specified before he could inherit his mother's share: he was legally married. Buckner estimated the value of William Ellison's personal property at just over $42,000 and the extent of his land at 430 acres, "more or less." His estimates illustrate his distance from his uncles' management of the estate, which actually contained more than twice that many acres.

Two days after Buckner filed suit, Sheriff Thomas Jefferson Coghlan served the Ellison brothers with a summons to appear in court the first Monday in April "to show cause, if any you have, why the prayer" of Buckner "should not be granted." The brothers won a brief delay until mid-April, when Judge C. M. Hursh ruled that William Ellison's land be divided among the three men. Judge Hursh did not parcel out any personal property, most likely because it had evaporated with emancipation and the collapse of the government that guaranteed the Ellison's Confederate paper. The judge named five commissioners to survey the Ellison land and present the court with an equitable partition. Among them were Dr. W. W. Anderson, R. J. Brownfield, who had married into the Sumter family, and A. P. Vinson, the white man who farmed for the brothers and presumably knew the property as well as anyone else outside the family.

By late August the commissioners had completed their work, and Judge Hursh accepted their proposal. In February 1872 he awarded John Buckner slightly more than 300 acres and each of the brothers slightly less, indicating that the value of the land was considered in the decision. Buckner also received his mother's half-interest in "Drayton Hall." His uncles, as directed by William Ellison's will, retained "Wisdom Hall" and the six-acre shop lot. For the first time in his life, John Buckner owned land. He obtained it by unraveling the estate a half-century after 1822, when his grandfather had begun to stitch it together by purchasing the shop lot from General Sumter.

Although Buckner's lawsuit fractured the estate, his uncles were responsible for the breakup. They reaped what they had sown. Since their father's death they had treated their nephew less than generously. During the war they hired him just for occasional odd jobs. Afterward, they permitted him to manage the gin shop and farm a little land, but Buckner barely squeaked by. Despite his uncles' stinginess, Buckner remained on good terms with them so long as his mother lived. In 1864 he named his first son John William Buckner for himself, his grandfather, and his uncle. Two years later he named a second son Henry Ellison Buckner.[144] But after his mother died and his uncles refused to give him his due, he had no choice but to sue. His uncles may well have been a bit jealous of Buckner. As a youngster he had been the apple of his grandfather's eye, William Ellison's first, and for fourteen years his only, grandchild. As adolescents during the 1830s, Henry and William Jr. had to toe the line for their father, while the young John Buckner romped and received indulgences from his grandfather. William Ellison trained Buckner to the gin maker's craft, just as he did his sons, and he looked forward to having Buckner extend the family business another generation into the future. That dream shattered in the early 1870s, the casualty of family strife.

Eliza Ann's death severed the Ellisons' ties to her husband, James M. Johnson. Without his wife, Johnson had no place at the crossroads. He owned no land and had no claim on the

house in which he had lived since 1845. Whether his stepson
John Buckner dispossessed him or he simply decided it was
time to go, Johnson left Stateburg shortly after he buried his
wife and returned to his father's home in Charleston. The
move scarcely improved his prospects as a tailor, however.
Postbellum aristocrats struggled to buy another mule, not a
hand-sewn suit of clothes. When his father James Drayton
Johnson died in 1871, he inherited three-quarters of his property, consisting principally of the houses at 7 and 9 Coming
Street. The other quarter of the estate went to Gabriella Miller
Johnson, whose husband Charley had died in Canada sometime during the 1860s.[145] Within a few years Johnson, who
was fifty-one when his father died, drifted away from Charleston and disappeared from the historical record.

The rest of the Ellisons stayed at the crossroads. Their houses,
tracts of land, and work made physical separation impossible,
but they were no longer laced together by affection. John
Buckner and his growing family lived in "Drayton Hall" and
Henry and William Jr. nearby in "Wisdom Hall."[146] Economic necessity made some cooperation imperative. To keep
their gin and blacksmith shop open, the brothers had no choice
but to rely on Buckner. The specifics of the arrangement have
been lost, but Buckner continued to run the shop his uncles
owned. Buckner still called himself a gin maker in 1880, when
the brothers identified themselves again as general merchants.[147] The two brothers continued to work as a team, but
John Buckner went his own way.

Buckner put all the distance he could between himself and
the rest of the Ellisons. He and his family quit Holy Cross
Episcopal Church for High Hills Baptist Church, the spiritual home of his wife's family, the Oxendines, and many other
Sumter Turks.[148] Buckner evidently sought a new form of
freedom, away from the Ellison brothers' scrutiny, and, perhaps, unwelcome avuncular advice. Nonetheless, Buckner did
not thrive. His gin business gradually petered out, and his
farming paid few rewards. When Buckner died in 1895, he was
still a poor man, despite his inheritance. His family buried
him in the Baptist cemetery, not in the Ellison family graveyard.[149] His eight children became small farmers in the neighborhood. A local historian reports that they assimilated into

the Turk community.[150] The census of 1910 lists one son, Samuel, his wife, and seven children as Turks. Another son, Henry Ellison Buckner, was a tenant farmer married to an illiterate woman named Bricky.[151]

Despite Buckner's defection, life at the crossroads did not turn sour. Resilient men, the Ellison brothers established new families early in the 1870s. After two decades as widowers, Henry and William Jr. remarried. In the 1840s they had married within a year or two of each other, and in the 1850s they both lost their Charleston wives within the space of eighteen months. Now they moved again in tandem into new marriages. In July 1870, just four months after the death of his sister, Henry wrote James D. Johnson in Charleston that "my loneliness makes me feel every thing but happy." He mentioned a recent visit to the city and remarked, "the time did seem very short, as being so agreeably entertained by all, the *Ladies* in particular. . . ." In gratitude, he sent along some home-grown melons, one especially for "Miss Shrewsbury."[152]

Amelia Ann Shrewsbury, twenty years Henry's junior at thirty-three, was from a well-established free mulatto family in Charleston. Her brother, Henry L. Shrewsbury, was a Republican state legislator, and she taught in one of the schools established in Charleston by the American Missionary Association shortly after the city fell to the Union army.[153] James Redpath, the abolitionist who had tried to woo the city's free colored population to Haiti on the eve of the war, was now superintendent of education in the city. The principals of Amelia's school were Thomas, and later F. L., Cardozo, sophisticated free mulattoes in antebellum days.[154] When Amelia applied to Thomas Cardozo for her teaching position, he asked her a series of specific questions, to which she replied: she was an Episcopalian; she was unmarried; she had taught privately in Charleston for five years; for four months she taught at the Ashley Street public school; she now sought a higher salary; and, yes, she was willing to teach freedmen.[155]

The staff she joined included representatives of several other old mulatto families—Sasportas, Holloway, and Weston. In July 1865 Thomas Cardozo praised his "southern Teachers" as "very faithful . . . good Christian young ladies of respectable parentage."[156] Two years later a woman who visited Cardozo's school complained that the student body was comprised almost "entirely of freemen's children, many of whom *owned slaves* before the war."[157] She feared that special treatment for "free browns" would "make the difference between them & the freed people even greater than it was in slavery."[158] Old distinctions died slowly, especially in Charleston. In 1875 another observer reported that the "light *colored* people of the city are quite as much prejudiced against the *Negro* as many of the whites."[159] By that time, Amelia Shrewsbury had left Charleston, married Henry Ellison, and settled into "Wisdom Hall" in Stateburg.

While Henry courted Amelia, William Jr. established a new relationship to an old friend. After Charley Johnson died in Canada during the 1860s, his widow Gabriella returned to Charleston, the city of her birth. The daughter of Eliza Vanderhorst, who claimed to be half-Indian, and George Miller, a white man, Gabriella was considered a colored woman in Charleston.[160] Thirteen years younger than William Jr., she was thirty-eight in 1870. "I told William nothing about Mrs. Gabriella Johnson's letter," Henry wrote James D. Johnson in July 1870. "I hope you did not, as you know there was nothing secret in it, but you know how some females will not accept a gift, when there is any publicity about it, as it broaches too much upon their delicacy."[161] The precise meaning of Henry's remark cannot be deciphered, but it is clear that his brother was courting Gabriella. Evidently just after Henry married Amelia, William brought his new wife home to the family compound.

William Jr. and Gabriella had no children, but Henry and Amelia had four. With Dr. W. W. Anderson attending, Amelia gave birth to Henry Shrewsbury in 1873, Louisa in 1875, George in 1877, and Amelia G. in 1881.[162] When young Amelia was born, Henry was sixty-four. She was only two years old when he died on August 20, 1883.[163] His obituary in the Sumter *Watchman and Southron* identified him as a man "known to many of our planting friends throughout the country, and the firm of which he was a member has built gins for hundreds of farmers, not only in Sumter, but also in surrounding counties." Henry was still very much the son of William Ellison in the eyes of local whites. "His father," the obituary pointed out, "who was a free colored man before the war, built up a thriving business as a gin maker at Stateburg, and Ellison's gins were known far and wide for their superior qualities."[164] Although Henry had not worked in the gin shop for almost twenty years, his father's reputation as a gin maker still clung to him.

Amelia and her children, the oldest of whom was only ten when Henry died, did not find the next few years easy. Amelia had two sources of income—rents from the 300 acres of land she inherited and proceeds from Henry's share of the store trade.[165] William Jr. was sixty-four in 1883, and for the first time in his life he worked without his brother and partner. Amelia received $174.81 from the store in 1885, but as her brother-in-law aged, the store income and her receipts declined. In the mid-1890s they ceased entirely. Amelia's rental income also dwindled. William Ellison's land still helped sustain his family, but by the end of the century it was wearing out. In 1894, for example, Amelia collected just $183 from ten renters. In that year's annual report of her administration of her late husband's estate, Amelia declared, "I have exceeded limit of rents received this year, to the amt. of one hundred and sixty four dollars."

Education expenses were the primary reason for Amelia's red ink. She scrimped on many things, such as paying 75 cents to "renovate [a] bonnet" instead of buying a new one. On education she did not cut corners. As a former teacher, she was fiercely committed to giving all her children an education. When they were small, they learned at home, taught by their mother and by Miss Mary Dereef, whom Amelia employed as a tutor. When the children grew older, Amelia sent them to proper boarding schools, sometimes as far away as Raleigh, North Carolina. It is impossible to document how much schooling her children received, but her son Henry was still a student when he was eighteen. All of Henry and Amelia's children evidently received at least high-school diplomas. Although William Ellison never knew his new daughter-in-law, he surely would have approved of her close attention to the education of his grandchildren. Gin making and planting held no promise in the 1890s, and Ellison children had to learn new ways to survive.

Other Ellison children lived in "Wisdom Hall" during the

last decades of the century. "Billy John," William Ellison, Jr.'s eldest son, returned home after 1865 from Philadelphia, where his father had sent him and his sisters for safety in 1860. His sisters also came back, although they evidently married in the 1870s, left the family compound, and disappeared from view. Billy John went to Canada soon after the war, where he met and married a young Irish woman named Catherine. Kate, as she was known, returned to Stateburg with Billy John in the mid-1870s. They had five children, and Billy John tried to support them by keeping bees and raising silkworms, a short-lived fad in Sumter District in the early 1880s.[166] Local tradition has it that Kate chafed at the "social isolation" she encountered as the white wife of a Negro man in South Carolina, and that she induced her husband to take her and the rest of the family back to Canada.[167] Although Billy John was a member of the Stateburg Democratic Club in 1890, in 1892 his name is scratched through and followed by "Republican."[168] It is logical to suspect that Republican sympathies and a white wife gave Billy John reason enough to desert Stateburg for the harsher weather and more benign social relations of Canada. But he died in Stateburg in 1894.[169] Only then, apparently, did Kate and the children depart for Canada.

On July 24, 1904, his father, the last of William Ellison's children, died.[170] The Sumter *Watchman and Southron* gave eighty-five-year-old William Ellison Jr. a long, glowing obituary. This "highly respected colored citizen of Stateburg," the notice read, along with his brother Henry "succeeded their father, William Ellison, who was the inventor and maker of the well known Ellison gin, and continued the business in the same shop, which is still standing in Stateburg." The entire "family has always been highly respected as colored citizens," the item reported. William's death, the paper suggested, was brought on by a failing of the Ellisons—a constitutional inability to quit working. "His health was never robust," the report said, "and a walk to his fields on one of the very hot days during the preceeding week brought on the attack which at his advanced age, was necessarily fatal." The old man "was twice married, his second wife being from Canada. She survives him and lives at the old homestead with his brother's widow and children."[171]

Gabriella had lived in Canada as the wife of Charley Johnson, but she encouraged the rumor that she was a white Canadian. For several years after her husband's death she shared "Wisdom Hall" with Amelia and her children. The census of 1910 captured the two old widows together for the last time— Gabriella, 77 and Amelia, 72. Both listed themselves as farmers who owned their farms outright. All four of Amelia's children were unmarried. Henry S., 37, was a teacher in the Graded School. Louisa, 35, and George, 33, did not claim occupations. Amelia G., 29, carried on in her mother's footsteps and taught at the high school. The column designating the Ellisons' race identified them as neither blacks, mulattoes, or whites. They were "other," a term reserved in Sumter District for Turks.[172]

In the next decade young Amelia died, and the three other children scattered east and west, far away from Stateburg. No Ellison had to return to the village to inherit and dispose of property, for William Jr.'s will directed that, after Gabriella died, the estate should be sold and the money divided among the surviving family members. All William Jr. insisted on preserving was the small plot of land for which his father had also made special arrangements in his will, the family "Burying Ground."[173]

Within a few years Amelia returned to Charleston after more than forty years in the upcountry. Gabriella lived on in "Wisdom Hall," alone, infirm, and later helpless.[174] In an upstairs bedroom at the back of the empty house, she was attended by a little girl who was a descendant of one of William Ellison's slaves. After 1914 Gabriella also had the assistance of a white family who moved next door into what had once been "Drayton Hall." The white man came over to Gabriella's each evening to lock up and returned each morning to open the house. His wife occasionally went upstairs to Gabriella's room and wrote letters for the old woman. His young daughter carried meals to Gabriella every day. In the evenings the deserted house was spooky as the girl climbed the steep stairs at the back. Sometimes, when Mrs. Ellison felt spry, she would open her bureau and show the young girl a beautiful piece of lace, which she said she intended for her shroud. Twice the girl became impatient with the old woman's repeated questions and answered her sharply. Each time Gabriella remembered to mention the incident to the girl's mother, and she received her two worst spankings for disrespect to Mrs. Ellison.

On December 14, 1920, when she was eighty-eight, Gabriella died in "Wisdom Hall." Only one member of the Ellisons' far-flung family returned for the funeral, Henry Shrewsbury Ellison, Henry and Amelia's eldest son, who traveled from Greensboro, North Carolina. A Stateburg resident recalled that white friends carried Gabriella's casket on their shoulders down to the family graveyard, where she was buried near her husband. After the funeral, members of the Ellison family in Greensboro wanted to express their appreciation for the care Gabriella had received from white friends nearby. To the white family who had looked after Gabriella they sent a silver spoon.

APPENDIX

TABLE 1
POPULATION OF SUMTER DISTRICT, SOUTH CAROLINA,
1790–1860

	WHITES	SLAVES	FREE NEGROES
1790	4,228	2,712	Not reported
1800	6,239	6,563	301
1810	7,128	11,638	288
1820	8,844	16,143	382
1830	9,184	18,721	372
1840	8,644	18,875	373
1850	9,813	23,065	342
1860	6,857	16,682	320

SOURCE: *Ninth Census, The Statistics of the Population of the United States* (Washington, 1872), 60–61.

TABLE 2
SLAVES OF WILLIAM ELLISON, *1820–1860*

	AGE	MALES	FEMALES	TOTAL
1820	26–45	2	0	2
1830	10–23	1	0	4
	24–35	2		
	35–54	1		
1840	<10	5	3	30
	10–24	2	1	
	24–35	8	2	
	36–54	6	2	
	55–99	0	1	
	Total	21	9	
1850	<10	10	1	36
	10–19	2	2	
	20–29	5	6	
	30–39	5	0	
	40–49	2	1	
	50–99	2	0	
	Total	26	10	
1860	<10	15	5	63
	10–19	6	3	
	20–29	9	3	
	30–39	4	6	
	40–49	4	1	
	50–99	3	4	
	Total	41	22	

SOURCE: Manuscript Census Schedules, Sumter District, South Carolina, 1820–1860.

TABLE 3
POPULATION OF THE CITY OF CHARLESTON, SOUTH CAROLINA, *1790–1860*

	WHITES	SLAVES	FREE NEGROES
1790	8,089	7,684	586
1800	9,630	9,819	1,024
1810	11,568	11,671	1,472
1820	10,653	12,652	1,575
1830	12,828	15,354	2,107
1840	13,030	14,673	1,558
1850*	20,012	19,532	3,441
1860	23,376	13,909	3,237

*The boundaries of the city were extended in 1848 to include population on Charleston Neck.

TABLE 4
MONTHLY ARRESTS IN CHARLESTON, *1858–1861*

Month	FREE NEGROES FOR NONPAYMENT OF CAPITATION TAXES			SLAVES FOR WORKING OUT WITHOUT BADGES		
	M	F	Total	M	F	Total
June 1858	0	0	0	3	0	3
July	0	0	0	3	1	4
August	1	0	1	3	0	3
September	3	1	4	1	1	2
October	27	26	53	1	0	1
November	3	1	4	3	0	3
December	0	0	0	1	0	1
January 1859	0	0	0	0	0	0
February	1	1	2	2	0	2
March	2	1	3	13	3	16
April	1	3	4	7	8	15
May	3	0	3	5	2	7
June	4	7	11	5	1	6
July	2	0	2	0	0	0
August	0	0	0	0	3	3
September	0	0	0	0	0	0
October	0	0	0	0	0	0
November	4	3	7	11	3	14
December	12	20	32	8	2	10
January 1860	2	2	4	0	0	0
February	0	4	4	0	0	0
March	0	0	0	0	0	0
April	3	0	3	14	13	27
May	8	17	25	17	28	45
June	9	16	25	12	20	32
July	6	14	20	9	31	40
August	5	10	15	39	54	93
September	0	0	0	0	0	0
October	0	0	0	6	0	6
November	1	0	1	2	2	4
December	1	0	1	1	0	1
January 1861	1	1	2	0	0	0
February	0	0	0	0	0	0

SOURCE: Monthly Report of the Chief of Police to the mayor of Charleston, in Proceedings of the City Council printed in the Charleston *Courier* toward the end of the month following the month summarized in the report.

TABLE 5
OCCUPATIONS OF FREE NEGRO MEN IN CHARLESTON, *1850* AND *1860*

	1850	*1860*	CHANGE
Carpenter	101	139	+38
Tailor	84	55	−29
Carter, Drayman	53	41	−12
Laborer	49	45	− 4
Shoemaker, Bootmaker	39	19	−20
Barber, Hairdresser	24	22	− 2
Fisherman	22	16	− 6
Butcher	13	22	+ 9
Wheelwright	14	11	− 3
Bricklayer	14	19	+ 5
Porter	13	27	+14
Millwright	12	13	+ 1
Painter	12	24	+12
Blacksmith	10	16	+ 6
Baker	1	12	+11
Upholsterer	2	10	+ 8
Other	81	118	+37
Total	544	609	+65
Farmer, Shopkeeper, Merchant	19 (3%)	33 (5%)	+14
Skilled Trades	370 (68%)	420 (69%)	+50
Carter, Drayman	53 (10%)	41 (7%)	−12
Common Labor	102 (19%)	115 (19%)	+13

SOURCES: 1850 and 1860 Population Schedules, Charleston, South Carolina.

TABLE 6
FREE NEGRO REAL ESTATE OWNERS IN CHARLESTON, *1860*

REAL ESTATE VALUE	NUMBER OF OWNERS	PERCENTAGE OF FREE NEGROES
$0	404	56
$1–999	74	10
1,000–1,999	126	17
2,000–2,999	49	7
3,000–3,999	27	4
4,000–4,999	9	1
5,000–5,999	10	1
6,000–7,999	6	1
8,000–9,999	7	1
10,000 and over	9	1
Total	721	

SOURCE: *List of the Taxpayers of Charleston, 1860* (Charleston, S.C., 1861), 315–34.

TABLE 7
FREE NEGRO SLAVEOWNERS IN CHARLESTON, SOUTH CAROLINA, *1860*

NUMBER OF SLAVES	SLAVEHOLDERS			PERCENTAGE OF SLAVEHOLDERS (N = *122*)	PERCENTAGE OF FREE NEGROES (N = *721*)
	MALE	FEMALE	TOTAL		
1	20	29	49	40	7
2	13	13	26	21	4
3	9	8	17	14	2
4	4	5	9	7	1
5	4	5	9	7	1
6	2	1	3	2	0.4
7	3	0	3	2	0.4
8–9	0	0	0	0	0.0
10–11	1	1	2	2	0.2
12–14	2	2	4	4	0.6
Total	58	64	122		

SOURCE: *List of the Taxpayers of Charleston, 1860* (Charleston, S.C., 1861), 315–34.

TABLE 8
CHARLESTON FREE NEGROES SUBJECT TO CAPITATION TAXES, *1858–1862*

	1858	*1859*	*1862*	PERCENTAGE OF CHANGE, *1859–62*
Men, 14–50	649	636	452	−29
Women, 16–60	980	998	866	−13
Total	1,629	1,634	1,318	−19

SOURCE: Reports of City Revenues published annually in Charleston *Courier,* except 1860, 1861; Charleston Free Negro Tax Book, 1862, CLS.

TABLE 9
CHARLESTON FREE NEGROES WHO PAID MUNICIPAL TAXES, *1860*

	1860	*1862*	CHANGE *1860–1862*	PERCENTAGE CHANGE
$10,000 and over	9	6	− 3	−33
$5,000–9,999	23	25	+ 2	+ 9
$2,000–4,999	85	77	− 8	− 9
Under $2,000	254	160	− 94	−37
Total	371	258	−113	−30

Note that this table includes all individuals who paid municipal taxes, even if they did not pay tax on real estate.

SOURCE: *List of the Taxpayers of Charleston, 1860* (Charleston, S.C., 1861), 315–34; 1862 Charleston Free Negro Tax Book, CLS.

TABLE 10
OCCUPATIONS OF CHARLESTON FREE NEGROES,
1860 AND *1862*

	1860	1862	CHANGE 1860–1862
Men			
Carpenter	139	68	− 71
Tailor	55	46	− 9
Laborer	45	40	− 5
Carter, Drayman	41	24	− 17
Porter	27	36	+ 9
Painter	24	10	− 14
Barber, Hairdresser	22	21	− 1
Butcher	22	24	+ 2
Shoemaker, Bootmaker	19	14	− 5
Bricklayer	19	22	+ 3
Blacksmith	16	20	+ 4
Fisherman	16	24	+ 8
Millwright	13	4	− 9
Baker	12	0	− 12
Wheelwright	11	9	− 2
Upholsterer	10	3	− 7
Other	118	59	− 59
Total	609	424	−185
Women			
Dress Maker, Mantua Maker, Tailoress	220	332	+112
Seamstress	158	192	+ 34
Laundress, Washer	150	142	− 8
Servant	46	32	− 14
Cook	14	38	+ 24
Nurse	21	26	+ 5
Milliner	4	5	+ 1
Total	613	767	+154
Total Men and Women	1,222	1,191	− 31

SOURCE: 1860 Population Schedules, Charleston, South Carolina; 1862 Charleston Free Negro Tax Book, CLS.

Abbreviations in Notes

CLS	Charleston Library Society, Charleston, South Carolina
LC	Library of Congress, Washington, D. C.
RSSL	Robert Scott Small Library, College of Charleston, Charleston, South Carolina
SCDAH	South Carolina Department of Archives and History, Columbia, South Carolina
SHC	Southern Historical Collection, University of North Carolina, Chapel Hill, North Carolina
SCHS	South Carolina Historical Society, Charleston, South Carolina
SCL	South Caroliniana Library, University of South Carolina, Columbia, South Carolina
WRPL	William R. Perkins Library, Duke University, Durham, North Carolina

NOTES

1. For an annotated edition of the letters, see the authors' *No Chariot Let Down: Charleston's Free People of Color on the Eve of the Civil War* (Chapel Hill, N. C., 1984).

2. Daniel R. Hundley, *Social Relations in Our Southern States,* ed. William J. Cooper, Jr. (Baton Rouge and London, 1979; orig. ed., New York, 1860).

3. Among the important studies are Jeffrey R. Brackett, *The Negro in Maryland: A Study in the Institution of Slavery* (Baltimore, 1899); Ulrich Bonnell Phillips, "Slave Labor in the Charleston District," *Political Science Quarterly* 22 (1907), 416–39; John H. Russell, *The Free Negro in Virginia, 1619–1865* (Baltimore, 1913); Ulrich Bonnell Phillips, *American Negro Slavery* (New York, 1918), 425–53; James M. Wright, *The Free Negro in Maryland, 1634–1860* (New York, 1921); Charles S. Sydnor, "The Free Negro in Mississippi before the Civil War," *American Historical Review* 32 (1927), 769–88; Ralph B. Flanders, "The Free Negro in Antebellum Georgia," *North Carolina Historical Review* 9 (1932), 250–72; E. Franklin Frazier, *The Free Negro Family: A Study of Family Origins before the Civil War* (Nashville, Tenn., 1932); E. Horace Fitchett, "The Traditions of the Free Negro in Charleston, South Carolina," *Journal of Negro History* 25 (1940), 139–51; Fitchett, "The Origins and Growth of the Free Negro Population of Charleston, South Carolina," *Journal of Negro History* 26 (1941), 421–37; James M. England, "The Free Negro in Ante-Bellum Tennessee," Ph.D. diss., Vanderbilt University, 1941; Luther P. Jackson, *Free Negro Labor and Property Holding in Virginia, 1830–1860* (New York, 1942); John Hope Franklin, *The Free Negro in North Carolina, 1790–1860* (Chapel Hill, N. C., 1943); E. Horace Fitchett, "The Status of the Free Negro in Charleston, South Carolina, and His Descendants in Modern Society," *Journal of Negro History* 32 (1947), 430–51; Morris R. Boucher, "The Free Negro in Alabama Prior to 1860," Ph.D. diss., State University of Iowa, 1950; Donald E. Everett, "The Free Persons of Color in New Orleans, 1830–1865," Ph.D. diss., Tulane University, 1952; Edward F. Sweat, "The Free Negro in Antebellum Georgia," Ph.D. diss., University of Indiana, 1957; Leonard P. Stavisky, "The Negro Artisan in the South Atlantic States, 1800–1860: A Study of Status and Economic Opportunity with Special Reference to Charleston," Ph.D. diss., Columbia University, 1958; Leon F. Litwack, *North of Slavery: The Negro in the Free States, 1790–1860* (Chicago, 1961); James Hugo Johnston, *Race Relations in Virginia & Miscegenation in the South, 1776–1860* (Amherst, Mass., 1970); Herbert E. Sterkx, *The Free*

Negro in Antebellum Louisiana
(Rutherford, N. J., 1972); Letitia
Woods Brown, *Free Negroes in the
District of Columbia, 1790–1846* (New
York, 1972); Marina Wikramanayake, *A World in Shadow: The Free
Black in Antebellum South Carolina*
(Columbia, S. C., 1973); Leonard P.
Curry, *The Free Black in Urban
America 1800–1850: The Shadow of the
Dream* (Chicago and London,
1981).
4. A landmark study that synthe-
sizes, reinterprets, and extends the
work to date is Ira Berlin, *Slaves
Without Masters: The Free Negro in
the Antebellum South* (New York,
1974). Other studies that examine
the activities of free Negroes
include William Ransom Hogan
and Edwin Adams Davis, eds., *Wil-
liam Johnson's Natchez: The Antebel-
lum Diary of a Free Negro* (Baton
Rouge, 1951); Davis and Hogan,
The Barber of Natchez (Baton
Rouge, 1954); Gary B. Mills, *The
Forgotten People: Cane River's Creoles
of Color* (Baton Rouge and London,
1977); T. H. Breen and Stephen
Innes, *"Myne Owne Ground": Race
and Freedom on Virginia's Eastern
Shore, 1640–1676* (New York and
Oxford, 1980); David O. Whitten,
*Andrew Durnford: A Black Sugar
Planter in Antebellum Louisiana*
(Natchitoches, La., 1981); Willard
B. Gatewood, Jr., ed., *Free Man of
Color: The Autobiography of Willis
Augustus Hodges* (Knoxville, Tenn.,
1982); Juliet E. K. Walker, *Free
Frank: A Black Pioneer on the Ante-
bellum Frontier* (Lexington, Ky.,
1983).

CHAPTER ONE

1. Court of Equity, Sumter District,
June 20, 1820, Miscellaneous Records, Book D, 369, SCDAH.
2. *Fifth Census . . . 1830* (Washington, D. C., 1832), 14–15. For a summary of Sumter District population
data, see table 1 in the Appendix.
3. Ellison family graveyard, Stateburg. We are indebted to Captain
Richard Anderson, Mrs. Mary
Anderson, and Will Anderson for
permitting us access to the graveyard.
4. For a good description of Fairfield early in the nineteenth century,
see Robert Mills, *Statistics of South
Carolina . . .* (Charleston, 1826),
536–56.
5. 1790 Census Schedules, Fairfield
District, South Carolina, 172.
6. Ibid.
7. Information about the Fairfield
Ellisons is sparse, but see John B.
Adger, *My Life and Times, 1810–1899*
(Richmond, Va., 1899), 21–41;
David Duncan Wallace, *The History
of South Carolina* (New York, 1934),
Biographical Volume, Part II, 897;
Fitz Hugh McMaster, *History of
Fairfield County, South Carolina*
(Columbia, S. C., 1946).
8. White William Ellison of Fairfield corresponded with James
Chesnut at least once, sending
greetings to the Chesnut family as if
their relationship went beyond a
nodding acquaintance. W. Ellison
to James Chesnut, February 16,
1821; see also James J. Deas to James
Chesnut, December 30, 1822. Chesnut Family Papers, 1782–1896
(microfilm), Division of Archives
and Manuscripts, State Historical
Society of Wisconsin, Madison,
Wisconsin; C. Vann Woodward,
ed., *Mary Chesnut's Civil War* (New
Haven and London, 1981), 31, 72.
9. Ira Berlin, *Slaves Without Masters:
The Free Negro in the Antebellum
South* (New York, 1974), 151–52,
266–67; Joel Williamson, *New People: Miscegenation and Mulattoes in
the United States* (New York and
London, 1980), 5–33; James Hugo
Johnston, *Race Relations in Virginia
and Miscegenation in the South, 1776–
1860* (Amherst, Mass., 1970); John
Donald Duncan, "Servitude and
Slavery in Colonial South Carolina,
1670–1776," Ph.D. diss., Emory
University, 1971; John Livingston
Bradley, "Slave Manumissions in
South Carolina, 1820–1860," M. A.
thesis, University of South Carolina, 1964.
10. 1800 Census Schedules, Fairfield
District, South Carolina, 228; 1810

Census Schedules, Fairfield District, South Carolina, 193.

11. Robert Ellison did bequeath "a young Yellow fellow named Narcy" to a grandson. Will of Robert Ellison, April 22, 1806, Will Book 5, 33–35, South Carolina Will Transcripts, 1782–1868, Wills of Fairfield County, SCDAH.

12. 1800 Census Schedules, Fairfield District, South Carolina, 204.

13. Another one of Ellison's slaves was evidently an ancestor of the eminent American novelist and man of letters, Ralph Ellison. The incomplete record makes it impossible to speak with certainty, but it appears that Ralph Ellison's paternal grandfather, Alfred Ellison, was born a slave about 1845, and that he belonged to Mary Ann Ellison, the widow of William Ellison, the owner of April. White William Ellison of Fairfield District (April's owner until 1816) died in 1833, leaving his plantation, his slaves, and everything else to his wife, Mary Ann Ellison. Fifty years old at the time of her husband's death, she continued to live in Fairfield. In 1840 she owned twenty-seven slaves, nine males, at least six of whom were old enough to have been Alfred Ellison's father, Greene, and eighteen females, at last ten of whom were old enough to have been Alfred's mother. In 1850 she owned forty-one slaves, two of them five-year-old boys, one of whom was probably Alfred. In 1855, when she was about seventy-two, Mary Ann Ellison sold her plantation in Fairfield to David Aiken and moved to Abbeville Court House, where she lived with one of her granddaughters, Mary A. Hoyt, the wife of Presbyterian minister Thomas A. Hoyt. She took some of her slaves to Abbeville with her, and it is likely that Alfred was among them. However, two years later when she made her will, she did not mention Alfred by name as one of the twelve slaves she bequeathed to her daughter, Harriet Harrison. By that time, she may have already given Alfred and other

slaves to Mary A. Hoyt, Harriet Harrison's daughter, who was not provided for in the will. Both Harriet Harrison and Mary Ann Ellison resided with the Hoyts in Abbeville in 1860, when Mrs. Ellison died. Evidence of Alfred Ellison's whereabouts during the 1860s does not exist. Presumably he lived in Abbeville and obtained his freedom in the general emancipation in 1865. In 1870, Alfred Ellison, a twenty-five-year-old propertyless, illiterate black man, lived in Abbeville with his wife Harriet, a nineteen-year-old black woman, and a ten-year-old black boy named William Ellison, who attended school. Alfred and Harriet Ellison both worked as domestic servants. By 1880 Alfred (now a farmer) and Harriet (now listed as a mulatto washerwoman) had a growing family of three young daughters and a three-year-old son, Lewis Alfred, who would become the father of Ralph Ellison. Taken together, this evidence indicates that Alfred Ellison and April Ellison and their ancestors belonged to the same white family, although the two men and their ancestors probably bore no blood relationship. 1810 Census Schedules, Fairfield District, South Carolina, 193; Will of William Ellison, Fairfield Wills, Book 14, 14–15, SCDAH; 1840 Census Schedules, Fairfield District, South Carolina, 511; 1850 Slave Schedules, Fairfield District, South Carolina, 704; Conveyance of Real Estate, Mary A. Ellison to David Aiken, November 6, 1855, Hugh Kerr Aiken Papers, SCL; Will of Mary A. Ellison, Ellison Family Miscellaneous File, SCHS; 1860 Population Schedules, Abbeville Court House, Abbeville District, South Carolina, dwelling 295; 1870 Population Schedules, Abbeville District, South Carolina, p. 12; 1880 Population Schedules, Abbeville District, South Carolina, p. 5; Stewart Lillard, "Alfred Ellison of Abbeville," unpublished paper generously made available to us by Mr. Lillard; Ralph Ellison to authors, November 23, 1982.

14. Miscellaneous Records, Book 4C, 843–44, SCDAH. At least three other slave sales by William Ellison were recorded: on April 27, 1798, he sold Belfast and Phillis (Misc. Records, 3C, 52); on June 8, 1813, he sold Jack to the trustees of his wife (Misc. Records, 4H, 88); and on December 17, 1814, he sold for $700 the Negro woman Molly and the Negro woman Morris, and for $265 he sold a thirty-five-year-old African man named Peter (Misc. Records, 4J, 278–79).

15. Rachel Klein, "The Rise of the Planters in the South Carolina Backcountry, 1767–1808," Ph.D. diss., Yale University, 1979, 4–20; Anne King Gregorie, *History of Sumter County, South Carolina* (Sumter, S. C., 1954), 8–21.

16. Robert D. Bass, *Gamecock: The Life and Campaigns of General Thomas Sumter* (New York, 1961), 226.

17. Klein, "The Rise of the Planters," 137–38.

18. Adger, *My Life and Times,* 22–27.

19. Ibid.

20. Ibid., 27–28; McMaster, *History of Fairfield County,* 25, 96.

21. Adger, *My Life and Times,* 29–36; McMaster, *History of Fairfield County,* 36, 173.

22. One country boy remembered years later that the long evenings picking cotton were made tolerable because there were "plenty of pindars and sweet potatoes" roasting in the fire. Edwin J. Scott, *Random Recollections of a Long Life* (Columbia, S . C., 1884), 10.

23. The story of the invention of the cotton gin has been told many times. See Jeannette Mirsky and Allan Nevins, *The World of Eli Whitney* (New York, 1952), 68–78; Harold C. Livesay, *American Made: Men Who Shaped the American Economy* (Boston and Toronto, 1979), 22–34; Charles S. Aiken, "The Evolution of Cotton Ginning in the Southeastern United States," *The Geographical Review* (April 1973), 196–99; F. L. Lewton, "Historical Notes on the Cotton Gin," *Annual Report of the Board of Regents of the Smithsonian Institution* (Washington, D. C., 1937), 549–54.

24. Pierce Butler to Nathaniel Hall, September 16, 1793, Pierce Butler Letterbook, SCL.

25. Pierce Butler to Joseph Eve, March 25, 1794, Pierce Butler Letterbook, SCL.

26. Quoted in Mirsky and Nevins, *The World of Eli Whitney,* 127. From Columbia, South Carolina, Eli Whitney reported in 1801 that the "use of the machine here is amazingly extensive & the value of it beyond all calculation." Eli Whitney to Josiah Stebbins, December 20, 1801, Eli Whitney Papers, Sterling Memorial Library, Yale University.

27. Convenient abstracts of the legislative records of South Carolina's purchase of the patent rights are included in D. A. Tompkins, *The Cotton Gin: The History of Its Invention* (Charlotte, N. C., 1901). The quotation is from p. 49.

28. Klein, "The Rise of the Planters," 289, 293; Alfred Glaze Smith, Jr., *Economic Adjustment of an Old Cotton State: South Carolina, 1820–1860* (Columbia, S. C., 1958), 1–8. For the impact of cotton on one upcountry town, see Judith Jane Schulz, "The Rise and Decline of Camden as South Carolina's Major Inland Trading Center, 1751–1829: A Historical Geographical Study," M. A. thesis, University of South Carolina, 1972.

29. Gregorie, *History of Sumter County,* 109.

30. 1800 Census Schedules, Fairfield District, South Carolina; McMaster, *History of Fairfield County,* 88, 121, 163, 178.

31. Writing from Camden in 1831, Joshua Reynolds pointed to one of the reasons why slaves were eager to become artisans. "Negroes are fond of acquiring trades," he said, "as it gives them an opportunity of making something for themselves." Joshua Reynolds to John B. Miller, December 24, 1831, Miller-Furman-Dabbs Family Papers, SCL. Eugene D. Genovese, *Roll, Jordan, Roll: The World the Slaves Made* (New York, 1974), 388–98; Leonard Price Stav-

isky, "The Negro Artisan in the South Atlantic States, 1800–1860: A Study of Status and Economic Opportunity with Special Reference to Charleston," Ph.D. diss., Columbia University, 1958.

32. For the evolution of cotton gin technology, see Charles A. Bennett, *Saw and Toothed Cotton Ginning Developments* (Dallas, ca. 1960), 1–79; Park Benjamin, ed., *Appleton's Cyclopaedia of Applied Mechanics: A Dictionary of Mechanical Engineering and the Mechanical Arts*, vol. 1 (New York, 1880), 386–89. An excellent description of the work of a nineteenth-century "mechanician" is Anthony F. C. Wallace, *Rockdale: The Growth of an American Village in the Early Industrial Revolution* (New York and London, 1978), 237–39.

33. This description is based on the work that April Ellison did immediately after he was freed in 1816, discussed below.

34. For a description and illustrations of the evolution of gin houses before the Civil War, see Bennett, *Saw and Toothed Cotton Ginning Developments*, 1–4.

35. Subsequent events, discussed in chapter 3, proved April trusted McCreight.

36. Will of Robert Ellison, April 22, 1806, Will Book 5, 33–35, SCDAH.

37. Biographical information about Matilda and Eliza Ann Ellison was gathered from their tombstones in the Ellison family graveyard, Stateburg; Sumter County Records, Deeds of Conveyance, 1835–1838, Book K, 67, SCDAH.

38. David J. McCord, ed., *The Statutes at Large of South Carolina*, vol. 7 (Columbia, S. C., 1840), 440–43.

39. Wm. H. Bowen, "A Case in South Carolina," *Saturday Evening Post*, April 19, 1856.

40. April testified to the fact and date of his manumission when he petitioned to change his name (see note 1). Unfortunately, no formal record of April's emancipation has survived. Either of two documents—the deed of emancipation or the certificate that the magistrate

and freeholders were required to file to demonstrate that they had satisfactory proof of the character and skills of the slave to be manumitted—might have recorded a word or phrase that would establish beyond doubt whether April bought his freedom.

41. For a series of bills from William McCreight to Richard Singleton, see the Singleton Family Papers, SHC.

42. The best descriptions of early Stateburg are in Gregorie, *History of Sumter County,* and Thomas Sumter, *Dedicated to the Past, the Present, and the Future Inhabitants of Stateburg* (2nd ed., Sumter, S. C., 1949).

43. David Ramsay, *History of South Carolina from Its First Settlement in 1670 to the Year 1808* (Newberry, S. C., 1808), 304.

44. Mills, *Statistics of South Carolina,* 743.

45. Gregorie, *History of Sumter County,* 63; Thomas McAlpin Stubbs, *Early History of Sumter Churches* (Sumter, S. C., n.d.).

46. On the merger of the upcountry and tidewater aristocracies, see William W. Freehling, *Prelude to Civil War: The Nullification Controversy in South Carolina, 1816–1836* (New York and Evanston, Ill., 1965), 1–48.

47. The stories of these first families are lovingly told in Josie Platt Parler, *The Past Blows Away: On the Road to Poinsett Park* (Sumter, S. C., 1939); John R. Sumter, *Some Old Stateburg Homes* (Sumter, S. C., 1934); M. L. Parler, "The High Hills of the Santee," *The State*, May 11, 1930; "Storied Old Mansions Are Stateburg's Pride," *The State*, April 29, 1928; Brenda Shipley Moulton, *Sumter County Historical Vignettes* (Columbia, S. C., 1970).

48. Anna Waties to Miss Harriet H. Simons, August 28, 1834, Simons Family Papers, SCL.

49. See note 39 and Elizabeth Allen Coxe, *Memories of a South Carolina Plantation during the War* (privately printed, 1912).

50. *Census for 1820* (Washington, D. C., 1820).

51. *Fifth Census . . . 1830* (Washington, D. C., 1832), 14–15.

52. Gregorie, *History of Sumter County,* 467–70; Gregorie to Ellen Perry, January 20, 1943; Gregorie to Edward Price, September 30, 1950, Anne King Gregorie Papers, SCHS; Brewton Berry, *Almost White* (New York and London, 1963), 35–39, 186–90.

53. 1820 Census Schedules, Sumter District, South Carolina, 106.

54. Bill, A. Ellison to Richard Singleton, August 1819, Singleton Family Papers, SHC.

55. Several saws made in the gin shop of William Ellison are in the possession of Captain and Mrs. Richard Anderson of Stateburg.

56. Bill, April Ellison to Judge Waities, October 6, 1817, Thomas E. Richardson Papers, SCL.

57. Sumter County Records, Deeds of Conveyances, 1835–1838, Book K, 67, SCDAH.

58. Henry Ellison was born January 14, 1817; William Ellison, Jr., on July 19, 1819; and Reuben Ellison, on December 10, 1821. Sumter County Records, Deeds of Conveyance, 1835–1838, Book K, 67, SCDAH.

59. Bill, April Ellison to Judge Waities, October 6, 1817, Thomas E. Richardson Papers, SCL.

60. 1820 Census Schedules, Sumter District, South Carolina, 106.

61. For a brief contemporary description of the intended insurrection, see Scott, *Random Recollections,* 17. "The whole community was greatly excited," he remembered. Several slaves were executed for the plot. "I saw four or five of them hanged at one time and another afterwards upon the same gallows," Scott said.

62. Deed, March 6, 1822, Sumter Conveyances, Book FF, 1821–25, 173–74, SCDAH.

63. Court of Equity, Sumter District, June 20, 1820, Miscellaneous Records, Book D, 369, SCDAH.

64. August 6, 1824, Minutes and Records of the Claremont Episcopal Church (Church of the Holy Cross, Stateburg, South Carolina), 1788–1842, 15–16, SCL. The church historian Albert Sidney Thomas thought the event notable enough to include in his discussion of Holy Cross in *A Historical Account of the Protestant Episcopal Church in South Carolina, 1820–1957* (Columbia, S. C., 1957), 431–35.

65. Holy Cross Episcopal Church Register, 1808–1863, SCHS.

66. The after-service social activities at Holy Cross are described in Sumter, *Dedicated to Inhabitants of Stateburg,* 21–22.

67. Gregorie, *History of Sumter County,* 31, 57, 64, 469.

68. Sumter, *Dedicated to Inhabitants of Stateburg,* 7; Parler, *The Past Blows Away,* 33; Moulton, *Sumter County Historical Vignettes,* 20.

69. February 24, 1824, Account Book, Dr. W. W. Anderson, The Borough House Papers, SHC.

70. *William Ellison v. George McSwain,* March 17, 1821, Court of Common Pleas, Roll 1943, Sumter County Court House.

CHAPTER TWO

1. See Edmund S. Morgan, *American Slavery, American Freedom: The Ordeal of Colonial Virginia* (New York, 1975), 154–57, 331–37; Peter H. Wood, *Black Majority: Negroes in Colonial South Carolina from 1670 through the Stono Rebellion* (New York, 1974), 3–9, 157, 159.

2. See especially T. H. Breen and Stephen Innes, *"Myne Owne Ground": Race and Freedom on Virginia's Eastern Shore, 1640–1676* (New York, 1980).

3. The best general history of free Negroes in the antebellum South is Ira Berlin, *Slaves Without Masters: The Free Negro in the Antebellum South* (New York, 1974). On the Revolution, see Benjamin Quarles, *The Negro in the American Revolution* (Chapel Hill, N. C., 1961). On Jefferson's experience, see William Cohen, "Thomas Jefferson and the Problem of Slavery," *Journal of American History* 66 (1969–70), 503–26.

4. For an example of a slave who successfully petitioned the Virginia

legislature to grant him freedom for his wartime service, see Willie Lee Rose, ed., *A Documentary History of Slavery in North America* (New York, 1976), 61–62.

5. Derived from population data in Berlin, *Slaves Without Masters*, 46–47, 136–37.

6. See Gordon Wood, *The Creation of the American Republic, 1776–1787* (Chapel Hill, N. C., 1969), 1–124.

7. Derived from population data in Berlin, *Slaves Without Masters*, 46–47, 136–37.

8. Douglas Southall Freeman, *George Washington: First in Peace*, Vol. 7, (New York, 1957), completed by John Alexander Carroll and Mary Wells Ashworth, 585; John C. Fitzpatrick, ed., *The Writings of George Washington from the Original Manuscript Sources, 1745–1799* (Washington, D. C., 1940), Vol. 37, 276–77.

9. Berlin, *Slaves Without Masters*, 176.

10. Ibid., 35–36.

11. John Livingston Bradley, "Slave Manumissions in South Carolina, 1820–1860," M. A. thesis, University of South Carolina, 1964; John Donald Duncan, "Servitude and Slavery in Colonial South Carolina, 1670–1776," Ph.D. diss., Emory University, 1971, 398. On miscegenation, see James Hugo Johnston, *Race Relations in Virginia & Miscegenation in the South, 1776–1860* (Amherst, Mass., 1970), 165–268.

12. Berlin, *Slaves Without Masters*, 35–36, 40. See also C.L.R. James, *The Black Jacobins: Toussaint L'Ouverture and the San Domingo Revolution* (London, 1980; orig. ed., 1938); Eugene D. Genovese, *From Rebellion to Revolution: Afro-American Slave Revolts in the Making of the Modern World* (Baton Rouge, 1979), 19–24, 82–125.

13. The free Negro population of New Orleans in 1860 was 10,689. *Population of the United States in 1860*, 195; H. E. Sterkx, *The Free Negro in Antebellum Louisiana* (Rutherford, N. J., 1972), 91–95; Berlin, *Slaves Without Masters*, 35–36, 40; Marina Wikramanayake, *A World in Shadow: The Free Black in*

Antebellum South Carolina (Columbia, S. C., 1973), 140–42, 159–60. We are indebted to David C. Rankin for information from his forthcoming study of the free colored community of New Orleans.

14. Berlin, *Slaves Without Masters*, 178. See also Joel Williamson, *New People: Miscegenation and Mulattoes in the United States* (New York, 1980), 5–58.

15. Derived from population data in Berlin, *Slaves Without Masters*, 46–47, 136–37.

16. *Population of the United States in 1860*, 598–605; Berlin, *Slaves Without Masters*, 136–37, 397–99.

17. Orlando Patterson, *Slavery and Social Death: A Comparative Study* (Cambridge, Mass. and London, 1982).

18. On the racial prejudice of whites, see Winthrop D. Jordan, *White Over Black: American Attitudes Toward the Negro, 1550–1812* (Chapel Hill, N. C., 1968); George M. Fredrickson, *The Black Image in the White Mind: The Debate on Afro-American Character and Destiny, 1817–1914* (New York, 1971); Fredrickson, *White Supremacy: A Comparative Study in American and South African History* (New York, 1981). On slavery, see John W. Blassingame, *The Slave Community: Plantation Life in the Antebellum South* (New York, rev. ed., 1979); Paul A. David et al., *Reckoning With Slavery: A Critical Study in the Quantitative History of American Negro Slavery* (New York, 1976); Eugene D. Genovese, *Roll, Jordan, Roll: The World the Slaves Made* (New York, 1974); Robert W. Fogel and Stanley L. Engerman, *Time on the Cross: The Economics of American Negro Slavery* (Boston, 1974); Kenneth M. Stampp, *The Peculiar Institution: Slavery in the Ante-Bellum South* (New York, 1956). On proslavery ideology, see Drew Gilpin Faust, ed., *The Ideology of Slavery: Proslavery Thought in the Antebellum South 1830–1860* (Baton Rouge and London, 1981).

19. On slave culture, see Herbert G. Gutman, *The Black Family in Slavery and Freedom, 1750–1925* (New York,

1976); Thomas L. Webber, *Deep Like the Rivers: Education in the Slave Quarter Community, 1831–1865* (New York, 1978); Lawrence W. Levine, *Black Culture and Black Consciousness: Afro-American Folk Thought from Slavery to Freedom* (New York, 1977); Leslie Howard Owens, *This Species of Property: Slave Life and Culture in the Old South* (New York, 1976); George P. Rawick, *From Sundown to Sunup: The Making of the Black Community* (Westport, Conn., 1972); Blassingame, *The Slave Community;* Genovese, *Roll, Jordan, Roll;* Stanley M. Elkins, *Slavery: A Problem in American Institutional and Intellectual Life* (Chicago, 3rd ed., 1976).

20. A notable exception was North Carolina, where mulattoes—but not blacks—were legally presumed to be free. John Hope Franklin, *The Free Negro in North Carolina, 1790–1860* (Chapel Hill, 1943), 52–53.

21. David J. McCord, ed., *The Statutes at Large of South Carolina* (Columbia, S. C., 1840), Vol. 7, 440–43. On other states, see Berlin, *Slaves Without Masters,* 91–95. See also Donald J. Senese, "The Problem of Citizenship and the Free Negro in South Carolina Before the Fourteenth Amendment," M. A. thesis, University of South Carolina, 1966.

22. *Monk v. Jenkins,* cited in Wikramanayake, *A World in Shadow,* 54.

23. Helen Tunnicliff Catterall, ed., *Judicial Cases Concerning American Slavery and the Negro* (Washington, D. C., 1929), Vol. II, 350.

24. McCord, ed., *Statutes at Large,* Vol. 7, 459–60. For one of the rare exceptions to the ban on manumissions, see Fairfield Deeds, Book EE, 258–59, SCDAH.

25. Berlin, *Slaves Without Masters,* 46–47, 136–37.

26. Ibid., 136–57.

27. The account of the Vesey conspiracy is based on: Lionel H. Kennedy and Thomas Parker, *An Official Report of the Trials of Sundry Negroes, Charged with an Attempt to Raise an Insurrection in the State of South Carolina* (Charleston, S. C., 1822); Robert S. Starobin, ed., *Denmark Vesey: The Slave Conspiracy of 1822* (Englewood Cliffs, N. J., 1970); John Oliver Killens, ed., *The Trial Record of Denmark Vesey* (Boston, 1970); John Lofton, *Insurrection in South Carolina: The Turbulent World of Denmark Vesey* (Yellow Springs, Ohio, 1964); Wikramanayake, *A World in Shadow,* 133–51; Marion L. Starkey, *Striving to Make It My Home: The Story of Americans from Africa* (New York, 1964), 152–212; Vincent Harding, *There Is a River: The Black Struggle for Freedom in America* (New York and London, 1981), 65–72; Genovese, *From Rebellion to Revolution,* 44–50; William W. Freehling, *Prelude to Civil War: The Nullification Controversy in South Carolina, 1816–1836* (New York and Evanston, Ill., 1965), 51–63. For a dissenting view, see Richard Wade, "The Vesey Plot: A Reconsideration," *Journal of Southern History* 30 (May 1964), 148–61.

28. Kennedy and Parker, *An Official Report,* 177.

29. James, *The Black Jacobins,* 38.

30. Eugene D. Genovese has noted that artisans, drivers, and preachers—the privileged strata of slaves—provided the leadership for Southern insurrections. Drawing on the work of Franz Fanon, Genovese argues that these elite slaves, being most exposed to assimilation by the dominant culture, are the least likely to equivocate on political issues. "That is, either they identify with their oppressors and seek individual advancement or they identify with their people and place their sophistication at the disposal of rebellion. They thus produce a high percentage of leaders and traitors. Individually, they play a central role on both sides; collectively, however, they do equivocate and attach themselves to one or the other." Genovese, *From Rebellion to Revolution,* 28.

31. Kennedy and Parker, *An Official Report,* 95.

32. Berlin, *Slaves Without Masters,* 316–40.

33. McCord, ed., *Statutes at Large,* Vol. 7, 461–62.

34. Berlin, *Slaves Without Masters,* 215.

35. Ibid., 317, 319, 327–33.

36. Wikramanayake, *A World in Shadow,* 65–67.

37. For warrants for the sale of Hetty Baron in 1840 and Maria Silanneau in 1849 for nonpayment of capitation taxes, see Charleston Miscellany, 1700–1950, SCDAH.

38. Sumter County Guardians of Free Blacks, 1823–1842, Sumter County Historical Society, Sumter, S. C. We are indebted to Mr. Esmond Howell for access to this document. For other examples of guardianships, see Fairfield Deeds, Book MM, 51, 107, 119, 146, 149, 447, 562, SCDAH.

39. Ibid.

40. Berlin, *Slaves Without Masters,* 144–45; Wikramanayake, *A World in Shadow,* 10–13.

41. John Belton O'Neall, *The Negro Law of South Carolina* (Columbia, S. C., 1848), 11.

42. Catterall, ed., *Judicial Cases,* II, 381–83.

43. O'Neall, *Negro Law,* 12.

44. Ibid.

45. Ibid.

46. Ibid., 35.

47. Ibid.

48. Clippings from the Columbia *Telegraph,* December 25, 1848 and January 6, 1849; and the Columbia *Advocate* (undated), bound in the back of the copy of O'Neall, *Negro Law,* in the University of California, Berkeley library.

49. Michael Stephen Hindus, *Prison and Plantation: Crime, Justice, and Authority in Massachusetts and South Carolina, 1767–1878* (Chapel Hill, N.C., 1980), 139–40. See also Donald J. Senese, "The Free Negro and the South Carolina Courts," *South Carolina Historical Magazine* 68 (July 1967), 140–53.

50. O'Neall, *Negro Law,* 34–35.

51. Ibid., 13.

52. Catterall, ed., *Judicial Cases,* II, 350.

53. Ibid.

54. O'Neall, *Negro Law,* 38–42; see also Howell M. Henry, *The Police Control of the Slave in South Carolina* (Emory, Va., 1914).

55. O'Neall, *Negro Law,* 12–13.

56. See for example, Catterall, ed., *Judicial Cases,* II, 283.

57. O'Neall, *Negro Law,* 13.

58. Ibid., 12–13.

59. All the data on families, race, occupation, and wealth discussed in this chapter were derived from an analysis of every free Afro-American household in South Carolina listed in the manuscript schedules of the 1860 federal census, excluding the city of Charleston, which is discussed in later chapters. In all, there were 1,387 free Afro-American households outside Charleston. Men headed 66 percent of the households. This is similar to the proportion of male-headed households in the free Negro community of Cincinnati in 1860, as reported in Paul J. Lammermeier, "The Urban Black Family of the Nineteenth Century: A Study of Black Family Structure in the Ohio Valley, 1850–1880," *Journal of Marriage and the Family* 35 (August 1973), 440–55; see also E. Franklin Frazier, *The Free Negro Family: A Study of Family Origins Before the Civil War* (Nashville, 1932); Frazier, *The Negro Family in the United States* (Chicago, 1939); Gutman, *Black Family,* 486–87, 496–97, 530; Theodore Hershberg, "Free Blacks in Antebellum Philadelphia: A Study of Ex-Slaves, Freeborn, and Socioeconomic Decline," in Hershberg, ed., *Philadelphia: Work, Space, Family, and Group Experience in the Nineteenth Century* (New York, 1981), 368–91.

60. Households headed by males without co-residing spouses accounted for 18 percent of all free Afro-American households.

61. The estimate is based on the assumption that the proportion of households headed by men without spouses but with co-residing children represented approximately the proportion of women without spouses who were either widows or had slave husbands. That is, there was little likelihood that the children in the households of a free Negro man were born to a white woman. Just over a quarter (28 percent) of the male-headed house-

holds without spouses had co-residing children. Since 72 percent of the female-headed households without spouses had co-residing children, 44 percent (72 percent minus 28 percent) would be the maximum estimate, but it is undoubtedly too high. Since the mortality rate was higher for men than women, and since free Negro women would be less able than men to afford to buy their slave spouses, a rough estimate is that concubines were about a third of the women who had children but no co-residing spouse. Even this estimate may be too high.

62. O'Neall, *Negro Law*, 13.

63. It is possible that the census enumerators or the clerks who copied the enumerators' field notes made a mistake in recording the race of one or more individuals in these families. We have included here only those families whose race did not appear to be recorded carelessly or mistakenly. Although the accuracy of the racial data is still open to doubt, we believe that the race indicated for the family members in these seventy-one families was not the result of simple copying errors. That is, these are not instances in which the census enumerator failed to make a ditto mark for "M" or "B," the abbreviations for mulatto and black. Instead, they are families in which the enumerator unambiguously indicated that both white and Negro persons with the same surname were present in the household. In 1812, citizens in Orangeburg District petitioned the legislature for penalties against miscegenation. Their petition said that the "softening" conditions of slavery had caused slaves to forget their place and attempt "to exercise among some of the lower classes of white peoples freedom and familiarities which are degrading to them and dangerous to society. We allude to attempts which are made and some of them with success at sexual intercourse with white females." The current problem, the petitioners said, "is that instances do now

occur in which not merely the dregs of society are concerned but some reputable families are disgraced and covered with infamy by the advances of a slave or free Negro." Petition from Orangeburg (December 12, 1812) requesting laws to penalize slave and free Negroes for miscegenation, General Assembly Petitions, SCDAH.

64. 1860 Population Schedules, St. Peter's Parish, Beaufort District, South Carolina, dwelling 251.

65. 1860 Population Schedules, Charleston District (outside the city), S. C., dwelling 312.

66. Wikramanayake, *A World in Shadow*, 76–77; Berlin, *Slaves Without Masters*, 160–64.

67. Berlin, *Slaves Without Masters*, 98–99.

68. See for example, Catterall, ed., *Judicial Cases*, II, 274, 289, 302, 307, 317, 334, 339, 346, 358, 385, 400, 450.

69. Ibid., 317.

70. Ibid., 358–59; see also 334–35.

71. O'Neall, *Negro Law*, 6.

72. Ibid., 12–13.

73. The 1860 population schedules listed 1,733 male and female free Afro-Americans outside the city of Charleston who had occupations.

74. See Luther Porter Jackson, *Free Negro Labor and Property Holding in Virginia, 1830–1860* (Washington, D. C., 1942), esp. 102–36.

75. Lee Soltow, "The Distribution of Real Estate Among Nonslave and White Males 20 Years Old and Older in the United States in 1850, 1860, and 1870," unpublished table generously provided us by Lee Soltow.

76. Nationwide, the mean value of real estate owned by free men who owned real estate in 1860 (almost all of whom were white) was $2,618. This was 3.2 times the mean for free Afro-Americans in South Carolina. These figures, of course, exclude those individuals who owned no real estate. The mean real estate value of all free men in the nation in 1860 was $1,492; that for all South Carolina free Negroes was $243, only one-sixth the national mean. The national means were calculated

from Soltow, "Distribution of Real Estate."

77. The mean wealth of white families in South Carolina was estimated by dividing the aggregate wealth of the state (minus that owned by free persons of color) by the number of families in the state (minus those of free persons of color). The data are in *Statistics of the United States, (Including Mortality, Property, &c.,) in 1860* (Washington, D. C., 1866), 312, 348. The mean wealth of all free Afro-American households (outside the city of Charleston) was obtained by dividing the aggregate wealth of all free persons of color in the state by the number of free Negro households. This method slightly overstates the wealth per head of household since the wealth of every wealth holder is included, regardless of whether the person was a head of household.

78. Franklin, *Free Negro in North Carolina*, 237.

79. Carter G. Woodson, comp., *Free Negro Owners of Slaves in the United States in 1830* (Washington, D. C., 1924), 27–31.

CHAPTER THREE

1. See, for example, Sumter County Deeds of Conveyance, Book K, 1838–40, 64, SCDAH.

2. Alfred Glaze Smith, *Economic Adjustment of an Old Cotton State: South Carolina, 1820–1860* (Columbia, S. C., 1958), 7.

3. Ibid., 10–38. Writing from Mobile, Alabama in 1840, J. C. Nott commented on his recent trip back to his native South Carolina: "You have no idea how poor & worn out the lands appeared to me. . . . There is no mistake in the great superiority of the West for a planter. . . . Carolina *is done* as a Cotton State. . . ." J. C. Nott to James Henry Hammond, July 21, 1840, James Henry Hammond Papers, SCL.

4. The article from the Camden *Journal* was reprinted in the Charleston *Courier,* December 2, 1835.

5. Edwin J. Scott, *Random Recollections of a Long Life, 1806 to 1876* (Columbia, S. C., 1884), 20.

6. Smith, *Economic Readjustment of an Old Cotton State,* 55–63.

7. Ibid., 40.

8. Anne King Gregorie, *History of Sumter County, South Carolina* (Sumter, S. C., 1954), 134; Bill, September 3, 1825, Singleton Family Papers, SHC.

9. Sumter *Banner,* March 31, 1847, and other local newspapers thereafter.

10. Bill, September 14, 1836, Singleton Family Papers, SHC.

11. Caleb Rembert to John B. Miller, March 10, 1836, Miller-Furman-Dabbs Family Papers, SCL.

12. Caleb Rembert to John B. Miller, September 25, 1836, Miller-Furman-Dabbs Family Papers, SCL.

13. Receipt, October 17, 1836, Miller-Furman-Dabbs Family Papers, SCL.

14. H. Vaughan to John B. Miller, March 20, 1836, Miller-Furman-Dabbs Family Papers, SCL.

15. Thomas S. Sumter, *Stateburg and Its People* (2nd ed., Sumter, S. C., 1949), 30.

16. Josie Platt Parler, *The Past Blows Away: On the Road to Poinsett Park* (Sumter, S. C., 1939), 32.

17. Gavin Wright, *The Political Economy of the Cotton South* (New York, 1978), 96.

18. Bill, September 3, 1825, Singleton Family Papers, SHC.

19. Bills, September 2, 1822; August 27, 1823; September 3, 1823; August 24, 1824; September 3, 1825, Singleton Family Papers, SHC.

20. Gregorie, *History of Sumter County,* 134; Sumter *Southern Whig,* June 2, 1832.

21. See for example, Sumter *Gazette,* July 23, 1845; Sumter *Banner,* December 13, 1848; *Black River Watchman,* May 11, 1850; Sumter *Watchman,* August 29, 1855; *Tri-Weekly Sumter Watchman,* June 23, 1860.

22. *Population of the United States in*

1860 (Washington, D. C., 1864), 454.

23. Judith J. Schulz, "The Rise and Decline of Camden as South Carolina's Major Inland Trading Center, 1751–1829: A Historical Geographical Study," M. A. thesis, University of South Carolina, 1972, 81.

24. Sumter, *Banner,* May 24, 1848.

25. Sumter, *Banner,* June 30, 1847.

26. Sumter *Banner,* December 13, 1848.

27. Bills, July 1845 to September 1852, Singleton Family Papers, SHC.

28. Sumter *Banner,* December 13, 1848.

29. Sumter *Banner,* April 23, 1851.

30. *Tri-Weekly Sumter Watchman,* June 23, 1860.

31. *Black River Watchman,* June 28, 1853.

32. Our search of the *Patents for Inventions Issued by the U. S. Patent Office, 1790–1873* (Washington, D. C.) failed to turn up an Ellison patent.

33. Bill, September 4, 1836, Singleton Family Papers, SHC.

34. James Boatwright to James Edward Calhoun, May 20, 1831, James Edward Calhoun Papers, SCL.

35. William Ellison Estate Papers, Sumter County Estate Papers, Box 151, Package 8, SCDAH.

36. Bill, September 3, 1823; Receipt, January 22, 1824, Singleton Family Papers, SHC.

37. January 22, 1849, Dr. W. W. Anderson Account Books, The Borough House Papers, SHC.

38. Ibid.

39. See, for example, January 30, 1847, Dr. W. W. Anderson Account Book, The Borough House Papers, SHC.

40. In the 1830s a lawyer in Alabama explained why his profession was so remunerative and, incidentally, why tradesmen had such difficulty collecting from planters. "They all run in debt—invariably," he said, "never pay cash, and all always one year behind hand. They wait for the sale of their crops. The roads are bad, the prices low, they cannot pay. They all wait to be sued. A suit is brought—no defence is made—an execution is taken out and is paid with all the costs and they even think it a good bargain. The rate of interest allowed is but 8 pr. cent." Quoted in James Oakes, *The Ruling Race: A History of American Slaveholders* (New York, 1982), 61–62.

41. William Ellison to Henry Ellison, March 26, 1857, Ellison Family Papers, SCL.

42. *William Ellison v. William H. Killingsworth,* November 1, 1834, Court of Common Pleas, Sumter County Court House, Sumter, S. C.

43. *William Ellison v. Oran D. Lee,* February 27, 1843, Court of Common Pleas, Sumter County Court House, Sumter, S. C.

44. Thomas S. Sumter, *Stateburg and Its People,* 30–31.

45. Robert W. Andrews, *The Life and Adventures of Capt. Robert W. Andrews of Sumter, South Carolina* (Boston, 1887), 25.

46. 1850 Population Schedules, Sumter District, South Carolina, dwelling 1225.

47. 1850 Population Schedules, Sumter District, South Carolina, dwelling 1223.

48. August 19, 1833, to February 7, 1861, Moody Family Papers, SCL. For additional examples of blacksmithing and carpentry work done in Ellison's shop between 1852 and 1867, see the eighteen items in the William Ellison Business Papers, SCL.

49. April 18, 1834, and February 21, 1860, Moody Family Papers, SCL.

50. 1850 Manufacturing Schedules, Sumter District, South Carolina, 636.

51. Until 1820 the census schedules record only the number of slaves. From 1820 through 1840 the census schedules report the number, sex, and age within large age groups (e.g., 36–54). In 1850 and 1860, the slave schedules list the color, age, and sex of each slave. Slaves' names were never recorded in the census.

52. 1820 Census Schedules, Sumter District, South Carolina, 106. Three other Sumter District free Negroes

owned slaves in 1820. Each of them owned two slaves, but none owned two adult males, like Ellison.

53. Bill, J. W. Dinkins to William Ellison, November 1822, Court of Common Pleas, Sumter County Court House, Sumter, S. C.

54. October 24, 1826, Dr. W. W. Anderson Account Book, The Borough House Papers, SHC.

55. Ibid., December 1825.

56. Ellison was the only free Negro slaveholder in Sumter District in 1830. 1830 Census Schedules, Sumter District, South Carolina, 82. A fragment of a document indicates that Ellison owed a white man $400 and $120 for purchases made in 1827. These amounts may reflect the balance due on slaves Ellison bought from the man. See *Richard B. Harrison v. William Ellison,* December 27, 1828, Court of Common Pleas, Sumter County Court House, Sumter, S. C.

57. Bill, September 14, 1836, Singleton Family Papers, SHC.

58. February 1, December 6, 1832, Dr. W. W. Anderson Account Books, The Borough House Papers, SHC.

59. 1840 Census Schedules, Sumter District South Carolina, 3.

60. Ibid.

61. Sumter County Deeds of Conveyances, Book K, 1838–1840, 64, SCDAH.

62. Ibid.

63. Sumter County Deeds of Conveyances, Book KK, 87, 129, SCDAH.

64. Thomas S. Sumter remembered that the general built his first house at Davis Hill. Sumter, *Dedicated to the Past,* 27.

65. 1840 Census Schedules, Sumter District, South Carolina, 3.

66. Ibid.

67. Appraisement Bill, January 6, 1862, William Ellison Estate Papers, Sumter County Estate Papers, Box 151, Package 8, SCDAH.

68. Susan J. Moody to Burrel Moody, January 9, 1846, Moody Family Papers, SCL.

69. Historian Carl N. Degler has observed that "historians today know more about the slave family than they do about the free Negro family of the nineteenth century." Degler, *At Odds: Women and the Family in America from the Revolution to the Present* (New York and Oxford, 1980), 112.

70. Bertram Wyatt-Brown, *Southern Honor: Ethics and Behavior in the Old South* (New York and other cities, 1982), 54.

71. Michael P. Johnson, "Planters and Patriarchy: Charleston, 1800–1860," *Journal of Southern History* 46 (February 1980), 45–72.

72. James M. Johnson to Henry Ellison, April 24, 1860, Ellison Family Papers, SCL.

73. Elisabeth Muhlenfeld, *Mary Boykin Chesnut: A Biography* (Baton Rouge and London, 1981), 24.

74. Emma Cantey to John L. Manning, July 14, 1839, Williams-Chesnut-Manning Papers, SCL.

75. Rebecca T. Singleton to Marion and Angelica Singleton, May 16, 1830, Singleton-Deveaux Collection, SCL.

76. Gabriella Huger to Mrs. Marion Singleton Deveaux, June 12, 1844, Singleton-Deveaux Collection, SCL.

77. Lizzie to Mrs. Marion Singleton Deveaux, May 20, 1846, Singleton-Deveaux Collection, SCL.

78. Catherine Clinton points out that aristocratic white girls were seldom trained to keep house, the task that occupied them after they were married. Clinton, *The Plantation Mistress: Woman's World in the Old South* (New York, 1982), 19. See also Wyatt-Brown, *Southern Honor,* 156; Johnson, "Planters and Patriarchy," 65–66.

79. May 13, 1830, Record of the Claremont Parish, 1808–1866, Church of the Holy Cross, Stateburg, South Carolina, SCHS.

80. Marion Singleton to Angelica Singleton, November 20, 1832, Singleton-Deveaux Collection, SCL.

81. In 1820 and 1830 three white families named Buckner lived in the South Carolina low country, two in Beaufort District and one in Charleston District, each of whom owned numerous slaves. It is possi-

ble that Willis Buckner had been a slave of one of these families and had recently obtained his freedom, perhaps after the 1820 ban on manumission, which could account for why he did not appear in the census as a free man. 1820 Census Schedules, Beaufort District, South Carolina, 36; 1820 Census Schedules, Charleston County, South Carolina, 67A, 91; 1830 Census Schedules, Beaufort District, South Carolina, 297; 1830 Census Schedules, Charleston District, South Carolina, 109. We are indebted to Anne E. Johnson for this information.

82. Aurora Greland to Marion Singleton, March 20, 1832, Singleton-Deveaux Collection, SCL.

83. Sumter County Records, Deeds of Conveyances, 1835–1838, Book K, 67, SCDAH.

84. *John Wilson Buckner v. Henry Ellison and William Ellison [Jr.]*, February 18, 1871, William Ellison Estate Papers, Sumter County Estate Papers, Box 151, Package 8, SCDAH.

85. Wyatt-Brown, *Southern Honor,* 247; Clinton, *Plantation Mistress,* 33, 38.

86. November 22, 1840, Record of the Claremont Parish, 1808–1866, Church of the Holy Cross, Stateburg, South Carolina, SCHS.

87. After having three sons within four years, William and Matilda had no more children. When their last child, Reuben, was born in 1821, William was thirty-one, and Matilda, twenty-six. It is possible that Ellison disciplined his intimate life by the same self-conscious planning that characterized all the rest of his behavior.

88. W. F. DeSaussure to John B. Miller, May 20, 1825, Miller-Furman-Dabbs Family Papers, SCL.

89. Johnson, "Planters and Patriarchy," 58–60; Wyatt-Brown, *Southern Honor,* 156.

90. June 17, 1835, The Diary of Mrs. Louisa Penelope Preston, SCL.

91. M. C. to James Chesnut, Jr., July 5, 1834, Williams-Chesnut-Manning Papers, SCL.

92. Richard Singleton to Alan Bradford, December 23, 1833, Singleton Family Papers, SCL.

93. Richard I. Manning to his mother, November 27, 1837, Williams-Chesnut-Manning Papers, SCL.

94. E. Merton Coulter, *College Life in the Old South* (Athens, Ga., 1928), 89; Wyatt-Brown, *Southern Honor,* 162–69.

95. Gregorie, *History of Sumter County,* 135. We believe it is likely that local tradition has confused William Ellison's sons with his grandchildren, some of whom did spend time in Canada. See chapter VIII.

96. See, for example, Henry Ellison to James Drayton Johnson, July 24, 1870, Ellison Family Papers, SCL.

97. William Ellison, Jr., to Henry Ellison, October 31, 1860, Ellison Family Papers, SCL. The only surviving evidence of Reuben's literacy is mention of a letter he wrote in, S. Benenhaly to "Dear Sir," April 18, 1858, Ellison Family Papers, SCL.

98. C. W. Birnie, "The Education of the Negro in Charleston, South Carolina, Prior to the Civil War," *Journal of Negro History* 12 (January 1927), 13–21.

99. 1830 and 1840 Census Schedules, Sumter District, South Carolina; Dr. W. W. Anderson Account Books, 1832–1845, The Borough House Papers, SHC.

100. James Henry Hammond to Marcus C. M. Hammond, March 19, 1840, James Henry Hammond Papers, SCL.

101. James Henry Hammond to John Hammond, February 10, 1845, James Henry Hammond Papers, SCL.

102. See the fine biography, Drew Gilpin Faust, *James Henry Hammond and the Old South: A Design for Mastery* (Baton Rouge and London, 1982).

103. Sumter County Deeds of Conveyances, Book K, 1838–1840, 64, SCDAH. The Ellison family home stands today, beautifully restored by its present owners, the Anderson family of Borough House.

104. Muhlenfeld, *Mary Boykin Chesnut*, 12–13.
105. Ibid., 14.
106. Woodward, ed., *Mary Chesnut's Civil War*, 411, 463–65.
107. Miller sold his plantation south of Camden to a white man. Muhlenfeld, *Mary Boykin Chesnut*, 14.
108. Parler, *The Past Blows Away*, 33; Brenda Shipley Moulton, *Sumter County Historical Vignettes* (Columbia, S. C., 1970), n. p.
109. We are indebted to Mrs. Gery Leffelman Ballou and her mother, Mrs. Pauline Leffelman, for a description of the house when they lived there in the 1930s. Interview with authors, May 29, 1980; Columbia *State*, October 4, 1931.
110. Sumter County Records, Deeds of Conveyances, 1835–1838, Book K, 67, SCDAH.
111. Wyatt-Brown, *Southern Honor*, xii, 12, 357.
112. Jack Thomas to "My Esteemed Friends," April 30, 1860, Ellison Family Papers, SCL.
113. James M. Johnson to Henry Ellison, May 30, 1860, Ellison Family Papers, SCL.
114. Wyatt-Brown, *Southern Honor*, 114.
115. Sumter, *Dedicated to the Past*, 26. Tradition has it that the tavern was made of red brick and its portico supported by large white pillars. Columbia *State*, October 4, 1931.
116. David M. Potter, *The South and the Sectional Conflict* (Baton Rouge, 1968), 15–16.
117. Robert Brent Toplin, "Between Black and White: Attitudes toward Southern Mulattoes, 1830–1861," *Journal of Southern History* 45 (May 1979), 185–200; Joel Williamson, *New People: Miscegenation and Mulattoes in the United States* (New York, 1980), 15–19.
118. Wyatt-Brown, *Southern Honor*, 345.
119. Jacob Stroyer, *My Life in the South*, 3d ed. (Salem, Mass., 1885), 17.
120. William Ransom Hogan and Edwin Adams Davis, *William Johnson's Natchez: The Ante-Bellum Diary of a Free Negro* (Port Washington, N. Y., 1968), 55.
121. January 7, 1828, Sumter County Guardianships of Free Blacks, 1823–1842, Sumter County Historical Society, Sumter, S. C.
122. Dr. W. W. Anderson Account Books, 1818–1827, The Borough House Papers, SHC.
123. Rev. I. E. Lowery, *Life on the Old Plantation in Ante-Bellum Days or a Story Based on Facts* (Columbia, S. C., 1911), 42–43.
124. Columbia *State*, October 4, 1931.
125. Sumter, *Dedicated to the Past*, 6, 32.
126. His first reference to "Mrs. Ellison" was September 17, 1847. Dr. W. W. Anderson Account Book, The Borough House Papers, SHC.
127. For this information we are indebted to Mrs. Mary Anderson, who now owns the biography. Mrs. Mary Anderson to authors, June 19, 1981.
128. John R. Sumter, *Some Old Stateburg Homes* (Sumter, S. C., 1934), 3–5; Anne King Gregorie, *Thomas Sumter* (Columbia, S. C., 1931), 247–67; Sumter, *Dedicated to the Past*, 10. On March 1, 1842, the estate of Thomas Sumter, Jr., paid William Ellison by note $118.71 for his work. Thomas Sumter, Jr., Estate Papers, Sumter County Estate Papers, Bundle 90, Package 4, SCDAH.
129. July 14, 1840, Natalie Delage Sumter Diary, 1840–1841, SCL.
130. Natalie Delage Sumter's diary mentions scores of the leading planter families of the High Hills. For the Chesnut family's admiration of this "beautiful and accomplished lady," see Woodward, ed., *Mary Chesnut's Civil War*, 281.
131. South Carolina Miscellaneous Records, Book G, 231–33, SCDAH.
132. 1810 Census Schedules, Fairfield District, South Carolina, 196–201.
133. 1830 Census Schedules, Fairfield District, South Carolina, 355.
134. Entry for June 11, 1837, James and Robert J. McCreight Cash Book & Misc. Accounts, 1827–1845, Winnsboro, SCL.

135. Ibid.

136. Entries for September 9, 1841, and December 18, 1843, ibid.

137. April's mother had to be at least fifty-five years old in 1830. Since the age categories for free women of color on the 1830 census schedules were thirty-six to fifty-four and fifty-five to fifty-nine, and since the ages were seldom recorded with pinpoint accuracy, we have made the most generous possible estimate and included all free women in either age category. Only one of the women headed a household and was thus named in the census, Peggy Ogilvie. Three other women lived in households headed by free men of color named Reason Collins, William Cole, and Robert Strother. The other five women lived in households headed by whites named John Starke, Elizabeth McMillan, Elizabeth Harris, John [illegible surname], and Benjamin Lakin. 1830 Census Schedules, Fairfield District, South Carolina. We are indebted to Anne E. Johnson for this information.

138. In 1830 William Ellison owned six slave women in the census age category thirty-six to fifty-four. Since the ages of slaves are notoriously unreliable in the early censuses, we assume the age of the oldest of these slave women might easily have been ten or fifteen years older than fifty-four. Ellison died in 1833, leaving all his slaves to his wife Mary Ann Ellison, who may have owned April's mother in 1837, when she died. Will of William Ellison, Fairfield Wills, Book 14, 14–15, SCDAH; 1830 Census Schedules, Fairfield District, South Carolina, 380.

139. 1840 Census Schedules, Sumter District, South Carolina, 3.

140. Dr. W. W. Anderson Account Books, 1823–1874, The Borough House Papers, SHC.

141. 1850 Population Schedules, Fairfield District, South Carolina, dwelling 234.

142. 1860 Population Schedules, Fairfield District, South Carolina, dwelling 5.

143. William Ellison Estate Papers, Sumter County Estate Papers, Box 151, Package 8, SCDAH.

144. Ibid.

145. "History of the Means Family," typescript, Means-English Family Papers, SCL.

146. Petition of James Patterson [1838], Slavery Petitions, SCDAH.

147. Ibid.

148. Report of the Committee on the Colored Population, December 11, 1838, Slavery Petitions, SCDAH.

149. At the time he bought Maria, McCreight owned seventeen slaves. 1830 Census Schedules, Fairfield District, South Carolina, 355.

CHAPTER FOUR

1. Charleston Free Negro Tax Book, 1844, SCDAH; Mary Thomson Ellison tombstone, Ellison family graveyard, Stateburg.

2. "List of Persons Admitted Members of the Brown Fellowship Society," *Rules and Regulations of the Brown Fellowship Society* (Charleston, S. C., 1844), 25–27, RSSL; Ellison family graveyard, Stateburg; Charleston Free Negro Tax Book, 1844, SCDAH; E. Horace Fitchett, "The Free Negro in Charleston, South Carolina," Ph.D. diss., University of Chicago, 1950, 48, 93, 162, 193–95.

3. Will of Thomas S. Bonneau, *Record of Wills*, Charleston County, Vol. 39, 905–7; Parish Register, St. Philip's Protestant Episcopal Church, 1810–1857 (typescript), SCL; *Rules and Regulations of the Brown Fellowship Society*, 25–27; Fitchett, "Free Negro in Charleston," 48, 93, 162, 193–95.

4. Mary Elizabeth Ellison tombstone, Ellison family graveyard, Stateburg.

5. Parish Register, St. Philip's Protestant Episcopal Church, 1810–1857, SCL.

6. Ibid.

7. 1843, Record of the Claremont Parish, 1808–1866, Church of the

Holy Cross, Stateburg, South Carolina, SCHS.

8. June 13, 1845, ibid.

9. Daniel Alexander Payne, *Recollections of Seventy Years* (Nashville, Tenn., 1883), 25, 36.

11. February 26, 1845, Record of the Claremont Parish, 1808–1866, Church of the Holy Cross, Stateburg, South Carolina, SCHS. Marina Wikramanayake states that "Both of William Ellison's daughters married white men. . . ." This statement is false. The mistake arises from Wikramanayake's confusion of the daughters of white William Ellison of Fairfield District with the free colored daughter of William Ellison of Stateburg. Wikramanayake, *A World in Shadow: The Free Black in Antebellum South Carolina* (Columbia, S. C., 1973), 76.

11. Charleston Free Negro Tax Books, 1838–1842, SCDAH.

12. The evidence for their friendship is discussed in chapter V.

13. At the time Johnson was confirmed, so were W. W. Anderson and Mary H. Anderson, children of William Ellison's white guardian, Dr. W. W. Anderson. June 20, 1843, Record of the Claremont Parish, 1808–1866, Church of the Holy Cross, Stateburg, South Carolina, SCHS.

14. "Taxes on House and Lot owned by Estate of Wm Ellison and J. D. Johnson," March 13, 1861, William Ellison Estate Papers, Sumter County Estate Papers, Box 151, Package 8, SCDAH.

15. 1850 Population Schedules, Sumter District, South Carolina, dwelling 1219.

16. 1850 Population Schedules, Sumter District, South Carolina, dwelling 1224.

17. For an example, see James M. Johnson to Henry Ellison, January 20, 1860, Ellison Family Papers, SCL.

18. December 12, 1847, Minutes and Records of the Vestry and Wardens of Holy Cross, Stateburg, South Carolina, 1770–1924, SCL; March 10, 1850, Record of the Claremont Parish, 1809–1866, Church of the Holy Cross, Stateburg, South Carolina, SCHS.

19. The wife of the free man of color Joseph J. Inglis was Henrietta McKensie Inglis. The couple sponsored the Holy Cross baptism of William Ellison, Jr.'s daughter Henrietta Inglis Ellison. On the same day, the Inglises' son John Mishaw was baptized, named for Mary Thomson Ellison's father, who was one of the sponsors of the baptism. March 10, 1850, Record of the Claremont Parish, 1809–1866, Church of the Holy Cross, Stateburg, South Carolina, SCHS.

20. April 12, 1847, Minutes of the Friendly Moralist Society, RSSL.

21. Ellison family graveyard, Stateburg; Josie Platt Parler, *The Past Blows Away: On the Road to Poinsett Park* (Sumter, S. C., 1939), 33; July 31, 1849, Register, Holy Cross Episcopal Church, 1808–1863, SCHS.

22. 1860 Agricultural Schedules, Sumter District, South Carolina, 21.

23. 1860 Slave Schedules, Sumter District, South Carolina, 181.

24. 1850 Slave Schedules, Sumter District, South Carolina, 911.

25. 1860 Slave Schedules, Sumter District, South Carolina, 181.

26. 1860 Agricultural Schedules, Sumter District, South Carolina, 21. In one 1858 transaction Henry received $484.86 for seven bales of cotton. Adams and Frost to "Mr Henry Ellison," November 13, 1858, Ellison Family Papers, SCL.

27. William Ellison, Jr., to Henry Ellison, March 26, 1857, Ellison Family Papers, SCL.

28. William Ellison to Henry Ellison, March 26, 1857, Ellison Family Papers, SCL.

29. Administration Papers, Estate of Reuben Ellison, Sumter District Estate Papers, Bundle 143, Package 4, SCDAH.

30. Dr. W. W. Anderson Account Book, 1844–1852, The Borough House Papers, SHC.

31. Inventory, Estate of Reuben Ellison, Sumter District Estate Papers, Bundle 143, Package 4, SCDAH.

32. Bills, June 15, 1851, July 1853, Moody Family Papers, SCL.

33. Bill, January 1851, Singleton Family Papers, SHC.

34. James M. Johnson to Henry Ellison, May 5, 14, 21, 1860, Ellison Family Papers, SCL.

35. James M. Johnson to Henry Ellison, May 14, 1860, Ellison Family Papers, SCL.

36. James M. Johnson to Henry Ellison, December 23, 1859, Ellison Family Papers, SCL.

37. James M. Johnson to Henry Ellison, January 20, 1860, Ellison Family Papers, SCL.

38. The earliest record of the "Ellison & Johnson" shoe business is an April 27, 1851, bill, Moody Family Papers, SCL. For itemized accounts, see the bills of March 10, 1854, March 10, 1856, and September 6, 1856, Moody Family Papers, SCL.

39. Wyatt-Brown, *Southern Honor,* 382.

40. See, for example, James M. Johnson to Henry Ellison, November 22, December 23, 1859; May 5, August 20, 1860, Ellison Family Papers, SCL.

41. Will of William Ellison, March 22, 1851, William Ellison Estate Papers, Sumter County Estate Papers, Box 151, Package 8, SCDAH.

42. Wyatt-Brown, *Southern Honor,* 117–18.

43. Will of William Ellison, March 22, 1851, William Ellison Estate Papers, Sumter County Estate Papers, Box 151, Package 8, SCDAH.

44. See Drew Gilpin Faust, *James Henry Hammond and the Old South: A Design for Mastery* (Baton Rouge and London, 1982). There is evidence that William Ellison may have tried to influence Henry Ellison's choice of a new bride after the death of his first wife. Although Henry's letters to James M. Johnson have not survived, Johnson referred to Henry's "frankness in unburdening yourself" about "disclosures" having something to do with his courtship. Johnson tried to bolster Henry's will by declaring, "I bid you God speed & would have you untrammelled in your choice when the Time comes. I hold it to be a personal affair, not subject to dictations. . . ." He advised Henry to "seek to find out whether the disposition & character of the object is adapted to your own before concentrating your affections." Whether Johnson's advice was prompted by William Ellison's pressure on Henry to marry some free woman of color that Henry had reservations about cannot be determined. Henry did not remarry until several years after his father's death. James M. Johnson to Henry Ellison, April 24, May 21, 30, 1860, Ellison Family Papers, SCL.

45. Sallie Clarke Manning to her mother, May 11, 1848, Williams-Chesnut-Manning Papers, SCL.

46. September 15, 1862, March 9, 1863, John F. Marszalek, ed., *The Diary of Miss Emma Holmes, 1861–1866* (Baton Rouge and London, 1979), 197, 236.

47. See, for example, James M. Johnson to Henry Ellison, December 23, 1860, Ellison Family Papers, SCL.

48. James M. Johnson to Henry Ellison, December 23, 1859, Ellison Family Papers, SCL.

49. Frances P. B. Holloway to "My Dear Minney," February 14, 1852, Ellison Family Papers, SCL.

50. Charleston *Courier,* October 14, 16–19, 1848; John F. Weston to Henry and Reuben Ellison, October 12, 1848, Ellison Family Papers, SCL.

51. Ibid.

52. Jacob Weston to Henry Ellison, June 25, 1855, Ellison Family Papers, SCL.

53. *List of Taxpayers of the City of Charleston, 1860* (Charleston, S. C., 1861), 316. The Ellisons commonly sent from the country small shipments of preserves, honey, grapes, melons, and potatoes to their city kin. Relatives in Charleston did what they could to assist the Ellisons, such as arranging for some peppers for Reuben and an order of leather for William Ellison.

54. William Ellison to Henry Elli-

son, March 27, 1857, Ellison Family Papers, SCL.

55. John B. Adger, *My Life and Times* (Richmond, Va., 1899), 21, 33, 36, 41.

56. William Ellison to Henry Ellison, March 27, 1857, Ellison Family Papers, SCL.

57. Samuel D. McGill, *Narrative of the Reminiscences in Williamsburg County* (Columbia, S. C., 1897), 97–98; 1860 Population Schedules, Sumter District, South Carolina, dwelling 1207.

58. S. Benenhaly to "Dear Sir," April 18, 1858, Ellison Family Papers, SCL.

59. Ellison family graveyard; January 6, 1850 [an obvious error, assuming the tombstone is correct], Record of the Claremont Parish, 1808–1866, Church of the Holy Cross, Stateburg, South Carolina, SCHS; Dr. W. W. Anderson Account Book, 1844–1852, The Borough House Papers, SHC.

60. Ellison family graveyard, Stateburg. Dr. Anderson visited Mary Elizabeth eight times in August 1852. Dr. W. W. Anderson Account Book, 1844–1852, The Borough House Papers.

61. Ellison family graveyard, Stateburg; June 4, 1853, Record of the Claremont Parish, 1808–1866, Church of the Holy Cross, Stateburg, South Carolina, SCHS. Between January 13 and 29, 1853, Dr. Anderson visited Mary Thomson almost daily. Dr. W. W. Anderson Account Book, 1853–1867, The Borough House Papers, SHC.

62. Ellison family graveyard, Stateburg, South Carolina.

63. December 7, 1853, Record of the Claremont Parish, 1808–1866, Church of the Holy Cross, Stateburg, South Carolina, SCHS. Between October 20 and December 6, 1853, Dr. Anderson came to see Harriett Ann almost daily, and on some days he came twice. On November 9, 1853, he attended her in "a case of difficult delivery." Dr. W. W. Anderson Account Book, 1853–1867, The Borough House Papers, SHC.

64. Ellison family graveyard, State-

burg, South Carolina; May 28, 1854, Record of the Claremont Parish, 1808–1866, Church of the Holy Cross, Stateburg, South Carolina, SCHS.

65. *Black River Watchman,* September 20, 1853.

66. The church has been carefully preserved and may be visited in Stateburg today.

67. September 27, 1852, Dr. W. W. Anderson Account Book, The Borough House Papers, SHC.

68. May 9, 1854, Dr. W. W. Anderson Account Book, The Borough House Papers, SHC.

69. April 18, 1857, February 13, 1860, Record of the Claremont Parish, 1808–1866, Church of the Holy Cross, Stateburg, South Carolina, SCHS.

70. 1860 Population Schedules, Sumter District, South Carolina, dwelling 695; March 25, 1858, February 13, 1860, June 22, 1860, Record of the Claremont Parish, 1808–1866, Church of the Holy Cross, Stateburg, South Carolina, SCHS; James M. Johnson to Henry Ellison, September 7, 1860, Ellison Family Papers, SCL.

71. 1850 Manufacturing Schedules, Sumter District, South Carolina, 636.

72. Ibid.

73. October–November 1860, Dr. W. W. Anderson Account Book, The Borough House Papers, SHC. We are indebted to Mrs. Mary Anderson for calling this item to our attention.

74. Sumter County Deeds of Conveyances, Book MM, 1846–48, 136–37.

75. 1850 Slave Schedules, Sumter County, South Carolina, 911.

76. Sale of Negroes, February 3, 1845, Thomas Sumter, Jr., Estate Papers, Sumter County Estate Papers, Bundle 132, Package 3, SCDAH.

77. 1860 Slave Schedules, Sumter County, South Carolina, 180.

78. Jacob Stroyer, *My Life in the South,* 3rd ed. (Salem, Mass., 1885), 31.

79. Charleston *Courier,* October 14, 1848; James D. Johnson to Henry

Ellison, December 28, 1858; James M. Johnson to Henry Ellison, February 25, 1860, Ellison Family Papers, SCL.

80. Isaac Lenoir to Gilbert & Fraser, December 22, 1853, Thomas Boone Fraser Papers, SCL.

81. Bill of sale, William W. Benbow and E. M. Anderson, March 2, 1857, Thomas Boone Fraser Papers, SCL.

82. Sumter County Deeds of Conveyances, Book NN, 1852, 481, 487, SCDAH.

83. 1860 Population Schedules, Sumter County, South Carolina, dwelling 694; 1860 Agricultural Schedules, Sumter County, South Carolina, 21.

84. In 1822 Ellison paid $375 for one acre; in 1835, $1,120 for 54½ acres; in 1838, $581.50 for 65½ acres; in 1839, $5,000 for 216 acres; in 1847, $270 for 22½ acres; and in 1852, $9,560 for 540 acres.

85. The total value of real estate owned by free persons of color in Sumter District in 1860 was $7,180; the mean real estate value was $100. The total value of personal estate owned by free persons of color in Sumter was $7,580; the mean personal property value was $105. Of course, these totals and means do not include the Ellisons. If the Ellisons had distributed their wealth equally to free colored people in Sumter District, each person would have been, on the average, five times richer. The data were compiled from the wealth reports in the 1860 census schedules of Sumter District.

86. The five districts in which the total wealth of all free people of color in the district exceeded that of the Ellisons were Barnwell, Beaufort, Georgetown, Charleston, and Richland.

87. Calculated from data in *Statistics of Mortality and Property in 1860,* 312–348.

88. *Agriculture in the United States in 1860* (Washington, D. C., 1864), 214, 237.

89. 1860 Population Schedules, Sumter District, South Carolina, dwelling 697; 1860 Slave Schedules,

Sumter District, South Carolina, 121.

90. 1860 Population Schedules, Sumter District, South Carolina, dwelling 748; 1860 Slave Schedules, Sumter District, South Carolina, 74.

91. The mean wealth of Southern men in 1860 was $3,978. Lee Soltow, *Men and Wealth in the United States, 1850–1870* (New Haven, 1975), 65.

92. Soltow, *Men and Wealth,* 134–35.

93. For data on free colored planters see Joseph Karl Menn, "The Large Slaveholders of the Deep South, 1860," Ph.D. diss., University of Texas, 1964, 209–10. See also Gary B. Mills, *The Forgotten People: Cane River's Creoles of Color* (Baton Rouge, 1977) and David O. Whitten, *Andrew Durnford: A Black Sugar Planter in Antebellum Louisiana* (Natchitoches, La., 1981).

94. We are indebted to Professor Loren Schweninger of the University of North Carolina, Greensboro, for this information from his forthcoming study of wealthy free Negroes in the nineteenth-century South.

95. Calculated from mortgage deeds, the totals are $16,906 for the purchase of 899½ acres.

96. At the very least, Ellison bought two slaves in the 1810s, two in the 1820s, sixteen in the 1830s, five in the 1840s, and ten in the 1850s.

97. 1850 Manufacturing Schedules, Sumter County, South Carolina, 63.

98. 1860 Agricultural Schedules, Sumter County, South Carolina, 21.

99. William Ellison to Henry Ellison, March 26, 1857, Ellison Family Papers, SCL. Adams and Frost advertised regularly in the Sumter District newspapers. See, for example, *Black River Watchman,* March 17, 1854.

100. 1860 Agricultural Schedules, Sumter County, South Carolina, 21.

101. Appraisal and Inventory, William Ellison Estate Papers, Sumter County Estate Papers, Box 151, Package 8, SCDAH.

102. Data on the age and sex of Elli-

son's slaves are summarized in table 2 in the Appendix.

103. Codicil, May 6, 1861, Will of William Ellison, William Ellison Estate Papers, Sumter County Estate Papers, Box 151, Package 8, SCDAH.

104. Robert William Fogel and Stanley L. Engerman, *Time on the Cross: The Economics of American Negro Slavery* (Boston and Toronto, 1974), 83.

105. 1860 Slave Schedules, Sumter County, South Carolina, 180.

106. Ibid, 181.

107. Thomas Jefferson wrote, "I consider the labor of a breeding woman as no object, and that a child raised every 2 years is of more profit than the crop of the best laboring man." He advised his manager "to inculcate upon the overseers that it is not their labor, but their increase which is the first consideration with us." Jefferson to Joel Yancey, January 17, 1819, Edwin M. Betts, ed., *Thomas Jefferson's Farm Book: With Commentary and Relevant Extracts from Other Writings* (Princeton, N. J., 1953), 43.

108. The most comprehensive statement of the complexities of paternalism is Eugene D. Genovese, *Roll, Jordan, Roll: The World the Slaveholders Made* (New York, 1974). For a succinct analysis of the rise of paternalism in the nineteenth-century South, see Willie Lee Rose, *Slavery and Freedom,* ed. William W. Freehling (New York and Oxford, 1982), 18–36.

109. Rev. I. E. Lowery, *Life on the Old Plantation in Ante-Bellum Days or a Story Based on Facts* (Columbia, S. C., 1911), 42.

110. J. K. Douglas to John B. Miller, February 20, 1848, Miller-Furman-Dabbs Family Papers, SCL. Some planters also sought to buy families rather than individuals. In 1825 Columbia planter Benjamin Franklin Taylor informed Richard Singleton that he would like to purchase fifteen of his slaves, adding, "I would prefer having them in families & young & the larger portion of them workers." Benjamin Frank-

lin Taylor to Richard Singleton, November 29, 1825, Singleton Family Papers, SCL.

111. Gregorie, *History of Sumter County,* 135. While doing research on black slaveholders early in this century, Calvin Dill Wilson discovered further evidence of William Ellison's reputation for harshness. "Dr. Hodges, of the Cincinnati Public Library, informed me that some years ago there was pointed out to him in Stateburg, South Carolina, a house, with iron-barred windows, in which he was told, a negro blacksmith, who had been noted for cruelty to his slaves, had been used to confine his blacks." It is difficult to know how much to credit these stories. Windows with iron bars are subject to more than one interpretation. They might have kept slaves out of a storehouse rather than (or in addition to) in a jail. Jacob Stroyer, a young slave in the 1850s on Mathew Singleton's plantation a few miles south of Stateburg, remembered that there was a "dungeon" under the overseer's house where his master punished recalcitrant slaves. Wilson, "Black Masters: A Side-Light on Slavery," *North American Review* 171 (November 1905), 688; Stroyer, *My Life in the South,* 74.

112. January 15, 1841, Natalie Delage Sumter Diary, SCL.

113. Jacob Stroyer remembered that as a boy on Mathew Singleton's plantation he wore only an osnaburg linen shirt during the summer, ate hard clabber and corn flour mush (except on Sundays when his parents managed to provide something better) and regularly received whippings from the white groom he assisted. Stroyer, *My Life in the South,* 10, 12, 27.

114. Sumter, *Dedicated to the Past,* 3–4.

115. 1850 and 1860 Population and Slave Schedules, Sumter District, South Carolina.

116. *Population of the United States in 1860,* 452.

117. Gregorie, *History of Sumter County,* 135. Our search failed to

locate a single advertisement Ellison placed for a runaway slave. Thomas Sumter claimed that "whenever any of their [the Ellisons'] slaves were rebellious, which was to be expected (though seldom occurring) they [the Ellisons] were promptly aided by some of their white friends in the insuring of order and obedience." Sumter, *Stateburg and Its People,* 31.
118. Andrews, *The Life and Adventures of Capt. Robert W. Andrews,* 25–26.
119. James Usher to Richard Singleton, April 19, 1822, Singleton Family Papers, SCL. One former Sumter District slave remembered that in the 1850s one local white man had a full-time job as a slave catcher. Planters used his services, but they worried that his pack of dogs would maim or kill their runaways. Stroyer, *My Life in the South,* 50.
120. Samuel D. McGill, *Narrative of Reminiscences in Williamsburg County,* 119.
121. Joshua Reynolds to John B. Miller, December 24, 1831, Miller-Furman-Dabbs Family Papers, SCL.
122. Tavern Account Book, Stateburg, S. C., April–May, 1837, The Borough House Papers, SHC. We are indebted to Mrs. Mary Anderson for bringing this item to our attention.
123. Dr. W. W. Anderson Account Books, The Borough House, SHC. These remarkable medical records indicate that from February 16, 1824, when Dr. Anderson extracted William Ellison's tooth, to October 4, 1902, when Dr. Anderson's son, also named Dr. W. W. Anderson, prescribed medicine for William Ellison's great-grandson, Frederick, the doctors Anderson continuously acted as the physicians of the Ellisons and their dependents.
124. Bill, January 20, 1833–January 7, 1834, Hampton Family Papers, SCL.
125. January 2–October, 1844, Dr. W. W. Anderson Account Book, The Borough House Papers, SHC.
126. While William Ellison saw to

the baptism of only six of his slaves, his neighbor Dr. Anderson had six of his slaves baptized in a single year. Holy Cross Episcopal Church Register, 1808–1863, SCHS.
127. In 1831 Rev. Converse reported, "Regular instruction was given to the colored people." Quoted in Albert Sidney Thomas, *A Historical Account of the Protestant Episcopal Church in South Carolina, 1820–1957* (Columbia, S. C., 1957), 431.
128. William Ellison to Henry Ellison, March 26, 1857, Ellison Family Papers, SCL.
129. James D. Johnson to Henry Ellison, December 28, 1858, Ellison Family Papers, SCL.
130. James M. Johnson to Henry Ellison, February 25, 1860, Ellison Family Papers, SCL.
131. James M. Johnson to Henry Ellison, December 23, 1860, Ellison Family Papers, SCL.
132. James M. Johnson to Henry Ellison, January 20, 1860, Ellison Family Papers, SCL.
133. James M. Johnson to Henry Ellison, December 23, 1859, Ellison Family Papers, SCL.
134. Codicil, May 6, 1861, Will of William Ellison, William Ellison Estate Papers, Sumter County Estate Papers, Box 151, Package 8, SCDAH.
135. See Genovese, *Roll, Jordan, Roll,* 84–85. For a different view, see James Oakes, *The Ruling Race: A History of American Slaveholders* (New York, 1982).
136. Joel Williamson emphasizes the difference between white attitudes toward mulattoes in the Upper South and the Lower South. Considered dissolute and contrary in the Upper South, mulattoes were favored and appreciated in the Lower South, where, he argues, they were treated as a third class, an intermediate element between white and black, slave and free. Williamson, *New People: Miscegenation and Mulattoes in the United States* (New York, 1980), 2–3, 14–23. See also Robert Brent Toplin, "Between Black and White: Attitudes toward Southern Mulattoes, 1830–1861,"

Journal of Southern History 45 (May 1979), 192.

137. Michael P. Johnson and James L. Roark, " 'A Middle Ground': Free Mulattoes and the Friendly Moralist Society of Antebellum Charleston," *Southern Studies* 21 (Fall 1982), 246–65.

138. See, for example, Michael Wayne, *The Reshaping of Plantation Society: The Natchez District, 1860–1880* (Baton Rouge and London, 1982), 24–26.

139. See Drew Gilpin Faust, ed., *The Ideology of Slavery: Proslavery Thought in the Antebellum South, 1830–1860* (Baton Rouge and London, 1981).

140. A diagram of the seating in Holy Cross in 1844 is reproduced among the illustrations in this book. It was obtained from Minutes and Records of the Vestry and Wardens of the Church of the Holy Cross, Statesburg, South Carolina, 1770–1924, SCL.

141. A. L. Converse to John B. Miller, January 25, 1837, Miller-Furman-Dabbs Papers, SCL.

142. December 12, 1847, Record of the Claremont Parish, 1808–1860, Church of the Holy Cross, Statesburg, South Carolina, SCHS.

143. Gregorie, *Thomas Sumter,* 264–65; Gregorie, *History of Sumter County,* 467–70; Sumter, *Dedicated to the Past,* 38, 69–70; Wikramanayake, *A World in Shadow,* 20–21.

144. Brewton Berry, *Almost White* (New York and London, 1963), 27–40; Calvin Trillin, "U. S. Journal: Sumter County, S. C.," *New Yorker,* March 8, 1969, 104–110.

145. S. Benenhaly to "Dear Sir," April 18, 1858, Ellison Family Papers, SCL; 1850 Population Schedules, Sumter District, South Carolina, dwellings 1207, 1308, 1311, 1315.

146. Ibid.

147. Frances P. B. Holloway to "My Dear Minney," February 14, 1852, Ellison Family Papers, SCL.

148. Brewton Berry observed that among the Turks "Marriage to a Negro has always been an unpardonable sin." Berry, *Almost White,*

187. Thomas Sumter claimed that, despite their dark skins, the Turks never made alliances with "colored people." Sumter, *Dedicated to the Past,* 70.

149. *John Wilson Buckner v. Henry Ellison and William Ellison,* February 18, 1871, William Ellison Estate Papers, Sumter County Estate Papers, Box 151, Package 8, SCDAH.

150. S. Benenhaly to "Dear Sir," April 18, 1858, Ellison Family Papers, SCL; September 26, 1883, Estate of Henry Ellison, Sumter County Estate Papers, Bundle 176, Package 35, SCDAH.

151. Benson J. Lossing, *Eminent Americans: Comprising Brief Biographies of . . . Men and Women Who Have Made American History* (New York, 1881), 236.

152. 1860 Population Schedules, Jefferson County, Mississippi, dwelling 575.

153. *Saturday Evening Post,* April 19, 1856.

154. Sumter *Watchman,* May 7, 1856. We are indebted to Carol Brown McShane, *Saturday Evening Post* archivist, for checking the extant records.

155. 1860 Population Schedules, Jefferson County, Mississippi, dwelling 575.

156. June 2, 1823, Sumter County Guardianships of Free Blacks, 1823–1842, Sumter County Historical Society, Sumter, S. C.

157. Gregorie, *History of Sumter County,* 236–39.

158. Woodward, ed., *Mary Chesnut's Civil War,* 77.

159. Vincent Harding, *There is a River: The Black Struggle for Freedom in America* (New York and London, 1981).

160. Gregorie, *History of Sumter County,* 136.

161. Inventory, Reuben Ellison Estate Papers, Sumter County Estate Papers, Bundle 143, Package 4, SCDAH.

162. 1860 Slave Schedules, Sumter District, South Carolina, 181.

163. Record of the Claremont Parish, 1809–1866, Church of the Holy

Cross, Stateburg, South Carolina, SCHS.

164. Gregorie, *History of Sumter County*, 136.

165. Record of the Claremont Parish, 1809–1866, Church of the Holy Cross, Stateburg, South Carolina, SCHS.

166. Will of William Ellison, William Ellison Estate Papers, Sumter County Estate Papers, Box 151, Package 8, SCDAH.

167. Ellison family graveyard, Stateburg, South Carolina.

CHAPTER FIVE

1. 1850 Population Schedules, Charleston, South Carolina, Ward 4, dwelling 414; 1860 Population Schedules, Charleston, South Carolina, Ward 4, dwelling 439; Charleston Free Negro Tax Books, 1816–1835, SCDAH.

2. 1810 Census Schedules, Sumter, South Carolina, 218, 222.

3. On October 19, 1871, an account was opened for James M. Johnson in the Freedman's Bank of Charleston by Richard E. Dereef. Records of the account give Charleston as Johnson's birthplace. However, the account card was not signed by Johnson, who was in Stateburg, and it may be in error. Registers of Signatures of Depositors in Branches of the Freedman's Savings and Trust Company, 1865–1874, National Archives Microcopy 816, Roll 23, Account numbers 8909, 9041, 9734.

4. 1830 Census Schedules, Charleston, South Carolina, Ward 4, 178.

5. Charleston Free Negro Tax Book, undated [before 1831], and subsequent years, SCDAH.

6. 1830 Census Schedules, Charleston, South Carolina, Ward 4, 178. See also 1840 Census Schedules, Charleston, South Carolina, Ward 4, 17.

7. George M. Keils to James M. and Charles J. Johnson, October 20, 1834, Conveyances, Book H10, 400; Thomas B. Elliot to Charles D. Carr, Trustee, January 31, 1837, Con-

veyances, Book Q10, 55, Charleston County Courthouse. Johnson evidently also owned an interest in a small lot on Charleston Neck as early as 1833 and possibly 1829. See James D. Johnson to Sarah Pencil, Quit Claim, December 6, 1848, Conveyances, Book A12, 476.

8. John Hunter to James D. Johnson, January 18, 1836; Johnson to Hunter, Mortgage, July 14, 1836, Conveyances, Book O10, 361, Charleston County Courthouse.

9. Richard E. Dereef to James D. Johnson, January 29, 1839; Johnson to Dereef, Mortgage, January 30, 1839, Conveyances, Book Z10, 87, Charleston County Courthouse.

10. Bill of Sale, Margaret J. and Catharine A. Pressly to James D. Johnson, August 18, 1834, Secretary of State, Recorded Instruments, Miscellaneous Records, Main Series, Bills of Sales Volumes, 1773–1840, SCDAH.

11. Bill of Sale, Matthew Muggridge to James D. Johnson, May 9, 1836, Secretary of State, Recorded Instruments, Miscellaneous Records, Main Series, Bills of Sales Volumes, 1773–1840, SCDAH.

12. Bill of Sales, Sarah G. Fuller to James D. Johnson, June 8, 1837, Secretary of State, Recorded Instruments, Miscellaneous Records, Main Series, Bills of Sales Volumes, 1773–1840, SCDAH.

13. "Taxes on House and Lot owned by Estate of Wm Ellison and J. D. Johnson," March 13, 1861, William Ellison Estate Papers, Sumter County Estate Papers, Box 151, Package 8, SCDAH.

14. James D. Johnson to Richard Lucas, July 31, 1846, Conveyances, Book X11, 48, Charleston County Courthouse.

15. James D. Johnson to James M. Howe, September 10, 1847, Conveyances, Book Z11, 226, Charleston County Courthouse.

16. Bill of Sale, James D. Johnson to Alexander H. Brown, April 5, 1842, June 8, 1837, Secretary of State, Recorded Instruments, Miscellaneous Records, Main Series, Bills of Sales Volumes, 1773–1840,

SCDAH; Bill of Sale, James D. Johnson to Edwin C. Steete, March 22, 1850, Secretary of State, Recorded Instruments, Bills of Sale, 1843–1872, SCDAH.

17. Francis Quinton McHough to James D. Johnson, November 15, 1850, Conveyances, Charleston County Courthouse. In 1856 Johnson, Richard E. Dereef, and William McKinlay jointly purchased several lots on Charleston Neck for $860. See Master in Equity to Dereef, McKinlay, and Johnson, February 26, 1856, Conveyances, Book K13, 195, Charleston County Courthouse.

18. *List of the Taxpayers of the City of Charleston for 1860* (Charleston, S. C., 1861), 324.

19. The 1830 and 1840 manuscript census schedules show that Johnson had two young free women of color in his household. Evidence cited below suggests that one of those women was his daughter Jane. The manuscript 1850 census schedules show that Johnson had a young woman named Humphretta Johnson in his household, apparently his daughter.

20. Evidence that Charley married in 1843 is in the Charleston Free Negro Tax Book (SCDAH) for that year, where Sarah first appeared in Johnson's household. Subsequent Free Negro Tax Books document Charley's continued residence with his parents. That Sarah was Johnson's wife is indicated by the Grace Church Parish Register (Grace Episcopal Church, Charleston), which records that they were the parents of an infant baptized April 4, 1851.

21. Grace Episcopal Church Parish Register, Grace Church, Charleston.

22. Ibid.

23. Holy Cross Episcopal Church Record, 1808–1863, Stateburg, South Carolina, SCHS; James M. Johnson to Henry Ellison, September 7, 1860; James D. Johnson to Henry Ellison, September 16, 1860, Ellison Family Papers, SCL.

24. Frederick A. Ford, *Census of the*

City of Charleston, South Carolina, For the Year 1861 (Charleston, S. C., 1861), 71; S. Benenhaly to "Dear Sir," April 18, 1858; James M. Johnson to Henry Ellison, December 23, 1859, Ellison Family Papers, SCL.

25. William Ellison, Jr., to Henry Ellison, March 26, 1857, Ellison Family Papers, SCL.

26. James D. Johnson to Henry Ellison, December 28, 1858, Ellison Family Papers, SCL.

27. Ibid.

28. William Ellison, Jr., to Henry Ellison, March 26, 1857; James D. Johnson to Henry Ellison, December 28, 1858, Ellison Family Papers, SCL.

29. James D. Johnson to Henry Ellison, December 28, 1858, Ellison Family Papers, SCL.

30. James D. Johnson to Henry Ellison, December 23, 1859; James M. Johnson to Henry Ellison, January 9, 1860, Ellison Family Papers, SCL.

31. James M. Johnson to Henry Ellison, December 23, 1859, Ellison Family Papers, SCL.

32. Ibid.

33. "Petition of Sundry Citizens of York District praying that all free persons of colour may be sold into slavery," undated, Slavery Petitions, General Assembly Petitions, SCDAH. Our belief that the petition was made in 1859 is based on the enslavement legislation introduced by the representative of York District, Edward Moore, discussed below.

34. "Sumter County petition against free persons of color," undated, Slavery Petitions, General Assembly Petitions, SCDAH. Again, we believe the proper date of the petition is 1859, based on the request that free Negroes be compelled to leave the state or be made slaves.

35. "Petition of Charles M. Pelot and Sundry Citizens of Abbeville praying relief upon the subject of free negroes," undated, Slavery Petitions, General Assembly Petitions, SCDAH.

36. "Petition of certain citizens of St. Helena Parish praying that the

legislature will consider the propriety of removing free persons of colour from the state," undated [ca. 1831–32], Slavery Petitions, General Assembly Petitions, SCDAH.

37. Thomas Jefferson, "Notes on Virginia" (1784) in *The Life and Selected Writings of Thomas Jefferson,* ed. Adrienne Koch and William Peden (New York, 1944), 256.

38. Ibid. For a subtle analysis of Jefferson's views of Afro-Americans, see Winthrop D. Jordan, *White Over Black: American Attitudes Toward the Negro, 1550–1812* (Chapel Hill, 1968), 429–81.

39. See George M. Fredrickson, *The Black Image in the White Mind: The Debate on Afro-American Character and Destiny, 1817–1914* (New York, 1971), 6–21; Vincent Harding, *There Is A River: The Black Struggle for Freedom in America* (New York and London, 1981), 66, 87, 118–19, 131, 184; Jane H. Pease and William H. Pease, *They Who Would Be Free: Blacks' Search for Freedom, 1830–1861* (New York, 1974), 20–23; Sheldon Harris, *Paul Cuffe: Black America and the African Return* (New York, 1972); P. J. Staudenraus, *The African Colonization Movement, 1816–1865* (New York, 1961).

40. Fredrickson, *Black Image in the White Mind,* 27–42; Leon F. Litwack, *North of Slavery: The Negro in the Free States, 1790–1860* (Chicago, 1961), 267–79.

41. Fredrickson, *Black Image in the White Mind,* 130–64; Eric Foner, *Free Soil, Free Labor, Free Men: The Ideology of the Republican Party before the Civil War* (New York and London, 1970), 261–300; C. Vann Woodward, *American Counterpoint: Slavery and Racism in the North-South Dialogue* (Boston, 1971), 140–62.

42. Litwack, *North of Slavery,* 66–74.

43. Roy P. Basler, ed., *The Collected Works of Abraham Lincoln,* 8 vols. (New Brunswick, N. J., 1953), V, 372.

44. Fredrickson, *Black Image in the White Mind,* 43–70; Drew Gilpin Faust, ed., *The Ideology of Slavery:*

Proslavery Thought in the Antebellum South, 1830–1860 (Baton Rouge and London, 1981).

45. George Fitzhugh, "What Shall Be Done With the Free Negroes; Essays Written for the Fredricksburg *Recorder,*" (Fredricksburg, Va., 1851), 6.

46. For the definitive work, see Don E. Fehrenbacher, *The Dred Scott Case: Its Significance in American Law and Politics* (New York, 1978).

47. Ibid., 341.

48. Basler, ed., *Works of Abraham Lincoln,* "Speech of June 26, 1857," II, 404.

49. Ira Berlin, *Slaves Without Masters: The Free Negro in the Antebellum South* (New York, 1974), 372–74.

50. See Stephen B. Oates, *To Purge This Land With Blood: A Biography of John Brown* (New York, 1970); David M. Potter, *The Impending Crisis, 1848–1861,* completed and edited by Don E. Fehrenbacher (New York and other cities, 1976), 356–84; Benjamin Quarles, *Allies for Freedom: Blacks and John Brown* (New York, 1967).

51. Berlin, *Slaves Without Masters,* 374–75.

52. "Petition of William Bass, a Free Person of Color, Praying to become a Slave," December 14, 1859, Charleston *Courier,* December 20, 1859. See also "Petition of Lucy Andrews, a free person of color praying to be permitted to go into slavery," Slavery Petitions, General Assembly Petitions, SCDAH; Marina Wikramanayake, *A World in Shadow: The Free Black in Antebellum South Carolina* (Columbia, S. C., 1973), 183.

53. Report of the Committee on the Colored Population, December 3, 1859, Slavery Petitions, General Assembly Petitions, SCDAH.

54. Charleston *Courier,* December 15, 16, 1859.

55. Charleston *Courier,* December 15, 1859.

56. Ibid.

57. Charleston *Courier,* December 16, 1859. Memminger's memory of

the Vesey conspiracy must have been vivid. In 1807, at the age of four, Memminger was placed in the Charleston Orphan House, after the death of his mother, who had moved with him to the city from Germany where he had been born. Memminger came to the attention of the prominent Charleston politician Thomas Bennett and in 1814 was taken into Bennett's household and treated as one of his children. Memminger attended South Carolina College between 1815 and 1819, then studied law in Charleston with a relative of Bennett's. As a young law student in 1822, he must have been near the center of discussions of the Vesey threat. Thomas Bennett was the governor of the state at that time and was residing in Charleston. Two of his slaves, Ned and Rolla, were among Vesey's lieutenants. See the biographical sketch in Christopher Gustavus Memminger Papers, SHC. On Vesey and Bennett, see Lionel H. Kennedy and Thomas Parker, *An Official Report of the Trials of Sundry Negroes, Charged with an Attempt to Raise an Insurrection in the State of South Carolina* (Charleston, S. C., 1822).

58. The Committee on the Colored Population recommended a $150 pension, but the full legislature was more generous. Petition asking for greater state bounty for Peter Desverney, 1857; Report of the Committee on Military and Pensions, General Assembly Petitions, SCDAH; Charleston *Courier,* December 9, 1857.

59. Charleston *Courier,* December 16, 1859.

60. Charleston *Courier,* December 15, 1859; *Reports and Resolutions of the General Assembly of South Carolina* (Columbia, S. C., 1859), 161, 163, 179, 211.

61. Charleston *Mercury,* December 4, 1835; Charleston *Courier,* December 17, 1835.

62. Charleston *Mercury,* December 10, 1835.

63. Charleston *Courier,* December 9, 1835. See, however, "The Slave

Law of 1834," Charleston *Courier,* October 10, 1835; "South Carolina Association," Charleston *Courier,* October 24, 1835.

64. Charleston *Courier,* December 9, 1835.

65. Charleston *Courier,* December 15, 1859.

66. James M. Johnson to Henry Ellison, January 9, 1860, Ellison Family Papers, SCL.

67. Ibid.

68. Grace Church Parish Register, Grace Episcopal Church, Charleston. For records of Memminger's purchase of a pew in Grace Episcopal Church in 1852, see Christopher Gustavus Memminger Papers, SHC.

69. Ford, *Census of Charleston, 1861,* 123; Charleston Free Negro Tax Books, 1827–1857, SCDAH.

70. 1860 Population Schedules, Charleston, South Carolina, Ward 5, dwelling 19; *List of the Taxpayers of Charleston, 1860,* 324; Minutes of the Brown Fellowship Society, January 7, 1869–July 6, 1911, RSSL.

71. James M. Johnson to Henry Ellison, January 9, 1860, Ellison Family Papers, SCL.

72. Charleston *Mercury,* October 8, 1858; Charleston *Courier,* October 11, 1858.

73. Charleston *Courier,* October 11, 1858.

74. "Petition of Mechanics and Workingmen of the City of Charleston Praying more effectual legislation for the prevention of slaves hiring out their own time and for other purposes," 1858; "The Petition of the South Carolina Mechanics' Association of Charleston . . ." 1858, Slavery Petitions, General Assembly Petitions, SCDAH; Presentment of the Grand Jury, Charleston District, October Term, 1858; Charleston *Courier,* November 15, 1858; *Report of the Committee on Colored Population . . . in reference to the Enactment of Laws Preventing Negroes From Hiring Out Their Own Time &c.* (Columbia, S. C., 1858).

75. See Robert S. Starobin, *Industrial Slavery in the Old South* (New

York and London, 1970), 128–37; Richard C. Wade, *Slavery in the Cities: The South, 1820–1860* (New York and London, 1964), 38–54; Leonard Price Stavisky, "The Negro Artisan in the South Atlantic States, 1800–1860: A Study of Status and Economic Opportunity with Special Reference to Charleston," Ph.D. diss., Columbia University, 1958, 84–150; Howell M. Henry, *The Police Control of the Slave in South Carolina* (Emory, Va., 1914).

76. Alexander Edwards, ed., *Ordinances of the City Council of Charleston . . . Passed Since the Incorporation of the City* (Charleston, 1802), 493–95.

77. George B. Eckhard, ed., *A Digest of the Ordinances of the City Council of Charleston From the Year 1783 to October 1844 . . .* (Charleston, S. C., 1844), 21–23. Charleston *Courier*, February 22, March 30, 1843.

78. A badge for a seller of fruits and cakes was five dollars; for a fisherman, four dollars; and for a fisherwoman, a house servant, or a washerwoman, two dollars. Ibid. These rates did not change during the antebellum years. See, for example, Charleston *Mercury*, December 31, 1860.

79. Eckhard, ed., *Digest of the Ordinances of Charleston, 1783–1844*, 21–23.

80. Edwards, ed., *Ordinances of Charleston (1802)*, 65–68.

81. *Report of the Committee on the Colored Population* (Columbia, S. C., 1858), 3.

82. See Christopher Silver, "A New Look at Old South Urbanization: The Irish Worker in Charleston, South Carolina, 1840–1860," *South Atlantic Urban Studies* 3 (1979), 141–72.

83. See Gavin Wright, *The Political Economy of the Cotton South: Households, Markets, and Wealth in the Nineteenth Century* (New York, 1978); Claudia Goldin, *Urban Slavery in the South, 1820–1860* (Chicago, 1976).

84. For the population of Charleston, 1790–1860, see table 3 in the Appendix.

85. John William DeForest to Andrew DeForest, November 9, 1855, John William DeForest Papers, Beinecke Rare Book and Manuscript Room, Yale University. We are indebted to Judith A. Schiff for making this material available to us.

86. Charleston *Courier*, July 14, 1859. In November 1859, Charleston hosted the South Carolina Institute Fair, which featured products manufactured by Southern artisans. See Charleston *Mercury*, November 15, 17, 19, 1859.

87. Charleston *Mercury*, February 2, March 17, 1858.

88. In addition, the legislature had just considered a bill to require the magistrates of each district to report all violators of the slave-hiring law at each term of the magistrate's court, along with the names of witnesses who could prove violations. A magistrate who failed to comply would have been subject to an indictment for a misdemeanor. The bill, prompted by a complaint of the Charleston Grand Jury about slaves hiring their own time, was tabled by a close vote (36 to 32). Charleston *Courier*, December 9, 1857.

89. Charleston *Mercury*, May 12, 1858.

90. The *Mercury* published an official weekly tabulation of yellow fever deaths during the epidemic. This analysis has been compiled from these reports between August 1 and November 13.

91. Charleston *Mercury*, September 9, 1858.

92. Charleston *Mercury*, December 6, 1858; Caroline Banks Black, "Aspects of the History of Yellow Fever Epidemics in Charleston, South Carolina," M. A. thesis, Duke University, 1943, 15–16, 60.

93. Charleston *Courier*, September 18, 1858.

94. Again, these figures were compiled from the weekly death reports in the *Mercury* between August 1 and November 13, 1858. See also, Todd L. Savitt, *Medicine and Slavery: The Diseases and Health Care of Blacks in Antebellum Virginia*

(Urbana, Ill., and other cities, 1978), 240–46.

95. Charleston *Mercury,* October 8, 1858.

96. For the names, see "Petition of Mechanics and Workingmen of the City of Charleston Praying more effectual Legislation for the prevention of slaves hiring out their own time and for other purposes," 1858, Slavery Petitions, General Assembly Petitions, SCDAH. The names of 95 of the 163 signers were listed in the city directory, the tax list, or the manuscript schedules of the federal census. A margin of error always exists when matching names on one list with those on another. When we located a person with the same surname and the same given name or first initial as a petition signer, we assumed the names matched. In a few cases there were several persons with the same name, but the occupational variation among the individuals was typically small.

97. More than a quarter of Charleston whites owned $5,000 or more; at the other extreme, 52 percent were propertyless. Michael P. Johnson, "Wealth and Class in Charleston in 1860," in Walter J. Fraser, Jr., and Winfred B. Moore, Jr., eds., *From the Old South to the New: Essays on the Transitional South* (Westport, Conn., and London, 1981), 65–80.

98. Ibid., 73.

99. *Report of the Committee on Colored Population;* Charleston *Mercury,* December 15, 1858.

100. *Report of the Committee on Colored Population.*

101. Ibid.

102. Ibid.

103. Charleston *Courier,* January 19, 1860.

104. Charleston *Courier,* March 1, 1860.

105. Ibid.

106. Charleston *Courier,* November 15, 1858.

107. "The Petition of the South Carolina Mechanics' Association of Charleston praying the passage of an Act more effectually to prevent slaves from hiring their own time

and for other purposes," Slavery Petitions, 1830–1859, Legislative Papers, SCDAH.

108. This statement is necessarily somewhat speculative, since the city treasurer's records of slave badge sales, which list the occupation of each slave with a badge, have not survived.

109. The exact figure is 69 percent. The data for this analysis of free Afro-American occupations were collected from the manuscript schedules of the 1860 federal census of the city of Charleston. Every free person of color who had an occupation listed in the census is included in this study. For a summary, see table 5 in the Appendix.

110. The exact percentage is 19.

111. See Leonard P. Curry, *The Free Black in Urban America, 1800–1850: The Shadow of the Dream* (Chicago and London, 1981), 258–66.

112. For a summary of the occupations of free Afro-American women in 1860, see table 5 in the Appendix.

113. The occupations of each free person of color in 1850 were collected from the manuscript schedules of the 1850 federal census. The comparison between 1850 and 1860 is necessarily limited to the occupations of men, since the 1850 census in Charleston did not list occupations of women. For a summary of the 1850 and 1860 occupational data, see table 5 in the Appendix.

114. The capitation tax was graduated by sex and age. Free Afro-American women between eighteen and fifty paid five dollars each; those between fourteen and eighteen, three dollars; and those under fourteen or over fifty were not taxed. Men between sixteen and twenty-one paid five dollars, those between twenty-one and sixty paid ten dollars, and those under sixteen or over sixty were exempt. See, for example, Charleston *Courier,* October 4, 1859.

115. The number of arrests for violations of the capitation tax and slave badge laws in each month between June 1858 and February 1861 was compiled from the monthly report

of the Chief of Police to the Mayor, contained in the proceedings of the city council published in the Charleston *Courier* toward the end of each month. The data are summarized in table 4 in the Appendix.

116. Vigilance to Editor, Charleston *Mercury,* November 11, 1859.

117. Charleston *Courier,* December 13, 1859.

118. Some of the Safety Committee to the Public, Charleston *Courier,* December 15, 1859.

119. A Vigilant Fireman to Editor, Charleston *Courier,* December 10, 15, 1859; Spectator to Editor, Charleston *Courier,* December 24, 1859; Charleston *Mercury,* November 2, 1859.

120. A Slaveholder to Editor, Charleston *Mercury,* October 25, 1859.

121. Another Slaveholder to Editor, Charleston *Mercury,* October 26, 1859.

122. A Resident and Native to Editor, Charleston *Mercury,* October 27, 1859. For similar sentiments, see also Many Voters to the Hon. Charles Macbeth and the Hon. John E. Carew, Charleston *Mercury,* October 21, 1859; Another Voter to Editor, Charleston *Courier,* October 26, 1859; Another Slaveholder to Editor, Charleston *Mercury,* October 27, 1859; Tout Bien Ou Rien to Editor, Charleston *Courier,* November 7, 1859; Charleston to Editor, Charleston *Courier,* November 7, 1859; A Mechanic to the City Council, Charleston *Courier,* November 29, 1859.

123. Charleston *Courier,* December 22, 1859.

124. Charleston *Courier,* January 5, 1860.

125. Charleston *Courier,* January 13, 1860.

126. Sumter *Watchman,* November 29, 1859.

127. Sumter *Watchman,* December 24, 1859.

128. Alfred Huger to Henry D. Lesesne, December 8, 1858, Alfred Huger Letterpress Books, 1853–1863, WRPL.

129. Ibid.

130. Alfred Huger to Robert Gourdin, August 23, 1859, Alfred Huger Letterpress Books, 1853–1863, WRPL.

131. Alfred Huger to W. T. Seale, August 8, 1854, Alfred Huger Letterpress Books, 1853–1863, WRPL.

132. Huger's supervision of Ned and George was so loose that he lost track of them for weeks at a time. Alfred Huger to Theodore Lewis Gourdin, June 21, 1858, Alfred Huger Letterpress Books, 1853–1863, WRPL.

133. Alfred Huger to Henry D. Lesesne, December 8, 1858, Alfred Huger Letterpress Books, 1853–1863, WRPL.

134. Ibid.

135. James M. Johnson to Henry Ellison, December 23, 1859, Ellison Family Papers, SCL.

CHAPTER SIX

1. Allan Nevins, *The Emergence of Lincoln: Volume II, Prologue to Civil War, 1859–1861* (New York and London, 1950), 203–28; Roy Franklin Nichols, *The Disruption of American Democracy* (New York, 1948), 18–32, 288–307; David M. Potter, *The Impending Crisis, 1848–1861,* completed and edited by Don E. Fehrenbacher (New York and other cities, 1976), 259–64, 407–12.

2. Charleston *Courier,* April 11, 1860; Laylon Wayne Jordan, "Police Power and Public Safety in Antebellum Charleston: The Emergence of a New Police, 1800–1860," *South Atlantic Urban Studies* 3 (1979), 122–40; New York *Times,* April 27, 1860.

3. James M. Johnson to Henry Ellison, April 24, 1860, Ellison Family Papers, SCL.

4. James M. Johnson to Henry Ellison, April 24, 28, 1860, Ellison Family Papers, SCL; Charleston *Mercury,* April 23, 1860.

5. Ibid.; Charleston *Mercury,* April 28, 1860.

6. James M. Johnson to Henry Ellison, April 28, 1860, Ellison Family Papers, SCL.

7. Ibid.; E. Horace Fitchett, "The Free Negro in Charleston, South Carolina," Ph.D. diss., University of Chicago, 1950, 48; Charleston Free Negro Tax Books, 1816–1848, 1850, SCDAH.

8. Between April and July 1860, 144 slaves were arrested for badge law violations, compared to 78 between June 1858 and March 1860. Nearly two-thirds (64 percent) of those arrested in 1860 were slave women, a reflection of their predominance in the city's slave population. However, by arresting slave women rather than slave men, city officials also reduced the impact of the crackdown on slaves (and masters) who competed with white working-men and magnified the symbolic meaning of the repression. There was relatively little competition from white women for the domestic jobs done by slave women who were hired out. For a monthly summary of the arrests, see table 4 in the Appendix.

9. For a monthly summary of the arrests, see table 4 in the Appendix.

10. James M. Johnson to Henry Ellison, May 14, 1860, Ellison Family Papers, SCL.

11. Ibid.

12. Ibid.

13. James M. Johnson to Henry Ellison, May 21, 30, 1860, Ellison Family Papers, SCL.

14. James M. Johnson to Henry Ellison, May 14, 1860, Ellison Family Papers, SCL.

15. James M. Johnson to Henry Ellison, May 30, 1860, Ellison Family Papers, SCL.

16. The census published the number of mulattoes and blacks in Charleston District rather than the city proper. Since the rice plantations in the district contained more than twice as many slaves as in the city, the total number of mulatto slaves in the city is difficult to estimate. If one assumes that all the mulatto slaves in the district lived in the city, then 21 percent of Charleston slaves were mulattoes. Since some mulatto slaves certainly lived outside the city, this figure is

doubtless too high. However, if one assumes that mulatto slaves were equally distributed throughout the district, then only 8 percent of Charleston's slave population were mulattoes. Regardless of which assumption is closer to the truth, the vast majority of slaves in the city were black.

17. Of the 721 free colored heads of household in the manuscript schedules of the 1860 census, 559 (78 percent) were propertyless. For a discussion of the distribution of wealth in the city, see Michael P. Johnson, "Wealth and Class in Charleston in 1860," in Walter J. Fraser, Jr., and Winfred B. Moore, Jr., eds., *From the Old South to the New: Essays on the Transitional South* (Westport, Conn., 1981), 65–80.

18. The data on real estate and slave-holding in this paragraph were derived from assessments for municipal taxes published in *List of the Taxpayers of Charleston, 1860* (Charleston, 1861), 315–34. For summaries of these data, see tables 6 and 7 in the Appendix.

19. According to the 1861 city census, free persons of color occupied 700 residences, of which 24 percent were owned by the occupants. Since a large number of free Afro-Americans emigrated from Charleston late in 1860, and since home-owners were probably underrepresented among the emigrants, the proportion of home-owners in the city in mid-1860 was probably somewhat less than 24 percent. Frederick A. Ford, *Census of the City of Charleston, South Carolina, for the Year 1861* (Charleston, 1861) lists the name of the occupant and the owner of each dwelling in the city, which made this estimate possible.

20. Of the 535 free colored renters in 1861, 425 rented from whites. The rest had free Negro landlords. Data derived from Ford, *Census of Charleston, 1861*.

21. In 1860, 317 free persons of color (44 percent of 721 free Negro households) paid municipal taxes on real estate. However, many of

the 74 whose property was assessed at less than $1,000 probably owned only unimproved lots. This was probably also true of some of the 126 individuals whose property was worth at least $1,000 but less than $2,000. It is unlikely that individuals who owned real estate valued at $2,000 or more were not homeowners. Data for this analysis were derived from *List of the Taxpayers of Charleston, 1860* (Charleston, 1861), 315–34.

22. Data derived from *List of the Taxpayers of Charleston, 1860*, 315–34. For a summary of the data, see table 7 in the Appendix.

23. For details on white wealth in Charleston, see Johnson, "Wealth and Class in Charleston," 65–80.

24. See Peter H. Wood, *Black Majority: Negroes in Colonial South Carolina from 1670 through the Stono Rebellion* (New York, 1974), 3–28, 95–103, 233–36; Marina Wikramanayake, *A World in Shadow: The Free Black in Antebellum South Carolina* (Columbia, S. C., 1973), 5–11, 72–85; Winthrop D. Jordan, *White Over Black: American Attitudes toward the Negro, 1550–1812* (Chapel Hill, N.C., 1968), 133–35, 145–47, 167–78, 408–409; Jordan, "American Chiaroscuro: The Status and Definition of Mulattoes in the British Colonies," *William and Mary Quarterly,* 3rd ser., 19 (1962), 183–200; Joel Williamson, *New People: Miscegenation and Mulattoes in the United States* (New York, 1980), 15–20. For comparisons with other slave societies in the New World see Carl N. Degler, *Neither Black Nor White: Slavery and Race Relations in Brazil and the United States* (New York and London, 1971); David W. Cohen and Jack P. Greene, eds., *Neither Slave Nor Free: The Freedman of African Descent in the Slave Societies of the New World* (Baltimore, 1972); Franklin W. Knight, *Slave Society in Cuba during the Nineteenth Century* (Madison, Milwaukee, and London, 1970), 85–120; Laura Foner, "The Free People of Color in Louisiana and St. Domingue: A Comparative Portrait of Two Three-Caste Societies,"

Journal of Social History 3 (1970), 406–30; Gad J. Heuman, *Between Black and White: Race, Politics, and the Free Coloreds in Jamaica, 1792–1865* (Westport, Conn., 1981).

25. Charleston population data are summarized in table 3 in the Appendix.

26. James M. Johnson to Henry Ellison, April 24, 1860, Ellison Family Papers, SCL.

27. For an incomplete diagram of some of the relationships, see Fitchett, "Free Negro in Charleston," following p. 283.

28. Since the published census reported only the total numbers of black and mulatto females of all ages, the exact numbers of free and slave mulatto women cannot be stated. The aggregate figures for Charleston District are 1,556 mulatto slave females and 1,618 free mulatto females. *Population of the United States in 1860* (Washington, D. C., 1864), 452.

29. Fitchett, "Free Negro in Charleston," 47–48.

30. *Population of the United States in 1860,* 448–49.

31. Ibid., 450–51.

32. The manuscript 1860 census schedules reported 425 households headed by free women of color. Information in this paragraph and the next was derived from an analysis of these households. They accounted for 52 percent of all free colored households; only 4 percent had a coresiding spouse.

33. Six out of ten female-headed households contained children. Only 4 percent of these households with children contained both parents.

34. Of the 143 black women who headed households, 97 were mothers who had a total of 174 coresiding children. Only five of these mothers had a coresiding spouse, and these two-parent households contained just 15 children.

35. Households headed by free mulatto women contained a total of 415 children. Of the 152 free mulatto mothers of these children, only five had a coresiding husband.

36. To cite just one example, Henry

Grimke, the brother of the famous Charleston-born feminists and abolitionists Sarah and Angelina Grimke, fathered three mulatto children with Nancy Weston, a mulatto slave woman. Gerda Lerner, *The Grimke Sisters from South Carolina* (Boston, 1967), 358–66; Williamson, *New People*, 48–49; Wikramanayake, *A World in Shadow*, 13–16, 76–77; Berlin, *Slaves Without Masters: The Free Negro in the Antebellum South* (New York, 1974), 265–67; Eugene D. Genovese, *Roll, Jordan, Roll: The World the Slaves Made* (New York, 1974), 398–431.

37. In Charleston District in 1860 there were 220 free colored boys and 241 free colored girls under five; 225 boys and 277 girls between five and ten; 229 boys and 275 girls between ten and fifteen. However, between 15 and 20, young men numbered 143, young women, 217; those in their twenties included 195 men and 348 women; those in their thirties, 159 men and 280 women; and so on. No other district in the state exhibited this pattern. *Population of the United States in 1860*, 448–49.

38. The manuscript schedules of the 1860 census reported 288 households headed by free black and mulatto men, from which the data for this paragraph were derived.

39. Of the 149 mulatto men with coresiding spouses, 137 had a mulatto spouse. Similarly, all 9 of the mulatto women who headed households and had a coresiding spouse had mulatto husbands. All of the 7 black women who headed households and had a coresiding spouse had black husbands.

40. Of the fifty-two black men who headed households and had a coresiding spouse, forty-three had a black wife. The proportion of black men with mulatto wives (13 percent) was more than twice that of mulatto men with black wives (5 percent). Though this evidence is hardly conclusive, it suggests that black men had a stronger preference for mulatto wives than mulatto men had for black wives. At least this evidence lends credence to the racial

data in the census by illustrating that census enumerators did not automatically indicate the same race for all members of free Negro households.

41. The data in this paragraph were derived from the wealth of free Negro heads of household reported in the manuscript schedules of the 1860 census. Rural free black women had the same mean wealth as their Charleston counterparts, while rural free mulatto women were slightly better off (with a mean wealth of $464) than those in the city. For a discussion of the rural wealth patterns, see chapter II.

42. *Rules and Regulations of the Brown Fellowship Society Established at Charleston, S. C., 1st November 1790* (Charleston, S. C., 1844), RSSL. See also, Berlin, *Slaves Without Masters*, 57–58, 312–13; Fitchett, "Free Negro in Charleston," 1–2, 163; Wikramanayake, *A World in Shadow*, 81–85.

43. *Rules and Regulations of the Brown Fellowship Society*, 11.

44. The uncertainty arises because the extant membership records contain a gap between 1844 and 1869. See ibid., and Minutes of the Brown Fellowship Society, January 7, 1869–July 6, 1911, RSSL.

45. *Rules and Regulations of the Brown Fellowship Society*, 19.

46. The most thorough study is Robert L. Harris, Jr., "Charleston's Free Afro-American Elite: The Brown Fellowship Society and the Humane Brotherhood," *South Carolina Historical Magazine* (1981), 289–310. Harris notes (p. 292) that one member, Malcolm Brown, was listed in the 1860 census as black. However, in the 1850 census Brown was listed as a mulatto. 1850 Population Schedules, Charleston Neck, dwelling 419.

47. *Constitution and Rules of the Humane Brotherhood, Organized June 19, 1843*, 2. We are indebted to Ms. S. Cornwell, Special Collections librarian, Langston Hughes Memorial Library, Lincoln University, Pennsylvania, for a copy of this document. See also, Harris, "Charleston's Free Afro-American

Elite," 29–30, for a convincing argument that the Humane Brotherhood did not begin in 1791 under the name of the Free Dark Men, as reported by James B. Browning, "The Beginnings of Insurance Enterprise Among Negroes," *Journal of Negro History* 22 (1937), 422–24.

48. Harris, "Charleston's Free Afro-American Elite," 296.

49. *Constitution and Rules of the Humane Brotherhood,* 6; Harris, "Charleston's Free Afro-American Elite," 298–300.

50. Browning, "Beginnings of Insurance Enterprise," 426.

51. Harris, "Charleston's Free Afro-American Elite," 295.

52. *Rules and Regulations of the Friendly Moralist Society* (Charleston, 1848), quoted in Fitchett, "Free Negro in Charleston," 126, no. 2.

53. Ibid.

54. Minutes of the Friendly Moralist Society, May 13, 1844, RSSL. We are indebted to Ralph Melnick, director of Special Collections, Robert Scott Small Library, College of Charleston, Charleston, South Carolina, for permission to use this document.

55. Minutes of the Friendly Moralist Society, May 13, 1844.

56. Minutes of the Friendly Moralist Society, March 9, 10, 20, 28, 1848.

57. During the years covered by the Minutes, 1841–56, some seventy individuals attended meetings. All of the forty-seven individuals for whom information could be located were mulattoes, according to the listings in the 1850 and 1860 manuscript census schedules. See Michael P. Johnson and James L. Roark, " 'A Middle Ground': Free Mulattoes and the Friendly Moralist Society of Antebellum Charleston," *Southern Studies* 21 (Fall 1982), 246–65.

58. Michael Eggart, "Anniversary Address," Minutes of the Friendly Moralist Society, June 11, 1848; the source of all quotations in this paragraph. For a transcription of Eggart's speech, see Johnson and Roark, " 'A Middle Ground.' "

59. Eggart, "Anniversary Address," Minutes of the Friendly Moralist Society, June 11, 1848; the source of all quotations in this paragraph.

60. Eggart's mother, Juliet Eggart, was illiterate. A free woman of color, she died when Michael was twelve, leaving him in the care of his two sisters, supported by a bequest of Juliet's house on St. Philip Street and by her slave girl Celia. Biographical information about Eggart was compiled from the Charleston Free Negro Tax Books, 1823–62, SCDAH, CLS; the manuscript schedules of the 1850 and 1860 censuses; Charleston Conveyances, Book B12, 425; and Book A14, 5; Wills of Charleston County, South Carolina, vol. 40, 1834–39, 138, SCDAH.

61. Minutes of the Friendly Moralist Society, June 11, 1848; Minutes of the Brown Fellowship Society, April 7, May 5, June 2, November 3, 1870, RSSL.

62. See also, Johnson and Roark, " 'A Middle Ground.' "

63. *African Repository and Colonial Journal* 33 (May 1857), 154.

64. *African Repository and Colonial Journal* 23 (June 1847), 190–91.

65. Ibid.

66. Eggart, "Anniversary Address," Minutes of the Friendly Moralist Society, June 11, 1848.

67. Eggart called the Friendly Moralists' attention to an account in the New York *Herald* (May 30, 1848) of a "war of color" in Haiti in which the black president murdered leading mulatto politicians, merchants, and professionals. Many mulattoes fled the country. A Dutch schooner made port in Jamaica with 127 Haitian refugees. New York *Herald,* June 9, 1848.

68. *African Repository and Colonial Journal* 33 (May 1857), 154. Another large contingent emigrated to Liberia a decade and a half earlier. Between May and November 1832, a total of 200 free Negroes left South Carolina for Liberia. In all the other years between 1820 and 1856 only 24 emigrated to Liberia, according to ibid. For a firsthand account of the

1832 emigrants, see *African Repository and Colonial Journal* 8 (May 1832), 74–77; (October 1832), 239–43. For other studies of emigration see Berlin, *Slaves Without Masters,* 169–71; Wikramanayake, *A World in Shadow,* 171–78; Philip J. Staudenraus, *The African Colonization Movement, 1816–1865* (New York, 1961); Randall M. Miller, ed., *'Dear Master': Letters of a Slave Family* (Ithaca, N. Y., 1978); Bell I. Wiley, ed., *Slaves No More: Letters from Liberia, 1833–1869* (Lexington, Ky., 1980).
69. *Rules and Regulations of the Brown Fellowship Society,* 22–23; Minutes of the Friendly Moralist Society, August 2, 1848.
70. Minutes of the Friendly Moralist Society, January 5, April 12, June 14, 1847; April 19, August 2, 1848.
71. The Ellison letters contain considerable evidence of a colony of Charlestonians in Canada; see especially James D. Johnson to Henry Ellison, December 28, 1858; James M. Johnson to Henry Ellison, August 28, 1860; James D. Johnson to Henry Ellison, September 16, 1860, Ellison Family Papers, SCL.
72. Edward Holloway to Charles H. Holloway, March 16, 1857, Holloway Scrapbook, RSSL.
73. For example, see James D. Johnson to Henry Ellison, December 28, 1858; James M. Johnson to Henry Ellison, November 22, 1859; James M. Johnson to Henry Ellison, January 9, 1860, Ellison Family Papers, SCL.
74. [Jack Thomas] to "My Esteemed Friends," April 30, 1860, Ellison Family Papers, SCL. The last section of Thomas's letter has not survived, unfortunately. The last lines in the extant letter are, "Now I suppose you all would like to know what sort of a place Jamaica is. Well in the first place, if you like Negro Company, you may go." Then the page ends. For testimony of a Charleston carpenter who emigrated to Liberia and became disillusioned, see *Examination of Mr. Thomas C. Brown, A Free Colored Citizen of South Carolina, As to the Actual State of Things in Liberia in the Years 1833 and 1834 . . .* (New York, 1834).
75. James M. Johnson to Henry Ellison, April 24, 1860, Ellison Family Papers, SCL.
76. Memorial of Thomas Cole, P. B. Mathews, and Mathew Webb, quoted in Wikramanayake, *A World in Shadow,* 52–53.
77. Ibid.
78. C. W. Birnie, "Education of the Negro in Charleston, South Carolina, Prior to the Civil War," *Journal of Negro History* 12 (January 1927), 15. Birnie mentions several other societies of Charleston free people of color, including the Friendly Union, the Brotherly Society, the Unity and Friendship Society, the Cumberland Society, the Asbury Association, the Capers Missionary Society, and the Bonneau Library Society. Ibid., 15–16.
79. *Seventeenth Annual Report of the Executive Committee of the Christian Benevolent Society: A Society Organized by Colored Men of Charleston, South Carolina in the Year 1839* (Charleston, 1856), Holloway Scrapbook, RSSL.
80. Ibid.
81. Fitchett, "Free Negro in Charleston," 48, 193–95; Birnie, "Education of the Negro in Charleston," 18–19; Wikramanayake, *A World in Shadow,* 87.
82. Fitchett, "Free Negro in Charleston," 48.
83. There were at least four or five other schools for free colored children. Birnie, "Education of the Negro in Charleston," 18–21; Fitchett, "Free Negro in Charleston," 193–203; Daniel A. Payne, *Recollections of Seventy Years* (Nashville, Tenn., 1883), 14–16, 19–26.
84. Payne, *Recollections,* 25–40.
85. New York *Tribune,* November 10, 1860.
86. James M. Johnson to Henry Ellison, May 14, 1860, Ellison Family Papers, SCL.
87. Sumter *Watchman,* May 7, 1860, reprinted in Charleston *Courier,* May 9, 1860.
88. *African Repository and Colonial Journal* 23 (June 1847), 190.

89. For a map of free Negro residential distribution in Charleston in 1859, see Leonard P. Curry, *The Free Black in Urban America, 1800–1850: The Shadow of the Dream* (Chicago and London, 1981), 63. See also John P. Radford, "Social Structure and Urban Form: Charleston, 1860–1880," in Fraser and Moore, eds., *From the Old South to the New,* 81–91; Radford, "Race, Residence and Ideology: Charleston, S. C., in the Mid-Nineteenth Century," *Journal of Historical Geography* 2 (1976), 329–46; and Radford, "Delicate Space: Race and Residence in Charleston, S. C., 1860–1880," West Georgia College *Studies in the Social Sciences* 16 (1977), 17–37.

90. A total of 2,078 free people of color lived in Wards 5, 6, 7, and 8, some 64 percent of all free Afro-Americans in the city. *Population of the United States in 1860,* 452.

91. Coming Street housed 273 free people of color. The next most heavily populated street was Calhoun, with 185. On Coming, free Afro-Americans comprised 18 percent of the residents and occupied 23 percent of the dwellings, two and three times the concentration on the next most densely settled streets. Ford, *Census of the City of Charleston, 1861,* 9, 15–20, 68–73.

92. Wikramanayake, *A World in Shadow,* 113–31.

93. Parish Register, St. Philip's Protestant Episcopal Church (typescript), SCL. See also, Fitchett, "Free Negro in Charleston,"

94. James M. Johnson to Henry Ellison, January 9, May 14, 1860, Ellison Family Papers, SCL.

95. Holy Cross Episcopal Church Record, Stateburg, 1803–1863, SCHS.

96. James M. Johnson to Henry Ellison, September 7, 1860, Ellison Family Papers, SCL.

97. James M. Johnson to Henry Ellison, May 30, 1860, Ellison Family Papers, SCL.

98. James M. Johnson to Henry Ellison May 21, 1860, Ellison Family Papers, SCL; Charleston *Courier,* May 18, 19, 1860.

99. James M. Johnson to Henry Ellison, May 21, 1860, Ellison Family Papers, SCL.

100. For the text of the report of Memminger's committee, see Charleston *Courier,* May 13, 1859.

101. Charleston *Courier,* May 13, 1859.

102. Charleston *Courier,* May 19, 1860. The dispute continued in summer after the convention adjourned; see A. W. to Editor, Charleston *Courier,* May 29, July 2, 14, 1860; S. to Editor, Charleston *Courier,* June 13, July 2, 26, 1860.

103. James M. Johnson to Henry Ellison, January 20, 1860, Ellison Family Papers, SCL.

104. Payne made these remarks in St. Mark's in Baltimore, but he almost certainly said something similar in Charleston. *Southern Episcopalian* 6 (February 1860), 595–97.

105. James M. Johnson to Henry Ellison, May 14, 1860, Ellison Family Papers, SCL.

106. Holloway Scrapbook, RSSL; Payne, *Recollections,* 38–40; F. A. Mood, *Methodism in Charleston: A Narrative* . . . (Nashville, Tenn., 1856), 183–90.

107. Wikramanayake, *A World in Shadow,* 117–22; Mood, *Methodism in Charleston,* 106–107, 123, 130–33, 145–47. Other free people of color found their way into the folds of the Baptists and Presbyterians, but their numbers were small. Wikramanayake, *A World in Shadow,* 87, 110, 116, 128–29.

108. Mood, *Methodism in Charleston,* 130–33; John B. Adger, *My Life and Times, 1810–1899* (Richmond, Va., 1899), 52–55, 164–65; Wikramanayake, *A World in Shadow,* 122–28.

109. Mood, *Methodism in Charleston,* 133.

110. By the late 1820s there were over 3,000 black Methodists in Charleston, but the galleries of the churches could accommodate no more than about 1,500. A partition was constructed at the back of the main floor of each church, enclosing a space known as "The Box," for the overflow from the galleries. Before long, the boxes also over-

flowed. Mood reports that "it had become not an infrequent occurrence that some of the whites were compelled to leave the church, their seats in the lower part of the church being preoccupied by colored persons, who refused to surrender them." Ultimately, a group of young white men "forcibly ejected" the Negroes from their seats. The problem continued to bedevil the white Methodists even after a Quarterly Conference in 1833 offered a compromise requiring all slaves to sit in the galleries and reserving the boxes for free people of color. Mood, *Methodism in Charleston,* 146–57.

111. James M. Johnson to Henry Ellison, May 30, 1860, Ellison Family Papers, SCL.

112. James D. Johnson to Henry Ellison, August 4, 1860, Ellison Family Papers, SCL.

CHAPTER SEVEN

1. This account of Johnson's itinerary is based on James M. Johnson to Henry Ellison, August 28, 1860; James D. Johnson to Henry Ellison, September 16, 1860, Ellison Family Papers, SCL. For an excellent map of the railroad route, see George Rogers Taylor and Irene D. Neu, *The American Railroad Network, 1861–1890* (Cambridge, Mass., 1956).

2. James D. Johnson to Henry Ellison, September 16, 1860, Ellison Family Papers, SCL. See also, H. Shirley Smith, *The World's Great Bridges* (New York, 1953), 72; and David Plowden, *Bridges: The Spans of North America* (New York, 1974), 108–9.

3. James D. Johnson to Henry Ellison, September 16, 1860, Ellison Family Papers, SCL.

4. James M. Johnson to Henry Ellison, August 28, 1860, Ellison Family Papers, SCL.

5. James D. Johnson to Henry Ellison, September 16, 1860, Ellison Family Papers, SCL; the source of all quotations in this paragraph. The visit of the Prince of Wales is recounted in stupefying detail in the Toronto *Daily Globe* between mid-August and late September.

6. Canada West Census, 1861 (microfilm), Toronto, St. John's Ward, District 3, reel 178, folio 598, Public Archives, Ottawa, Canada. St. John's Ward contained 626 persons born in the United States out of a total population of 8,034. St. James's Ward had the next largest group of U. S. natives with 333. Regrettably, the published Canadian census did not specify the race of these individuals, although information about race, marital status, and religion was collected on the manuscript census forms. *Census of Canada, 1861: Origins and Religions* (Quebec, 1862), 48. For an excellent general history, see Robin Winks, *The Blacks in Canada: A History* (New Haven and Montreal, 1971).

7. See, for example, the advertisements in the Toronto *Daily Globe,* August 4, September 12, and October 17, 1860.

8. James M. Johnson to Henry Ellison, November 22, 1859, Ellison Family Papers, SCL.

9. James M. Johnson to Henry Ellison, February 25, 1860, Ellison Family Papers, SCL.

10. James M. Johnson to Henry Ellison, May 14, 1860, Ellison Family Papers, SCL.

11. James D. Johnson to Henry Ellison, September 16, 1860, Ellison Family Papers, SCL.

12. Canada West Census, 1861 (microfilm), Toronto, Reel 178, folio 598.

13. James M. Johnson to Henry Ellison, August 28, 1860, Ellison Family Papers, SCL.

14. James D. Johnson to Henry Ellison, September 16, 1860, Ellison Family Papers, SCL.

15. Ibid.; the source of all quotations in this paragraph.

16. Charleston *Courier,* August 9, 1860.

17. James M. Johnson to Henry Ellison, August 20, 1860, Ellison Family Papers, SCL.

18. Ibid.

19. Ibid.

20. Ibid.

21. Ibid.

22. Ibid. The most likely meaning of this statement is that four slaves who belonged to the Dereefs but whom they had allowed to live as free persons were required to have slave badges, and the Dereefs, as their owners, were fined for failing to obtain the badges earlier. There are other possible interpretations, however. See the authors' *No Chariot Let Down: Charleston's Free People of Color on the Eve of the Civil War* (Chapel Hill, N.C., 1984), letter of August 20, 1860, note 16.

23. Sumter County Guardians of Free Blacks, 1823–1842, Sumter County Historical Society, Sumter, South Carrolina.

24. McCreight died November 4, 1859. See the obituary in Charleston *Mercury,* November 10, 1859. Ideally, it would be possible to identify the men who served as trustees and guardians of Charleston's free mulatto elite. Unfortunately, few pertinent records are extant.

25. For examples of special treatment, see entries for July 1807, November 1, 1808, and November 1809, Plowden Weston Ledger, 1802–1820, RSSL. For other biographical details, see 1860 Population Schedules, Charleston, Ward 5, dwelling 137; Fitchett, "Free Negro in Charleston," 31–32, 102–3.

26. Plowden Weston Will, Record of Wills, Charleston County, vol. 37 (typescript), 165–85, CCL.

27. Ibid.

28. *List of the Taxpayers of Charleston, 1860,* 332.

29. James M. Johnson to Henry Ellison, August 20, 1860, Ellison Family Papers, SCL.

30. James M. Johnson to Henry Ellison, August 28, 1860, Ellison Family Papers, SCL.

31. The estimate of seven hundred Negroes who were forced to buy slave badges is based on a comparison of city tax revenues for 1859 and 1860. Conveniently, the city's fiscal years ended August 31. During the fiscal year ending August 31, 1860, the city received $16,808 from the sale of slave badges, $3,109 more than in the previous fiscal year. Most of the difference can reasonably be attributed to the badges sold during the enslavement crisis. However, since badge fees varied depending on the slave's occupation, the dollar figure cannot be converted into the exact number of badges sold. Badges cost $7 for tradesmen; $5 for sellers of fruits, cakes, and other articles; $4 for carters, draymen, fishermen, porters, and day laborers; and $2 for fisherwomen, washerwomen, and domestic servants. Since there is no reliable information about the proportions of slaves who were hired out in these several occupations, one must make an assumption about the mean badge fee. If one assumes that the mean badge fee was about $4, then the $3,109 in additional badge revenues in 1860 was produced by the sale of 777 new badges. For city revenue data, see Charleston *Courier,* October 4, 1859; November 29, 1860. For badge prices, see Charleston *Mercury,* December 23, 1859; January 21, 1860.

32. James M. Johnson to Henry Ellison, August 28, 1860, Ellison Family Papers, SCL.

33. James M. Johnson to Henry Ellison, August 20, 1860, Ellison Family Papers, SCL.

34. *List of the Taxpayers of Charleston, 1859,* 387; *List of the Taxpayers of Charleston, 1860,* 319.

35. *List of the Taxpayers of Charleston, 1860,* 326; 1860 Population Schedules, Charleston, Ward 7, dwelling 84.

36. Fitchett, "Free Negro in Charleston," 345–46; 1860 Population Schedules, Charleston, Ward 4, dwelling 243.

37. James M. Johnson to Henry Ellison, August 20, 1860, Ellison Family Papers, SCL.

38. James M. Johnson to Henry Ellison, August 28, 1860, Ellison Family Papers, SCL.

39. James M. Johnson to Henry Ellison, September 3, 1860, Ellison Family Papers, SCL.

40. James M. Johnson to Henry Ellison, August 28, 1860, Ellison Family Papers, SCL.

41. James M. Johnson to Henry Ellison, August 20, 1860, Ellison Family Papers, SCL.

42. Ibid.

43. The records of the Charleston Court of General Sessions, to which cases from the magistrate's and free-holders' court could be appealed, do not exist for the years from 1840 to 1865, and a search of related records proved fruitless. We are indebted to Marion Chandler of the South Carolina Department of Archives and History for expert guidance in this matter.

44. James M. Johnson to Henry Ellison, August 28, 1860, Ellison Family Papers, SCL.

45. Ibid.; Charleston Free Negro Tax Book, 1862, CLS.

46. James M. Johnson to Henry Ellison, August 28, 1860; Ferslew, *Directory of Charleston, 1860*, 60; *List of the Taxpayers of Charleston, 1860*, 25.

47. Charleston *Courier,* June 28, 1860. For other cases of free Negro insolence, see Charleston *Courier,* August 23, November 1, 1860.

48. James M. Johnson to Henry Ellison, September 3, 1860, Ellison Family Papers, SCL.

49. Ibid.

50. Ibid.; the source of all quotations in this paragraph. For information about the Thompsons, see 1860 Population Schedules, Charleston, Ward 6, dwelling 129.

51. Ibid.; 1860 Population Schedules, Charleston, Ward 4, dwelling 161.

52. Ibid.; the source of all quotations in this paragraph not otherwise attributed.

53. Charleston *Courier,* September 1, 1860.

54. Ibid.

55. See, for example, Singleton's $200 bill for twelve days during Charleston's races, February 11 to 23, 1823. Singleton Family Papers, SHC.

56. Petition in Behalf of Jehu Jones, November 6, 1827, General Assembly Petitions, SCDAH. The petition had 120 signatures, including those of some of the most prominent white Charlestonians. The law was also strictly enforced against Morris Brown and Henry Drayton after the Vesey conspiracy; see Wik-ramanayake, *A World in Shadow: The Free Black in Antebellum South Carolina* (Columbia, S. C.), 1973, 126–28. See also F. C. Adams, *Manuel Periera: Or, The Sovereign Rule of South Carolina* (London, nd [1852]), 94–96.

57. 1860 Population Schedules, Charleston, Ward 6, dwelling 32; Ford, *Census of Charleston, 1861,* 204; *Southern Patriot,* January 8, 1848.

58. James M. Johnson to Henry Ellison, September 3, 1860, Ellison Family Papers, SCL.

59. Ibid.; the source of all quotations in this paragraph.

60. James M. Johnson to Henry Ellison, August 20, 1860, Ellison Family Papers, SCL; the source of all quotations in this paragraph.

61. Ibid.

62. Fitchett, "Free Negro in Charleston," 345–46.

63. James M. Johnson to Henry Ellison, August 20, 1860, Ellison Family Papers, SCL; the source of all quotations in this paragraph.

64. Ibid.; the source of all quotations in this paragraph.

65. James M. Johnson to Henry Ellison, August 28, 1860, Ellison Family Papers, SCL; the source of all quotations in this paragraph.

66. "Up-Town" John to Editor, Charleston *Courier,* August 4, 1860.

67. 1860 Population Schedules, Charleston, Ward 2, dwelling 355; Ferslew, *Directory of Charleston, 1860,* 97; *List of the Taxpayers of Charleston, 1860,* 172.

68. James M. Johnson to Henry Ellison, August 20, 1860, Ellison Family Papers, SCL; the source of all quotations in this paragraph.

69. James M. Johnson to Henry Ellison, August 28, 1860, Ellison Family Papers, SCL; the source of all quotations in this paragraph. For data regarding Whaley, see Ferslew, *Directory of Charleston, 1860,* 148; *List of the Taxpayers of Charleston, 1860,* 297.

70. James M. Johnson to Henry Ellison, August 28, 1860, Ellison Family Papers, SCL. On Schnierle,

see 1860 Population Schedules, Charleston, Ward 4, dwelling 796; Ferslew, *Directory of Charleston, 1860,* 124; *List of the Taxpayers of Charleston, 1860,* 253.

71. James M. Johnson to Henry Ellison, September 3, 1860, Ellison Family Papers, SCL; the source of all quotations in this paragraph. On Webb, see 1860 Population Schedules, Charleston, Ward 8, dwelling 64; Ford, *Census of Charleston, 1861,* 64, 228.

72. James M. Johnson to Henry Ellison, August 28, 1860, Ellison Family Papers, SCL.

73. Ibid.; the source of all quotations in this paragraph.

74. For a monthly summary of arrests, see table 4 in the Appendix.

75. James M. Johnson to Henry Ellison, September 3, 1860, Ellison Family Papers, SCL; also the source of the next two quotations in this paragraph.

76. James M. Johnson to Henry Ellison, August 28, 1860, Ellison Family Papers, SCL; also the source of the next quotation in this paragraph.

77. James M. Johnson to Henry Ellison, September 3, 1860, Ellison Family Papers, SCL.

78. Ibid.

79. James M. Johnson to Henry Ellison, September 7, 1860, Ellison Family Papers, SCL; the source of all quotations in this paragraph. On the sickness in the city, see Charleston *Courier,* September 3, 1860.

80. James M. Johnson to Henry Ellison, September 24, 1860, Ellison Family Papers, SCL.

81. James M. Johnson to Henry Ellison, October 12, 1860, Ellison Family Papers, SCL; the source of the subsequent quotations in this paragraph.

82. James M. Johnson to Henry Ellison, September 24, 1860, Ellison Family Papers, SCL.

83. James D. Johnson to Henry Ellison, September 16, 1860, Ellison Family Papers, SCL. Johnson may have recalled that in June 1859, when a free man of color named Stephen Maxwell tried to return to Charleston, he was arrested and ordered to leave or be sold into slavery. Charleston *Mercury,* June 9, 1859.

84. James M. Johnson to Henry Ellison, September 24, 1860, Ellison Family Papers, SCL; the source of all quotations in this paragraph.

85. James M. Johnson to Henry Ellison, October 8, 1860, Ellison Family Papers, SCL.

86. Ferslew, *Directory of Charleston, 1860,* 76.

87. On Lincoln's election, see David M. Potter, *The Impending Crisis, 1848–1861,* ed. and completed by Don E. Fehrenbacher (New York and other cities, 1976), 405–47; Allan Nevins, *The Emergence of Lincoln, Volume II, Prologue to Civil War, 1859–1861* (New York, 1950), 287–317.

88. On secession in South Carolina, see Steven A. Channing, *Crisis of Fear: Secession in South Carolina* (New York, 1970); Charles E. Cauthen, *South Carolina Goes to War, 1860–1865* (Chapel Hill, N.C., 1950); Philip M. Hamer, *The Secession Movement in South Carolina, 1847–1852* (Allentown, Pa., 1918); Harold S. Schultz, *Nationalism and Sectionalism in South Carolina, 1852– 1860: A Study of the Movement for Southern Independence* (Durham, N. C.,1950); James G. Van Deusen, *Economic Bases of Disunion in South Carolina* (New York, 1928).

89. 1860 Population Schedules, Charleston, Ward 7, dwelling 344; *List of the Taxpayers of Charleston, 1860,* 84; Charleston *Courier,* August 25, 1860.

90. Charleston *Courier,* August 25, 1860; the source of all quotations in this paragraph.

91. Charleston *Courier,* August 17, 22, 25, 29, 31, September 3, 7, 12, 1860.

92. Charleston *Courier,* August 17, 1860.

93. See, for example, Charleston *Mercury,* September 24, 1860.

94. Charleston *Courier,* October 6, 1860; Charleston *Mercury,* October 6, 1860.

95. Charleston *Mercury,* September 26, October 5, 1860. Robert Duryea also courted mechanic voters; see

Charleston *Courier,* October 8, 1860.

96. Charleston *Mercury,* September 25, 1860.

97. "Sympathy" to Editor, Charleston *Mercury,* September 29, 1860.

98. For detailed election returns, see Charleston *Mercury,* October 11, 1860.

99. For a discussion of voter turnout, see Charleston *Courier,* October 16, 1860.

100. Peake and Coffin did almost as well. Coffin polled 2,092 votes; Peake, 1,939. The ballots of the last candidate to be elected (who came in twentieth in a field of thirty-six) totaled 1,533. Charleston *Mercury,* October 11, 1860.

101. The quoted phrase is from James M. Johnson to Henry Ellison, August 20, 1860, Ellison Family Papers, SCL.

102. William Ellison, Jr., to Henry Ellison, October 31, 1860, Ellison Family Papers, SCL.

103. Charleston *Courier,* January 30, 1860.

104. William Ellison, Jr., to Henry Ellison, October 31, 1860, Ellison Family Papers, SCL; the source of subsequent quotations in this paragraph.

105. Ibid.; the source of all quotations in this paragraph.

106. Janice Sumler Lewis, "The Fortens of Philadelphia: An Afro-American Family and Nineteenth-Century Reform," Ph.D. diss., Georgetown University, 1978; Ray Allen Billington, ed., *The Journal of Charlotte Forten: A Free Negro in the Slave Era* (Toronto, 1961).

107. Benjamin C. Bacon, *Statistics of the Colored People of Philadelphia* (Philadelphia, 1859), 8.

108. William Ellison, Jr., to Henry Ellison, October 31, 1860, Ellison Family Papers, SCL.

109. Lewis, "The Fortens of Philadelphia."

110. Charleston *Mercury,* November 8, 1860.

111. Charleston *Courier,* November 17, 1860; Charleston *Mercury,* November 17, 1860.

112. William Kaufman Scarborough, ed., *The Diary of Edmund Ruffin,*

Vol. I, Toward Independence, October 1856–April 1861 (Baton Rouge, 1972), 495–97.

113. Philadelphia *Evening Bulletin,* November 2, 1860. See also *National Anti-Slavery Standard,* November 17, 1860; *The Liberator,* November 23, 1860.

114. New York *Tribune,* November 10, 1860; the source of all subsequent quotations in this paragraph. The *Courier* (November 19, 1860) reprinted an item from the *Southern Presbyterian* that responded to the reports of the Philadelphia refugees by pointing out that the emigrants had chosen to leave to avoid the enforcement of the law against manumission, and concluded, "The good of the whole community, both white and black, at the South, requires that the two races sustain their present relation to one another. And hence South Carolina forbids emancipation on the soil."

115. Charleston *Courier,* November 15, 1860.

116. New York *Tribune,* November 22, 24, 27, 30, 1860; Philadelphia *Inquirer,* November 29, 1860.

117. "Caution" to Editor, Charleston *Courier,* October 29, 1860. See also Charleston *Courier,* September 29, October 9, 30, 1860. For a detailed account of the experience of Catherine Bottsford, a white woman from New York who was arrested by Charleston authorities as an abolitionist emissary and tossed in jail, where she spent October and November of 1860, see her letter in the New York *Tribune,* March 22, 1861, and the related notes on March 26 and 30, 1861. Her arrest was mentioned in Charleston *Courier,* September 29, 1860.

118. For a good discussion of Charleston late in November, see New York *Tribune,* December 3, 1860. The *Tribune* had an excellent anonymous correspondent in the city, whom the city police hunted for weeks, without success.

119. Charleston *Mercury,* November 30, 1860.

120. For a copy of the bill, see Charleston *Mercury,* November 24, 1860. For a discussion of similar

laws in other states, see Ira Berlin, *Slaves Without Masters: The Free Negro in the Antebellum South* (New York, 1974), 370–80.

121. Charleston *Mercury,* November 24, 1860.

122. "Aristides" to Editor, Charleston *Mercury,* November 27, 1860.

123. Charleston *Mercury,* December 6, 1860.

124. Charleston *Mercury,* November 30, 1860; see also Charleston *Mercury,* December 1, 1860.

125. Charleston *Mercury,* November 28, 1860.

126. "A Master Mechanic" to Editor, Charleston *Courier,* December 7, 1860; the source of all quotations in this paragraph.

127. Charleston *Mercury,* December 6, 1860.

128. Charleston *Courier,* December 13, 1860.

129. The quoted phrase is from James M. Johnson to Henry Ellison, December 7, 1860, Ellison Family Papers, SCL; the source of the information in this paragraph, unless otherwise noted.

130. 1860 Population Schedules, Charleston, Ward 6, dwelling 73; *List of the Taxpayers of Charleston, 1860,* 318; Ford, *Census of Charleston, 1861,* 72; Parish Register, Grace Episcopal Church, Charleston.

131. James M. Johnson to Henry Ellison, December 7, 1860, Ellison Family Papers, SCL.

132. The actual petition has not survived, but the text was printed in the Charleston *Mercury,* December 12, 1860.

133. Charleston *Mercury,* December 18, 1860.

134. James M. Johnson to Henry Ellison, December 7, 1860, Ellison Family Papers, SCL; the source of all quotations in this paragraph.

135. The petition has not survived. James Rose was the president of the South West Rail Road Bank. He reported $10,000 in real estate and $1,200 in personal property to the federal census, and he paid municipal taxes on fifteen slaves. It is likely that Rose's petition was signed by many of the same men who signed

an 1857 petition urging the legislature to increase the annual pension the state paid Peter Desverney, the Negro man who had alerted authorities to the Vesey conspiracy in 1822 and who had been awarded his freedom by the state, along with an annual stipend. Fifty-six Charleston white men signed the Desverney petition, and only one, Henry T. Peake, was a mechanic or tradesman. All the rest with identifiable occupations (fifty-one of fifty-six) were commission merchants (eleven), bankers or bank employees (thirteen), factors (six), attorneys (four), physicians (three), planters (three), general merchants (three), or city officeholders. As a group, the men were wealthy slaveholders. Almost half of them (46 percent) paid city taxes on real estate valued at more than $10,000, and nearly one in five (18 percent) owned at least twice that amount. More than nine out of ten (92 percent) owned slaves, and a third of them (31 percent) owned twelve or more slaves. Their wealth was reflected in their ownership of carriages in the city. Six out of ten (61 percent) paid taxes on a carriage, and one out of five (20 percent) paid taxes on two carriages. The data for this analysis were compiled from "Petition of Peter Desverney, a free person of colour, for increase of the annual bounty . . . ," 1857, General Assembly Petitions, SCDAH; Ferslew, *Directory of Charleston, 1860; List of the Taxpayers of Charleston, 1860.*

136. Curiously, the South Carolina newspapers gave no attention to Read's speech. The best coverage is in the Baltimore *Sun,* which had a correspondent in Columbia who witnessed Read's remarks and reported several passages in the December 18, 1860, issue, the source of all quotations in this paragraph. The correspondent noted, "It is generally conceded that the only slaves overworked in the State are those owned by free negroes; they work them much harder and manage to make a good deal more out

of them than do the white owners."
137. See Charleston *Mercury,*
December 18, 1860.
138. Ideally, it would be possible to
reconstruct the legislative history of
Eason's bill. However, the normally
haphazard record keeping of the
state legislature deteriorated in the
1860 session as the state readied
itself for secession. *Journal of the
House of Representatives, Session of
1860–61* (Columbia, S. C., 1860), 11,
131, 196, 386; Charleston *Mercury,*
December 6, 7, 15, 1860.
139. James D. Johnson to Henry
Ellison, December 19, 1860, Ellison
Family Papers, SCL.
140. James M. Johnson to Henry
Ellison, December 7, 1860, Ellison
Family Papers, SCL.
141. See, for example, Charleston
Mercury, December 21, 1860.
142. Ibid.; Charleston *Mercury,*
December 22, 1860; Scarborough,
ed., *Diary of Edmund Ruffin,* I, 511–
14.
143. James M. Johnson to Henry
Ellison, December 23, 1860, Ellison
Family Papers, SCL.
144. Ibid.; the source of all quota-
tions in this paragraph.
145. James D. Johnson to Henry
Ellison, December 19, 1860, Ellison
Family Papers, SCL.
146. James M. Johnson to Henry
Ellison, December 23, 1860, Ellison
Family Papers, SCL.
147. Ibid.; the source of all quotations in this paragraph.
148. James D. Johnson to Henry
Ellison, December 19, 1860, Ellison
Family Papers, SCL.
149. *National Anti-Slavery Standard,*
November 17, 1860.
150. Philadelphia *Evening Bulletin,*
November 26, 1860; Philadelphia
Inquirer, November 27, 1860.
151. James Redpath, ed., *A Guide to
Hayti* (Boston, 1861), 172.
152. James Redpath to G. R. Hey-
ward, in "Report of James Redpath
. . . to the Hon. M. Pleisance, Secretary of the State of Exterior Relations of the Republic of Haiti,"
n.d., though evidently written in
late March 1861. James Redpath
Papers (microfilm), Manuscript

Division, LC. Within months, Redpath himself became disillusioned
with the experience of the Haitian
emigrants.
153. James D. Johnson to Henry
Ellison, December 19, 1860, Ellison
Family Papers, SCL.
154. James M. Johnson to Henry
Ellison, December 23, 1860, Ellison
Family Papers, SCL.
155. Ibid.

CHAPTER EIGHT

1. See especially Charles Edward
Cauthen, *South Carolina Goes to
War, 1860–1865* (Chapel Hill, N.C.,
1950), 63–138; E. Milby Burton, *The
Siege of Charleston, 1861–1865*
(Columbia, S. C., 1970), 1–65. For
national developments, see David
M. Potter, *The Impending Crisis,
1848–1861,* ed. and completed by
Don E. Fehrenbacher (New York
and other cities, 1976), 555–83;
David M. Potter, *Lincoln and His
Party in the Secession Crisis* (New
Haven, 1942); Kenneth M. Stampp,
And the War Came (Baton Rouge,
1950).
2. New York *Tribune,* January 16,
1861.
3. Mary Boykin Chesnut kept a
diary while she was in Charleston,
but during the 1870s and 1880s she
revised it; the statements quoted
here are from her revised journal.
C. Vann Woodward, ed., *Mary
Chesnut's Civil War* (New Haven
and London, 1981), 36, 37, 42, 45.
4. Many Merchants to Editor,
Charleston *Mercury,* November 17,
1860.
5. Charleston *Mercury,* November
17, 19, 26, 29, 30, 1860.
6. Charleston *Mercury,* November
30, 1860.
7. New York *Tribune,* December 3,
1860.
8. New York *Tribune,* December 13,
1860.
9. Philadelphia *Inquirer,* January 2,
1861.
10. New York *Tribune,* January 4,
1861.

11. New York *Tribune,* January 17, 1861.

12. Burton, *The Siege of Charleston,* 22.

13. New York *Tribune,* January 22, February 4, 1861.

14. New York *Tribune,* January 22, 1861.

15. New York *Tribune,* January 28, February 8, 1861.

16. Burton, *The Siege of Charleston,* 22; New York *Tribune,* January 19, 1861.

17. New York *Tribune,* January 19, 1861; the source of all quotations in this paragraph. For other accounts, see New York *Evening Post,* January 18, 1861; Philadelphia *Evening Bulletin,* January 18, 1861; Philadelphia *Inquirer,* January 19, 1861. Free people of color did not forget the enslavement crisis. When Howell M. Henry investigated South Carolina slavery early in the twentieth century he found that "Old negroes of that day who are still living recall the talk . . . about re-enslaving the free negro and feel now that this agitation was taken advantage of by the white man to hold it over the colored free man as a threat." Almost thirty years later E. Franklin Frazier reported a reminiscence of a woman whose grandfather was one of the refugees. The woman said her grandfather "conducted the largest tailor establishment" in Charleston in the antebellum years: "During the slavery agitation my grandfather was walking with his son one day down the street and a white man struck him with a cane. He had been insulted on several occasions but this was the last straw. They sold everything and went to X (a northern city). Men, coming out of the South, came to the home of my widowed grandmother to pay their respects because they had learned their trade in the shop of my grandfather." Howell M. Henry, *The Police Control of the Slave in South Carolina* (Emory, Va., 1914), 189; E. Franklin Frazier, *The Negro Family in Chicago* (Chicago, 1932), 233.

18. New York *Tribune,* March 19, 1861.

19. New York *Tribune,* February 11, 1861.

20. For a summary of the comparison, see tables 8, 9, and 10 in the Appendix. The estimate of over a thousand refugees from Charleston is based on the fact that in 1860 only about 1 out of 10 free persons of color in the city paid real estate taxes. Thus, since 113 taxpayers were absent in 1862, the total number of refugees was probably at least ten times as great. The principal problem with using the 1862 Free Negro Tax Book to determine the number and character of the emigrants is that the list was compiled more than a year after emigration had become impossible. Regrettably, the 1861 Free Negro Tax Book is not extant. Even if it were, however, the only individuals required to be listed were men between fifteen and fifty and women between sixteen and sixty; both the young and the old, who comprised well over half of the 1860 population, would not appear. In addition, by 1862 a large number of free women of color had evidently moved into Charleston to sew clothing for civilians and soldiers (see table 10 in the Appendix), while some free men of color may have left the city for the countryside. Despite these problems, there is no reason to doubt the general conclusion about the large number of emigrants and their poverty. Curiously, these data corroborate a note in the *Liberator* (November 23, 1860) from "A Man," and are within range of the other newspaper reports. It is likely that the New York *Tribune* correspondent's estimate of 2,000 refugees was correct, though it included free Afro-Americans from throughout the state, not just from the city of Charleston. The data for this analysis were compiled from *List of the Taxpayers of the City of Charleston, 1860;* Charleston Free Negro Tax Book, 1862, CLS.

21. Memorial to Thomas J. Gantt, January 10, 1861, Francis Wilkins Pickens Papers, Manuscript Division, LC. The *Tribune* correspondent identified the memorialists as

"black men." New York *Tribune,* January 18, 1861.

22. Memorial to J. H. Boatwright, January 10, 1861; Memorial of Free Negroes to His Excellency Gov. Francis W. Pickens, January 10, 1861, Francis Wilkins Pickens Papers, Manuscript Division, LC.

23. Memorial to Thomas J. Gantt, January 10, 1861, Francis Wilkins Pickens Papers, Manuscript Division, LC. In her eloquent history of her family, Pauli Murray notes, "Anyone who has been part of a family of mixed bloods in the United States or West Indies has lived intimately with the unremitting search for whiteness. To deny that is part of one's heritage would be like saying one had no parents." Pauli Murray, *Proud Shoes: The Story of An American Family* (New York, 1978), 88.

24. Ibid.

25. Ibid.

26. Memorial to Gov. Pickens, January 10, 1861, Francis Wilkins Pickens Papers, Manuscript Division, LC.

27. The Charleston refugees made this remark to the New York *Tribune* reporter when they arrived in mid-January aboard the *Marion.* New York *Tribune,* January 19, 1861.

28. James Redpath to Francis W. Pickens, January 31, 1861, Francis Wilkins Pickens Papers, Manuscript Division, LC. As the federal government comandeered virtually all available ships, Redpath's efforts to obtain steamers for emigrants to Haiti became extremely difficult. See April 6, 16, 1861, Report of James Redpath to Hon. M. Pleisance, James Redpath Papers, Manuscript Division, LC.

29. Charleston *Mercury,* January 3, 1861; New York *Tribune,* January 7, 1861.

30. New York *Tribune,* January 14, 1861.

31. New York *Tribune,* March 22, 23, 1861.

32. Dr. Anderson's bill for his visits to the Ellison home between August 5 and December 5 was $110. Dr. W. W. Anderson's Account

Book, 1853–1867, The Borough House Papers, SHC.

33. Ellison family graveyard, Stateburg, South Carolina.

34. December 6, 1861, Record of the Claremont Parish, 1808–1866, Church of the Holy Cross, Stateburg, South Carolina, SCHS.

35. James D. Johnson to Henry Ellison, December 9, 1861, Ellison Family Papers, SCL.

36. Burton, *Siege of Charleston,* 71–80; Cauthen, *South Carolina Goes to War,* 136–38.

37. James D. Johnson to Henry Ellison, December 9, 1861, Ellison Family Papers, SCL.

38. Ellison family graveyard, Stateburg, South Carolina.

39. Reuben Ellison had died in March, nine months before his father. Since he died without a legal wife or legitimate heirs (see chapter IV), his portion of his father's estate was shared among the survivors. Henry served as administrator of Reuben's meager property. Through 1864 Henry collected several hundred dollars due Reuben and paid some taxes on the estate. However, Reuben's belongings did not add substantially to the Ellison family wealth, although his absence made for bigger shares for the survivors. Reuben's purported slave wife, Hannah, received nothing. By 1864 she had given birth to two more slave children. Reuben Ellison Estate Papers, Sumter County Estate Papers, Bundle 143, Package 4, SCDAH.

40. Unless otherwise noted, the following discussion of the Ellisons' Civil War experience is based on William Ellison's estate papers, particularly the careful accounts that Henry filed annually with the Probate Court in Sumter. William Ellison Estate Papers, Sumter County Estate Papers, Box 151, Package 8, SCDAH.

41. *Tri-Weekly Watchman,* January 8, 1862.

42. Elizabeth Allen Coxe, *Memories of a South Carolina Plantation during the War* (privately printed, 1912), 9–10.

43. James L. Roark, *Masters without*

Slaves: Southern Planters in the Civil War and Reconstruction (New York, 1977), 38–41.

44. R. M. Durant to "H and W Ellison," December 8, 1863, William Ellison Business Papers, 1852–1867, SCL.

45. Roark, *Masters without Slaves*, 39–45.

46. 1860 Agricultural Schedules, Sumter County, South Carolina, 21.

47. Coxe, *Memories of a South Carolina Plantation*, 75. See also, Mary Elizabeth Massey, *Refugee Life in the Confederacy* (Baton Rouge, 1964).

48. Paul W. Gates, *Agriculture and the Civil War* (New York, 1965), 370–73.

49. Coxe, *Memories of a South Carolina Plantation*, 9.

50. Anne King Gregorie, *History of Sumter County, South Carolina* (Sumter, S. C., 1954), 256; Cauthen, *South Carolina Goes to War*, 171.

51. Gregorie, *History of Sumter County*, 259.

52. Cauthen, *South Carolina Goes to War*, 184–87.

53. Gregorie, *History of Sumter County*, 256.

54. Bell Irvin Wiley, *Southern Negroes, 1861–1865* (Baton Rouge, 1965), 115–17.

55. Cauthen, *South Carolina Goes to War*, 147, 178.

56. Wiley, *Southern Negroes*, 116; Cauthen, *South Carolina Goes to War*, 178–183.

57. Jacob Stroyer, *My Life in the South*, 3d ed. (Salem, Mass., 1885), 35.

58. Eliza C. Ball to William J. Ball, June 2, 1863, Ball Family Papers, SCL.

59. Louisa P. Weston to "My Dear Brother," March 23, 1864, Ellison Family Papers, SCL. See also Ella Lonn, *Salt as a Factor in the Confederacy* (New York, 1933).

60. Bills, Moody Family Papers, SCL.

61. Burrel Moody to "Ellison and Johnson," April 27, 1851, Moody Family Papers, SCL.

62. Oscar Lieber to his parents, April 18, 1861, Francis Lieber Papers, SCL.

63. George D. Terry, "From Free Men to Freedmen: Free Negroes in South Carolina, 1860–1866," unpublished seminar paper, University of South Carolina. We are grateful to Dr. Terry for making his paper available to us.

64. Charles H. Wesley, "The Employment of Negroes as Soldiers in the Confederate Army," *Journal of Negro History* (July 1919), 239–53; Mary F. Berry, "Negro Troops in Blue and Gray: The Louisiana Native Guards, 1861–1863," *Louisiana History* 8 (1967), 165–90. In general, see the incomparable documents in Ira Berlin, Joseph P. Reidy, and Leslie S. Rowland, eds., *Freedom: A Documentary History of Emancipation, 1861–1867. Series II, The Black Military Experience* (Cambridge, England, and other cities, 1982).

65. Terry, "From Free Men to Freedmen."

66. Confederate Military Records, SCDAH.

67. *The Watchman and Southron*, August 28, 1895, in Yates Snowden Papers, SCL.

68. H. C. Roberts to Henry Burn, July 12, 1859, Burn Family Papers. SCL.

69. *The Watchman and Southron*, August 28, 1895, in Yates Snowden Papers, SCL.

70. Cassie M. Nichols, *Historical Sketches of Sumter County: Its Birth and Growth* (Sumter, S. C., 1975), 136–38. John Buckner's experience runs contrary to Bell Wiley's generalization that "If persons with Negro blood served in Confederate ranks as full-fledged soldiers, the per cent of Negro blood was sufficiently low for them to pass as whites." Wiley, *Southern Negroes*, 160.

71. John F. Marszalek, ed., *The Diary of Miss Emma Holmes, 1861–1866* (Baton Rouge and London, 1979), 202.

72. Cauthen, *South Carolina Goes to War*, 111.

73. Bernard H. Nelson, "Legislative Control of the Southern Free Negro, 1861–1865," *The Catholic Historical Review* 32 (1946–47), 34.

74. Terry, "From Free Men to Freedmen."

75. *Tri-Weekly Watchman,* July 6, 1863.

76. June 28, 1863, Record of the Claremont Parish, 1808–1866, Church of the Holy Cross, Stateburg, South Carolina, SCHS.

77. John G. Barrett, *Sherman's March Through the Carolinas* (Chapel Hill, N.C., 1956), 23–99.

78. Gregorie, *History of Sumter County,* 260–71.

79. Marszalek, ed., *The Diary of Miss Emma Holmes,* 399–439.

80. Ibid., 439.

81. Joel Williamson, *After Slavery: The Negro in South Carolina during Reconstruction, 1861–1877* (Chapel Hill, N.C., 1965), 3–31; Leon Litwack, *Been in the Storm So Long: The Aftermath of Slavery* (New York, 1979).

82. William Ellison Estate Papers, Sumter County Estate Papers, Box 151, Package 8, SCDAH.

83. Roark, *Masters without Slaves,* 94–141; Maj. Gen. Charles Devens to Lt. Col. W. L. M. Burger, December 28, 1865, National Archives Record Group 393, Department of the South and South Carolina and 2d Military District (P), 1862–1883, General Records, Correspondence, E–4112, Letters and Reports Received Relating to Freedmen and Civil Affairs, January 1865–January 1867, National Archives, Washington, D. C.; Francis Butler Simkins and Richard Hilliard Woody, *South Carolina During Reconstruction* (Chapel Hill, N. C., 1932).

84. William S. McFeely, *Yankee Stepfather: General O. O. Howard and the Freedmen* (New York, 1970); Martin L. Abbott, *The Freedmen's Bureau in South Carolina, 1865–1872* (Chapel Hill, N.C., 1967).

85. Tax Returns, Additional Returns of freedmen, Sumter District, 1865, 28, Comptroller General, South Carolina, SCDAH.

86. James D. Johnson to Henry Ellison, December 28, 1858, Ellison Family Papers, SCL.

87. Tax Returns, Additional Returns of freedmen, Sumter District, 1865, 1, 2, 18, Comptroller General, South Carolina, SCDAH.

88. Rev. I. E. Lowery, *Life on the Old Plantation in Ante-Bellum Days; or a Story Based on Facts* (Columbia, S. C., 1911), 104–5, 125.

89. Roger L. Ransom and Richard Sutch, *One Kind of Freedom: The Economic Consequences of Emancipation* (Cambridge, England, 1977), 56–99.

90. The discussion of the Ellisons' postwar agricultural reorganization is based on the 1870 Agricultural and Population Schedules, Sumter District, South Carolina; William Ellison Estate Papers, Sumter County Estate Papers, Box 151, Package 8, SCDAH.

91. Williamson, *After Slavery,* 164–165.

92. Gregorie, *History of Sumter County,* 267–68.

93. R. R. Briggs to H. & W. Ellison, August 13, 1866, and Isham Moore to H. & W. Ellison, October 17, 1867, William Ellison Business Papers, SCL. In September 1866 J. E. Adger & Company of Charleston, who had supplied the Ellisons with items of hardware for many years, wrote to explain that the "belting" the Ellisons ordered was on its way to Stateburg. J. E. Adger & Co. to Mr. H. Ellison, September 26, 1866, Ellison Family Papers, SCL.

94. Bernard E. Powers, "Black Charleston: A Social History, 1822–1885," Ph.D. diss., Northwestern University, 1982, 113.

95. 1870 Population Schedules, Sumter District, South Carolina, dwelling 111.

96. Tax Returns, Additional Returns of freedmen, Sumter District, 1865, 7, Comptroller General, South Carolina, SCDAH. The manufacturing schedules of the 1870 census in Sumter District are not extant.

97. Jack Bowen to R. Moody, January 1869, Moody Family Papers, SCL.

98. March 7, 1867; January 1, 1868, Dr. W. W. Anderson Account Books, The Borough House Papers, SHC.

99. 1870 Population Schedules, Sumter District, South Carolina, dwelling 111.

100. 1870 Population Schedules, Sumter District, South Carolina, dwelling 112.

101. *Acts and Joint Resolutions of the General Assembly of the State of South Carolina, 1865* (Columbia, S. C., 1866), 279.

102. Williamson, *After Slavery,* 77; Thomas Holt, *Black Over White: Negro Political Leadership in South Carolina during Reconstruction* (Urbana and other cities, 1977), 19–20; Powers, "Black Charleston," 98.

103. William Ellison Estate Papers, Sumter County Estate Papers, Box 151, Package 8, SCDAH.

104. Charles S. Aiken, "The Evolution of Cotton Ginning in the Southeastern United States," *Geographical Review* 63 (April 1973), 210–16.

105. Ransom and Sutch, *One Kind of Freedom,* 44–47.

106. Mark Reynolds, MD, to editor, New York *Albion,* February 22, 1870, Reynolds Family Papers, SCL.

107. R. L. Burn to H. C. Burn, March 22, 1866, Burn Family Papers, SCL.

108. Harold D. Woodman, *King Cotton and His Retainers: Financing and Marketing the Cotton Crop of the South, 1800–1925* (Lexington, Ky., 1968), 243–314. Also see Thomas D. Clark, *Pills, Petticoats and Plows* (Indianapolis, 1944), and Lewis Atherton, *The Southern Country Store, 1800–1860* (Baton Rouge, 1949).

109. Bills, 1872–1874, Moody Family Papers, SCL.

110. Interview with Mrs. Julia Simons Talbert, June 9, 1980, Stateburg, South Carolina.

111. February 14, 1868, Dr. W. W. Anderson Account Book, The Borough House Papers, SHC.

112. Receipt, H. and W. Ellison to B. Moody, January 27, 1874, Moody Family Papers, SCL.

113. H. & W. Ellison to R. J. Moody, October 21, 1876, Moody Family Papers, SCL.

114. Bills, December 15, 1881; March 9, 1882, Moody Family Papers, SCL.

115. Woodman, *King Cotton and His Retainers,* 301–2.

116. R. H. Anderson to "My dear Son," June 24, 1873, Blanding-Anderson Family Papers, SCL.

117. R. H. Anderson to "My dear daughter," October 27, 1878, Blanding-Anderson Family Papers, SCL.

118. Ransom and Sutch, *One Kind of Freedom,* 303.

119. Ibid., 126–48.

120. See especially, Jonathan M. Wiener, *Social Origins of the New South: Alabama, 1860–1885* (Baton Rouge and London, 1978).

121. Henry Ellison to "My Dear & Honoured Little Miss," October 16, 1870, and Henry Ellison to [illegible], date illegible, Ellison Family Papers, SCL.

122. Ransom and Sutch, *One Kind of Freedom,* Appendix G, 306–15.

123. H. & W. Ellison, November 25, 1872–February 1880, Dun Credit Ledgers, Baker Library, Harvard University. We are indebted to Professor David Carlton for this information.

124. Holt, *Black Over White;* Williamson, *After Slavery;* William C. Hine, "Frustration, Factionalism and Failure: Black Political Leadership and the Republican Party in Reconstruction in Charleston, 1865–1877," Ph.D. diss., Kent State University, 1979, 63, 69.

125. Holt, *Black Over White,* 37, 46, 234.

126. Ibid., 228–40.

127. Voter Registration, Headquarters Second Military District, Charleston, South Carolina, 1868, SCDAH.

128. See especially Carol R. Bleser, *The Promised Land: The History of the South Carolina Land Commission* (Columbia, S. C., 1969). For an analysis of a community that was established on such land, see Elizabeth Rouh Bethel, *Promiseland: A Century of Life in a Negro Community* (Philadelphia, 1981).

129. J. Morgan Kousser, *The Shaping of Southern Politics: Suffrage Restriction and the Establishment of*

the *One-Party South* (New Haven and London, 1974), 49, 85, 91; Edwin S. Redkey, *Black Exodus: Black Nationalism and Back-to-Africa Movements, 1890–1910* (New Haven, 1969).

130. Minute Book and Roll of the Stateburg Democratic Club, 1890–1910, Borough House Papers, SHC.

131. William J. Cooper, Jr., *The Conservative Regime: South Carolina, 1877–1890* (Baltimore, 1968), 34–35.

132. Ibid., 93.

133. Ibid., 108; Kousser, *The Shaping of Southern Politics,* 49, 85, 91.

134. Cooper, *Conservative Regime,* 109.

135. Sumter *Watchman and Southron,* August 28, 1895, Yates Snowden papers, SCL.

136. Albert Sidney Thomas, *A Historical Account of the Protestant Episcopal Church in South Carolina, 1820–1857* (Columbia, S. C., 1957), 433.

137. Sumter *True Southron,* August 16, 1881.

138. Sumter *True Southron,* October 25, 1881.

139. Cash-Shannon Duel, 1878–1880, SCL; Thomas J. Kirkland and Robert M. Kennedy, *Historic Camden: Part Two, Nineteenth Century* (Columbia, S. C., 1926), 237–48; 431.

140. Ellison family graveyard, Stateburg, South Carolina.

141. William Ellison Estate Papers, Sumter County Estate Papers, Box 151, Package 8, SCDAH.

142. 1870 Population Schedules, Sumter District, South Carolina, dwelling 112.

143. The following discussion of Buckner's suit is based on *John Wilson Buckner v. Henry Ellison and William Ellison,* William Ellison Estate Papers, Sumter County Estate Papers, Box 151, Package 8, SCDAH.

144. 1870 Population Schedules, Sumter District, South Carolina, dwelling 112.

145. Ibid.; Will and Estate Papers of James D. Johnson, Charleston, South Carolina, Bundle 215, Package 1, Probate Court, Charleston County Courthouse, Charleston, South Carolina; 1870 Population Schedules, Charleston, South Carolina, Ward 4, dwelling 904.

146. 1870 Population Schedules, Sumter District, South Carolina, dwellings 111, 112.

147. 1880 Population Schedules, Sumter District, South Carolina, dwellings 432, 471.

148. Gregorie, *History of Sumter County,* 469.

149. Tombstone, High Hills Baptist Church. When we visited Stateburg in 1980, Buckner's tombstone served as a steppingstone on the path to the Baptist Church privy.

150. Cassie Nicholes, *Historical Sketches of Sumter County,* 137. Nicholes incorrectly states that in their marriages beyond the original colony, the Turks "have confined the choice of a husband or wife to the Caucasian race." Ibid.

151. 1910 Population Schedules, Sumter District, South Carolina, dwellings 75, 287.

152. Henry Ellison to James D. Johnson, July 24, 1870, Ellison Family Papers, SCL.

153. Holt, *Black Over White,* 34–38, 70.

154. Williamson, *After Slavery,* 211.

155. A. A. Shrewsbury to Thomas Cardozo, June 22, 1864 [1865], American Missionary Association Manuscripts, South Carolina (microfilm), Amistad Research Center, Dillard University, New Orleans, Louisiana.

156. Thomas Cardozo to M. E. Strieby, July 1, 1865, American Missionary Association Manuscripts, South Carolina (microfilm), Amistad Research Center, Dillard University, New Orleans, Louisiana.

157. S. W. Stansbury to Rev. Mr. Smith, January 30, 1867, American Missionary Association Manuscripts, South Carolina (microfilm), Amistad Research Center, Dillard University, New Orleans, Louisiana.

158. S. W. Stansbury to Rev. Mr. Smith, February 16, 1867, American Missionary Association Manuscripts, South Carolina (microfilm),

Amistad Research Center, Dillard University, New Orleans, Louisiana.

159. J. T. Ford to E. M. Cravath, April 17, 1875, American Missionary Association Manuscripts, South Carolina, Amistad Research Center, Dillard University, New Orleans, Louisiana.

160. *The State,* October 4, 1931.

161. Henry Ellison to James D. Johnson, July 24, 1870, Ellison Family Papers, SCL.

162. Dr. W. W. Anderson Account Book, Borough House Papers, SHC; 1880 Population Schedules, Sumter District, South Carolina, dwelling 432.

163. Ellison family graveyard, Stateburg, South Carolina.

164. Sumter *Watchman and Southron,* August 28, 1883.

165. The following discussion is based on the extensive Henry Ellison Estate Papers, Sumter County Estate Papers, Bundle 176, Package 35, SCDAH.

166. William Ellison, Jr., to Henry Ellison, October 31, 1860, Ellison Family Papers, SCL; *The State,* October 4, 1931; 1880 Population Schedules, Sumter District, South Carolina, dwelling 432; Will of William Ellison, Jr., Sumter County Probate Court, Sumter County Courthouse, Sumter, South Carolina.

167. *The State,* October 4, 1931.

168. Minute Book and Roll of the Stateburg Democratic Club, Borough House Papers, SHC.

169. He was buried on February 11, 1894 in the family cemetery. Ellison family graveyard, Stateburg, South Carolina; Register of the Holy Cross Episcopal Church, 1866–1937, SCHS.

170. Ellison family graveyard, Stateburg, South Carolina.

171. Sumter *Watchman and Southron,* July 27, 1904.

172. 1910 Population Schedules, Sumter District, South Carolina, dwelling 374.

173. Will of William Ellison, Jr., Sumter County Probate Court, Sumter County Courthouse, Sumter, South Carolina.

174. The following account is based on interviews with residents of Stateburg; *The State,* October 4, 1931; Ellison family graveyard; Register, Holy Cross Episcopal Church, 1866–1937, SCHS.

Acknowledgments

SCHOLARSHIP is often said to be a lonely enterprise, and there is enough truth to the observation to justify the appearance of authors' names on title pages. However, even the most reclusive writer works in a social context. Writing this book has been less lonely than usual because we have collaborated from the very beginning and because we have constantly (and shamelessly) depended on family, friends, colleagues, archivists, publishers, and funding agencies for advice, ideas, support, encouragement, and patience. Aid has flowed in one direction—from them to us. Only the telephone company has demanded punctual repayment. We know this book bears the mark of all the favors we have received, and we hope all those who helped us will recognize it as a statement of our indebtedness.

Although we did not know it at the time, the book began to take shape at a picnic table in the back yard of Bill and Hilma Wire in Richmond, California, where we spent two April days trying to decipher certain passages of the Ellison family letters that had remained inscrutable to us for almost a year. At that time each of us was involved in another, independent project, and neither of us intended to do much more than read and understand the Ellison letters. Over the next several months, as we stole time from other matters to locate a clue or track down a lead, we realized that we needed to spend some time together in the archives in Columbia, South Carolina, where, if anywhere, we might find answers to questions that would not go away. With the help of John G. Sproat we settled into a spacious apartment near the University of South Carolina campus in the summer of 1980 and began to work in earnest on the history of William Ellison. In a few days we had stumbled across enough information to begin to joke, after a pitcher of beer, that we could write a book about Ellison. The interest and encouragement of James L. Mairs persuaded us that we should and helped us decide we would.

Our research in South Carolina benefited from the expert guidance and shrewd advice of numerous archivists and librarians. Marion Chandler and Joel Shirley aided our search through the labyrinth of state records in the South Carolina Department of Archives and History and, along with other members of the staff, helped refine our ill-informed questions into a sensible research strategy. Again and again, Allen Stokes steered us into the right collections in the rich holdings of the South Caroliniana Library and, more than anyone else, became a co-collaborator in our search for information about William Ellison. E. L. Inabinett and the staff of the Caroliniana provided congenial surroundings and ready access to the unparalleled resources of the library. Tom Terrill, Walter Edgar, Lacy Ford, David Carlton, Peter Colcanis, Debra Busbie, and Cynthia Miller included us in the community of historians in Columbia and gave us a sounding board for our ideas plus tips on everything from the best archival materials to the best barbeque.

For help with the Charleston side of the Ellison story we are indebted to Gene Waddell and David Moltke-Hansen of the South Carolina Historical Society and to Ralph Melnick, director of Special Collections of the Robert Scott Small Library at the College of Charleston. Our work in Charleston also benefited from the advice of Robert L. Harris, Jr., Nan Woodruff, Richard Coté, Lee Drago, and Susan Bowler. Rector Benjamin Bosworth Smith and Barney Snowden gave us access to the parish records and other items at Grace Episcopal Church. The staffs of the Charleston City Archives, the Charleston Library Society, the City Hall, and the Courthouse were invariably helpful in trying to make indexes and documents yield their secrets.

Nothing did more to bring the Ellison story to life than a trip to Ellison's former home in Stateburg. Captain Richard and Mrs. Mary Anderson and their son Will welcomed two strangers into "Borough House," their magnificent home. They encouraged us with their recollections of people and events related to the Ellisons, permitted us to roam over the former Ellison property and visit the Ellison family graveyard, introduced us to other knowledgeable Stateburgians, and showed us items from their family archives. They also let us examine a cotton gin similar to, if not one of, those built by William Ellison and his sons, as well as several gin saws definitely manufactured in Ellison's shop. We were also the recipients of the generous hospitality of Mrs. Julia Simons Talbert and of Mrs. Emma Fraser, each of whom recounted memories of members of the Ellison family. Former Stateburg residents Mrs. Gery Leffelman Ballou and her mother Mrs. Pauline Leffelman told us about the discovery of the Ellison family letters and their life in the former home of the Ellisons during the 1930s. In nearby Sumter, Esmond Howell permitted us access to valuable materials in the Sumter County Historical Society and made arrangements for us to examine old court records in the attic of the Sumter County Courthouse.

While we were in South Carolina we began to piece together the information we had gathered. Evidence from each day's research served as the beginning point of intense conversations that continued late into the night. Our notes on those conversations became the first draft of the book and the agenda for subsequent research and rewriting over the next three years. During the course of that work we received aid from many archivists and librarians whose willing and prompt answers to our queries we have acknowledged in the notes.

We received financial support from the Weldon Spring Endowment of the University of Missouri, a Regents Faculty Fellowship and a Humanities Faculty Fellowship from the University of California, Irvine, and—most important of all—Research Fellowships from the National Endowment for the

Humanities. Although each of us received the NEH fellowship for an independent project that got pushed aside by the accelerating momentum of our Ellison research, officials of the Endowment raised no objection, for which—in addition to the grants—they have our everlasting gratitude.

Colleagues gave us essential intellectual support, including the invaluable resource of informed skepticism. Ira Berlin, Carl Degler, Barbara Fields, George Fredrickson, Gary Mills, Spencer Olin, George Rawick, and Theodore Rosengarten read portions of our work and gave us helpful comments. Dan T. Carter, John P. Diggins, Jonathan Prude, and David C. Rankin took time away from their own studies to read the entire manuscript and suggest revisions. Jonathan Wiener provided a constant source of good historical judgment and practical wisdom about word processing. Charles Aiken, Theodore Hershberg, William Hine, Anna Rutledge, Loren Schweninger, and Lee Soltow generously shared the results of their own research. At a critical moment, C. Vann Woodward gave us renewed direction and a spiritual boost.

Although our efforts to compile a complete genealogy of the Ellison family were foiled by incomplete evidence, the accuracy of what we have been able to reconstruct has been aided enormously by Ralph Ellison, Stewart Lillard, and Dr. Henry S. Ellison, the only direct descendant of the Stateburg Ellisons whom we have been able to locate. We feel certain that additional information about the Stateburg Ellisons exists, though we have been unable to find it. Perhaps this book will spur someone to open a trunk or rummage through an attic and discover fresh evidence of William Ellison and his family. We hope so, for although we have learned what we can from the extant evidence, we are eager to learn more.

Harold H. Norvell, Charles Gay, George Terry, and Chris Kolbe made photographs of people, places, and things associated with the Ellisons. Karin Christensen skillfully transformed confusing sketches and contemporary maps into clear guides to the physical and social geography of Stateburg and the High Hills.

From the beginning, this book has received the steadfast support of James L. Mairs. His insightful reading challenged emphases, illuminated blind spots, and questioned obscure formulations. His colleagues at W. W. Norton, Robert Kehoe and Steven Forman, have also encouraged us by their enthusiasm for the project, and Janet Byrne gave us the benefit of her superb red pencil.

Finally, we are grateful to our families for their patience, which frayed but endured.

INDEX